# UNDONE

The Revealed Series – Book Four

Alice Raine

Published by Accent Press Ltd 2016

ISBN 9781910939734

Copyright © Alice Raine 2016

The right of Alice Raine to be identified as the
author of this work has been asserted by the author
in accordance with the Copyright, Designs and
Patents Act 1988.

# ONE

My mind was swirling as I sprinted away from the studios in a panicked daze, still able to smell the lingering acrid odour in the air.

Smoke.

Flames.

Fire.

*Jack.*

Oh God. Jack. I could barely believe it; the *Fire Lab* stage had burnt to the ground, but there was no news on Jack except for the fact that he had been taken away by ambulance. *An ambulance.* That didn't sound particularly positive.

I stopped just outside the studio gates, my hands shooting into my hair and scraping my fingers across my scalp in a desperate attempt at grounding myself before completely freaking out. I failed, of course, and felt anxiety crawling up my spine and wrapping around my veins like tiny, poisonous tentacles.

*Stay calm.* I pinged the elastic bands on my wrist and winced as they bit into my skin far too hard. Ouch. Jack hated this habit, and would have tried to stop me if I'd done it in front of him … but he wasn't here.

He was in hospital.

Unfortunately, thinking about him merely made me snap the bloody bands until my wrist bore a bright red ring.

My throat started to close up with panic as I tried to

1

push away images of his face screwed up in pain, but the visions wouldn't cease. Was he injured? Or worse?

*Stay calm.* Panicking wouldn't help, would it? And neither would incapacitating my wrist by numbing it with over-the-top snaps. What I needed to do was get back to the house and look up the hospital address, and get down there to see him.

The woman on reception had told me Jack had been taken to Lakeside Hospital, but I hadn't actually thought to ask the specific address before taking off. Idiot.

Setting off again, I took up the same rapid pace and, after dodging across the main road in an obvious jaywalk, I quickly found myself at my housing complex. Flashing my ID to Security, I then forced my lungs to work overtime as I sprinted down the street to my house.

In my rush, I stumbled over my own feet, crashing through the front door and straight into Allie. 'Goodness Cait! Slow down! What's wrong?'

I was so breathless from running I could barely speak. 'I just ...' *Wheeze.* 'There was ...' *Wheeze.* God, I was so out of breath I gave up and simply breathed his name. 'Jack.'

Crossing her arms, Allie gave an annoyed tut and threw me an irritated look. 'Cait, he works in the same studio as you so you'll see him from time to time, but you've told him you're not interested and I'm sure he respects that.' Confused, I paused for a second as I tried to work out what was she was talking about. She thought I was upset because I'd seen Jack? I suppose that made sense, seeing as I usually *was* freaking out because of some encounter with him. If only that were the case.

Pushing her hair away from her face, she shook her head, looking as exasperated as I felt. 'He's a good guy, Cait, I really don't think he'll try and push you. It's not as big a deal as you're making it out to be, I promise.'

'I know.' Sucking in another breath, my lungs filled

with a blessed rush of air and I finally felt marginally more capable of speech. 'That's not the matter.'

The frown now creasing Allie's brows said that she didn't entirely believe me, but she licked her lips and thoughtfully tilted her head anyway. 'So it's not Jack that's upset you?'

My elastic bands got a ping and I bit my lip as pain spread to my wrist and caused me to ball my fist tightly. It helped settle me – just – but didn't entirely manage to quell the anxiousness rearing up inside me. 'Well, it does involve Jack, but not in the way you're thinking.' Seeing one of Allie's eyebrows rise again, I hurried to finish my stilted explanation. 'There was a fire on one of Jack's stages and he's injured. I'm ... I'm ... worried about him.'

Allie's face immediately transformed into one of concern as she reached out and ran a hand up my forearm supportively.

'Oh my God, that's awful.'

Nodding, I swallowed to try and ease my dry throat. 'I know. And it's stupid to be this worried about someone I barely know but ...' I shrugged helplessly, my emotions towards Jack so confusing that I could hardly keep up with them myself, let alone expect Allie to understand. '... But I am.'

'You care about him, it's OK to feel that way. It's perfectly normal.'

She'd hit the nail right on the head. I *did* care about him, it had just taken this shock to make me accept it. Sniffing back some errant tears, I leant back, feeling well and truly miserable. Why couldn't I develop feelings for a man that was vaguely in my league? Why did it have to be mega-rich, ultra-famous, sinfully handsome Jack Felton?

Before I'd even seen her move, Allie was suddenly throwing her arms around me and smothering me in a

3

bear hug. It was just what I needed, so I buried my face into the crook of her neck and wrapped my arms around her tightly in return.

As we embraced I felt her fingers dig into my ribs as she clung to me, and I realised that her hug seemed just as desperate as mine. It suddenly occurred to me that this was the first time I'd seen her since her trip to LA to find Sean after his disappearing act.

'How's Sean? Did you find him?'

Allie leant back and nodded, and I noticed that her eyes were puffy and red. 'I did, he's OK … *ish.*' She paused, her face scrunching up slightly before she blew out a long breath. 'We're still on a break. It's … well, it's complicated.' Shoving her hair from her face, she gave me a firm look. 'But we can talk about that later, it's hardly the most important issue at the moment. Jack is injured, how badly?'

My stomach dropped again. 'I don't know, that's the problem.' Shaking my head, I sighed and recounted the story of how Jack had saved the cameraman but gained some injuries in the process.

'Wow, it sounds like he saved that guy's life,' Allie whispered in awe. 'Have you called him?'

My head immediately began a frantic nodding. 'Yeah, but there was no answer.'

Giving me an exasperated stare, Allie's mouth briefly hung open, 'Well, get your phone out and try again!'

I was fairly sure that once I knew he was OK, I'd be able to relax, but the possibility that he might *not* be OK made dread simmer in my belly until I felt close to throwing up.

Pulling my phone out of my bag, I swallowed hard and stared at it as if it were some alien device. Several seconds passed, and when my trembling hand still hadn't managed to do anything useful, Allie tutted, removed it from my grasp, sorted through it until she found his

4

number, and then thrust it at me. 'Call him.'

I paused, all my insecurities and panic rearing up in one huge tidal wave. 'I can't.' Seeing Allie's exasperation reaching an all-time high, I flushed and drew in a breath through my nose, before expelling it in a long puff from my lips as I tried to pinpoint exactly what was causing me to hesitate. 'We're friends ... but it's such a weird situation because we've admitted to having feelings for each other.' I paused and flicked my elastic bands to get the soothing sting I needed. 'I ... I think I want more with him,' I admitted, my eyes dropping away from Allie's as I whispered my confession. 'I have no idea how to go about it, though. It's crazy. What should I do?'

Allie crossed her arms and gave an understanding nod. 'This may sound a little blunt, but I think you need to hear it. You're one of the sweetest, most considerate people I've ever met, but you need to get over your fear. Call him. This isn't about you, or the future. This is about *now*, and whether or not he's hurt. Forget the other shit and call him.'

Well, that was me told.

# TWO

## JACK

The beeping of my phone woke me from my doze and I instinctively went to reach for it before hissing at the pain that shot up my left arm. Wincing, I blinked my eyes open and blearily assessed it – bandaged from the tips of my fingers all the way up to mid-bicep and it felt like it had been treated to a manicure from a cheese grater. What the hell?

Grimacing at the throbbing pain, I looked around and saw the sterile white suite, pale green curtains, and medical machines beside me.

Oh yeah. I was in hospital. Either that or a hotel with an exceptionally bad interior designer. The pain medication was making my brain sluggish, and each time I woke from a doze it took me a few seconds to recall where I was.

Now I was more alert I was all too aware of precisely *why* I was here.

The fire.

My heart rate accelerated as memories flooded back and I felt the hairs on my scalp rise. We'd been mid-way through a take, I was reciting my lines, then *boom*, a flash of blue sparks had come from nowhere, flaring up into a fireball to my right within seconds. The place had quickly filled with choking black smoke, panicked screams, and the acrid smell of burning plastic before I'd realised I could hear Brent yelling that he was trapped.

Thank God our show featured an arson unit, because

7

it had meant that we had extinguishers on set as props – thankfully they were full, and not fake ones – and I had immediately grabbed one and tried to douse the flames around Brent. Between myself and Fiona the line editor, we'd supressed the blaze enough to drag Brent out, but from the hacking coughs he'd been making I bet he was a damn sight worse for wear than I was.

Talk about fiction becoming reality; I'd literally ended up doing the rescuing that my *Fire Lab* character did on a daily basis.

Shaking my head, I began to gingerly shift myself more upright. I eyed my right arm with distaste as I saw the cannula there, the little plastic tube piercing my skin and connected to an IV bag of fluids hanging by my side. Ugh. I didn't mind needles, but I disliked cannulas immensely. Just the thought that it was stuck inside my body was enough to make me feel queasy.

Turning my eyes away, I saw that someone, presumably Flynn, had been to the studios and retrieved my things for me, because my wallet and phone were now sat on my bedside table. I saw several missed calls and a new text on my mobile screen, so reaching for it I went straight for the message.

> *From: Duncan Maywear*
>
> *Jack, how are you feeling? I spoke to your consultant and he said you should be released later this week. Don't worry about the bandages, I have the script writers already working on an episode that will incorporate your injuries into the season. Call me when you're out so we can discuss when you'll be back on set. Duncan.*

Duncan Maywear, my producer and all round idiot. It was typical that he seemed more concerned about delays to the schedule than my actual health. No doubt all the missed calls were from him too, desperately trying to find out when I'd be back at work.

I didn't bother to reply, or look at the missed calls, and instead chucked the phone beside me and rested my head on the pillows. I found it ironic that he was apparently so concerned but couldn't be bothered to visit. Arsehole. And 'Don't worry about the bandages' was pretty unfeeling too. I couldn't give a flying fuck if the bandages affected the show. Right now my main concern was the damage beneath them.

I could understand his concerns about the filming schedule, though. *Fire Lab* was one of those shows where the first episode aired before we'd filmed the entire season, so any major delays could cause us to postpone broadcasts. While I didn't mind inconveniencing Duncan a little, I couldn't upset the fans. They were the reason I got to do what I loved every day.

A visit from my director would have been a nice touch but not something I'd hold my breath for. Not that I could hold my breath for that long anyway – my lungs still felt decidedly dodgy from inhaling the smoke, even after the oxygen mask I'd been forced to wear in the ambulance.

Closing my eyes, I absorbed the sounds of the busy hospital corridor outside my room. The place didn't smell of disinfectant as hospitals often do because the burn shield gel that had been applied to my arm smelt strongly of aloe vera, surrounding me in a calming scent and almost masking the fact that I was in hospital. *Almost*. The scratchy blankets, needle in my arm, and constant beeping of my heart rate monitor were fairly annoying reminders.

I was broken from my miserable thoughts by the door opening as my nurse came swanning in again. Miriam had been seeing to my burns since I'd been admitted, re-applying cream and bandages and sorting out my IV fluids, all the while attempting to flirt with me rather outrageously even though she was old enough to be my mother. She was hilarious, though, and definitely making today far better than it could have been.

'Mr Felton, let's check that wrist again, shall we?' Unfortunately, I'd been wearing a watch when the fire had started, and as I'd been attempting to douse the flames the nylon strap had melted onto my skin. Fantastic. The fact that it didn't hurt was causing the doctors to worry that there was nerve damage and that the burns below would be more severe than the rest of my arm, which although painful and unsightly, was mostly covered in superficial blisters.

Miriam had been using a gel like Vaseline on my wrist to loosen the melted nylon, and was hopeful it could be removed within the next twenty-four hours.

Just as Miriam had finished and was popping the lid back on the tub, my phone began to ring. I let out a long sigh as I reached for it, deciding that if it was Duncan then I was definitely going to ignore it.

To my surprise, and complete delight, it wasn't Duncan's name flashing on my screen, but Caitlin's. My breath hitched as I blinked and double checked I'd seen it correctly. And I had, my screen was still illuminated with the words: *Incoming call from Caitlin Byrne.* This was a real turn-up for the books.

I felt my cheeks heat with excitement, and embarrassingly, my heartrate monitor sped up so a rapid *beep, beep, beep* suddenly filled the quiet of the room causing Miriam to look up and gave me a grin.

'Someone special calling?' she enquired with a smirk, cutting off any answer by flashing a wink and heading to the door. 'I'll leave you in peace, I'm all done here for now. I'll be back to check on that wrist in an hour or so.'

As soon as the door had closed I accepted the call. 'Hello?' My voice was croaky, partly from the smoke inhalation but mostly from the fact that I was nervously holding my breath.

Finally, I had to pull in a wheezy breath, because, as long as I waited, there was no response. 'Hello? Is anyone there?'

After some muffled rustling, I heard a breath and then a voice. 'Jack?' I'd recognise Caitlin's sweet, soft tone anywhere, and it was most certainly not Caitlin on the other end of the line. I pulled the mobile away from my ear to check the screen again before speaking.

'This is Jack,' I replied, attempting to reel in my skittering emotions and get my voice back under control.

'Hi, Jack, this is Allie.' Allie. Caitlin's friend and the girlfriend Sean was so enamoured with. Or were they still broken up? I wasn't sure, but disappointment settled in my gut.

Realistically, I should have known that Caitlin wouldn't call me. She was attracted to me, but she seemed adamant in her denial, so why would she call? Allie, on the other hand, didn't seem phased by anything, famous people included.

'I thought it was Caitlin,' I murmured, my voice not hiding the disappointment that laced my words.

'It was, but I grabbed the phone because she had to … uh … sneeze,' Allie blurted, sounding completely unconvincing. She had to sneeze? Yeah, right. Presumably Caitlin hadn't wanted to speak to me, but Allie had either forced her to call me, or had grabbed her phone and done the calling herself.

I wasn't surprised at how disappointed that made me feel. I liked that girl more than I should. My lips twitched as I recalled her drunken announcement of how she liked me 'way more than she should', a sentiment I definitely returned, even if it looked like it would never lead anywhere.

There was the noise of muffled voices down the line and several seconds of rustling before Allie spoke again. 'Anyway, Cait's here, she was hoping to speak to you.'

I doubted that. There were more muffled noises and a few seconds of silence which were finally followed by the soft notes of Caitlin's voice.

'Jack, hi.' My eyes closed as I absorbed her voice, the sound of it causing me to feel warm inside. She paused and I again wondered if Allie had forced the phone into her hands. 'I ... uh ... I heard about the fire and I just wondered if you're OK.'

I suddenly didn't feel so bad, just knowing that Caitlin was worried enough about me to ask made the pain and discomfort feel a whole lot better.

'I'm not too bad, all things considered. Some burns to my arm and hand, and a bit of smoke inhalation. Nothing too serious.' I didn't want to upset her, so I left out the more gruesome details of my mangled wrist.

A breath whistled down the line, followed immediately by a deep sigh. 'That's a relief. I still can't believe the set caught fire. It must have been so scary. What caused it?'

'Yeah, it was certainly unexpected,' I murmured. What a huge under-exaggeration. When I'd seen the flash of the fire starting I'd thought it was a bomb exploding. It had been utterly terrifying. 'Last I heard they still weren't sure. I suspect electrical problems, but there are some investigators in there at the moment looking into it.'

There was a pause, followed by a quiet snapping noise, and my eyes narrowed as I pictured Caitlin giving her elastic bands a ping. 'I ... I'm really glad you're OK.'

Her confession meant far more to me than it should,

especially as I knew how closed-off she could be. But still, as I ran her words through my mind I got a lump in my throat and had to take a sip of water before I could speak again.

'I'm really pleased you called,' I replied, to which I definitely heard a small intake of breath followed by a loud swallow. Perhaps I wasn't the only one with a lump in my throat.

'Yeah, well ... that's the sort of thing a friend would do ... isn't it?'

As much as I respected her request that we be just friends until I knew for sure she wanted more, I quickly realised that I could turn this situation to my advantage.

'It is. Thank you for the concern,' Licking my dry lips, I prepared to try my plan. 'A friend might also pop into the hospital for a visit, you know, especially as I'm stuck here on my own and don't have any family around.' OK that was a bit of an exaggeration. It was true that my family weren't around, but I had plenty of friends I could call up if I wanted some company. The problem was, the only company I *really* craved recently was Caitlin's. I just didn't think she was ready to return the sentiment in quite the same way.

Fully expecting her to find an excuse, I was astounded by the next words from her mouth. 'Um ... I could come down for a bit this afternoon?'

My eyebrows shot up, and I immediately felt guilty about my underhanded coercion. 'It's fine, I'm sure you must be busy. I was just kidding.'

Caitlin cleared her throat several times before she spoke again, and this time I was sure I could detect the hint of a smile in her voice. 'No, I'm free, I finished work at two. Which ward are you in?'

She seemed ... *keen*. Practically speechless, I quickly told her the ward details and visiting times before she rang off, promising to be here in the next few hours.

Wow. For several seconds after she hung up all I could do was sit there in stunned silence with the phone pressed to my ear.

# THREE

## ALLIE

Cait had totally frozen up when Jack had answered her call, so of course I'd had to grab the phone from her and take over. But then, after flashing me a thoroughly unimpressed look, she had hesitantly begun chatting. Initially her eyes had flashed around nervously and her answers had been stilted and edgy, but then she'd stepped away so she could continue the conversation with a little privacy.

I wouldn't usually try and push a romantic notion, but I could tell how much Cait liked Jack. It was practically written all over her face every time his name came up. I'd never seen her so flustered about a man before. Not to mention the way she'd blushed when she had described his kiss – *that* flush had spoken for itself.

As much as I'd have loved to see more developing I wasn't holding out too much hope. Cait appears fairly shy, but under that quiet veneer she is incredibly tough and extremely bloody stubborn, and if she'd decided not to advance things with him, then she would stick to it.

I was pleased that they were trying friendship though. Thrilled really. If Cait could take some steps towards a serious friendship with someone like Jack then it could help her rebuild some of her trust in men.

I know getting a boyfriend isn't the be all and end all, but Cait is so sweet and loving and I just wished that she could open up and share that side of herself with someone.

Watching as Cait finished the call, I saw her lower the phone, ping the elastic bands on her wrist once, and straighten her shoulders before turning around. Her face was flushed, but her hazel eyes had a wary look to them as she approached me.

'Is he OK?'

'Kind of, he's got some burns and smoke inhalation but he seemed OK.' Shoving her phone back in her bag, Cait began fidgeting and then checked her watch, which I took as a very unsubtle sign that she was keen to end the conversation.

As tempted as I was to push it, I let her have her way. For the time being, anyway. 'So, seeing as I've just got back and found the fridge bare, I think we need to pop out and do a food shop. Wanna come?'

Licking her lips, Cait hesitated, then she cleared her throat and averted her eyes as her cheeks flushed again. 'Actually, I can't this afternoon, sorry.'

Frowning, I checked my watch then looked back to my bestie. 'Why? I thought you'd finished work for the day.'

'I have, it's just that I, um … I told Jack I'd go visit him in the hospital.' Blinking in surprise, my jaw briefly hung open before I clenched my teeth together and tried my hardest to supress a grin of delight. The urge to do a happy dance right there and then was almost overpowering but I didn't want her to see how excited I was in case it put her off.

Wow. I hadn't expected that. Ever. Maybe I'd been wrong about her not progressing her relationship with Jack.

'He's on his own and they're keeping him in for a few days so I think he's bored.'

'Did you offer, or did he ask you to visit?'

Her eyes darted to mine and narrowed. 'Don't read too much into this, I'm just trying to be supportive. He knows the deal.' Hmm. He might know what Cait had told him about being 'just friends', but he definitely had a soft spot for her. 'Anyway, I said I was calling to check up on him because that's what friends do, and he said friends also go and visit in the hospital, especially when the patient was feeling lonely.'

Once again I felt my lips twitching with the urge to smile. Jack Felton, you cunning man. The more I got to know about him, the more I liked him.

'I can do the shopping on my own, it's fine. When are you going?' Considering how excited I was about this developing bravery from Cait, I congratulated myself on how calm I sounded.

'Now, I guess.' Pulling out a fold-up map from her bag, Cait spent a few minutes consulting it. 'The hospital is here, Wiltshire Boulevard. It's in a different direction to the supermarket though, so maybe we need separate cabs. Or do you want to share and do the longer route?'

What I *really* wanted to do was become a fly on the wall of Jack's hospital room so I could witness Cait's visit, but instead I settled for nodding my head and linking my hand through Cait's elbow. 'We can get separate, its fine. But let's walk to the main road together.'

# FOUR

## CAIT

My visit began with an awkward stop in the hospital shop – awkward because a) I had no idea what to take when visiting someone you barely knew but fancied like crazy, and b) I wasn't sure I should even be buying anything in the first flipping place. Would a 'friend' buy grapes, balloons, or chocolates?

Snorting out a frustrated breath, I ditched the idea of balloons and chocolates straight away. They would look *waaay* too forward, and I wanted to avoid anything that would look too over the top.

The very fact that I was even considering what would look too forward probably indicated that I was thinking about this far too much, but I pushed that thought aside with a frown and huffily grabbed a bunch of grapes.

Stepping into a lift, I gave my elastic bands a ping to try and calm myself, and had to grab the hand rail to steady myself after my legs went wobbly. Perhaps my coping mechanism wasn't quite as effective as it used to be.

Gripping the rail with a clammy fist, I vaguely toyed with the idea of scarpering. As soon as the lift stopped I could press the ground floor button again and make a run for it, tell Jack I had a prior arrangement I'd forgotten about … That option was taken away two seconds later, however, as the lift reached Jack's floor and the doors opened to reveal a suited man. 'Miss Byrne?'

Bugger. There would be no swift escape to the

freedom of the ground floor, then. As I flicked my gaze over him I recognised him as Jack's bodyguard. I'd met him briefly a few times, but put on the spot like this I couldn't for the life of me remember his name.

Great, I had practically collapsed in the lift in a clammy mess and now I was met with this guy's steely gaze and unfaltering calm. I was getting myself far more worked up than I needed to, but really, what the hell was I doing visiting a movie star in hospital? In what universe was that a good idea?

I saw him give me a brief assessment, a small smirk curling his lips as he saw the bag of grapes in my hand, before clearing his expression. 'I'm not sure if you remember me. I'm Flynn, I work for Mr Felton. He asked me to keep an eye out for you.'

Flynn. That was it. 'I remember you, you've been kind enough to drive me home a few times now.'

My cheeks flushed as I remembered the first time he'd given me a lift home – the night I'd met Jack at the theatre and agreed to go for a drink with him. The conversation we'd had in the car that night had been pretty embarrassing – he'd asked me out, and I'd said no – all of which had been overheard by Flynn.

Flynn ushered me into a room but as soon as I crossed the threshold I stumbled over my own feet and flinched at the click behind me as he pulled the door closed. A second later my initial self-consciousness was forgotten as I became focused on Jack sitting in the bed in front of me. Smiling hesitantly, I moved forwards as I quickly ran my eyes over him to assess his injuries.

One of his arms and hand were bandaged and he was hooked up to various monitors and tubes, but apart from that he didn't look too bad.

My heart kicked up a beat as I moved from his injuries and took in the man. He looked pretty damn good, with his hair all tousled, his handsome face as devastating as ever, and a bright, happy smile on his lips.

My throat dried up when my eyes briefly strayed to his chest. The sheet was pulled up high, but there was no mistaking the fact that he was topless. Maybe even naked. I swallowed hard and quickly tried to distract myself from that line of thought, because it really couldn't go anywhere good.

Quite clearly the soft, brown hair that covered his forearms extended over other areas of his body, although it seemed to be trimmed short and neat on his pecs. I wondered if it was trimmed on his belly too, but that just led me back to thinking about where that hair might lead to. Oh God. The idea of Jack Felton stark naked nearly made my knees buckle.

Considering I avoided physical contact with men, it was quite surprising just how tempted I was to lean in and see how firm his muscles would feel under my fingertips. Licking my lips, I ripped my gaze away from his body and looked around the room, hoping he hadn't caught my ogling. He no doubt had. Especially seeing as I could feel his gaze burning into me, making my skin tingle.

When I was finally brave enough to lift my eyes to his, there was a smile on his face, but not smug like I had expected. Instead, it was that sweet, soft, affectionate look that I'd seen in my house when he'd brought me a hangover breakfast. That look was quite something, and it made my stomach tumble with some emotion I couldn't even begin to name.

Suddenly I felt completely overwhelmed. I really shouldn't have come here.

'Caitlin, you came.'

*Breathe.* My lungs either didn't listen or my brain was speaking a foreign language, because it took another second or two for me to actually draw in a breath and connect my vocal chords.

'Hi, Jack.' Thankfully, my voice came out relatively smooth and nowhere near as shaky as I felt inside. 'Of course I did, I said I would.' I didn't mention that I'd very nearly chickened out fewer than five minutes ago.

This man really had thrown my life into complete turmoil. I'd been through the cycle of denial, then avoidance, eventually slipping into grudging acceptance, and now here I was ... stood at the bedside of a man I liked.

A lot.

Way more than I should.

Way more than I'd ever liked *any* man.

Would it be possible to build a friendship with him knowing I was ridiculously attracted to him? Knowing that *he* was attracted to *me*? I couldn't see how I could date him, it was beyond my boundaries to consider, but he made me feel safe, and relaxed and ... happy.

I realised I was still silent and he was sitting there gazing at me in quiet expectation, so clearing my throat I tried another shaky smile. 'Uh ... how are you?'

'I'm fine.' Jack's reply was a little too speedy for my liking, so I narrowed my eyes and gave him a stern look that I'd perfected back in my teaching days.

He chuckled. Clearly my attempt at strictness hadn't been particularly successful, but at least it had made him smile. 'Honestly, Caitlin, considering I was in a fire, I really am doing OK. Thank you for coming.'

'You're welcome.' Licking my lips, I fidgeted before remembering the small bag I was carrying. 'Oh yeah, I, er, I bought you some grapes.' As I said it I realised how clichéd it was, and dumped them down on his table feeling embarrassed and wondering why I'd bothered.

'Thanks,' Jack smiled, but as he spoke I saw his eyes flick to behind me and I turned to see a gigantic basket of fruit on a shelf. Bugger. I felt my shoulders slump with a sigh and gave him a rueful smile. 'Ah, looks like someone beat me to it.'

Jack's smile extended into a grin as he looked at the fruit basket and back to me. 'Don't worry about it, the hospital provided that but grapes are much better, I mean look ...' He gingerly lifted his bandaged arm and indicated the fruit basket again. 'What good are oranges and bananas? I'm one handed, can't even peel the things.' As if wanting to prove his point he raised his good arm, plucked off one of my grapes, and popped it in his mouth with a wiggle of his eyebrows as he chewed.

The fact that he was trying to make me feel better instantly made me smile. He really was a decent guy. *Genuinely nice*, as Allie kept reminding me.

I was filled with the ridiculous urge to pluck off another grape and offer to feed him, but, thankfully, I was stopped as the door behind us opened and two nurses strode in, one with a small tray of medicines and the other with a jug of water.

The younger nurse placed the water down and made a show of placing a hand on Jack's bare shoulder before giving it a little rub and fluttering her eyelashes with a grin. 'How's the patient? It must be so difficult for a strapping man like you to be stuck in bed.'

Strapping man? She might as well have bent down and nuzzled his chest.

'You need me to get you anything, Jack?' she added, her voice all breathy and pathetic. Her obvious flirting really riled me for some reason. I felt my shoulders stiffen and my teeth clench. All I could think was *get your hands off him*, but before I embarrassed myself by clambering over the bed and smacking her round the face, Jack shifted so her arm fell away and then locked his gaze with mine, flashing me the tiniest of winks.

I couldn't decide if I'd imagined the wink or not, but the eye contact instantly soothed my hackles. Either he was oblivious to her charms or not bothered at all, because his eyes only left mine for a split second as he thanked her and then immediately looked back at me. Ha! If it was a competition I definitely would have won that round.

Frigid freak one, sexy nurse zero.

A small, smug smile curled my lip as the younger nurse left the room, looking rather disgruntled. The other nurse – Jack introduced her as Miriam – began to undo his bandages before pausing and looking at me. 'This isn't a pretty sight. You might want to leave the room if you're squeamish.'

Immediately I frowned and glared at Jack. 'I thought you said you were fine?'

Jack flushed before shrugging guiltily. 'I am. Mostly.' He grinned at Miriam and looked at me again. 'So, are you squeamish …?'

# FIVE

## JACK

Miriam peeled back the final loose bandage to expose my wrist to the cool air and I sucked in a quiet breath. It was aching and stinging, the entire area still feeling hot. A shocked gasp sounded in the room before small, warm fingers wrapped around my good hand and squeezed tightly. Really tightly.

'Oh my God. *Jack.*'

My discomfort from the burn was immediately forgotten as I focused my attention on where Caitlin was gripping my hand. She was touching me of her own accord. Looking at her face, I saw it was blanched of colour, her hazel eyes staring at my opposite wrist in distress.

A second later she practically yelped as she realised she was holding onto me and yanked her hand away as if *she* was the one getting burnt.

I'd been sorely tempted to tighten my grip so she couldn't escape, but I'd never trap her to me like that. Besides, knowing how stubborn Caitlin could be she probably would have struggled and I didn't want to have a tussle with her in front of Miriam, who was already watching us both with interest, so I reluctantly let her fingers slide from mine as she pulled back.

It was a shame, really. I could have done with the contact to help me deal with the discomfort as Miriam began to carefully prod at my watch strap.

As she hit a particularly tender patch it felt like

someone had put a blow torch against my wound, and I couldn't help but wince and suck in a hissed breath.

'Have you been using your clicker for the pain?' Miriam asked with a frown. I eyed the clicker which lay on the bed beside me and felt my eye flinch with guilt. I was supposed to press it any time I needed relief to administer a top-up of pain medication.

Trying not to look too guilty, I nodded. Which was a complete lie, because as soon as I knew Caitlin was coming to visit I'd stopped self-administering the drugs so I wouldn't be drowsy. I hadn't wanted to be bleary for her and they were seriously starting to wear off.

'Hmmm,' was all Miriam said, and I would have placed money on the fact that she'd seen straight through my lie.

Glancing at Caitlin, I found her gripping the bed rail like her life depended on it, and grimacing as she looked over to where Miriam was working on my nauseating arm. And it really was gross. Red skin surrounded my watch strap and below that several deep sores were visible which were weeping a yellowy liquid. All in all, it was quite a frightful sight.

I saw Caitlin's eyebrows flicker with concern before she swallowed hard and looked at me with a slightly tense smile. Her fingers briefly lifted from the bar and hovered above mine before falling back to grip the bar so tight that her knuckles turned white.

It seemed she wanted to reach out, but wasn't allowing herself to comfort me. In fact, now she looked distinctly like she was about to bolt from the room. As soon as Miriam left I was going to gently press her on the progress we'd been making recently and see if maybe she would consider going for a drink with me once I was out of the hospital. I might consider myself a gentleman, but I wasn't above playing a situation to my advantage. If I could use Caitlin's sympathy to get her to relax her boundaries a little then I would definitely pursue that possibility.

As soon as Miriam finished tending to my arm, Caitlin pulled in a breath and straightened her back, keeping her hands glued to the bed rail. 'I'm so glad you're OK, but I think I should go now.'

Damn. I'd been right about her fleeing then.

'What? You only just got here,' I blurted, my face falling with disappointment. Apparently my expression was pitiful, because from the way she suddenly sucked her lower lip into her mouth and chewed, it looked like her resolve was crumbling.

'Stay? Just for a little longer?' I cajoled softly.

Caitlin was obviously torn, her eyes flicking between mine and her clenched knuckles. Finally she released a long breath and fixed her stare on mine. 'I'm just going to be honest with you, Jack. You've already spotted that I have ... issues ... with men. It's relationships in general really, they aren't something I'm good at ...'

I went to interrupt her, but she silenced me with a shake of her head. 'The thing is ... well ... I've begun to get quite attached to you.'

My eyebrows jerked up in surprise at this turn in the conversation. She was attached to me? And admitting it sober? How was that a problem, exactly? It was like music to my ears, and if I hadn't been confined to a hospital bed suffering from some fairly intense pain I would have jumped up and down with happiness. The panicked expression on Caitlin's face stopped me from reacting though, because obviously she had more to say.

Caitlin flicked her elastic bands and I winced before she spoke again. 'You've probably already guessed, but there's a "but".'

Sighing, Caitlin swept her hair from her face and exchanged the elastic band flicking for chewing on her lower lip again. 'I really enjoy spending time with

27

you …' As she paused for breath I could practically hear the 'but' hanging in the air.

'*But* I feel like I'm taking advantage of the fact that you make me feel good, and happy, and safe, when I can't give you what you want.' She swallowed loudly and lowered her eyes. 'I don't think I can give you more. Does that mean I'm leading you on?'

I zeroed in on the fact that she had said 'I don't *think* I can give you more,' not a definitive *can't*.

'Have I ever pushed you for more than you felt comfortable with, Caitlin?' I asked, desperately hoping she wouldn't bring up the time when I had kissed her in the park – the one instance where I had pushed her and a day I regretted and treasured in equal measure.

'No, but …'

'No more buts.' I shook my head, pleased that her eyes were still locked on to mine. She looked like she was teetering on the cusp of opening up, but was still hesitant to take such a leap.

Perhaps if I led the way and clearly laid out my feelings it might make her feel more sure. 'I enjoy spending time with you too, Caitlin.' I declared. 'Were you worried when you heard I'd been involved in the fire?'

An expression of fear seemed to pass across her face, but before she'd even spoken, Caitlin snapped her teeth together and gazed towards the window, giving nothing more than a vague shrug. Damn, she was still holding herself behind those walls. The frown on her brows told me she was confused by my change in conversation, but now I had started on this route I was determined to get her to open up.

'If things had been reversed, if it had been *you* in the fire, I would have been beside myself with worry,' I confessed quietly. Her eyes flew to mine, wide and curious as she licked her lips.

28

'Really?' she whispered, her face losing some of its tightness as she waited for my reply. This tactic seemed to be working. She obviously wanted to explore the bond between us but seemed hesitant to expose herself first. That was fine by me, I had no issues laying my feeling on the table.

'Really,' I nodded and chose to risk it and go one step further. 'In all honestly, I'm rather attached to you too.' This was such an understatement that I nearly laughed. It seemed to cause a brief happiness to spread across her face before panic followed, her eyes dilating and shoulders tensing. 'You can trust me, Caitlin. I swear I don't, and won't, ever expect anything more than what you're willing to give.'

There was a long, heavy pause, and she parted her lips hesitantly. 'Terrified,' she murmured.

She was terrified? Of what? Me? A relationship?

'I mean … I *was* terrified. When I heard about you being in the fire I was a mess. The idea of you being hurt …' Her eyes flickered shut.

My heart rate rocketed, embarrassingly projected around the room via the damn monitor, but Caitlin was so focused on my face that she didn't seem to notice.

'Let's try something,' I said. 'We're going to play the Yes or No game.'

I was totally winging it, but all I could do was hope that this might help Caitlin relax and get me some of the answers I needed in the process. In response to her confused frown I grinned and settled back against my cushions. 'I get to ask you some questions, and the only reply you can give is a yes or a no. The only rule is that you must answer honestly. Then you can return the favour and ask me. OK?'

## CAIT

A game? I hadn't expected this. Jack didn't wait for me to agree; instead he started immediately.

'Question one. Do I scare you?' That wasn't a question I'd been expecting at all, and my eyes flashed to his, wary and unsure where he was going with this. 'Truthful answers, remember, and you can only say yes or no.'

Truthful answers … that was pretty easy then. 'No.'

Jack's eyes widened in pleasant surprise, but it was true – the way he affected my senses scared me, the uncontrollable way I responded to him scared me, but Jack didn't. I somehow knew he would never hurt me.

Giving a nod, his face softened as he smiled. 'I'm glad,' he whispered. I lowered my eyes, suddenly worried that he could somehow see through me to my carefully hidden secrets. Pulling in a deep breath, he cleared his throat. 'Question two. Did you feel jealous when you saw that nurse flirting with me?'

My expression hardened at his cheek. It was embarrassing because he had obviously clocked the way I'd wanted to batter the woman.

'No,' I blurted, but my tone was hurried and sulky and probably gave away the fact that I'd broken his stupid 'honest answers only' rule.

My eyes were now trained on the bedsheet, hoping to hide my fib, but I heard Jack make a soft tutting noise as if he didn't believe me for a second. Why was I such a crappy liar?

'Look at me, Caitlin.' The edge of command in his tone had my head rising without consent, but by the time

I'd realised, it was too late, because he had caught me in his potent gaze again and I couldn't drag my eyes away.

Those eyes. Man alive, they were something else.

'Question three …' I was both relieved and surprised that he was letting me get away with my lie, but I found myself holding my breath as I waited to see what he had in store for me. 'This one should be easy because I've already asked you this,' he murmured. 'Do you feel this thing developing between us?' He wafted his hand in the gap between our bodies where I could swear there was electricity jumping at that very moment.

*Do you feel this thing between us?* I was instantly transported back to that day in the Getty Centre where he'd asked me the same question and I'd accidentally replied with a nod of confirmation.

My teeth clenched with the effort of holding in an instantaneous response. There *was* a connection between us. Whether it was just strange chemistry or more, I didn't know, but it was definitely there. Not that I should be admitting that out loud. For whatever reason, Jack made me want to open up, like I was trained to respond to him, and going against that instinct took serious determination.

'I barely know you,' I whispered. Surprisingly, my voice sounded relatively stable, but I wasn't able to keep eye contact as I avoided his question. True, we didn't know each other well, but regardless, the connection was there. Some strange pull that tugged at me whenever Jack was near.

'Caitlin.' This time my eyes edged back to his gaze to find brown pools of determination staring at me. 'That wasn't what I asked. I let the last lie go, but no more fibs. Do you feel this thing between us, yes or no?'

Surely he could detect my attraction a mile off. He'd probably had his fair share of women falling for him over the years, so it must be pretty obvious that I was affected by him. Screamingly obvious, if the burning of my cheeks was anything to go by, not forgetting how lost I'd got in his kiss. Remembering how good his lips had felt, I shivered as a delightful tingling skittered across my skin. Admitting it wouldn't really change anything, so I sighed and gave a nervous shrug.

'Yes. But …' Jack cut me off by raising a hand and smiling.

'No buts. This is the Yes or No game. Not the Yes, No, or But game.' I couldn't help but give a tiny smile in return. I'd expected a smug smirk, but if anything, he actually looked relieved.

'Ask me the same question,' Jack urged, his eyes so focused on me that I could hardly breathe from the intensity.

There was no point carrying on with this stupid game, regardless of our connection. Nothing could ever come of it because I was damaged goods. Or could it? Jack had me so jumbled up that even I was starting to doubt the conviction of my long-held single status.

'Do you … do you feel it?' After forcing the words out I swallowed hard, but it sounded more like a rasping gulp in the silence.

'I do. Yes. From the tips of my toes to the top of my head. When you're near it's like something inside of me comes alive.' Oh God. I'd been worried he would say yes, but he'd gone and said so much more. My mouth fell open in surprise, until I felt like a gawping idiot. His word choices had really hit home because something inside of me came alive when he was near too.

What on earth did I do now?

Jack tilted his head and smiled that soft, affectionate smile that was quickly becoming my favourite expression. 'Now it's your turn to ask your earlier question.'

This was so surreal that my mind had gone totally

blank. What question? Seeing my confusion, Jack leant across and whispered in my ear. His warm breath on my cheek made me quiver and my eyes briefly fluttered shut. 'You asked if you were leading me on.'

'Oh.' My voice was hoarse, so I cleared my throat and asked again. 'Am I ... am I leading you on?' I whispered, too intrigued not to, because I desperately wanted to know the answer.

'No.' Licking his lips, Jack shifted so he was marginally closer to me and gave me a hopeful smile. My heart was pounding so quickly I had no words, so I just stood there staring at him like an idiot. 'You have been totally clear right from the start, but that's OK, because this thing we feel between us ...' he jerked a hand between the two of us, '... is worth waiting for. I'll be patient and wait as long as you need me to,' he finished, his eyes burning into mine with such intensity I could almost feel his words imprinting into my very soul.

A desperate gasp broke from my throat that almost sounded like a sob, and I suddenly felt tears building behind my eyes. I seemed to have gone from zero to emotional wreck in under sixty seconds.

I *so* wanted what he was offering me, but it seemed beyond anything I could give. God, I had so much to process. I pinged my elastic bands and blinked my tears away.

'So what do you say? Are you willing to try and let me in a little?' he asked gently, his unwavering gaze never leaving mine for a second.

# JACK

I could see that Caitlin was torn from the torrent of emotions passing over her face, and from the nervous pinging of those damn elastic bands around her wrist. God, I hated those things. I hated that she hurt herself with them.

'Don't overthink it,' I murmured. 'We don't have to define our relationship with such strict boundaries like *friends* or *more*. We can just be two people who enjoy each other's company and are getting to know each other.' I probably sounded desperate, but that was because I *was* desperate. I knew it, and Caitlin most likely did too, but I didn't care. The only thing I cared about was making sure she didn't put distance between us.

I had no idea why she'd been brought into my life, but this girl was important to me – I'd known it from the first moment we'd met. There was a powerful connection between us, which didn't occur often, and I wasn't willing to walk away from it.

My eyes dropped to where her hands were resting on the side of the bed and I felt my eye twitch as she looped a finger under one elastic band and pulled it from her wrist. The skin below was bright pink and I couldn't stop myself from reaching across and tucking my finger under the band as she let it go. Instead of snapping onto her skin, the band landed on the crook of my finger, the back of my knuckle just brushing her forearm as her eyes dropped down in surprise.

'I'm sorry. I hate seeing you hurt yourself with those.' They were obviously a coping mechanism, and as

I thought about that a crazy idea sprung to my mind. She'd grabbed my hand once before – at the batting cages when the noise of the falling chairs had shocked her – so I wondered if she subconsciously found comfort in my touch.

'I have one final question. Instead of flicking those elastic bands, would you like to squeeze my hand like you did at the batting cages?'

After several long seconds, Caitlin raised her eyes to mine and I noticed the flush now colouring her cheeks. 'Squeeze my hand,' I urged her. 'Instead of hurting yourself, squeeze my hand to relieve your stress. Could you do that?'

There was another lengthy pause, and then Caitlin slowly nodded. 'Yes,' she croaked. Shocking me, she made the first move by reaching down and sliding her trembling fingers around mine.

Warmth climbed through my body from the contact and I felt a contented sigh fill my lungs. I couldn't have been more thrilled, and after allowing her to get used to the contact I shifted our hands so our fingers were interlinked. It was a small change, but far more intimate, and even though I knew this gesture was definitely moving away from *friends* towards *more*, I didn't point it out to her.

Caitlin blinked and glanced at her spare hand and the elastic bands around the wrist before tucking the hand into her pocket with a shrug. 'They're meant as a distraction but sometimes I get carried away.'

I wanted to press her on the reasons she wore the bands, but I sensed that now wasn't the time. What was she distracting herself from?

'Distract yourself with me,' I whispered. Watching her eyes flick to our joined hands and then my eyes, I could tell I was treading some seriously thin ground, until Caitlin's lips twitched into a flicker of a smile.

'So instead of hurting myself you want me to hurt you?'

Sensing the tension between us passing and transforming into something promising, I smiled, but managed to keep the excitement from my voice. 'I'm pretty tough. I promise I can take it.'

'You're already in the wars, I don't think you need to add "broken knuckles" to your list of injuries,' she replied, still maintaining a gentle hold on my hand.

Shrugging, I gave my fingers a small wiggle. 'Think of it like an oversized stress ball.' This earned me an even bigger smile, which warmed me to my core and made my chest puff with pride.

We sat there like that for several minutes, holding hands and enjoying the sensations that being connected brought with it. It felt like every nerve ending in my body had simultaneously been ignited as her fingers gave a firmer squeeze before she let out a shaky breath.

I felt like a teenager again. My neck was clammy, my stomach was churning with nerves, and below the bedsheets my groin had shot to life and was attempting to escape my pyjama trousers like a thing possessed, causing me to bend my knee across to conceal it.

Now was not the time to lose control. Caitlin was holding my hand and accepting that we meant something to each other, which were both major developments and something that I wasn't going to ruin. Her fingers were rhythmically gripping mine, seeming to take out her nerves on my hand just as I had asked.

'See? It's not so bad,' I murmured, my voice embarrassingly hoarse.

'It's nice,' she paused, wincing as if she realised how bland the word 'nice' could be. 'Really, er … good, but it feels a lot like *more* to me,' she observed quietly as she continued to stare at our joined hands.

It felt a lot like more to me too, but I would do

anything and everything in my power to keep her calm, so I stayed silent.

After a few minutes of contented quiet, Caitlin looked at me inquisitively. 'So ... uhh ... what does this mean?' she asked quietly, her eyes darting between mine and our entwined fingers. I could see anxiety on her face but curiosity too, and maybe even a tiny trace of hope.

'It means whatever we want it to. Please stop overthinking. Remember what we said earlier – there is no *friends* or *more* between us. We're just two people who enjoy spending time together and are getting to know each other.'

Another smile curved her lips, bigger and more confident, but her eyes stayed fixed on our fingers. 'It's not exactly a catchy title, but OK, I'll roll with it.'

I couldn't keep the smile from my face as we sat in silence, absorbing the skin on skin contact. OK, I wasn't dragging Caitlin into my arms and kissing her like I wanted to, but right now, the simple act of holding hands was filling me with a roaring sense of hope.

I noticed Caitlin's eyes narrowing and she began to fidget as if thinking something through. From the frown forming on her face, it wasn't something good.

'Can I ... um ... can I assume that you won't be "getting to know" anyone else while we're doing this? Whatever *this* is ...' she mumbled awkwardly, her cheeks flushing the most gorgeous shade of pink.

Blinking rapidly, I ran her words through my mind, realising to my joy that she seemed to be asking for exclusivity.

'No, and I hope you won't either?'

Caitlin actually laughed, the corners of her eyes crinkling as she looked at me with a wry smile. 'Hardly. Just attempting to deal with you is stressful enough.'

Perfect. That was settled then. Caitlin and I were a sort of, not quite defined, but exclusive couple.

It made for a mouthful, but I had to admit, I loved the ambiguity and excitement.

Caitlin's thumb was now tentatively moving against the back of my hand and I couldn't help but look down and grin at our entwined fingers. It was a small, almost insignificant connection, but for me, this hand-holding status was perfect. For now. Caitlin certainly seemed to have come around to the idea of more in the long run. She was a little fragile, but I had every intention of being the man to help her escape her self-imposed boundaries.

# SIX

## CAIT

I left the hospital feeling ... well, actually, I wasn't entirely sure how I felt, because I was pretty sure my brain had short circuited somewhere back in Jack's room.

What word would suitably sum up my emotions? Hopeful, perhaps? Happy? Loved up? Exuberant? None really seemed momentous enough to describe all that had occurred.

Was I in a relationship now? Grinning, I bit down on my lower lip to try and stop myself looking like a complete loon. I think I *was* in a relationship. Which was flipping crazy. Me, Caitlin Byrne, spinster specialist, was in a 'taking-it-slow-and-seeing-how-it-goes' kind of relationship, which was still by definition a relationship, I suppose. Maybe I'd be able to ditch the spinster title soon.

One thing was for sure – whatever the feelings swirling inside of me were, they lasted all through my cab ride back and were still with me as I approached the house. Pulling in a refreshing breath of the cool evening air, I walked through our small front garden with a broad grin on my face, hoping that Allie would be in so I could share my exciting news.

An ironic laugh slipped from my lips. Ha! Listen to me, actually wanting to talk about a man for a change. Allie would be in for a shock.

I was a complete newbie to this – I needed advice,

and I needed it quick, but I also wanted to press her on the issues with Sean, and check she was OK. Just because I'd had a spectacularly exciting afternoon didn't mean I would forget that my bestie was going through some tough times at the moment.

Pushing open the front door, I saw Allie on the sofa, staring into space with a cup of tea grasped in her hands. She was home. Perfect.

Tamping down my excited nerves, I was about to gently push her on the developments with Sean when she beat me to it. 'Hey. How's Jack? Tell me what happened, I want the deets.'

'I thought we could talk about you and Sean first,' I offered, slipping onto the sofa beside her.

'Nope, that can come later. I want gossip first. Come on, how did it go?'

Her keen eyes and adamant refusal gave me the push I needed, and I felt something flip-flop in my belly as I suddenly set off, splurging out everything I had been holding inside me.

'It was good. He's OK. I mean, he's not fully OK, obviously. He's got burns, and his wrist ... ugh ... you should have seen it, his watch strap had melted and fused to his skin. It was gross. But they're confident they can remove it in the morning so that's really goo –'

'Cait, take a breath, woman.' Allie had placed a hand on my arm and I suddenly realised that I was talking a mile a minute and really did need to breathe. Oops. I may have gotten a little carried away. Pausing, I drew in several breaths and released them through my nose.

'So I take it the visit went well? You're glad you went to see him?'

Clearing my throat, I tried to control the blush I could feel flaming my cheeks. 'Yeah. I'm really glad I went. He was in good spirits, all things considered.'

'That's probably because you went to see him.'

Annoyingly, my cheeks reddened further. Damn it. At this rate, my lousy face would give away my news before I'd even managed to say it. Suddenly feeling really nervous, I shrugged and stood up to fetch some wine from the kitchen. I needed a drink to calm myself down.

'So are you going to give the guy a break and try a date with him yet?' she enquired, her tone laden with curiosity.

My cheeks were now so hot that I was amazed they hadn't actually ignited.

Jack and I hadn't used the term 'date', or even dating, but I think it had been implied. 'Actually, we did talk about us maybe moving things on,' I confessed, returning with a bottle of red and two glasses.

'Really?' Allie squeaked, suddenly sitting very upright and looking as shocked as I felt.

'Yeah. I was so nervous when he said it I couldn't decide if I wanted to run away, throw up, or dive into his arms.'

'What did you do?' she pressed desperately.

'It was a close run thing, but obviously I stayed and talked it through with him.'

'*And?*'

'*And* I totally panicked when he mentioned us being more than friends. So …' I shrugged.

'*So* …? Cait this is unbearable! I wish you'd spit it out!' Allie was clearly losing patience, because she was now urging me on with some very exasperated hand flapping.

'So … Jack suggested we try being two people who like one another and want to get to know each other.'

'Right,' Allie agreed, but I could tell from the tone of her voice that she didn't quite understand it the way Jack and I did. He'd immediately understood that the idea of a formal relationship scared me, so this was his way of helping me relax by not putting the pressure of a label on it … whatever *it* was.

'Anyway, he knows that slow steps is all I can manage right now … but … well, I'm kind of dating him now.' Allie's eyes flared with the same kind of happiness I was feeling in my belly and then, suddenly, she flapped her arms, unable to keep her excitement contained for a second longer.

'Oh my God! This is so exciting, Cait!'

And it was, but my excitement and happiness were mixed with overwhelming anxiety. Was I nuts trying to date a Hollywood actor who was over ten years my senior? I guess I'd find out soon enough. 'I'm feeling pretty dazed, it's all such a mix of happiness and fear, but amazing too. Nothing really happened apart from talking, but we did hold hands for a bit.' It had been more like an hour, but I kept that part to myself.

'You held hands?' Allie asked, her eyebrows lifting in pleasant surprise. Considering I was talking about a man and actually openly discussing the way I felt about him – pretty much a first where Spinster Cait was concerned – Allie was managing to contain her glee surprisingly well, apart from her arm flapping episode, bless her.

Nodding, I gave a small hum as I recalled how I'd seen his injuries and grabbed his hand. I was the least touchy-feely person I knew, but *wham*, put Jack Felton within spitting distance and I became all grabby like a frigging octopus. Not that that would be a bad thing any more, now we were kind of dating.

'I didn't think I'd ever find someone I could trust like this again,' I added, slowly absorbing the enormity of this new reality, and as a result there was a nervous shake to my hand as I poured the first glass of wine.

'Tell me about the hand holding,' Allie asked keenly as she accepted the glass.

I shrugged, suddenly embarrassed. 'Jack noticed my habit of flicking these,' I said, pointing to my elastic bands. 'Apparently he doesn't like the idea of me hurting myself. He said to squeeze his hand instead, like an oversized stress ball.'

Allie's eyes opened wide and she blinked several times before sighing. 'Wow. That's really romantic. I think I like him even more.'

'Yeah.' I replied, knowing with certainty that I *definitely* liked him more than I did before. 'It was nice.'

'Just nice?' she replied with a glint in her eye.

Giggling, I shook my head. 'OK, it was more than nice.' Opening up about my feelings seemed to be far easier now I'd made my decision with Jack.

I took a sip of wine and waggled my eyebrows. 'So, that's my gossip. Fill me in on Sean while we're settled.'

Allie winced, gulped some of her drink and held out her glass for a top up. 'Let's have a few drinks first.' Uh-oh. That didn't sound particularly promising.

'Before we change topics, I just want to say I'm really glad Jack's OK, and I'm really proud of you.'

The blush that had receded from my cheeks popped back up and I tried to hide my reddening face by nodding and turning my head. It was almost starting to sink in … I was dating Jack Felton.

I really couldn't have been any happier about it.

# SEVEN

## ALLIE

The sun was slowly beginning to sink in the sky, but it was still warm enough to move out to the deck and enjoy the evening. The house I shared with Cait was on the small side, but it was worth it just to get this deck. It had probably seen more use than the other rooms in the house combined.

As a treat, we had ordered a Chinese takeaway – courtesy of Cait's first pay check – and the delicious goodies were spread across the small table in front of us, making me salivate. BBQ ribs, prawn toast, sweet and sour chicken, duck in black bean sauce, spicy chilli beef … the dishes went on and on.

'Consider this an early birthday meal,' Cait grinned, lifting her wine glass in a toast.

I smiled, happy that Cait had remembered my birthday, which was in two days' time, and clinked my glass against hers before taking a swig. Sean and I might be on a break, but at least I could celebrate with my best friend. 'Thanks, Cait, this looks amazing. I thought with the fire and everything that's been going on with Jack, you might have forgotten.'

Cait made a dismissive raspberry noise and shook her head. 'No chance. This is the first time in ages I actually get to see you on your birthday. I've taken the day off work, so is there anything particular you'd like to do?'

Looking back at the food, I topped up my chilli beef. There was way too much food here for just the two of us, but I suspected this was Cait's way of trying to perk me up because she knew just how much of a sucker I was for a decent Chinese meal.

'Not really. Maybe mooch around the shops and get lunch somewhere?'

'Sounds good.'

Over the next half-hour we continued to stuff ourselves while I gave Cait an update of my break with Sean. I explained, in painful detail, the course of my last few days; discovering his beach house empty but full of beer bottles and smelling like perfume, flying to LA and finding him sick, meeting his sister Evie, and then lastly, with flaming cheeks, I told her how I'd accidentally ended up sleeping with him.

At this tit-bit, Cait dropped her chopsticks and raised both eyebrows. 'How do you "accidentally" sleep with someone? "Oops, sorry, I tripped and fell on your dick?"' she joked, still not looking best impressed. It was hardly surprising, because I wasn't best impressed with myself, either.

Dropping my eyes, I fiddled with the hem of my shorts. 'It wasn't like that. He woke me up by doing … *stuff* to me, and I was sleepy and confused. By the time I'd fully come to my senses it was too late.'

'The deed had been done,' Cait concluded with a sage nod.

'Yeah.' Recalling Sean's distraught face that day, I put my chopsticks down as any remaining appetite I had vanished. 'He looked crestfallen when I said I didn't want to have any contact with him until the Savannah fiasco is sorted. I felt terrible,' I admitted. 'I still do.'

Cait resumed her dinner, chewing thoughtfully on a spring roll. Pushing my plate away, I leant my elbows on my knees as my sudden guilt made the food I'd eaten feel like a sack of rocks in my stomach. On the table, Cait's phone beeped with a message alert and she

46

opened it up before making a face and dropping the phone. 'Ugh. My fingers are so greasy.'

As she wiped her hands clean I picked her phone up and used my napkin to clean the smears for her before glancing at the screen.

'Don't worry, I can clean that. Here, let me have it,' Cait said, her voice higher than usual. My eyes strayed across the screen again and I saw a message from someone called Phillip. I frowned, and instinctively pulled the phone back.

Cait didn't have male friends, so that made it weird to start with, but what was really bugging me was the content of the message.

'Who's Phillip?' I asked, my tone tight.

Cait scrabbled at my hand as she attempted to snatch the phone back, which was very un-Cait-like. 'Uhhh … just … a friend. Someone from … the studio. Give me my phone. Please.'

Something in my gut told me she was lying, so instead, I swivelled out of her reach and read the message.

*From: Phillip*

*Thanks for letting me know she got back to L.A. safely. I appreciate it. S*

It didn't take a genius to work out what was going on.

'This is from Sean, isn't it?'

Cait didn't even attempt to deny it, crumpling, nodding once, and leaning forwards to bury her face in her hands. 'Yeah. Shit, Allie. I'm sorry.'

'Cait, what the hell? Why are you and Sean texting? Are you spying on me?' My heart rate had rocketed. I wasn't jealous, I knew neither Cait nor Sean would ever cheat on me, but I couldn't believe they'd been talking behind my back.

'He was going out of his mind. I mean, he had a real, proper panic attack.'

That brought me up short. Sean had had another panic attack? I knew he had them, but I hadn't thought they'd been such an issue recently.

'When?' I croaked, my voice suddenly losing its force.

'After you two had the bust-up at the studios, he came to the house looking for you.' Cait ran a hand through her hair, her meal also abandoned on the table. 'I didn't know you'd broken up, and he was ranting, barely making any sense. He explained what had happened and had this panic attack.' Cait swallowed hard, as if struggling with her composure, and she wasn't the only one.

Seeing me on the verge of crumbling, Cait gave my forearm a supportive squeeze. 'He asked if I would text him updates, but I swear I said no. He was in such a state though, so I took his number in case of emergencies, then he messaged me today. He must have got my number from Jack.' Cait looked worried I wouldn't believe her, but I did, completely.

He'd had a panic attack because of me. As if I didn't feel bad enough about the monumental 'accidental shag' in Vegas, I had this to add to it. *Fuck.*

'It's not been a regular thing, I promise. He messaged me this morning to see if you had got back from Vegas OK, and I replied, that's all,' Cait whispered, her eyes wide and imploring.

'I believe you, Cait.'

Chewing on my lip, I let out a long, low breath. So he was still my man with over-protective tendencies, which reassured me a little. But his panic attacks had come back. Wasn't that just fan-bloody-tastic?

# EIGHT

## JACK

Sucking in a deep lungful of air, I smiled. It couldn't quite be described as 'fresh air' because it was humid as hell, but still, it was real, outside air, and not the recycled air-conditioned stuff I'd had to deal with in the hospital.

Tipping my head back, I gazed at the clear blue sky. It felt so bloody good to be out of the confines of that suffocating room.

In the end I'd been kept in for observation for three days, and to my surprise, Caitlin had visited me each day, growing in confidence and even being the one to initiate a hand hold on two occasions.

I'd been released just after lunchtime, and as much as I wanted to use my freedom to explore my relationship with Caitlin, I was aware that I needed to tread carefully. And anyway, from the text she had sent me earlier, I knew she was working.

Ensuring I gave her space was going to be an uphill battle; I'd already practically inundated her with messages. I was so enamoured with her that I wanted to spend every minute of every day getting to know her.

Not to mention night times. A small groan escaped my throat as my eyes fluttered shut. I wanted to feel Caitlin curled up in my arms more than I wanted my next breath. I knew the physical side of things would take a long while to develop, and I was completely fine with that, but it didn't mean I couldn't dream about it.

Which I did frequently. I was a hot-blooded male,

after all.

She had an innocence about her that was quite rare, reminiscent of the shy, blushing beauties from a Jane Austen novel. Women in Hollywood were a whole different kettle of fish: done up to their eyeballs with make-up and wearing the teeniest, tiniest clothes while they twerked their way through life hoping to snag a rich guy in the process.

But not Caitlin. In fact, I'd place money on the fact that she'd only had a few lovers in her life. One or two, tops. Probably a high school sweetheart and then some tentative college guy who was equally as shy and nervous.

I was neither shy nor tentative in bed. I might have been selective about the women I'd slept with, but I'd had enough sex in my relationships over the years to know what I was doing, and I'd been told on several occasions I did it pretty damn well. I loved sex. Loved exploring the soft curves of a woman's body and working out what made her tick. I loved being the man to make her breath hitch, skin flush, and body clench as I made her lose control. The idea of doing those things with Caitlin was so exciting I could barely wait. But wait I would.

Holding off would only make it all the sweeter in the end.

My good mood was soured slightly by the ongoing issues between Sean and Allie. He'd texted me last night to say he was back in LA and at a loose end if I fancied meeting up. As I'd read his message I realised that he probably didn't even know I'd been involved in the fire. I had got the distinct impression that he was feeling sorry for himself, so I'd replied saying I'd go over for a beer.

This was the first time I'd been to his new place, and from the outside it looked pretty amazing. I loved houses near the sea. My home in the UK was in the remote Scottish wilderness and overlooked a windswept cove and beach. I loved it, but for my LA house Flynn had suggested something a little more secure, as I had a much bigger fan following over here, so we'd picked the house in the all-singing, all-dancing gated compound designed specifically for the ultra-rich and famous.

Just seconds after Flynn had dropped me outside, the front door opened and I was greeted by Sean, clad in just running shorts and trainers, dripping with sweat.

My eyes narrowed as I saw the bandages on one of his hands, and I laughed dryly as I saw him mirroring my expression and looking at my own bandaged arm.

'Twins!' he murmured wryly, wiggling his bandage at me. 'Come on in. It looks like we've got a lot to catch up on.'

I entered his new place and nodded my appreciation as I followed him through to a light lounge with a stunning sea view. It was lovely. Simple design, sparse on furniture, but almost exactly the type of style I liked.

'I need a quick shower after my run, I won't be long. Make yourself at home.'

I took him at his word, and so by the time Sean emerged, I had a soda water in my good hand and was reclining in one of the sun loungers on his deck, listening to the waves break on the beach below.

Raising my bottle to him, I smiled. 'This place is awesome.'

'Thanks.' Sean looked pleased and joined me on the other lounger after grabbing a bottle of water. 'I've got beer in the fridge, you want one?' he offered.

'Thanks, but I gotta drive home later.' *And maybe pop in to see Caitlin.* The idea sprung to my mind without prompting and immediately caused a grin to spread on my lips. If there was even a remote possibility I could be seeing her, I definitely wanted to be one hundred per cent sober.

'So what happened exactly?' Sean asked, indicating my arm and oblivious to my suddenly flushed skin.

Thinking of the fire quickly doused my lusty thoughts, and so with a grimace I explained about the studio fire and my burns, and by the time I'd gone into the gruesome details of my mangled wrist, Sean was sitting upright, listening intently.

'Jeez. Sounds like you were quite the hero.'

'Not really. I was just closest to him,' I replied, brushing off his compliment. As far as I was concerned, I had done what anyone would have in that situation. 'So enough about me, what happened to *your* hand?'

It was comical, both of us sitting here with almost matching bandages.

'When Allie broke things off with me I punched a sign,' Sean confessed with an embarrassed shrug. 'Broke two knuckles.'

When I'd first met him – probably getting on for thirteen years ago now – Sean had had a bit of a temper. His on-off girlfriend, Elena, (more like a friend with benefits, by all accounts) had just died in an accident, and from what I could gather it had sent him off the rails. The young man I'd known then was a fighter, drinker, and serial seducer, and a million miles away from the man I now classed as one of my closest friends.

Perhaps he could tell I was about to give him a lecture on controlling his temper, because Sean grinned and held up a hand. 'It was accidental, Jack, I swear. I threw my arms up and caught this one on a big studio board. Hurt like a fucker.'

'I'll bet.' Now we were settled I decided it was time to broach the elephant in the room. 'So, how are things between you and Allie?'

Sean slugged on his water like it was beer and let out a frustrated sigh. 'We're on a break until I get the situation with Savannah resolved.' He sighed heavily and gave me a miserable look. 'It hurts so fucking much, but I understand why she needs the space. Savannah is a soul sucking parasite, the quicker I can get her away from both Allie and me, the better. Finlay's arranged a press conference for tomorrow, so hopefully Allie and I can work things out then.'

'That sounds pretty positive,' I commented, feeling a bit useless with regards to what advice to give.

'Yeah. Ah, fuck it. Do you want to crack open a few beers to take my mind off things? You can crash in the spare room.'

My plans of seeing Caitlin vaporised before my eyes, but mates in need were mates in need, and Sean clearly needed me. It wasn't like I'd actually made plans anyway.

Nodding, I settled in for the evening. 'OK, sounds good.' I felt a little bad for being so happy when Sean was so down, so it was the least I could do.

'I'll grab some beers.' Sean disappeared, leaving me with my thoughts. Swilling the bottle in my hand, I watched the clear liquid bubble and froth. Cocking my head to the side I listened as Sean turned on a familiar song on the radio in the kitchen and found myself smiling as my heart sped up a little.

It was Adele's 'One and Only', a track that had reminded me of Caitlin every single time I heard it. I felt like a complete sap comparing my life to a song, but the lyrics had completely summed up the state of things between us since meeting.

Maybe I'd make her a copy of this song and tell her how I thought of her when I heard it.

'Hey, what's with the sappy smile?' Sean asked as he rejoined me and held out a beer.

Busted. My cheeks flamed with embarrassment. Make her a copy? Jeez, what was I, a teenager making a mix tape for the girl he was crushing on?

'I was just thinking about Caitlin,' I admitted sheepishly.

Sean raised an eyebrow and grinned at me. 'Just because my love life is temporarily screwed up doesn't mean we can't discuss yours. Come on, dish the dirt, what's happened?'

I ran a hand through my hair as I thought back to her visits. We'd only held hands and talked, but it had been amazing. 'We're sort of at the really early stage of a relationship.'

Sean gave me a pleasantly surprised look and then smirked. 'The "fucking like bunnies" stage?'

Ha. Hardly. 'No, not quite. This is Caitlin we're talking about.'

'Ah, of course.' Sean sobered his features as he sipped his beer. 'Has she told you why she's so jumpy?'

Letting out a deep breath, I shook my head. 'Not really. She's hinted it's to do with her ex so I'm guessing he was really overbearing and that put her off relationships.'

'Given how skittish she is … did you ever think maybe he was abusive?' Sean ventured tentatively.

My teeth ground together so hard I saw Sean wince in sympathy. 'Yeah, I thought that was a possibility.'

'Sorry, I didn't mean to spoil your excitement. So what's happened between you?' he asked, sipping his beer and letting out a contented smacking noise with his lips.

With a self-conscious shrug I recounted our kiss on the studio run and told him about Caitlin's visits to the hospital.

'So you've only kissed once in the woods, and held hands at the hospital?' he asked in disbelief.

When he described it like that, it sounded so insignificant. But it wasn't to me – it was monumental

55

and I was savouring every precious moment. 'Yeah.'

God. First mix tapes and now "precious"? What the heck had gotten into me?

*Caitlin*. That's what. Because if I had to take it slow and just hold hands for the next year, I would, and what's more, as long as I had Caitlin by my side I would be perfectly content with that.

My embarrassment must have shown on my face, because Sean leant forwards to land a friendly punch on my shoulder. 'Hey, lose the face. Taking it slow in a relationship can be great,' he nodded, before his face split into a grin. 'So I've heard, anyway,' he added. 'Nah, seriously, it's pretty romantic.'

Pretty romantic.

Yeah, I liked that summary. I liked it lot.

# NINE

## SEAN

After making sure Jack had everything he needed for the night, I stumbled to my bedroom feeling just a little tipsy. I'd only had three or four bottles over the entire evening, but after the exertion of my run it had been enough to take the edge off my stress.

Jack really was a good mate, and such easy company that I'd almost managed to forget the looming press conference and my issues with Allie for an hour or two.

As I closed my bedroom door, I dragged my T-shirt over my head and kicked my shorts off in the general direction of the wash basket. I was about to head to the en suite to brush my teeth when I spotted my laptop on the bed.

I'd decided this morning that it would be wise to print off a paper copy of my contract before the press conference, just in case Finlay decided to get arsy with me afterwards. At least if I had my contract in my hand, my lawyer could check the fine print and make sure he didn't screw me over. The only problem had been that my personal records were stored on my home computer in the UK, and I'd been having trouble accessing them remotely.

I'd contacted David back home, my most trusted tech guy, and asked him if he could sort the issue, which luckily he had, so I could once again log on to my UK computer from here, all the way across the ocean. Technology was bloody amazing. I remember when I was a kid and had to load my computer games using a tape player. Jeez, that made me feel old. Would kids these days even know what a cassette was?

Shoving my hair back from my forehead, I dropped onto the bed and opened up the laptop lid. The screen glowed to life with a message box illuminated in the centre.

*Downloads complete.*

Once I'd downloaded my contract this morning I'd been skimming through my documents, and the file for my security footage had caught my eye. That was the footage that contained the videos of Allie and I having sex, the ones she'd found out about, freaked out about, and then demanded we watch together. Unfortunately, we'd broken up before we'd had the chance.

I'd decided to copy it across to my laptop and erase it from my home computer like I'd told her I would. I'd started the download before I'd gone to work out, and I could see it had completed downloading sometime during my session.

Curiosity got the better of me and I clicked the "open" button to see if the file transfer had worked properly. Once the egg timer on my screen stopped spinning, I was presented with a list of dated files.

It wasn't hard to find the one I most wanted to see, because I thought it was the most memorable encounter between Allie and me, taken last Christmas Eve. Loading the file, I licked my lips and held my breath.

The screen opened full-size and I was met with the sight of Allie sat in my lounge in England. God, it was surreal to see this footage after so much had happened between us.

Knowing we were still apart, on a 'break', I knew I should close down the computer and go to bed, but I couldn't help myself and I fast forwarded to where I entered the room. My face was dark, and shoulders

59

hunched. I looked like such a grouchy bastard.

Had I really been that moody with her? It was a fucking miracle she'd stayed with me as long as she had.

Settling myself more comfortably on the bed, I let out a long breath as I watched the scene play out. I'd entered the room and caught Allie reading about Elena on her laptop. I'd made some remark about keeping Allie on her toes and she'd called me an arsehole. Which I probably deserved. After that I had confessed my secrets about Elena, then I'd kissed her.

Watching as her tentative response turned more passionate, I shifted and leant closer to the screen. Allie was so beautiful. On the screen she arched her body to my touch and a groan left my lips. Watching us together was such a turn-on that I was now completely hard, my cock poking eagerly out my boxers.

I eyed my erection for a second before pushing aside any guilt and wrapping a palm around my solid shaft. Hissing at the ache in my busted knuckles, I swapped hands and looked back at the screen. My left hand smoothed up and down my cock, feeling awkward and unfamiliar, but it was all I had tonight so I'd have to make do.

I watched as Allie shook her head. Her eyes had been dilated and her cheeks flushed, but I could recall clearly how she had played hard to get, and how much of a fucking turn-on it had been. It still was. She'd repeatedly claimed she didn't want me while her body had said the complete opposite by rubbing against mine.

Watching as she leant back and accused me of only being able to communicate through a 'quick fuck', I began to move my hand quicker. I'd taunted her that night, making her repeat her crude words, and damn if hearing her use dirty talk hadn't been the hottest thing I'd ever experienced.

Aware that Jack was down the corridor, I turned the

volume up just enough so I could hear her breathy pleas. *'Oh God, don't stop, Sean ... take me again ... I want you to fuck me ... fuck me better than any man ever has ...'* I groaned long and low as my hand jerked up and down and pleasure began to build in my tightening balls.

Allie capitulated, giving her consent, and the Sean on the screen went wild, ripping her clothes off and descending on her like a man possessed. Allie arched beneath my touch as I pinched her nipples and nibbled on her neck before sliding a hand between her legs. As if in sync with the video, my cock released a small pulse of pre-come onto my fingers to ease the smoothness of my strokes.

My hand continued to rub up and down with repeated urgency. It still wasn't as smooth as usual, and not as experienced as my right when it came to servicing myself, but this video was the sexiest thing I'd ever seen. I could probably come from just watching the footage. I watched avidly as on the screen I grabbed Allie's hips and virtually impaled her on my desperate cock. Her head rolled backwards as she let out a long, low groan of pleasure and greedily wrapped her legs around my hips.

My gorgeous girl.

I think she'd expected me to ram back inside of her like I had done the previous times we'd fucked, but this was the day I'd realised that Allie meant far more to me than just a casual lay, and instead of my usual force, I'd taken her by surprise and pressed my length inside her slowly. Almost lovingly. The look of surprise on her face was priceless, as was the knowing look in her eyes that followed shortly after. It was more than just sex between us, and in that moment she knew it too.

My hips bucked on the empty bed, desperately wishing that Allie were here with me and not just on my laptop screen. As of tomorrow, after the press conference, that would hopefully be a different matter.

My computer self was reaching climax, the muscles on my back straining as I tried to hold on for Allie. Her face reddened, as it always did before she came, and keeping her eyes fixed on mine I watched as she cried out her orgasm, pleasure so intense it almost looked like pain sweeping her face as her nails bit into my shoulders and she bucked insatiably against me.

Back in real time I felt my orgasm nearing, and as I rammed inside Allie on the screen and climaxed, I simultaneously came into my hand with a muffled groan.

Looking down at my heaving chest muscles and the sticky mess of come that now covered my fist, boxers, and stomach, I felt a brief flicker of guilt that I had just pleasured myself to images of Allie, but it was short-lived as I felt relaxation sweep through my muscles.

I really needed that.

Looking at the screen, I paused the image and gently swept my index finger over her face.

Tomorrow, my gorgeous girl.

I'll make you mine again tomorrow.

# TEN

## ALLIE

The irritating beeping woke me for a second time, and with an accepting sigh I blinked my sleep-heavy eyes and rubbed my face. It would seem my mobile didn't want me to have a lie-in today.

Not that I really minded – it was my birthday, after all.

The first message to wake me had been from my parents, so wondering who this was from, I rolled over to reach for my phone, assuming it was another friend or a relative wishing me happy birthday.

*Message from Sean P.*

Instinctively, my heart leapt in my chest. As much as I wanted to hear from him, the opposite was also true – I didn't want to hear from him until things were sorted.

Perhaps he'd seen my birthday as a reason to break our no-contact rule?

I stared at the tiny illuminated letters and drew in a sharp breath to try and calm my suddenly hammering pulse. My heart hurt just from looking at his name – how ridiculous was that? The extent to which this man affected me was astounding.

Sitting up, I drew my knees in and chewed on my lip as I delayed opening the message. Even without any contact, he had constantly been on my mind.

The last two and a half days since I'd left Vegas had passed in a blur of tears and stress. Cait had tried her best to distract me, but I still felt like a bit of myself had been removed. Not just removed, but torn away from my soul. I missed him so much.

I was scared, no, *terrified*, of getting irreparably hurt by Sean's glamorous lifestyle, which, let's face it, was poles apart from mine. But I loved him so much I didn't see how I could do without him.

Taking a deep breath, I finally clicked the 'Open Message' button and read his words without breathing.

*From: Sean P*

*Allie, I know I said I wouldn't pressure you or contact you, but I thought you would want to know that the press conference is today. Your name will not be mentioned. I miss you. S x*

As I skimmed his words a second time, a huge breath flooded from my lips, causing me to make a raspberry sound. Well, it hadn't been the 'Happy Birthday' message I had been expecting, but *'I miss you'* certainly hit all my pressure points at once.

The press conference was today? On my birthday? I couldn't decide if that was brilliant timing or the worst ever. Should I go? Would that be weird? Not to mention stressful, having to see Savannah again.

Sighing, I dropped my mobile onto the duvet and only just resisted the temptation to call him so I could hear his sexy as sin voice.

Instead, I chewed on my lip while pondering what to do, then, feeling none the wiser, I got out of bed to have a shower … a cold one.

After drying off and chucking some shorts and a T-shirt on I headed downstairs. Cait was off work today, so she would be able to advise me on what to do.

Bless her, I found her in the kitchen preparing a birthday breakfast. A stack of thick pancakes was steaming on the counter and Cait was just putting the finishing touches to some crispy bacon.

'Good morning, happy birthday!' she exclaimed, pulling me into the most gigantic hug ever. 'I thought as we were in America, we'd do your breakfast American-style: pancakes with all the trimmings.'

Pancakes were my favourite breakfast, so that was just fine by me. As well as maple syrup, on the table there was a bowl of chopped strawberries, some sliced banana, chocolate sauce, and a huge pot of coffee. Perfect.

Cait had obviously put in a huge effort to make this special, but even with her infectious happiness, I was struggling to smile as I sat down on one of the chairs at the kitchen table. I did though, for her sake, and even added an enthusiastic rub of my stomach as I took in the banquet before me. 'Wow, Cait, this looks amazing, thank you!'

Turning to me with a narrow-eyed look, Cait placed the bacon down and joined me at the table. 'Good effort, kiddo, but I know you too well to fall for that fake smile. What's got you so grumpy on your birthday?'

Sighing, I explained about the text.

After mulling it over, Cait nodded slowly and got up. 'I thought this would be good news, but you don't look too happy,' she commented as she flipped two pancakes onto her plate and stacked them high with bacon.

'It *is* good news, and I am happy, but I'm really nervous,' I confessed, taking a huge gulp of coffee. 'I mean, this is like D-Day for our relationship, isn't it? His director is probably furious that he's had to do the press conference, which will cause issues for Sean at work … what if he decides that because of all this I'm too high maintenance and not worth the bother?'

Cait laughed so hard that several chunks of bacon flew out of her mouth. 'As if! He's crazy about you!

66

Surely the fact he's willing to piss off a man as influential and intimidating as Finlay James proves how committed he is?'

She had a point. Sean's director would score a twenty out of ten in the intimidation department. Maybe even a thirty. Even just witnessing a tiny snippet of Finlay's temper at the studios had been scary, so Sean *was* risking a lot to make this stand.

Cait had been nothing but supportive these last few days, but it was obvious she was firmly on Team Sean, and had used every available opportunity to convince me of his dedication ... much in the same way I had engineered ways to point out Jack's positives to her.

'You were doing pretty great together before this came up. There's no reason it can't get even better.' Cait licked the maple syrup from her fork. 'Eat up, we need to get going,' she said, with a definite twinkle in her eye, as I gave her a confused look. 'You just told me the press conference is today. You don't think I'm going to miss that spectacle, do you?'

'I wasn't sure I should attend,' I confessed.

Cait made a dismissive noise in the back of her throat. 'Little Miss Smarty Pants Savannah Hilton getting her come-uppance in front of a room full of people? You bet you should be attending!' And then Cait did something I'd never seen her do before. She cackled. Rather loudly and wickedly.

Wow. She was really excited about this. As I thought about it, I felt butterflies settle in my own stomach. After this, Sean and I could be together for real. Like an actual couple. In public. That sounded almost too good to be true.

Biting my lip nervously, I nodded and made up my mind. I'd definitely regret it if I missed out on Savannah being publicly told she wasn't the woman Sean wanted to be with. 'Sod it, you're right. If I go and put a bit of make-up on, do you think you can find out the time of the press conference?'

Beaming from ear to ear, Cait shooed me off towards my bedroom and nodded. 'I think one or two of my colleagues are probably in the know about this. You go and get ready, I'll make some enquires.'

And just like that I was leaping up the stairs, desperate to see Sean again.

The press conference turned out to be in one of the smaller stages on Sean's studio complex, and even though I rushed to get ready, we still arrived with just five minutes to spare.

I'd wanted to speak to Sean beforehand to make sure he was definitely OK with upsetting his director, but getting behind the scenes proved trickier than I'd hoped.

A big, burly security guard stood between us and the room where Sean was waiting, and when I say big, I mean gargantuan; I'd never seen a man as tall and broad as this one. He was having none of my attempted distractions (which came in the form of some outrageous compliments), and merely shook his head disapprovingly at Cait's attempt at a bribe, so reluctantly we headed to the public seating area.

Shortly after we took our seats, a thrum of excitement passed through the air, and then Sean and a sour-faced Savannah made their way out, each flanked by a PR representative.

Beside me, Cait drew in a gasp and grabbed my forearm. 'God, Allie, look what you've done to him – he looks awful!' she whispered. 'Did he look that bad in Vegas?'

Remembering how sick Sean had looked when I'd arrived in Vegas, I nodded and allowed my eyes to really soak in his appearance.

Cait was right; Sean looked miserable, not to mention

haggard. Still drop dead gorgeous of course, but more than a little worse for wear. The weeks' worth of stubble I'd seen in Vegas had now developed, almost resembling a full on beard. I had to say, I didn't mind it.

Once the media were seated, Sean wasted no time getting started, and leant forwards to tap the microphone in front of him several times.

'Thank you, everyone, for coming. I'd like to start by thanking the fans of *LA Blue,* who have made the series the hit it is. We all really appreciate your support.' Niceties out of the way, Sean rolled off his shoulders and inhaled a long, deep breath. 'The reason for this press conference is to clear up a few facts about mine, and Savannah's, personal lives,' Sean paused as a murmur ran through the crowd. 'There's been a lot of speculation about our relationship recently, but I'd like it to be clear and on the record that Savannah and I are no longer together.'

My gaze shifted to Savannah, and I watched as she pouted and allowed her gaze to drift off sideways towards the windows as if bored to death.

'This was an entirely mutual decision and we're still friends, but that's all there is to it. We thought our fans deserved to know.'

Savannah's sour pout didn't make it look like the decision had been mutual, but now the news was out, I didn't waste a second longer looking at her. Instead, I focused my stare upon Sean.

It was irritating that Sean couldn't confess how he'd been practically blackmailed into going along with the engagement farce, but I was starting to understand how Hollywood worked, and coming clean just wasn't an option.

Now that Sean had finished his speech, the front four rows became a mass of frantically waving hands and whirling cameras as each journalist tried to get the best shot and attract Sean's attention so they could fire questions at him.

'Sean, are either of you in serious relationships with anybody else right now?' I was on the edge of my seat, and mildly tempted to stand up and yell 'He's mine! All mine!'

A flicker of something flashed in Sean's eyes … desperation? But before he could answer, Savannah leant into her microphone with a pucker of her fat lips.

'He is,' she drawled, flashing Sean a taunting look as if punishing him for making her go through the press conference. To give him credit, Sean barely even reacted to her behaviour, merely sitting back and keeping his gaze away from her.

All eyes rotated to Sean like some bizarre tennis match as an expectant silence fell over the crowd.

'Is it true, Sean? Is it the blonde we've seen you with recently?' called a journalist, breaking the silence and shouting his questions in a rapid fire.

'Yes, I am seeing someone …' Sean confirmed, but then hesitated, looking uncertain, and my stomach all but dropped from my body.

Was he having second thoughts about me?

About *us*?

'Well, I hope I am, anyway,' he muttered, before taking a sip of his water. Thank goodness. His words soothed my terror and I licked my lips, wishing I could swig on his drink to wet my parched mouth.

This was so bizarre, I was quietly sitting in an audience listening to a conversation about myself.

Sean's answer clearly had the press curious, but once again Savannah waved them off dismissively.

'Oh, Sean, stop being such a drama queen,' she purred, giving a roll of her eyes. 'They've had a little bit of a falling out. His girlfriend isn't in the acting business and she's having a hard time adjusting to his celebrity lifestyle.' Savannah abruptly stopped when Sean shot her a look. God, talk about nerve-wracking.

I was so tense that my fists were clenched in my lap and I hardly dared to blink for fear of missing something. Cait had been right, though; I was glad we'd come along.

'Can we assume that you're hoping you can work things out with your girl, Sean?' pushed a particularly inquisitive journalist from the back row and I felt my heart accelerate until it was almost bursting from my ribs.

The look Sean threw at the crowd was one of frustration, his brows drawn together and lips in a tight line. 'Yes. If she still wants me.'

'Anyway, don't you want to know about me? I've just started dating someone too ...' Savannah announced, which caused the attention to immediately move to her as the press sensed another storyline waiting to be written.

All attention was on Savannah now as she primped her hair and fluttered her eyelashes, well and truly enjoying the spotlight. I rolled my eyes at her desperation for attention, but couldn't drag my eyes away from Sean for more than a few seconds. I felt my heart leap as I noticed how he discretely took his phone out of his shirt pocket and checked the screen, before letting out a sigh and placing it on the table in front of him.

Had he been hoping for a reply from me?

I was suddenly overwhelmed with the inappropriate urge to text him just to see his reaction. It was hardly the time or place, but before I knew it I was dragging my phone out of my bag and opening up my messenger app.

Would he get in trouble if his phone beeped? Surely he'd have it on silent? Besides, the focus was well and truly on Savannah now and she was off and running with her story and its ridiculous details.

I quickly composed a message and pressed send before I could change my mind, all the while secretly praying that his phone wasn't about to beep loudly.

*To: Sean P*

*For goodness sake, smile. You look miserable – it doesn't suit you. x*

My eyes were focused on Sean so intently that I hardly blinked, and a second or so later I saw the screen on his mobile glow pale blue as my message arrived. *Phew* – it had been on silent. Looking slightly puzzled, Sean discreetly checked that everyone was still focused on Savannah before casually moving his phone towards himself and reading the text.

A confused frown settled on his brow, but as the realisation hit that I was in the audience, his head shot up and his eyes began to scan the rows.

Things then seemed to happen in slow motion; I held my breath as his eyes passed over the room, row by row, until he saw me and our eyes met, and I saw hope blaze in his big blues. He raised an eyebrow as if to say *'What are you doing here?'*

The connection of our gaze was so strong that the hairs on my arms stood up to attention and my heart was banging out such a fast rhythm in my chest I was starting to feel dizzy with expectation.

Deciding to throw myself fully into the moment, I gave a teasing shrug and a tiny smile as if to give a *'Just thought I'd drop in'* response.

His face noticeably perked up, but Sean didn't text back. I suppose it would have looked pretty unprofessional, but he did risk a small smile – just as I had instructed in my text – and I instantly felt my heart melt.

God, I loved this man.

Teasing was all very well, but I was terrible at playing it cool so as soon as he smiled I felt a blush run to my cheeks and I couldn't stop myself from breaking out into a grin. Sean's response was immediate; his dejected body language morphed into his usual confidence as he sat up straight in his seat and allowed a self-assured, determined look to overtake his handsome features.

Ooohh … Sean Phillips looking at me with focus and a tiny bit of dominance. Yummy. I'd always found confident men attractive, but when Sean looked like this, I practically melted.

Before I could stop myself, my fingers were flying over my phone screen again as I frantically typed out another message.

Cait leant over to read along, her eyebrows rising in a mix of amusement and worry as she realised I was typing to the man of the hour in the middle of his own press conference.

*To: Sean P*

*Don't stare, you'll give me away.*
*P.S. You look very sexy now you're smiling. x*

Sean read the text eagerly and I could have sworn I saw him blush a fraction, before another smile cracked at the corner of his mouth. He looked at me before making a deliberate effort to spread his gaze around the audience, pausing occasionally at various parts of the room.

As I sat gazing at him with my heart almost bursting with love, I couldn't help but think back to his desperate words on the day we'd decided to take a break. *'You have to believe me when I say that I am unconditionally one hundred per cent yours, Allie.'* Even though it was ridiculous to keep firing messages at him, I had a desperate urge to tell him we were OK, and found my fingers composing one final message. I needed to make this a good one. I pondered for a couple of seconds before finally sending:

> *To: Sean P*

> *That's better, much less obvious, thank you. x*
> *P.S. Of course I still want to be with you, you silly sod.*
> *P.P.S. I am 100% yours.*

After reading the message, Sean surprised me by laughing out loud.

*Oops*. I may have gone a bit far with that, but hopefully he wouldn't get into trouble. He looked like a complete lunatic, sitting back in his chair and guffawing before grinning from ear to ear, and I had to wonder what everyone else in the room was making of his behaviour.

My stomach did a flip of happiness and I found myself biting down on my lip as an excited murmur ran through the crowd of journalists. Their attention careened away from Savannah and back to Sean, much to Savannah's obvious annoyance, and a journalist wearing a jacket emblazoned with the logo of *LA Glamour* stood up.

'Care to tell us why you're suddenly looking so perky, Sean?'

Sean gave a self-satisfied smile but remained silent, his eyes glittering with an arrogance that instantly turned me on.

'Can we assume from your grin that it was your

mystery lady … and that things are back on track?'

Sean's eyes flitted across the room before imperceptibly resting on me to seek my go-ahead to say more. Considering he looked so cocksure it was amusing that he wanted my blessing. I gave a nod and Sean's attention returned to the journalist.

'Yes, Rick, it was. Things are certainly looking more positive. I'm sure you'll understand I don't wish to say anything more at this point,' Sean announced with a happy smile.

'No name for us?' pushed Rick, who seemed to be a seasoned pro at this type of thing, and I felt the hairs on the back of my neck raise. Now that we were free to be a couple, I suddenly felt really nervous about people finding out about me, which was stupid, because an up-front, honest relationship was what I'd wanted from the start. Still, I couldn't deny that there was an underlying quiver of nervousness in my belly.

Thankfully, Sean must have guessed how I would be feeling, because he grinned at Rick and then shook his head. 'Afraid not, Rick.'

A few more questions were aimed at Savannah, until one of their publicity agents stepped in and announced the end of the press conference, stating that Sean and Savannah were due back on set. The four of them stood, waved at the crowd, and left the stage.

It was over.

A relieved breath left my lungs. Bloody hell, that had been intense.

Standing up, Cait linked her arm through mine as we started to make our way towards the back and I found myself very glad of the support because my legs actually felt a bit shaky.

Pulling me close, she grinned happily. 'You look like a different person already! The colour has come back to your cheeks and everything. Maybe this won't be such a bad birthday after all, eh?'

I nodded, still feeling a bit dazed. As it sunk in, one thing stuck in my mind and caused frustration to rise in my belly – Sean was due back on set, which meant I couldn't see him until later. Damn it. I really wanted to get things back on track once and for all.

'I wish I could talk to Sean, but it sounded like he was due back at work.' I murmured dolefully.

'Yeah, it did,' Cait agreed. 'Tell you what, let's go for some birthday cocktails instead. The time will fly by and you can see him once he's finished.' I was immediately cheered by the idea of birthday drinks, and we began to head towards the studio exit.

# ELEVEN

## CAIT

As we were jostled by the throngs of people trying to leave, I felt my phone vibrate in my handbag. Once we had reached the relative calm outside, I pulled it from my bag and immediately felt my cheeks heat.

'Aww, did somebody get a message from their boyfriend?' Allie teased in a sing-song voice. It would seem my bestie was back to her usual self. Grinning, I nodded as I opened the text.

*From: Jack F*

*Hey, sweetheart, I know you're not working today, but I was wondering if you had time for a coffee? J x*

Biting my lip, I re-read the message and began to type my reply as excited butterflies settled in my stomach. I still couldn't believe that a man like Jack wanted little ol' me. But it would seem that he did, and the more I adjusted to that fact, the closer I would come to moving things along physically.

We were four days in, and with him being in hospital it had limited us to remaining at the hand-holding stage. He messaged me though, *a lot*, and I found it amusing that he put kisses on his texts when we hadn't yet properly kissed in real life. Not since the encounter in the park, anyway. The electricity between us was potent though, making my skin tingle and body heat whenever we were near each other. To be honest, if I weren't so cautious, I suspect we'd already be humping like bunnies by now regardless of his hospital accommodation.

As of the day before he was out of hospital, and keen to see me, which made my stomach do a loop-the-loop of happy nervousness.

*To: Jack F*

*Hi ☺ I'm with Allie at the moment, just about to start her birthday celebrations. Sorry. I'll be in later though if you want to pop round? x*

I felt a bit silly putting a smiley face, but he always, *always,* wrote 'Hi, sweetheart' in his messages, and replying with a plain 'hi' seemed to be a bit lacking. I didn't have a pet name for him, and I couldn't bring myself to write 'babe' or 'darling', so I'd started to add the emoticon instead.

Once I'd pressed send I looked up to find Allie still grinning at me. Apparently the press conference had acted like a stress reliever, because she looked positively radiant.

'All done, *sweetheart*?' I couldn't help but roll my eyes. After the ribbing I'd given Allie for Sean calling her 'gorgeous girl' she clearly loved returning the favour. Before I could come up with a smart remark my phone gave another buzz in my hand.

*From: Jack F*

*OK, sweetheart. I finish filming at 6, I'll come after that. Looking forward to seeing you. x*

This would be our first 'date' outside of the hospital. Would we kiss? My pulse thumped in my ears as I considered the idea of Jack laying his lips upon mine.

Wanting to avoid more soppy comments from Allie, I quickly pushed the images away, shoved my phone in my bag, and tried distracting her the only way I could think of – booze.

'Yep. What kind of mood are you in? Cocktails? Beer? Wine? Maybe we could grab some snacks too.' It worked a treat, and a second later her teasing was forgotten and she began dragging me towards the studio gates professing a sudden need for a Strawberry Daiquiri followed by cheeseburger and fries.

# TWELVE

## SEAN

I couldn't bloody believe I had to go to work. After Allie's surprise appearance at the press conference, all I wanted to do was see her.

I also wanted to kiss her senseless. My heart sped up and my groin gave a twitch as I realised my understatement. I didn't just want to kiss her senseless, I wanted to bury myself inside of her and fuck her senseless. Oh God, I would definitely do that as soon as humanly possible. As I thought about her soft lips parting below mine, a groan rose in my throat, causing my director to flash me a look. *Oops.* I'd been so lost in thought I'd almost forgotten he was here. My cheeks burned as I cleared my throat, trying to pretend my groan had been linked to a cough.

Unfortunately, after my jaunt to Las Vegas and my week off work, we were now behind schedule, so Finlay was on my back to catch up. My knuckles were still strapped up, but we had been managing to get the majority of the shots done with some clever camera angles so my hand wasn't featured.

Glancing at my watch, I saw I had just under twenty minutes until I was due on set. Finlay was blathering on about some scene he wanted to adapt, but I was still buzzing from Allie's messages and could barely focus.

*P.S. Of course I still want to be with you, you silly sod.*

That line had been particularly great, but a grin as

wide as the Grand Canyon split my lips as I recalled the one which had followed it.

*P.P.S. I am 100% yours.*

Damn right she was. Frustration was buzzing in my system, because I was stuck here when all I wanted to do was see her. Did I have time to squeeze in a visit? Glancing at my watch, I realised I probably would if Finlay would piss off.

After what felt like an eternity, Finlay finally fell quiet, and I tensed in anticipation of his departure. Taking the hint, he left, thank fuck, with a barked command not to be late to set.

I immediately pulled my phone from my pocket, but just as I was about to dial Allie's number, a plan formed in my mind and instead, I dialled Cait.

As the ringing tone sounded I prayed Cait wouldn't say my name when she answered. Finally she accepted the call. 'Hello?'

'Cait, it's Sean. Don't let Allie know, I want to surprise her. Just say "yes" if you're still with her.'

There was a pause, and then Cait hummed. 'Mmm-hmm, yes.'

'Brilliant. OK. I was hoping you'd bring her backstage. I'll only have a few minutes but I really need to see her. If I arrange for Security to let you through, would you do that for me?'

There was another pause. 'I see. OK, I could do that.' She was playing along. Relief flooded my system.

'Thank you, Cait. Pretend that someone from your studio was at the press conference and needs you to do them a favour or something.'

Dropping further into the roleplay, I heard Cait hum and answer. 'I guess that won't take long. I'll pop around now. Bye.'

'Great! I'm in studio two, dressing room three. I owe you one, thank you.'

Dumping the phone down, I dashed to the corridor to let Security know to expect two female visitors. They smirked at me for my over exuberance, but I didn't care, I was going to see Allie again in mere moments and I could barely wait.

# ALLIE

We hadn't even made it out of the studio gates when Cait's phone rang for a second time. The first call had been a message from Jack, but this time she gave the screen a slightly odd look and then answered.

'Hello?' Her eyes narrowed, flicked towards me before bouncing rapidly away again, and then she nodded. What was stranger though, was that I could have sworn her cheeks flushed slightly. Who was calling her?

After talking for a few seconds she shrugged, gave a heavy sigh, and then hung up. Cait deposited her phone in her bag, all the while looking decidedly flustered, which further peaked my curiosity.

'I'm sorry, Allie, we need to nip to one of the studios, I've got a quick thing to do for work.'

Work? I really was confused. 'But you don't work at these studios.'

'I know. Uh … one of the … uh … managers was at the press conference and they're doing some work here this afternoon. He spotted me and wants to pick my brains on something. You can come too.'

With that she grabbed my arm and started charging off, leaving me stumbling at her heels as I saw my dream of a Strawberry Daiquiri disappearing before my very eyes. 'I'll get you one of those extra thick frozen Daiquiris to make up for it,' she promised, targeting my weakness for frozen cocktails.

Cait quickly examined the site map before dragging me to her left. 'Sorry to spoil your birthday afternoon, but this won't take long, I promise.'

We entered a studio and almost immediately came up

against two burly security guards. The taller of the two widened his stance, crossed his arms, and gave us a penetrating look. 'Can I help you, ladies?'

Cait fidgeted for a second – which wasn't surprising considering the intimidating glare she was receiving from the man mountain – pinged her elastic bands, then nodded. 'I'm Caitlin Byrne. My name should be on the list.'

The bodyguards immediately relaxed, sharing an amused look before both breaking out into grins that were completely incongruent with their harsh demeanours of a second ago, and then they parted like the red sea, stepping back and directing us to the third door down the corridor.

Passing the burly men, we exchanged a relieved look as Cait shook her head and whispered, 'Jeez, they were so tall.' Once we were outside a room labelled 'Dressing Room Three' Cait hesitantly raised her hand and knocked twice.

As the door swung open, Cait swiftly stepped away to the side and shoved me so I stumbled into the doorway with a yelp. 'Cait! What the heck!'

But then I was met by a very familiar sight. Sean.

My jaw dropped open, eyes as wide as saucers, but Cait was grinning from ear to ear, looking incredibly pleased with herself. 'Catch ya in a minute, kiddo. I'll go hang out in the sunshine with my book,' she announced before disappearing back down the corridor.

Cait was usually dreadful at keeping secrets so I could barely believe she'd managed to trick me like this, but thoughts of my friend's deception instantly left my mind as Sean ushered me into the room.

Closing the door behind me, he fixed his gaze on mine as he finished buttoning up what appeared to be a freshly ironed blue shirt. He was changing into the uniform he wore on the show, and as I ran my eyes from his booted feet, up the navy trousers, and across his form-fitting shirt I swallowed and couldn't help but bite on my lower lip. He looked stunning. I really was a sucker for a police uniform. Especially when it was Sean underneath the badges and buttons.

And cuffs.

My eyes lingered on the shiny metal loops on the utility belt at his waist and my brain almost malfunctioned.

Swallowing again, I leant back on the door, still slightly shell-shocked. As I drew in a deep breath and raised my eyes to his face, I found Sean rapidly closing the gap between us.

'Sorry about the trickery, but I wanted to surprise you before I get back on set. I've only got ...' he glanced at his watch, '... *damn*, eight minutes but I needed to see you after all that's happened.'

My head was spinning, but one thing was clear. The air around us was now thick with attraction. My body had responded as it always did when he was near: by heating up and coming alive with sensation. If it were possible for two bodies to create actual sparks, there would be some serious electricity flowing through this space.

Looking into his curious eyes, I knew I had made the right decision to come to the press conference today. We were meant to be. I'd have to learn to deal with my jealous streak, and his high profile career would mean that things would not always be smooth sailing, but there was no other option, because there was no way I could give this man up.

Without speaking a single word, I threw myself at Sean. The quicker I kissed him, the quicker I could banish the last clingy images of Savannah kissing him from my mind. In my haste to reunite us, our noses bumped together clumsily and teeth briefly clashed, but I eventually settled on his parted lips and kissed him furiously.

Sean groaned against my lips, the vibrations seeming to travel straight to my core. My hands found his hair and dug through the strands as I dragged him closer and moaned as his tongue met mine. In response, Sean's arms entwined around my waist and pulled me to him so desperately that the air was pushed from my lungs and I was lifted off my feet.

After several breath-taking moments, Sean pulled back, lowering me to the ground and I saw that his face was flushed, as mine surely was too. His hair was a mess thanks to my exploring fingers, but it looked so sexy that I left it as it was.

'What does this mean then?' he asked in a hopeful whisper, causing me to chuckle.

'Well … it means I have a few jealousy issues to deal with, but they are *my* problems, and I *will* overcome them. After lots of thinking, I understand that acting is your job, and I trust you completely when you say it doesn't go beyond the set.' I paused and chewed briefly on my lip. 'It also means that however proud of you I might be, I *never* want to be in the studio when you're filming a scene that involves kissing anyone else, ever again … otherwise I might have to kill them.'

Sean sighed in relief and gathered me to him, holding me so tightly I struggled to breathe. Giggling with relief and pleasure, I pushed myself away with another laugh. 'Finally, it means that … yes, of course I still want to be with you.'

Happiness flooded Sean's handsome features as he placed another light kiss on my lips.

'God, I wish I didn't have to be on set,' he said as he playfully pulled me against him to show just how much he wanted me. Judging by the rock solid shaft I could feel pressing into my stomach, he really, *really* wanted

88

time for us to reconnect.

'Huummmm … me too,' I murmured, eyeing his incredibly sexy uniform and plucking open the top button on his shirt.

'Don't start down that road, Allie …' Sean warned with a groan. 'You know I'd love to let you carry on, baby, but if you do I'll never make it to set and Finlay will go ballistic. I'm already in his bad books.'

I made a noise of protest, but just as I was about to be a good girl and do his button up, Sean let out a low, almost animalistic growl, and then he stepped towards me and slammed us both against the door.

'Fuck it …' His lips crushed onto mine, his tongue forcing its way into my mouth as I desperately tried to draw in a breath. 'This is going to have to be quick, my gorgeous girl,' he murmured, as one hand lowered between us and dragged my sun dress up my thighs until it bunched around my waist. His sudden advance sent a rush of heat between my legs and I started to squirm in his arms.

I didn't care where we did it, or how long it lasted, I just needed the re-connection. Sliding my trembling hands from his shoulders, I immediately joined his hurried movements by reaching down and tugging on his belt buckle and zipper.

With a groan his fingers dug inside my knickers and found my heat, where he began rubbing slick circles on my clitoris that caused me to gasp as pleasure swept through my body. I was so dizzy that it slightly hampered my attempts at undoing his trousers because my fingers were suddenly too shaky.

'So wet. You're so fucking perfect.' His murmurings only intensified my arousal and sent another thrum of desire to where his fingers were quickly working me towards my peak.

Finally I managed to open his zipper and dig my hand

inside his boxers to wrap around his erection. The silky hardness felt so good and I tugged it free with a soft gasp. His cock bobbed out of its confinement, prodding insistently at my stomach as I gave several impatient tugs. This certainly wasn't my most refined sexual repertoire, that was for sure, but primal need seemed to push finesse aside.

'Are you OK?' he asked urgently.

Dragging air into my lungs, I nodded frantically. 'I'm good to go.'

Without warning, Sean nodded, grabbed my hips, and spun me around to the dressing table where he swept several things aside and practically threw me backwards so I was laid out before him. I heard things crashing to the floor, but my focus was completely on Sean. We could clear up later.

With his hands on my thighs he shoved my legs apart and unceremoniously dug his fingers through the thin lace of my panties and ripped them clean off. My body jerked but the material seemed to give way relatively easily and was quickly tossed over his shoulder.

He paused briefly, groaning at the sight now before him, and holy cow was the look of determination on his face arousing. He really, *really* wanted me, and knowing that was undeniably powerful. He didn't stop for long though, his hands shifting to my hips as he stepped closer and thrust into me in one long, hard stroke that had me shooting backwards along the counter as I tried to mute my cry of pleasure.

'Fuck!' I think we both yelled at the same time as our fingers clutched at each other to deepen our connection.

He hadn't been kidding when he'd said this would be quick, because Sean set off at a pace so frantic that our bodies were slapping together furiously as he repeatedly dragged his cock in and out of me, hitting my g-spot on every one of his jerking thrusts.

I was already super sensitive, so it didn't take much to send me spiralling towards a climax. My muscles clenched around him, the spasms sending him over too and he barked out a groan, clutched my hips in desperation, and buried himself inside me as his cock jerked its release.

Talk about speedy. Well, he had said it needed to be quick, and I almost giggled, feeling high from the rush of adrenaline and endorphins now spreading around my body.

'God, I love you,' Sean muttered, dropping one last kiss on my lips before gently sliding from within me and grabbing a box of tissues.

Gently running one tissue between my legs, he looked up with regret. 'I'd like to do my usual routine, but I really have to get going. I'm sorry, my gorgeous girl.' He really did look regretful, bless him. Shaking my head, I dismissed his concerns and finished cleaning myself up while he quickly wiped himself off and righted his clothing.

'Sorry this is such a rush, but think of it this way – the quicker I get to the studio, the quicker I can finish and spend some time with the birthday girl. Are you free tonight?' Sean asked, fastening the buttons of his shirt.

I'd thought that with all that had been going on Sean would have forgotten my birthday, but clearly he hadn't, and I found myself grinning at him and nodding.

'You thought I'd forgotten, didn't you?' he tutted with mock disbelief. 'I didn't want to mention it in my text in case you thought I was trying to pressure you,' he explained as he dropped another kiss on my lips and reached into his back pocket to draw out a long, black velvet box.

'Happy birthday, Allie,' he murmured, and he pressed the box into my hand but left his lips lingering on mine. Suddenly I found it quite hard to breathe, let alone think straight, and as I moved my lips away I shakily looked at the box in my hand.

'OK, I am desperately late now, but could I tempt you into allowing me to cook you dinner tonight? I'll pick you up at seven o'clock?'

'That would be lovely, thank you,' I replied, my thumb caressing the velvet of the box.

'I really must go before Finlay has my nuts on a plate, so open your present before I go,' he urged as he adjusted the tie round his neck. Examining the box, I saw a small bronze clip on the side and flicked it open, the lid popping up to reveal a deep blue silk lining and the most stunning necklace I'd ever seen in my life. It was a silver chain with a circular pendant on the end. At first glance it looked like a solid sphere, but as I looked closer I realised it was made up of two thin strands of metal that had been intricately swirled and twisted together to form its circular shape.

'Sean, it's beautiful!' I exclaimed as tears instantly filled my eyes. 'I love it.' Sean seemed to observe my reaction with pleasure before he reached into the box and removed the necklace, stepping behind me so he could gently drape it around my neck.

'It's hand worked platinum, made by a designer I know. The pendant is called Unspoken Bond. When I saw it I knew I had to get it for you.' His words were no more than a whisper, but I felt his warm breath tickling my neck as he spoke.

'Unspoken bond?' I whispered hoarsely.

'Yeah ... that's how it feels to be with you,' he murmured, sounding almost embarrassed by his confession.

He turned me to admire his efforts. 'You look stunning. Right, I really must go, but I promise I'll see you tonight.' With that, he dropped the briefest of kisses on my lips and was gone, leaving me completely

92

overwhelmed. Not to mention a bit damp between my legs.

Talk about whirlwind.

I was a lost cause where that man was concerned – there was no point in denying it any more.

# THIRTEEN

## CAIT

After birthday cocktails of the much-anticipated Strawberry Daiquiris, and then burgers and chips – or fries, as I was now getting used to calling them – Allie and I were now home. I was in the kitchen, mid-way through icing a freshly baked birthday cake – carrot cake, Allie's favourite – when there was a loud banging on the front door.

Frowning, I turned towards the sound. Allie was upstairs primping for her date with Sean later and Jack had said he might pop in after six, but it was only 4.35 so I couldn't imagine he had finished filming yet. Only the four of us had clearance at the front gate, so unless one of our neighbours was knocking, I couldn't imagine who it could be.

Feeling a tingle of anxiousness in my belly, I paused by the sink to wipe the remnants of cream cheese frosting from my fingers, smoothed my hair from my face, and made my way cautiously through the lounge.

As I peered through the peephole, I felt my shoulders relax – it *was* Jack, obviously finishing up early. But before I could get nervous, I realised he had a small boy wrapped around his shoulders like a limpet. What the heck? Pressing my eye harder against the peephole, I saw there was also a pretty little girl clutching his hand and desperately jigging back and forth on her feet.

Children? Now I was confused. I leant back, somewhat surprised by their presence. Not being an expert on kids, I guessed that the boy was about five and the girl slightly older, but the age was irrelevant when compared to the more important question – who were they?

Even with my confusion, I couldn't help but break into a broad smile when I pulled the door open and took in Jack, looking at me with his trademark breathtaking grin. This man's smile was so good it could stop traffic.

'Hi, Jack.'

'Hey, sweetheart.' My cheeks flushed, and I rolled my eyes at my out of control blushing where this man was concerned.

'This is Eddie and Freya. We need to ask you a favour.' He smiled apologetically. 'Freya is desperate for the toilet – is there any chance she can use yours? I'm not sure we'd make it all the way home without an accident.' He narrowed his eyes and gave a smile, probably imagining his fancy car getting an impromptu interior valet.

Looking at Freya as she jigged from foot to foot, I grinned at her. 'Sure, sweetie. It's at the top of the stairs, do you want me to show you the way?'

Freya smiled politely before shaking her head. 'No thanks, I'll find it.' With that, she dropped Jack's hand and began to head inside before the boy interrupted her.

'Wait, Frey, let me come with you!' he exclaimed, struggling frantically to untangle himself from Jack's shoulders, keen on the idea of exploring a new house.

Jack's arm was still bandaged up, and as he struggled to help the boy down, I quickly reached over to help, taking hold of the boy under the arms, swinging him off, and causing him to shriek with joy. Once I had safely deposited him on the ground, he grinned at me, and as I returned his smile, I decided they must be brother and sister, because they both had floppy brown hair and chestnut brown eyes to match.

As I stepped back to gesture them towards the stairs, it occurred to me that they weren't the only person in the room with chestnut eyes and floppy brown hair ... their hair and eyes were *exactly* the same shade as Jack's.

My lungs suddenly felt tight, and a wheeze drew itself from my chest. Oh my God ... were these *his* kids? Did he have children I didn't know about? I suppose that was a possibility.

Suddenly feeling completely winded, I watched the children disappear upstairs and then turned back to Jack.

Closing the door, he gave me an apologetic look and stepped closer to me. 'Caitlin, I'm so sorry. I know we were supposed to be meeting later, but ...'

'You have children?' I blurted, completely losing the ability to regulate my conversation into something more polite. I suppose it wasn't a huge issue, but it certainly was a bit of a shock.

'What?' He looked completely confused, but after a brief moment, his eyes suddenly twinkled with recognition. 'Oh! They're not my kids, Caitlin, I would have told you!' he chuckled, stepping further inside.

Trying to ignore his distracting closeness, I jerked a thumb at the stairs. 'Well ... whose are they then?' Had he randomly picked them up from the street to impress me with his patience and way with kids?

'One of my co-stars, Jared, he's a good friend and his girlfriend was supposed to have them today, but she had a family emergency. He needed someone to watch them while he shot the rest of his scenes and kids aren't allowed to stay 'cause it's a closed set, so I ended up finishing early and offered to take them for an ice-cream,' he shrugged. 'I was going to call you and explain I couldn't make it later, but Freya got desperate for the loo.'

I had to admit, finding out they weren't Jack's was quite a relief. I'd barely managed to have a grown-up relationship yet, I was hardly the most ideal candidate for taking on the role of mother figure.

Now I understood, I relaxed and grinned, but as our eyes met, I found a much different emotion reflecting at me. Lust.

Oh God. One look like that and my insides were suddenly curled with heat. It was like Jack had managed to transform me into this open, relaxed, and wanton version of myself.

Given that this was our first meeting as a couple – well, as 'two people who liked each other and wanted to get to know each other' – I should have been consumed by nerves, but crazily enough, I wasn't.

I could do this: be with a man and not be terrified, and it was all because Jack had somehow made me trust him. I *knew* he wouldn't hurt me or push me, and that knowledge had me feeling liberated and carefree.

On top of that, I felt normal, and that was something I'd feared I would never get back.

'Umm … it's nice to see you outside of the hospital,' I mumbled, not sure what else to say when all I could focus on was the tingling of attraction running all over my skin.

Nodding slowly, he kept his gaze firmly locked with mine. 'It's good to be out.' Drawing in a long breath through his nose, he seemed to be trying to control himself, and then smiled softly. 'Can I come closer, would that be OK?'

My heart kicked with excitement at his words and after licking my lips, I plucked up the bravery to reply. 'That would definitely be OK.'

He looked thrilled by my response, and then, taking another step closer, he moved his body so that there was barely a scrap of distance separating us, but just enough that he was still respecting my fear of physical contact. I felt like my entire being was radiating with awareness.

The temptation to lean forward and give myself over to his strength was almost overpowering.

'I know we're taking it slow, but I really have to tell you how gorgeous you look.' Jack's voice was rough and low, and sexy as hell, and made the hairs on the back of my neck stand up.

Now we were finally alone together, it seemed that all our chemistry, connection, lust, and desire couldn't remain contained any more. It was a live, breathing thing, heightening my senses and depriving my lungs of air at the same time. I was so attracted to this man I could barely control myself.

Just as I was about to say, 'sod taking it slow' and grab him, Jack spoke again. 'You have something on your nose. Is that icing?' he asked, and he might have been talking about something as innocuous as icing sugar, but his voice seemed to travel straight through me and pool somewhere between my legs. I'd literally never experienced feelings like this before – I was so affected that I felt like every inch of my skin was being licked with burning flames, and all he was doing was talking. God knows how I'd cope when he touched me. Really touched me. I'd probably pass out.

Giving a wobbly nod of my head, Jack lifted a hand before pausing. 'Can I wipe it off?' Instead of being embarrassed by the way he asked for permission, I found myself touched, but like the lust-filled idiot I was I just nodded again.

Jack leant down so he was barely a few centimetres away, then gently wiped the tip of my nose with his forefinger before popping the digit into his mouth and taking his time to lick the icing off with a happy hum.

It was quite possibly the most erotic thing I had ever seen.

His eyelids became heavy as I watched his lips curl around his finger, and I desperately wanted to rip his finger from his mouth and suck on it myself. That really was a crazy thought for me, Caitlin Byrne, the woman who had barely any sexual experience, and I suddenly craved finger sucking.

Where had that come from?

As I continued to watch him, my entire body seemed to explode with horniness, and suddenly all I wanted to do was throw down my walls, grab his shirt, and kiss the life out of him.

'I *really* want to kiss you,' Jack muttered, as if reflecting my own thoughts, but just as I was about to tell him to do it, a bang from the landing upstairs had me pausing.

Bloody kids.

'We shouldn't really … the children …' I murmured, my tone far less convincing than it should have been, because truthfully, I wanted nothing more than for him to kiss me.

'They'll be a while yet, and we really, *really* should …' he whispered.

'Then you'd better do it quick before they come back,' I whispered huskily, amazed by my own confidence.

Jack looked almost as shocked by my offer as I felt, but then his head began to lower toward mine and my breath froze in my lungs as his soft lips brushed over mine.

Tingles flooded my system from the gentle contact, but just as I was rocking forwards onto my toes so I could wrap my arms around him, he suddenly pulled back, a look of frustration lingering on his features.

'I can't, Caitlin. Not when we're pushed for time like we are now. I want our first kiss to be amazing, not rushed.' Jack's face was close to mine, his breath warm and minty, and I nearly cried out in frustration and stamped my foot like a toddler having a tantrum.

Rolling back onto my heels, I nodded shakily and licked my lips, running my tongue across the skin where his had just been, all of which was watched by Jack as his eyes darkened with desire.

The next second there was a clattering of feet on the stairs as the children rejoined us in the lounge, proving Jack right for stopping and leaving us both flushed and more than a little wound up. I could still feel the chemistry between us lingering in the air, and my lips were almost buzzing from his brief touch as I replayed it over in my mind again.

Jack stepped close beside me and leant down to whisper in my ear. 'Breathe, Caitlin.'

I realised then that I was still holding my breath and gave an embarrassed laugh before pulling in a deep breath.

Jack flashed me a wink that was so intimate it very nearly stopped my breath all over again. 'Better. We can't have you passing out every time I kiss you, because once we venture down that path I'm going to be kissing you *a lot.*' His words had been whispered but I heard them loud and clear.

Holy hell. I was so hot I felt a distinct need to crank the air conditioner up to full blast.

Clearing my throat, I dragged my gaze away from Jack's and found two sets of curious eyes peering at me. The children. Blimey, in my lusty state I'd almost forgotten they were here.

'I can smell cake,' Eddie stated, his curious stare changing to one of hope as he sniffed the air again.

'Oh, yes! I have cake! Come on through!' My voice was higher than usual because of my flustered state, but cake was the perfect distraction, so I ushered them all to the dining table and then rushed into the kitchen.

I could hear Jack settling the children down so I took a moment to lean back on the counter to try and compose myself. It could take a while. I think to truly recover from that interlude I'd need a cold shower and a fresh pair of knickers. I swallowed hard and picked up a tea towel to fan my face.

Thankfully, after a few moments I felt more composed – just – and busied myself getting some plates out.

Luckily I'd had spare mixture and made two cakes, so I sliced one and carried it through to where Jack was sitting with two impatient children. Bringing in some glasses and a carton of milk to complete our impromptu picnic, I smiled at the domestic scene, and then pushed away an errant vision of Jack and I and our own children. Jeez. It was *way* too early to even consider that type of scenario.

I dished out some glasses of milk and plates and popped a slice each in front of Eddie, Freya, and Jack and watched as both children dived in with gusto. Smiling, I slipped into the last seat around the table as I served myself a slice.

As I tucked into my cake, I gradually became aware that two small sets of eyes were once again watching my every move. Smiling, I picked up the milk bottle. 'Anyone want more milk?' I asked, to resounding nods from Freya, Eddie, and a grinning Jack. He really did look like an overgrown child, and the image did nothing to help remove the goofy smile on my face.

As I popped the lid back on the milk, Eddie whispered something to Freya and then the girl turned her shrewd eyes onto me again. 'Eddie and me want to know if you and Uncle Jack are dating,' she asked as she wiped the milk from her upper lip.

'Uhhh ...' I think the answer was yes, but if I were honest, I wasn't entirely clear on specifically what position I held in Jack's life. I was seemingly the girl who he wanted to kiss, but that wasn't exactly something

I could say in this particular situation.

'Ummm …' I looked desperately at Jack for support, only to find him waiting keenly for an answer along with Freya and Eddie.

Great. What had his description been in the hospital? 'Just two people who enjoy each other's company and are getting to know each other.' Was that the same as being his girlfriend? Did it class as dating? We had mentioned we wouldn't see other people, but what if I said yes and he freaked out?

I didn't want to presume anything, so I cleared my throat and totally chickened out. 'Uhhh, well, we're good friends,' I stated, quite pleased with myself for sounding calm and coming out with what I thought was a safe, child-friendly answer, and one that wasn't likely to send Jack running for the hills.

'You can't be *very* good friends with him because we've never met you before and we see Uncle Jack all the time,' Freya responded with an assessing tilt of her head. How intelligent *was* this kid? Feeling more and more flustered by the second, I looked at Jack and he finally took pity on me.

'Well, Caitlin and I have known each other for a little while now, and we get on really well so you might be seeing more of her because I really like her.'

He really liked me. My heart pumped fast enough to make me dizzy, and then Freya and Eddie smiled broadly before Jack dropped his head and whispered something to them that caused them to giggle and nod frantically.

'Uncle Jack says we should ask you if you want to be his girlfriend.' As she spoke, Freya looked solemnly at me as if this was a life and death decision. Eddie picked at a crumb on his plate and Jack was smiling almost bashfully while staring at me expectantly.

My cheeks immediately flushed and began burning;

I'd never felt more like I was in an inquisition – but it was the best type of inquisition because I was being asked the very thing I craved. I hadn't been sure, but everything seemed to be falling into place.

I was ready to commit.

'I think you should say yes, then we can have loads more cake when you come to visit!' Eddie chimed in.

Smiling, I felt a bubble of happiness well up inside of me that felt too big for my body to contain. 'Well, in that case, I'd better say yes.' I wanted to jump up and down with joy at this declaration, but I managed to retain control and instead directed the children to a cupboard in the living room where they would find some games that had been left by the old tenants.

Once Freya and Eddie were safely out of earshot, I moved around the table and sat myself next to Jack. 'You coward, using the children to do your dirty work,' I chided him, but I couldn't keep the grin from my face, which totally gave the game away.

His eyes crinkled at the corners as he grinned and then reached for my hand, which I gladly gave. He twined our fingers together, staring at them for a second before raising his gaze. 'Yeah, but it worked, didn't it?'

Slowly lowering his head towards mine, Jack stared me in the eyes, his pupils visibly dilating as he closed the gap, but just when I thought he was going to kiss me on the lips he diverted and landed a gentle, lingering kiss on my cheek.

I wasn't sure whether to be pleased or disappointed. It was hardly the right moment to shove my tongue in his mouth, but bloody hell, I would have liked to.

My skin immediately tingled from his contact, and I drew in a small gasp of pleasure before smiling at him shyly. In response, he winked and turned to Freya as she ran over to show him some Lego she'd found.

My head was reeling and my skin still singing with

the pleasure of his brief kiss. Jack Felton was officially my boyfriend. That sounded a bit ridiculous when referring to a man who was nearly forty, but sod it, I didn't care, I fully intended to call him by that title.

This was hugely exciting, and definitely major progress, but I tried not to let myself get too excited. After all, he had yet to discover how messed up I really was.

# FOURTEEN

## SEAN

As I entered my bedroom I found Allie on my bed wearing nothing but the necklace I had given her earlier that day. She was wearing her birthday gift *in* her birthday suit? Jesus. It caused me to freeze in the doorway and stand there to appreciate her beautiful body.

Her skin was tanned and flawless, her hair was falling down her back, long and sleek, appearing like spun gold in the muted bedroom light.

God, she was beautiful.

I couldn't believe I had my girl back. It seemed too good to be true, but *finally*, the shit with Savannah was resolved and Allie and I could get on with making a life together.

I couldn't wait.

After I'd arrived, we'd celebrated her birthday with a barbeque and had now taken our celebrations upstairs.

When I'd popped out to top up our drinks, Allie had snuck on to my laptop and opened up the CCTV footage from my house in England. I'd mentioned the copies over dinner, but I hadn't banked on her being this keen to watch them with me.

But keen she was.

The laptop was on the end of the bed as Allie looked across at me with desire-filled eyes. I'd thought she might be embarrassed at the idea of watching herself on tape, but from her erect nipples and the bright flush to her skin, she was already aroused and as far from embarrassed as possible.

Swallowing hard, I tried to calm my suddenly dizzying pulse, but it was a losing battle. Kicking myself into gear, I ignored my swaying head and shed my clothes quickly. Joining Allie on the bed, I moved in close behind her and reached out to trail my fingers through her hair. I couldn't be near her and not touch, it simply wasn't feasible.

Tangling my fingers in the silky locks, I sighed contentedly. I loved her gorgeous strands so much I doubted I'd ever tire of the feel of it between my fingers.

Or wrapped around my wrist in the height of passion.

On the screen the video had loaded and things were already heating up; we were in the entrance to my kitchen, Allie wearing my T-shirt as a nightdress, and I was pinning her to the wall as our eyes remained glued together in a heated stare.

In the tape it didn't take long for me to peel the T-shirt from her body and start my assault on her by manoeuvring her towards the kitchen counter, causing her to gasp on screen just as the Allie in front of me gasped too.

Her eyes were glued to the screen as she watched me bending her over the kitchen counter and stretching her arms above her head.

Even through the small speakers of my laptop I could hear how aroused I was on the video when I gave her my command. 'These stay here.'

My cock leapt with the images on the screen. I loved this part of the tape. My gorgeous girl had offered me her body with no limitations and I could still remember how euphoric that had made me feel.

Bringing me back to the present, Allie swallowed loudly then licked her lips. 'Wow ... I'd almost forgotten how moody and domineering you were back

107

then,' she murmured huskily. Her voice held a definite note of longing, and I began to wonder if I'd become a bit too soft recently.

We were a couple, things were done as a pair, including sex; it had always been great – sometimes she led and sometimes I did. But hearing her tone, I started to think that perhaps she missed the way I used to take charge in the bedroom.

I'd missed it too.

Kneeling behind her, I scooped up her long hair and trailed it over her shoulder, leaving her neck exposed for my kiss. I began to trail my lips over the delicate skin below her ear as I ran my hands from her shoulders, down her arms, until I came to her wrists.

'Did you like it?' I asked breathily, my hands looping around her wrists to gently hold them captive. 'That side of me?'

Allie arched into my touch, tugging at her restrained arms and inadvertently thrusting her breasts into the cool of the room as her head fell back onto my shoulder. 'I … yes.'

Her admission made my cock throb and my head spin as the longing for control roared to the forefront of my thoughts.

*Mine*. She was mine to possess, mine to control.

Barely holding myself together, I lowered my lips to her ear before nipping at the skin with my teeth. 'Get on your hands and knees,' I commanded, my tone rough.

As soon as I released her wrists she immediately scrambled to do as I had requested. How she could be so confident and independent in life, but so willingly submissive in the bedroom was astounding.

Not to mention a real fucking turn-on.

On the laptop screen, video me was caressing Allie's pale, smooth back, so I tried to mimic the tape, aware that Allie was watching the recording too. She shivered beneath my touch, her breathing unsteady as a low moan slipped from her lips.

As I wrapped her long hair around one wrist on the screen, I did it in real life, relishing the feel of the sleek strands as they tightened around my arm and exerted pressure on her scalp, just hard enough that Allie arched her back toward me and lifted her arse up as if she were presenting it to me.

This position allowed me a perfect view between her legs and my head swum when I saw how excited she was.

As if on autopilot, my right hand traced its way down her spine, trailed through the crack of her arse – causing her to quiver below my touch – before the pads of my fingers made contact with her soft sex.

Tonight was about reconnecting. It was about claiming, and getting my girl back in the most primitive way possible. The quickie at the studios had been fantastic, but over far too fast. I needed to really claim her back and show her we were meant to be together.

Allie moaned, her hips shifting and causing two of my fingers to slip inside her opening. A groan left my throat and I couldn't resist adding a third finger and pressing them deeper as my thumb sought her clit. I loved the feel of her stretching to accommodate me. One brush across the swollen flesh had her squirming against me and caused her to ripple around my fingers in pleasure.

I had missed this, and I don't mean the sex; I'd missed sharing the incredible connection, the small noises she made when she was turned on, the way we responded to each other.

And yeah, I'd missed the actual sex too.

As I drew in a breath to try and steady myself, I realised I'd strengthened my grip on her hair in my urgency. Her back was arched even more now, but instead of complaining, Allie appeared to be lost in the heights of pleasure. Her eyes were rolled shut, lips parted, and hips thrusting against my hand harder and harder by the second. With barely any warning, her muscles suddenly clenched and she climaxed with a startled yelp, seemingly taking us both by surprise.

As she rode out her orgasm with a series of breathy whimpers I couldn't help but stare at her in wonder. Wild and so fucking beautiful that it almost hurt. It seemed my girl really had missed this side of our relationship as much as I had.

How I was managing to hold myself together was beyond me. Talk about an overstimulating experience – I was surrounded by her sexy body, both in real life and on the screen, where the old me was now pressing her to the counter until her gorgeous breasts flattened beneath her and she writhed excitedly.

On screen, I lined my cock up with her entrance and thrust in with almost brutal force. Her body shot forwards, both of us moaning as I continued to pound into her relentlessly.

I couldn't deny that the image had my cock throbbing with the need to be inside her again, but I winced, wondering how the hell Allie had ever fallen for me when I had treated her so roughly.

Underneath me, I felt Allie shift and I slowed my fingers to ease her down from her climax. Dragging my eyes away from the screen, I looked at her flushed face as she glanced over her shoulder at me. Her eyes were dilated, her face framed by several locks of hair that had escaped from around my wrist, and she had never looked so gorgeous.

She bit her lip before glancing at the laptop where I was still banging out my pleasure in her willing body. 'Fuck me, Sean. I want you to take me hard, just like that. Don't hold back.'

Holy hell, her words surprised me. They left me with little doubt as to who was really in control, but I didn't care – if my girl wanted me to fuck her hard, I would happily oblige.

Giving a small nod, I grinned at her wickedly and slid my fingers out of her, replacing them with the tip of my pulsing hard-on. 'As you wish.' Wasting no time at all, I copied the roughness of the scene on the tape and jerked my hips forwards so I was buried deep within her in one hard thrust.

'*Fuck.*' The curse hissed from my lips as my head spun and my entire body focused on the glorious sensations in my dick. She was so tight. So perfect.

Gripping her hair in one hand and her hip in the other, I began to thrust like there was no tomorrow. Each move had me buried inside her, my stomach banging against her arse on each thrust as she practically threw herself backwards to increase the intensity.

'Yes. Just like that.' I wasn't entirely sure if it was me who spoke or Allie, but this was so fucking perfect I could barely see straight. The scene on the laptop drew to its crescendo, the sounds of Allie and I coming through the speakers, but the video was all but forgotten as we focused on the then and there.

Looking down at where we were joined caused me to groan in pleasure. Watching my cock disappearing inside her was so erotic I felt it swelling in size even further. Allie moaned, and lifting one hand from the bed she tugged my hand from her hip and guided it towards her clit.

I began to rub slick, firm circles in time to my brutal thrusts, just how I knew she liked it, and was almost immediately rewarded with a long, drawn-out groan. 'Oh, God. I'm going to come, Sean.'

That made two of us. With my fingers at her clit and one hand in her hair, we moved in unison until suddenly she gasped, let out a low, gravelly moan as her body clamped around mine and began to climax in a series of convulsions so hard I thought my cock would be bruised the next day. For now I had no complaints, the hard grip exactly what I needed to send me chasing after her as my release shot from me in hot pulses that had me jerking against her for several seconds.

I was pleasurably exhausted, and so sated that I could already feel sleep pulling at the edge of my vision, but I was alert enough to fall to my side, bringing Allie's body with me. 'Mine.'

'You're mine too, you know.' Allie giggled softly, her words thrilling me as she snuggled against me, her breathing slowing as we both fell towards sleep with my length still buried inside of her.

# FIFTEEN

## ALLIE

I smelt the coffee before I'd even properly woken up, its rich aroma invading the lovely dream where Sean and I were back together, and Savannah didn't exist.

I sighed as my brain started to wake up. If only life could be as perfect as my dream world.

'Good morning, my gorgeous girl,' Sean's deep voice washed over me, infiltrating my senses and immediately causing me to peel my eyes open.

In my direct line of sight was a broad, naked chest, with a perfect six-pack and sprinkling of hair that had my eyes shooting upwards until I saw an even better view.

Sean.

Complete with a seriously sexy case of bed head and a night's worth of stubble he looked dark, dangerous, and deliciously sexy as he stared down at me smugly.

He was really here.

Blinking again, my sleepy haze began to lift and I remembered the previous day's hectic events: the press conference, Savannah's sour face, my birthday meal, and finally the incredible sex session where Sean had fucked me into a coma.

Wow. Actually, I think maybe reality *was* better than my dream.

'It's so good to have you back in my bed,' he murmured, dropping down beside me so he could place a gentle kiss on my lips.

'It's good to *be* back in your bed,' I replied with a giggle.

Wiggling his eyebrows, Sean returned my smile before rolling over to the bedside table. 'I made some coffee.' Pouring two mugs from the large jug, he settled himself against the headboard and waited for me to prop myself up next to him before passing me my mug.

We enjoyed a moment of silence as we sipped our coffees, and then Sean placed his mug down and turned towards me. 'So ... last night, I, uh ... I fell asleep before I could ask if you were OK. Sorry, that's a typical guy thing to do, huh?' he mumbled with a small smile. I could detect hesitancy in his murmured words, presumably he was worried he had been too rough, but he didn't need to have any such concerns – I had enjoyed every minute of it.

Laughing, I immediately set about reassuring him by also getting rid of my cup and placing a soft, lingering kiss on his warm lips. Hmm. He tasted of coffee and smelt like hot-blooded male mixed with citrusy shower gel. What a perfect mix.

'Don't worry, I passed out too. And I'm fine, really.' I felt my cheeks flush as I thought over the events of last night. The amazing, earth-shattering, double climatic events of last night.

'You enjoyed it?' he asked.

I had more than enjoyed it. Just remembering how he'd whispered for me to get on my hands and knees sent an immediate rush of warmth between my legs and I felt my nipples harden underneath the sheet. Jeez. It almost felt wrong to admit that I liked when he took control, as if I was somehow giving in to some weakness inside myself. But I loved it. As much as it went against my independent woman status, I truly loved it when Sean dominated me in bed.

Not quite sure how to voice this, I cleared my throat

and finally plucked up enough courage to look him in the eye. 'I really enjoyed it, Sean. We can definitely do that kind of thing again.'

I saw relief sweep his features and he smiled, released a breath, and nodded. I was just about to reach for my coffee when Sean gave a shake of his head, his eyes taking on a dark appearance. Throwing back the sheet to expose my naked body, Sean growled low in his throat, and as he reached for me I got the distinct feeling I would be drinking my coffee cold this morning.

# SIXTEEN

## JACK

The sun was shining, I had a coffee in one hand, and Caitlin's fingers curled around my other. All in all, things were pretty damn great.

My schedule was maddeningly busy at the moment, but we'd made the best of it and been gently progressing our time together, starting each day by meeting for coffee and later during another break if our schedules matched. We now held hands every time we were together, and I had continued my habit of kissing her on the cheek, which always brought a gorgeous flush to her skin. My kisses were straying closer and closer to her lips as each day passed, not that Caitlin seemed to mind in the slightest.

We were going physically slow, but the smouldering looks that now passed between us were practically X-rated. My girl could almost reduce me to my knees with one of her secret sexy smiles. I truly didn't think she had any idea just how gorgeous she was. I was like a teenager again, and seemed to have a permanent hard-on whenever she was near me. Despite my best efforts to hide it, I know she'd spied the bulge in my jeans on several occasions, so perhaps she was starting to get some idea of just how much she affected me.

My only real free time was late night when I got home and promptly collapsed into bed. As much as I'd have liked to suggest Caitlin wait beneath the duvet at my place for me, I sensed that would be pushing things, so I'd held off from even joking about it.

I was prepared to wait for the physical side of things to develop, but I was still desperate to spend as much time with her as possible, so I had decided that it was time to step it up to an evening date now I finally had a weekend off. A meal somewhere, maybe a moonlit walk along the beach. I fully intended to progress from a chaste kiss on the cheek too, and get my first real kiss from her.

'So, what are you doing Friday night?' I enquired, trying to keep my tone light but probably sounding like an excited teenager.

'Friday?' Caitlin smiled and her cheeks flushed in that way I adored, but before she could answer we were interrupted by the sound of a camera shutter nearby. Caitlin's attention was immediately drawn to it and a frown creased her brow. 'She just took a picture of us.'

Glancing at a retreating girl, I saw her giggling with a friend as they rejoined a group on a guided studio tour.

'Yeah? I didn't notice.' I shrugged. 'It happens so much I'm kind of oblivious to it now. It'll probably end up on some random star-spotting blog.'

I felt Caitlin's fingers tense around mine and then her eyes darted to mine in alarm. There were several seconds of silence as if her mind was working overtime. '*A blog?*'

Putting my coffee down, I tried to work out why Caitlin suddenly looked so horrified. Her cheeks had paled, her hazel eyes were wide and glazed, and her mouth was parted.

'Umm ... well, maybe. A lot of the people who do these tours like to spot as many celebrities as they can. Sometimes they put the pictures on Facebook, sometimes they end up on a blog. I'm sure it was just harmless, don't worry.'

Cait ripped her hand from mine and almost fell from

her stool as she stumbled backwards. 'I can't believe I didn't think of this earlier. Shit! I'm such an idiot.'

What the hell? To say I was stunned was an understatement.

'Why would you care if someone took a picture of us?' I asked softly, hoping to calm her down. As she remained staunchly silent, one thought came to my mind that made my stomach drop. 'Are you embarrassed to be seen with me?'

Caitlin pinged her elastic bands twice and huffed out a breath before turning on her heel and striding away without a single word, leaving me gaping at her retreating back. That hadn't exactly been the answer I'd been hoping for.

How had we gone from enjoying a nice coffee date to her running away? The horrified look on her face was now searing into my brain. I was about to go after her, but seeing as she'd rather publicly shunned me, I thought better of it and instead stormed back to my dressing room so I could stew in peace.

## CAIT

Gasping for breath, I came to a halt at the exit and sunk down onto one of the stone benches in the sunshine. I couldn't believe I'd run away from Jack. *Again.* I groaned, wincing as I tried to count how many times I'd done something similar in the short duration of our acquaintance. It was becoming too numerous to count, and Jack didn't deserve my appalling behaviour, especially not now we were a couple.

*Crap.*

Blowing out a long breath, I rubbed at my temples and replayed the last few minutes through my mind. The trigger had been when he'd said we might appear on a blog; it had hit me just how careless I was being with my behaviour. I'd been so wrapped up in the giddiness of spending time with Jack that I'd become sloppy. Jack was famous, his picture was in some paper, magazine, or gossip column practically every week.

And now my picture might be there too.

To be honest, now I'd considered it, it was a miracle I hadn't already been snapped with him. I'd probably only avoided it because he'd been so busy that we hadn't had the time to see each other much beyond our daily coffee breaks.

What if Greg ended up seeing the picture? He'd be able to trace where I was. Swallowing hard, I shook my head. I knew the chances of that happening were miniscule, but I hadn't lived the last three years without Facebook, Twitter, or Instagram for nothing, I wanted – *needed* – to stay under the radar. Being seen with Jack was the complete opposite.

No matter how slim the risk, I couldn't chance the press snapping a picture of Jack and I, and Greg seeing it. If he turned up it would destroy everything – my new job, my new relationship … my fresh start.

So I'd panicked and run away.

Slapping myself on the forehead, I buried my head in my hands. The expression on Jack's face had been one of complete confusion. There had been no trace of his usual jovial self. The one man I wanted to get closer to, and I was pushing him away at every turn.

I couldn't leave it like this. I was supposedly an adult, attempting a relationship. He deserved an explanation, and if we stood any chance of making things work, then I needed to dig up some bravery and tell him about my past, even if the thought of sharing it completely terrified me.

Swallowing down my fear, I decided to do it then before I chickened out.

# SEVENTEEN

## ALLIE

I'm not sure I'd ever held my breath for quite so long. Hearing the door close, I released my breath in a whoosh and looked at Sean with wide eyes. 'Holy shit, that was close.'

Sean had been practicing his knot-tying skills on me in the kitchen. When I say he was 'practising his knot skills', what I really mean is he had stripped me naked, attached my wrists together, and proceeded to tie me to the pan rack that hung from our ceiling.

And that's when the front door had opened.

So yeah, I'd been naked and trussed up in our kitchen and Cait had come home early. I was positive that she was supposed to be working until late, but thank goodness she hadn't come through to the kitchen or glanced in our direction, because I was in direct line of sight of the front door.

Sean, who was also naked, had flicked a glance to the opening door, and then raised a finger to his lips to signal my silence as he stepped into an alcove to hide.

Cait might have left again, but my heart was still galloping in my chest, and there was a film of nervous sweat building on my brow. As I raised my eyes to Sean, I saw none of my panic reflected on his face. He looked pretty goddamn gleeful, actually, and so did his groin, because he was still fully erect. He was unbelievable. I was a quivering wreck, but apparently he was still good to go.

Keeping my cool when I was basically hanging from the ceiling was incredibly difficult, but I gave it my best attempt by flashing a disbelieving glance towards his eager cock. 'You're like the frigging Duracell bunny.'

My breath caught as I watched Sean begin to strut towards me, his swagger indicating just how confident he felt, which immediately sent a shiver of anticipation running through my trussed-up body.

As I took in our surroundings I couldn't help but smile and think that kitchen sex was becoming a regular occurrence for us. Perhaps Sean had a culinary fetish I didn't know about.

My smile faded as I registered his determined expression, then he leant forwards and placed a hard kiss on my lips, closing in so tight I could feel the insistent nudging of his erection against my belly.

'Cheeky.' Kissing me again he raised his hands and began caressing my breasts, his thumbs circling my erect nipples and making me rise onto my tiptoes and arch into the delicious contact with a muffled moan. 'That mouth of yours will get you in trouble,' he added, before I felt a pinch on my right nipple that ripped a gasp of shock from my throat.

Sean took a step back, his eyes twinkling with mischief as they dropped to my chest while the painful pinch continued on my flesh. 'That should keep you in line.'

Looking down, I saw a plastic clothes peg was now attached to my nipple, and felt my brows shoot up into my hairline. What the heck?

'Found it on the shelves when I was hiding,' he murmured. 'Makeshift nipple clamp,' he explained, his face glowing with excitement. 'Is it OK? I tested it on my little finger first.'

Even with Sean's kinkiness recently, this was quite surprising, but it was actually not that painful. There was a spark of pain, but given how aroused I was, it simply added to the thrumming sensation between my legs and I found myself nodding as my cheeks flared. Not that I should be embarrassed in front of Sean any more, we'd done so much together; belts, balconies, hair gripping … Sean was pulling out all sorts of tricks with bondage and kink. Obviously from the moisture collecting between my legs, I was pretty fond of it too.

'Beautiful,' he whispered, his eyes travelling down my body and back up again. 'Shame there weren't two pegs. Perhaps I'll have to invest in some real clamps.' Closing the gap between us, he lowered his head to run the tip of his tongue over my trapped nipple, and any comment I'd wanted to make vanished into a breathy gasp. The sensation of his warm, wet kisses on the tight flesh was incredible as I threw my head back with pleasure and tugged uselessly on my restraints.

Continuing to kiss me, Sean briefly transferred his attention to the other breast, swirling around the tip before applying a similarly tight pinch with his finger and thumb. Once he had well and truly worked me up, he trailed his hand lower, drifting his fingertips over my belly and to the searing heat between my legs. A growl rose in his throat as he dipped a finger into my moisture before plunging two inside.

My head was swirling with desire and my hands repeatedly tugged on the restraints, wanting to touch him, but it was no good. Sean's knot work was proving to be as good as a top ranking Scout.

Leaning back, Sean stared into my eyes and simultaneously tweaked the peg on my nipple while pressing hard circles on my clit, a duel sensation that was so good it nearly threw me into a climax. 'Oh god …' My voice was hoarse, brow damp, and eyes unfocused. I couldn't believe how much one little peg could heighten the sensations, but god, did it.

'Fuck, you're so sexy, Allie. I can feel you tightening around my fingers.' Sean bit on his lower lip then increased the speed of his fingers as he crooked them and found my g-spot.

'Come for me, baby. Come all over my hand.' It was too much: his fingers, his skilled thumb on my clit, the dirty words, and then, as the first clenching spasm of my orgasm began to rip through me, he reached up and pulled off the peg. A rush of blood flooded the tip, causing a surge of pleasure to shoot through my body, flinging me into a huge climax that had me swinging from the ropes and yelping my release until he dived forward and caught my cries with a deep kiss.

Gripping my quivering arse, he squeezed the cheeks and started to lift me. 'Up you go,' he urged, and somehow I managed to prompt my shaky limbs to climb up his body and wrap around his waist. Supporting my weight with one hand, Sean reached up and unhooked my wrists from the pan holder and turned us towards the kitchen counter.

My wrists were still joined, but I looped them behind his neck and held on as he carried us across the room and placed me down. As my bum hit the cold marble Sean kissed me and trailed his lips to my ear. 'My turn.' And with those heated words he spread my thighs and plunged home with a yell.

Holding on to him as best as I could with my hands tied, I wrapped my legs around his waist and gargled out my pleasure as his next thrust went deep enough to make me see stars.

'Love … you … so … much …' His words were punctuated by four hard, deep thrusts, and then, gripping my arse, he dragged me right to the edge of the counter and tilted me back slightly so he was at the perfect angle to bury his entire length inside of me, root to tip.

Seeing as his entire length was pretty damn

impressive, I really frigging felt it when he ground in and paused for a second before pulling out and repeating the move.

'Fuck!' It was Sean who cried out first, but with the depth of that last penetration, I wasn't far behind him. It felt like he was trying to crawl his whole body inside of me.

'Not going to last much longer,' Sean panted as he landed another perfect hit to my g-spot that made my channel convulse around him as a second orgasm neared. 'Look at me, my gorgeous girl.'

As our eyes met and I saw the intensity in his gaze, I couldn't help but profess my love for him. 'I love you too, Sean.'

Growling at my words, he nodded and pulled his hips back again, sliding smoothly from within me before blinking once and jerking forwards with a roar and one final toe-curlingly good thrust that launched us both into explosive climaxes. He shuddered against me, gathering me into his arms as his hips flexed his cock in and out of my quivering sex while we both continued to shatter with the power of our joint release.

Wow. Just wow.

If kitchen sex inspired him this much, I'd have to make more effort to cook in the future.

# EIGHTEEN

## JACK

As I let myself into my dressing room I slammed the door with a satisfyingly loud bang and cursed as my mood descended to a diabolical low. Caitlin's departure stung like a whip lash and I sunk into a chair as I tried to work out what the fuck just happened.

First she hadn't wanted physical contact, and now she didn't want to be seen in public with me? It had to be said that this was another first for me. I'd thought things were going so well until that moment. Was it the age gap bothering her? Or was she just not as into me, *into us*, as I was?

I had quarter of an hour before I was due back on set – quarter of an hour that *should* have been spent with Caitlin, making plans for Friday night – and my mind was no way focused enough to concentrate on reciting my lines.

Treating myself to a scorching shower, I was just pulling on my trousers for the afternoon shoot when the phone on the counter rang. I padded across to the phone, frowning as I went because it was rare that this line got any calls.

'Hello?'

'Hey, Jack, this is Brandon on security, I've got a girl who says she needs to see you. She insists she's a friend of yours. Cait Byrne?'

My eyebrows popped up, and the corner of my mouth tweaked with a smile. No matter how upset I was, the thought that Caitlin was here instantly had me feeling just a little bit better.

The word 'friend' niggled at me far more than it probably should have, though. She was my girlfriend, why hadn't she said that?

Not voicing my annoyance, I levelled my tone. 'She is. Can you bring her round?'

'Sure thing.'

'Great, thanks, Brandon.' Hanging up, I quickly rubbed my hair dry and chucked the towel aside before dragging my shirt on and buttoning it up.

I was tempted to open the door and await her arrival like a keen puppy, but seeing as she'd snubbed me rather spectacularly, I forced myself to play it cool and leant up against the counter behind me instead.

She might be here to finish with me, who knew?

There was a timid knock and I took a moment to compose myself before calling out, 'Come in.'

I watched the door handle turn and tried to form my face to be as neutral as possible as Caitlin glanced nervously around the door and then stared directly at me. She froze for a second, her body tensing as she drew in a breath before she gave a tight smile and hurriedly shut the door behind her.

She looked far from relaxed, which certainly made two of us. I noticed she was clutching a folder to her chest in a white-knuckled grip too – what was in there?

'Do you have some time to talk?' she asked hesitantly, as her spare hand slid down her arm to the elastic bands. If she started to ping those bloody things, I would really find it difficult to hold back from reaching out for her.

Glancing at my watch, I nodded. 'I've got to be on set in ten minutes.'

Caitlin winced, and I wasn't sure if it was because she wanted longer or if my brusqueness upset her, but after the way she had freaked out earlier, I didn't exactly know where we stood.

'I … I'm sorry for earlier. After my rude behaviour, I wasn't sure you would even agree to see me.' She suddenly looked so fragile. The confidence and spunk I'd been getting used to seemed to have completely deserted her now.

Shaking my head at the ridiculous idea of me ever turning her away, I had to fold my arms to resist the urge of pulling her into a hug, as I desperately wanted to.

'Of course I would see you,' I murmured. Her huge eyes turned to mine and filled with relief. But what was the cause of her hesitancy? 'That's not to say I wasn't a little upset by the way you ran away from me,' I added. As much as I wanted to move on from today, I couldn't ignore how much it had affected me, and I needed her to know that. I did, however, gentle my tone so I didn't sound like a complete bastard.

Caitlin's chest lifted and fell in a huge sigh, and she gave the elastic bands at her wrist a pluck that made my teeth grate together. *I* was supposed to be her distraction technique, not those bloody elastic bands.

'I know, and I'm so sorry. I want to explain …'

Ushering her towards the small sofa, I took a seat beside her and watched as she fidgeted nervously. 'Let me start by saying my freak-out had nothing to do with you. You're … well, you're perfect,' she whispered, her cheeks flushing a deep pink. Her words made my heart speed up with hope. I was far from perfect, but I liked the fact she had chosen that word to describe me.

'It's me that's drowning in baggage,' she said quietly, swallowing hard, and I noticed her eyes were now glassy as if she were on the verge of tears. Seeing Caitlin like this made my chest clench. I hated that something was upsetting her. I wanted to comfort her, help her, but for now I supressed the urge and chose to remain quiet.

'I … I want to tell you about my past,' she whispered, and I felt my chest tighten at the enormity of her words. 'Ten minutes isn't enough time for that, so I'll leave some for another day.'

Pausing for a second, Caitlin closed her eyes, drew in a deep breath, and after expelling it through her nose, she looked at me. 'You've probably guessed as much, but my ex was abusive.'

The words rushed from her mouth, and even though I *had* guessed as much, I still found her blunt honesty shocking. Every muscle in my body tensed up as I bristled with hatred toward a man I had never even met.

'His name …' Her words were broken by a small sob before she collected herself and continued. 'His name was Greg. We were together a while. Around a year or so.' Another hiccupy noise escaped as she began to chew frantically on her lip, seeming to try to gather her control. 'There's a reason I don't want to be seen in public with you, but I swear it has nothing to do with what's developing between us.'

Pausing, she unclenched her grip from the folder in her hands and laid it on the table before looking at me with a sombre gaze.

My natural reaction was to protect her, but what from? All I could do was offer my hand, which she accepted immediately, and then give a reassuring squeeze.

Caitlin returned the gesture before sighing again. 'I finished with him over three years ago, but I haven't been able to move on because I think he might be looking for me. *Stalking me.*' She whispered the final two words so softly I barely heard them, but when they sunk in I felt my entire body bristle to alertness.

'He …' She cleared her throat, obviously uncomfortable, so I swivelled myself on the sofa and took hold of her other hand. Her fingers were trembling, but she managed to offer a weak smile of thanks. 'He sometimes sends me letters to my parent's house. They come from all around the world, as if he's trying to catch up with me.'

*Ho-ly fuck.* I wanted to kill this scumbag. How fucking dare he inflict this type of mental torture on to someone?

'I've avoided all social media for years so I don't give him an easy way to find me, and that's why I freaked out about being seen in public.' Her hands gripped mine even tighter. 'I know it's a small chance, but if a photograph of us together gets into the media, he might see it and be able to track me down.'

Bloody hell.

'I … I've been having such a great time with you that it just didn't occur to me.'

I hated the fear I could see in her eyes and I desperately wanted to wrap her in my arms, but I wasn't sure it would be the right thing to do – she already looked stiff and terrified, overwhelming her with physical contact might make it worse.

'Christ, Caitlin, you could have told me earlier, sweetheart.'

Caitlin nodded and then sniffed up a few strayed tears. 'I know, but it honestly didn't cross my mind until I heard the camera and thought about how famous you are.'

'We'll find a way to work around this, Caitlin.' My tone held an edge of demand, because I seriously couldn't even contemplate how I would cope if she finished with me over this, but Caitlin's face lit with relief and I finally felt the tension leave my body.

'I'm so glad you said that,' she said. 'I want to be with you, Jack. I really want it. You've got yourself a freak show of a girlfriend, though,' she whispered. 'I hate you knowing I'm so weak.'

I experienced a moment of joy at the way she had referred to herself as my girlfriend – that was far better than the 'friend' title – but my spine immediately straightened at her self-derogatory words. I shook my head vehemently. 'Don't ever say that. You are one of the strongest, bravest people I've ever met.'

Caitlin's eyes were averted, but her dejection was clear to see in her slumped posture. 'Yeah, so brave I don't want to be seen in public with you,' she muttered.

'What have the police done about this?' I demanded, trying to distract her from her unnecessary self-doubt. As Caitlin explained what had been done so far my brain immediately began trying to work out what contacts I had that might be able to help me track the fucker down.

'I … I ran back to the house to get these.' She reached out a palm and briefly rubbed the folder on the table. 'They're copies of letters he's sent,' Caitlin murmured. 'I keep them with me wherever I travel in case I ever need to go to the police. I wish I could burn them.'

My skin prickled and my eyes flicked from the folder to Caitlin, finding myself wanting to read them in case I could gain any clue to where her ex could be.

'You can look if you want. He made them look like love letters.' She shuddered and stood up. 'I'm going to use your toilet.'

Caitlin disappeared into the en suite and I sat with the folder in my hands, unsure if I should read it. Eventually, the desire to know more overwhelmed me and I opened it.

The first thing I pulled out was a colour photocopy of a postcard. The picture was a red heart and the writing on the back was minimal. 'I can't wait until we are back together again.' The veiled threat sickened me.

Next was a letter. This was obviously a copy made by the police because there were station details across the top. The handwriting was the same as the card, and although there was a date in the top right corner, there was no forwarding address. It wasn't signed. In lieu of a signature was simply a cross.

Reading the first few lines, I saw what Caitlin had meant about it appearing like a love letter. There were mentions of him missing her and wanting to be together again, but then, it started to get explicit. *'I'll tie you down and take you, because I know how much you love to tease me. All good whores love to be tied down and forced, and you're no different, are you, my little slut? You love the chase. And you'll love it until you beg me to stop. But I won't, not until I've had my fill this time ...'*

Holy fuck. I felt sick to my guts, and as my eyes skimmed the rest of the letter, my teeth clenched so hard I heard them squeak in protest.

Shoving the letter back into the folder, I threw it down and surged to my feet feeling totally helpless. Reading those letters just made me even more determined to protect Caitlin like she deserved.

After another minute, the toilet door opened and Caitlin re-emerged looking pale and anxious. She took a step toward me like she was about to step into my arms when a knock on the door interrupted us and caused her to jump back with a startled yelp.

'On set in one minute, Jack,' a runner called from behind the closed door. Fuck. Talk about shitty timing. I didn't want to leave her alone, not for a second.

'Damn it.' Swiping a hand through my hair, I stared at my watch and grimaced. 'I'm going to have to go.'

Caitlin nodded and wrapped her arms around herself almost defensively.

'I know I don't have the full story, but thank you for letting me in. I'll never let him hurt you again, Caitlin. I swear to God I'll keep you safe.' I wasn't quite sure it was the right time to pursue a date with her, but after her

136

emotional confession I was even more desperate to spend time with her and found my next words falling from my mouth unfiltered. 'Can I see you Friday night? We can do something under the radar, but I'd love to spend some time with you.'

Caitlin's cheeks started to get some colour back in them as she smiled shyly up at me and then nodded. 'I'd really like that, Jack. Thank you.'

My heart almost exploded with happiness at her acceptance, and I wanted to drag her into my embrace so badly that my arms ached from holding back. Instead, I settled for placing a kiss on her cheek, but she turned her face slightly into mine so my lips briefly brushed across hers, almost imitating the kiss we'd shared at her house.

Thrilled at her small advance, I reluctantly stood back, taking in her flushed cheeks and smile with a grin of my own, before heading for the door.

# NINETEEN

## JACK

It had been two days since Caitlin's meltdown about the photograph, and to my surprise she now seemed remarkably calm about it. After my promise to keep her safe she seemed to be taking me at my word, and instead of pulling away like I'd feared she would, she was still meeting me at the studio café daily, and still holding my hand at every chance she got.

It was a scorcher today, so instead of our usual Americanos, Caitlin and I were drinking iced coffees on our afternoon break and the refreshingly cool liquid was going a long way to cooling my heated skin.

'I should be finished by five on Friday, thank God. I can't wait to have a full weekend off,' I breathed, so excited by the prospect of my date with Caitlin that I could barely contain myself.

'I'm really looking forward to your weekend off too,' she replied with a shy grin. As I returned her smile she sipped her drink and licked a trace of coffee from her lips. It was an innocent enough gesture, but I found myself staring at her mouth and counting down the minutes until Friday when I was hoping to share many kisses with her.

Just two more days.

I could wait that long. Just.

Great. Thinking about kissing Caitlin had predictable results and beneath the table I now had a hard-on. Again. Luckily, with work keeping me frantically busy, I was so tired most nights that I hadn't given into the desire to turn up on her doorstep and throw myself at her.

Yet.

I might on Friday, if Caitlin was anywhere near as teasing as she had been when I'd last gone to her house. It had been as if being in her own space had emboldened her, and I was kind of hoping she might feel just as relaxed at my house and let us advance things a little bit.

'I'll come straight across after work and pick you up, if that's OK? Then we can have dinner at my place. Or Flynn can collect you?' I added quickly, thinking about her concerns about keeping our relationship under the radar.

'Uh, as long as there aren't loads of journalists around I don't see why you can't get me,' she offered, her cheeks flushing with colour and giving me a small hint that she might be just as excited about Friday as I was.

Beside me, Caitlin put down her coffee and started to dig through her handbag. 'Damn, I must have left my phone on the workbench. Let me run and grab it.'

After Caitlin had walked off, I relaxed in the sun, sipping my cool beverage, and tried to plan what I could cook on Friday. I was pretty good in the kitchen, if I did say so myself, but I wanted an easy meal that would allow me to spend plenty of time with Caitlin. Perhaps salmon baked in the oven – that was easy, and really tasty too.

After replying to a few emails on my phone, I glanced at my watch and realised it had now been ten minutes since Caitlin had headed inside. What was taking her so long? Wondering if she'd lost her mobile and needed help looking, I finished the last of my coffee and strolled towards the studio door to find her.

I took off my sunglasses as I entered the dim corridor and could just about make out the shape of two people at the far end. One was a male, facing away from me and blocking most of my view of his companion, but the long, brown hair that I could see was immediately recognisable to me as Caitlin, so I began to make my way towards them.

My footsteps obviously made my presence known because the man suddenly swung around to face me. 'We're trying to talk privately, buddy. Just give us a minute, OK?' he asked, but his tone was far from polite and I immediately felt my hackles rise.

Who was this guy? For a crazy second I panicked that it was her ex, but he had an American accent and a studio lanyard and ID tag around his neck. A work conflict perhaps? Was Caitlin behind on a deadline?

I saw she was as white as a sheet and I shook my head, knowing I wasn't moving a millimetre until I had Caitlin by my side. Whoever this guy was, he had clearly upset Caitlin, which in turn upset me.

'Actually, I work on this set,' I said. 'Who are you again?'

He didn't bother to respond. Instead, he just ran a hand through his hair and rolled his eyes. After fidgeting on the spot for a second, he murmured something under his breath then sent a narrow-eyed stare my way.

Something was definitely off, so I pulled my phone from my pocket ready to call site security if I needed to.

'Caitlin? Did you find your phone?' I asked, taking another step closer, but Caitlin barely seemed to notice my presence – she was just staring ahead in a dream. What the heck was going on?

'Caitlin?' I tried again, but as I went to go around the man, he threw out a hand.

'She's fine! Just fuck off.' In the blink of an eye the guy flew at me, his fist shooting towards my face.

*What. The. Fuck?*

Thank goodness my military skills kicked in and I

managed to dodge the punch so it only chipped the tip of my jaw. Howling at his miss, he tried to throw another punch and I ducked and stepped into him as I threw all my weight into an uppercut to his solar plexus.

My hit found its target spot-on and he dropped to his knees, gurgling and gasping as I raised my phone to call security. I went to bend to restrain him but a sob from Caitlin had me stopping in my tracks.

Her eyes were wide and blank, but tears were now streaming down her cheeks as her slim body slowly began sliding down the wall to the floor. Fuck.

'Caitlin? *Caitlin?*' Forgetting the spluttering man at my feet I immediately ran to her side, careful not to touch her.

Dropping to my knees, I watched as she curled herself into a ball with her knees pulled to her chest as silent tears continued to flow down her cheeks. 'Caitlin? Sweetheart, it's me, it's Jack. It's OK.'

The crash of a door opening behind me alerted me to the arrival of three security guards, but when I turned back I saw that the corridor just contained them.

The mystery guy was gone.

'Shit! There was a man here less than a minute ago. He swung at me; looked to be mid-thirties. Blond hair, chin-length, and an orange T-shirt.'

One of the guards ran out the door while a second bent down beside Caitlin and the third picked up his walkie-talkie. 'Control, this is Mike, I need you to check the feed on the CCTV by stage five for the last ten minutes. See if you can get any images of a young man with blond, chin length hair wearing an orange T-shirt. Try to find his location, he attacked someone.'

There was fuss going on all around us, but all I could focus on was the fact that I needed to try and help Caitlin, but that she was still non-responsive. How could I help when she wouldn't answer me? Christ, she was as white as a sheet, so pale I genuinely feared she was about to pass out.

'Are you OK? Can you speak, sweetheart?' The only response I got was a watery-eyed blink, still unfocused and glassy.

What had he said to her?

'Caitlin?' I sounded like a broken record, but short of grabbing her shoulders and shaking her, I didn't know what else to do. Her fingers were gripped into tight fists, so I very carefully laid a supportive hand on her shoulder. As soon as my fingers brushed against her she flinched to the side and a pitiful whimper left her lips.

I withdrew my hand as if I'd been scalded. 'Fuck!'

'Is she gonna puke?' The security guard beside me asked, shifting himself backwards out of the firing line. He called into the walkie-talkie on his lapel, 'Control, we need a paramedic. Corridor of stage five, we've an unresponsive employee.'

Flicking my thumb across the screen of my phone, I found Sean's number and pressed dial, hoping with all my life that he wasn't on set. He answered after three rings and I felt my chest decompress in relief.

'Sean? It's Jack, is Allie with you?'

'No, I'm at the studio. She's at their house writing. Why?'

'I don't have Allie's number, but something's wrong with Caitlin. Can you call Allie and ask her to come across to the studio? I'll have someone meet her by the gates.' I gave the security guard an intense look. He nodded and pulled out a pad for me to scribble Allie's name down and then hurried out of the door.

'Of course. Is Cait OK?'

'I'm not sure. I think she's having a panic attack, I'm hoping Allie will know what to do.'

'Shit. I'll call her now. Good luck.'

'Thanks. We're in stage five. Tell her to be quick.'

142

# TWENTY

## ALLIE

Sean's phone call had really shaken me up. Thank goodness I'd spent the morning writing and hadn't gone out shopping as planned, because otherwise I'd have been miles away in the middle of Wal-Mart juggling a trolley load of goodies right now.

Hot on the heels of a security guard, I rushed through a set of heavy doors and saw Jack's tall figure, pale and drawn as he frantically ushered me toward him.

Practically tripping over every step, I made it to his side and my stomach dropped as I saw Cait sitting on the floor, tiny and terrified with her arms around her knees as she gently rocked back and forth while a paramedic attempted to read her blood pressure. Jeez.

This didn't look good.

Dropping to my knees, I leant in close. 'Cait, it's Allie.' Even though I'd used my softest voice, she didn't respond at all.

Her eyes were open, but staring straight ahead sightlessly.

'What happened?' I asked, standing up next to Jack.

'We were on a coffee break when Caitlin realised she'd left her phone here. She went back to get it but she'd been gone a while so I came in to check on her.' Pausing, he ran a hand through his hair, looking completely stressed out. 'When I got back, she was talking to this guy. Well, he was talking to her. As soon as I tried to intervene he attacked me.'

'What?' I squawked. Jack was a sizable guy, tall and well-built. I'd imagine another man would have to be pretty confident to go for him. Or pretty crazy.

'Yeah, he tried to punch me in the face, but I managed to dodge it. I dropped him to the floor but while I was checking on Caitlin he managed to get away.'

'Oh my God. Who was it?' I whispered.

'No idea. He was wearing a tag that looked like a site pass, but I'd never seen him before.' At that moment, a security guard hurried to us with a sheet of paper that he thrust at Jack.

'We got this from the entry gate footage just over an hour ago. This the guy? The ID tag looks the wrong colour, might be a fake.'

Jack examined the image and nodded.

'We're checking it against the staff database, but if that tag is fake then whoever let him in is in serious trouble.'

As they we talking I leant in and glanced at the picture and the blood in my veins turned icy. Shit. His hair was longer, and the picture was quite grainy, but there was no mistaking that pointy face.

'He was here?' I stuttered, my voice high and wobbly as I tried to calm my spinning brain.

'Yes. You know him?' Jack asked, his frame immediately turning to me.

'I've not seen him for years, but that's …' I paused, casting a glance at Cait and lowering my voice to a whisper. 'That's Gregory Lambert.'

Greg.

'Cait's last boyfriend. Things didn't, um … didn't end very well. I think we need to call the police.'

'That *was* her ex?' Jack demanded, his eyes widening as his shoulders bunched in obvious annoyance. Had Cait told him about Greg?

145

'Yep.'

'Fuck! He had an American accent.' Jack pulled in a huge breath and shook his head. 'She won't speak. Did he hurt her? Has this happened before?'

Greg had certainly hurt Cait before, but I suspected this was a panic attack.

'I think she's having an anxiety attack. Did he touch her?'

'I don't think so, it didn't look like it when I arrived.' Frowning, Jack's left eye winced slightly as he chewed on his lower lip. 'I know how skittish she is about physical contact, but I did try to touch her shoulder.' Swallowing hard, he lowered his eyes. 'She, uh, flinched away from me and whimpered.'

The poor guy looked beside himself with worry. 'I think it must be the shock of seeing Greg after so long.'

'She's mentioned him to me, said he was abusive. What did he do?' Jack asked, lowering his voice this time. My eyes fluttered shut as I recalled the day, years ago, when Cait had called me from the police station once Greg had been arrested. Once we were through with the police and hospital checks I'd taken her back to the house we shared, but it had reminded her of Greg and she'd freaked out, so we'd driven across to her parent's house.

They were in Crete for a month, so it had been quiet and empty and seemed to calm Cait down, but she had been too traumatised to sleep alone for the first fortnight. That night, as I'd sat at the side of her bed while she tried to sleep, was when she had cracked and broken down into tears and let the whole story out between jagged sobs.

A long breath whistled from my lips as I finally opened my eyes and blinked back to reality. 'It needs to be Cait who tells you that.' It wasn't my story to tell, and as much as I knew Jack wanted to help, it had to be her choice whether she wanted to tell him or not.

Looking first to Cait and then to a concerned Jack, I wondered how long it was going to take her to recover this time.

One of the paramedics approached Jack and I. 'She's going to need to speak to the police, but for now we need to get her out of here and get her properly checked over.'

Crouching beside her, I cleared my throat of the tears that were building and tried to get through to her. 'Cait? Sweetie? Can you stand up? I want to take you home.' When I got no response, I carefully laid a hand on her arm, only to have her flinch away and ball her hands into fists with a whine.

I looked up to Jack and saw his expression was grim. Shaking his head, he came to my side and lowered into a crouch in front of Cait.

The paramedics had failed to get close enough to read her blood pressure, so after briefly chatting, one turned to us while the other brought over a wheelchair. 'We can take her to the medical centre on site, it's a three minute walk from here so we'll lift her into the wheelchair.'

As the paramedic's bent to shift Cait, Jack dropped to his knees and threw his hands out. 'Wait! She'll hate that. She has a phobia of physical contact.'

The paramedic exchanged a look with his partner and shook his head thoughtfully. 'There's really nothing else we can do, sir, she needs to be seen by the doctor, but as they're treating someone else at the moment we need to take her there. We'll limit the contact as much as possible.'

Before I could join in and support Jack's comments, I watched as the two paramedics knelt beside Cait and swiftly looped one hand under each of her armpits to lift her.

Ohhhh shit … Cait *hated* being touched by men, this was not good, and manhandling her was definitely not the way to go. This was like all her triggers rolled up into one great big ball, and then, seconds later, just as Jack had predicted, Cait suddenly went from non-responsive to completely animated and freaking out; her arms flailed, legs kicked, and eyes sprung open like saucers as she wriggled and writhed in their grip.

Holding his hands extended toward her thrashing figure, Jack began speaking to her, his voice loud but calm, even though I suspected that Cait was beyond hearing him. 'Caitlin, sweetheart, you're OK, I'm here. It's me, it's Jack. I'm right here.'

This was horrific to watch. Cait was sobbing loudly now, her struggling so forceful that the paramedics were practically wrestling with her, and not succeeding in getting her any closer to the wheelchair. Suddenly, one of her arms shot out and grabbed Jack's extended hand and in a blur of floundering limbs she dived out of the paramedic's grip and literally crawled into Jack's lap, almost knocking him backwards with her desperation.

Her body was still twitching and jerking, but she calmed almost immediately as he gently circled her with his arms and shot me a startled look. I was as shocked as he was.

Jack was amazing, so calm and controlled. He recovered from his surprise almost immediately and after looping an arm under her knees, he secured Cait to his chest and stood up. His head dipped next to hers as he talked to her reassuringly the entire time. 'You're safe, Caitlin. I promise you. You're safe with me.' His voice was soft and gentle, and at complete odds to his tense stance, but it was working, Cait was calming, her body losing its tension as she began to go lax in his grip.

'Do you want to put her in the wheelchair?' offered one of the paramedics, but Jack dismissed the idea with a scowl and a shake of his head.

'No. I've got her.'

148

Letting out a small, dry sob, Cait's hands then settled on his chest as she balled them in the material of Jack's shirt and clung on for dear life. Her fists were trembling and her eyes were scrunched shut but she rested her head on his shoulder and drew in several calmer breaths.

Wow. I would never in a million years have expected this to happen. Jack glanced across at me, apparently equally as shocked by Cait's capitulation, but then wasted no time in giving a sharp nod to one of the paramedics and starting off towards the studio doors.

'Let's get her to the doctor.'

With Cait suspended in his arms, Jack looked like an olden day knight in shining armour, saving his damsel in distress. It was a pretty accurate description, really.

Following close on Jack's heels, he refused the offer of a lift in a golf cart and instead strode the entire way to the medical centre with Cait cradled in his arms. His legs were so long that both myself and the paramedics struggled to keep up as he headed off purposefully, weaving between buildings and fences until he finally came to an abrupt halt next to the studio's medical block.

'Can you open the door, please, Allie,' he murmured, Jack's worried eyes focused solely on Cait as she rested in his arms.

I got quite a big lump in my throat as I watched just how careful Jack was with Cait as he carried her inside and gently laid her onto the doctor's bed. He whispered softly to her the entire time, words so quiet that I couldn't hear, but the reassuring sentiment was clear.

Seconds later, a doctor rushed in, thankfully female, which Cait might respond to slightly more favourably, and after Jack and I had given her a quick rundown of what had happened, she politely ushered us out of the room.

Stepping into the waiting area, Jack threw his hands up and ran them roughly though his hair. 'Fuck.' He whispered the curse softly but the bristling tension in his body made his anxiousness all too clear.

Guiding me to the waiting seats he fixed me with an intent stare. 'It wasn't just verbal abuse, was it? He hurt her, didn't he?' he stated, his jaw so tight I was surprised I hadn't heard his teeth squeaking. 'Or was it worse?' he pushed, his voice dropping to a rough whisper as his eyes filled with emotion.

I had never once broken Cait's confidence about the events of that awful day, but I was so tempted to do so now. It was obvious how much Jack cared about her, and I knew she felt something for him, but swallowing loudly, I just couldn't break my promise to her. Instead, I neither confirmed nor denied his questions, simply giving one single blink which caused Jack to let out another hissed curse.

'Like I said, it's not my story to tell. I'm sorry, I can see you care for her, but it's something Cait needs to tell you herself if she chooses to.'

I expected Jack to push for more, but instead his head slumped forward and he rested it on his balled fists as he took in several deep breaths before finally lifting his gaze to mine again. 'I understand. I can't believe I was there with him and let him get away. There's no way you two can stay in that house alone with him in LA.' His tone left no room for argument, but I was already in complete agreement. 'You can stay with me if you like, I have spare rooms.'

'If it's OK with you, I'd rather we go to Sean's beach house. I have some things there, anyway.' From the way Jack's mouth opened I could tell he was about to object. 'I won't feel as if we're intruding quite as much. I ... I know you two are together, and I can see you want to keep her close, but it's still really new. She might feel strange being at your house.'

Jack nodded reluctantly. 'OK, Sean's place it is.'

I sent Sean a text to let him know that Cait and I would be staying with him for a few nights, not that he would mind.

Checking his phone, Jack huffed out a breath. 'The security team have messaged me to say the police have arrived. They're going to run through the CCTV footage then interview both myself and Caitlin.'

Chewing on my lip, I frowned. 'I hardly think she's going to be in any fit state for that.'

'No. I agree. I'll try and get them to come to the house later instead. That should be a little less stressful for her.'

Both Jack and I jumped up when the consultation room opened, and the doctor indicated for us to come over.

'I think you were right with your speculation of a panic attack. Cait is lucid now, and she's spoken to me a little but she's still very much in shock. I'm happy to release her, but I've prescribed some medication to calm her and help her sleep, and I suggest she makes a follow up appointment with her own doctor and therapist, if she has one, for next week.'

'OK. Thank you so much.'

As the doctor was bagging up the pills, Cait appeared in the doorway looking ashen and unsure as she pinged her elastic bands repeatedly and stared at the floor.

Jack immediately dashed towards her, holding out his hands again as if she might require a steadying handhold, but she shook her head and wrapped her arms around her body. 'I can walk,' she whispered, her eyes still locked on the tiled floor.

The crestfallen expression on Jack's face was almost painful to witness, but he kept his cool, and after gently placing a blanket around her shoulders, led us both in the direction of the car park.

Jack opened the rear passenger door of his car so Cait

and I could ride together, before he slid into the driver's seat. Apart from nodding when I told her I was taking her to Sean's, Cait didn't respond throughout the short journey, but she let me hold her hand and I noticed her eyes gradually rising.

I was fairly sure I caught her gaze flicking in Jack's direction on several occasions, and I definitely saw him watching her in the rear view mirror whenever we were stopped in traffic.

# TWENTY-ONE

## CAIT

He was here.

In LA.

I couldn't believe it.

Greg was here. The mildly amusing title of 'the fuckwad' didn't seem quite as appropriate any more, it had been a silly distraction technique to lighten the impact of him, but there was nothing remotely amusing about this. He was here. And from the few disgusting words he'd muttered to me before Jack had burst in, he planned on finishing what he'd started all those years ago, and worse.

My blood ran cold as I allowed the reality to sink in. My fingers gripped at the leather of Jack's car seat and I felt my nostrils flaring as I tried to draw in some much needed air.

When I'd been stood by my locker and felt the tap on my shoulder, I had never in a million years expected it to be Greg when I jumped and turned around. But it was. Finally, after over three years, he'd found me.

The fight between Greg and Jack was a bit of a blur, and then chaos had seemed to erupt around me as Jack and the security guards had frantically spoken. In the end my legs had just given out and I'd slid down the wall, it had seemed the easiest option at the time.

Lights had become brighter, and sounds louder, but my focus had dimmed to just a tiny dot of light as if I were staring down a really long cardboard tube. Then I simply sat there staring at nothing and breathing raggedly as my world turned in on itself. The feel of the paramedics gripping my arms had been the final straw.

The only thing that had brought me back from complete hysteria had been Jack when he'd held his arms out to me. I couldn't believe I'd crawled into his lap like that, but the touch of his hand had felt good, offering me the security I desperately needed, and my body had seemed to act of its own accord. As he'd carried me out of the studio I'd realised that I'd never felt so safe in my entire life.

Jack made me feel safe.

The last hour might have been utterly horrific, but it had made one thing clear in my mind, it was time to let him in. Completely.

## ALLIE

Once we had arrived at Sean's and negotiated the
security gates, Jack pulled his car up outside the front of
the beach house, switched off the engine, and
immediately jumped out to help Cait. Leaning in to
assist her, Cait stopped him and shook her head jerkily.

'I'm OK,' she whispered. 'Thank you.' Her voice
sounded dry and quiet in the breezy afternoon, but I
couldn't help but feel proud of how brave she was. I
could see Jack wanted to do more, but instead of pushing
it he merely nodded and stood back while she lowered
herself from the Jeep's door.

With me on her arm and Jack acting like a shadow
behind us, we made our way up the steps and through
the front door until we were in the lounge. 'Would you
like a drink? Tea?' I asked Cait, hoping to start her
talking.

'Yes, please,' she replied, her voice a mere whisper
as she let go of my arm. I noticed she was avoiding eye
contact with myself and Jack, but at least she was
standing on her own and starting to talk again.

Stepping away to make my way to the kitchen, I saw
Jack shuffle on his feet. 'Do you want me to leave you
two alone now, or stay until the police arrive?' he asked
hesitantly. When Cait didn't speak Jack sighed and
began to turn for the hallway.

Suddenly Cait's gaze lifted. 'No. Jack, wait,' Jack
paused, turning back to Cait, who was now watching
him with wide, unsure eyes. 'Thank you. Please stay,'
she murmured, her voice still reedy and dry, and then, to
my complete amazement, Cait swallowed loudly and

hesitantly stepped into Jack's chest, resting her cheek on his shirt and sliding her trembling hands around his waist.

Holy crap. I'd never seen Cait initiate contact with a man since her relationship with Greg, and now she'd voluntarily gone into Jack's arms twice in the last two hours. I felt my mouth drop open and watched as Jack gaped down at her as she clung to his frame like a limpet.

The gentleness with which he encircled Cait with his arms and began to lightly stroke her hair made me bite down on my lower lip as my emotions quickly began to get the better of me. It would appear I wasn't the only one though, because Jack scrunched his eyes shut for a second as if holding in tears.

A huge lump was forming in my throat, so before I sobbed loudly and spoilt their sweet embrace, I quietly slipped away from the room.

# TWENTY-TWO

## CAIT

I'd wanted to touch Caitlin for so long, and now, I'd held her in my arms twice within the last few hours. I couldn't ever remember feeling quite so exhilarated.

My contentment at this new development was marred by the fact that I'd met the arsehole that had caused Caitlin's issues with men. I was convinced Gregory fucking Lambert had physically hurt Caitlin in the past. Allie's face had basically supported my suspicions and I was furious with myself for letting him get away.

I wish I'd knocked him out instead of just knocking the wind out of him. That fucker had done something horrific to this beautiful, sweet girl. My jaw tensed as I tried to reign in my rage.

At any other point, the feel of Caitlin pressing her body against mine would have led to some serious constriction in my trouser region. But not today. My anger at Lambert and fear for Caitlin were all-consuming, and desire was just about the furthest thing from my mind.

I'd long known that Cait was cautious around the opposite sex and wary about being touched, and even though I'd briefly considered that perhaps something had happened to her in her past, I'd dismissed the idea and put her behaviour down to her being overly shy. Then she'd shown me those letters and I'd started to piece it together.

Things were becoming clearer, and as much as I

wanted to be here comforting Caitlin, another side of me wanted to get on the street with the police and hunt that fucker down.

Her head moving brought me back to the present and I looked down as Caitlin shifted slightly within my gentle embrace so she was resting her forehead just above my sternum.

The police had called me, and told us that they were finishing up at the studios and would be heading over to interview her in an hour, which gave us all some more time to recover. As far as I was concerned, I wanted to spend every second of those sixty minutes with her in my arms.

I could feel her warm breath through the cotton of my shirt, and I realised with a grimace that her hands were still trembling against my back as she slid them around to sit on my hips.

Moving one of my hands with infinite care so as not to startle her I began to gently rub her shoulders, hoping to settle her. My words had seemed to work at the studio, so I tried them again. 'Shhh. It's OK, Caitlin. I'm here, sweetheart. You're safe.'

Gradually, I felt Caitlin begin to soften even more, her breathing becoming slower and deeper and her trembling subsiding until finally she lifted her head and gave me a timid smile.

Smiling back, I instinctively smoothed some stray hairs away from her face but I felt Caitlin tense as I touched her cheek and immediately dropped my hand.

Fuck. She was so fragile, but I wanted to touch her so badly. I had to tread really, really carefully.

Behind us, I heard a soft knock on the lounge door and turned to see Allie with a tray in her hands watching the two of us. It seemed she was bringing us drinks, but I also suspected she was rather protective of Caitlin and was using the refreshments as a means of checking up on

159

us too.

'I brought some tea.' As Allie entered, Caitlin took a step away from me, tucking her hands into the pockets of her jeans and dropping her gaze to the tray that Allie had placed on the coffee table. I immediately missed her warmth, and it took every shred of my self-control not to follow her and wrap her in my arms again.

Caitlin cleared her throat and looked at her friend, and I noticed that her cheeks finally seemed to have more colour in them.

'Thanks, Allie. And, uh … thanks for coming to get me.' Lifting a hand to her mouth, Caitlin chewed on the thumb nail and then dropped her hand when Allie stepped forward and embraced her.

'You don't need to thank me, Cait. You have my back and I have yours, babes.' Their closeness was rather touching, almost like that of family, and reminded me a lot of the bond my brother and I shared.

The girls stepped apart and Caitlin cleared her throat nervously. 'And you too, Jack.' She was animated in her nervousness: staring at the floor again, nudging the rug with her toe, and pinging the elastic bands on her wrist. 'Thank you for getting me out of there.'

I wanted to respond the same way Allie had and pull Caitlin into my arms, but I didn't dare, so instead I shook my head. 'It wasn't a problem, Caitlin,' I murmured, my voice rough from the intensity of the feelings I had for this woman. I wished that I had detained Gregory and knew the whole story of her past so I could properly console her. Reining in my frustration, I felt a surge of hope as she raised her head and met my eyes.

'Allie, I promise we'll talk later, but would you mind giving me some time to talk to Jack, please?' I was as surprised by Caitlin's words as Allie looked, but she nodded and turned for the door.

'No problem, I'll be in the kitchen if you need me.'

160

Once we were alone, Caitlin moved to one of the large leather sofas and took a seat, tucking one leg underneath herself and patting the seat to her side. She wanted me near her, which thrilled me, and I found my heart was suddenly galloping in my chest.

Indicating at the tray containing a tea pot, two mugs, and two bottles of water, I looked to Caitlin. 'Would you like a drink?'

Her eyes skimmed the tray and then wandered to the small bar in the corner of the room. 'I'll have a whiskey.'

My eyebrows jumped, then I chuckled at the playful look on her face and nodded. 'Your wish is my command.'

I knew Sean didn't drink spirits any more, usually sticking to one glass of wine or a bottle of beer, but I walked over to check in case he had any for guests. As I suspected, the surface contained a wine rack with several very decent bottles and nothing more, but exploring the mini fridge and cupboard to its right, I discovered beers, juices, water, and three bottles of port, whisky, and brandy. Pouring a decent measure for Caitlin, I made up a brandy for myself and glanced over to find her watching me with that same smile on her face.

Seeing that look on her lips because of me would never grow old.

'Ice?' God, my voice sounded high pitched and adolescent. I seriously needed to get a grip on myself.

'Just a touch of water, please.' Cracking open one of the bottles, I added a splash to both drinks and made my way back to the sofa. As much as I wanted to sit as close to her as possible, I left a gap, respecting her space.

I tried not to stare at her mouth as she took a sip of the amber liquid, but as her tongue darted out to capture a drop of moisture on her lower lip, it was impossible. Her lips were too irresistible not to watch. God, I wanted to kiss her so badly. I wanted to kiss her until her bad memories went away and only the two of us existed.

Grabbing a pillow as a distraction, I pulled it onto my lap and fiddled with the zip to stop myself staring. I took a sip of my own drink, trying to calm my hammering pulse, and followed her lead by placing my glass on the table.

'You've been so patient with me, Jack,' she murmured quietly. Looking across, I could see an apprehensive expression on her face. 'I've held you off, knocked you back, and completely freaked out on you, but you're still here.'

'I told you I was willing to take things slow, and I meant it.'

She nodded thoughtfully as if absorbing my words. 'I'll be honest, at first I thought that was just a line. I figured that, being who you are, you were hoping for a quick shag before moving on.' Her admission made my eyebrows rise in surprise, but to be fair she had a point – a vast majority of actors I knew were exactly like that, moving from one woman to the next at every opportunity.

'I'm glad I proved you wrong,' I murmured.

'I'm the one who's glad,' she added.

'I'm too old to be playing games like that, Caitlin. I'm not looking for a quick fling,' I confirmed. 'I told you I wanted you properly, and I meant it. I feel a connection I've never felt before and as far I'm concerned, that's something worth exploring.'

'And that's still the case? Even after today?' she asked quietly, her eyes wide and wary.

If anything, seeing her so vulnerable had increased the intensity of my feelings. I wanted to protect and love her and help her blossom, but I didn't say any of that. Nodding my head, I kept it simple. 'It's still very much the case, Caitlin.'

Caitlin nearly killed me by flicking out her tongue and licking it across her lower lip as she processed my words. Swallowing hard, I had to tamp down the instant flood of blood that rushed to my cock at her accidentally seductive move. Thank fuck I had this pillow. I seriously didn't think she knew how sexy or appealing she was, but I was now rock solid inside my jeans. Uncomfortably so.

'I ... I feel the connection. It's amazing. *You're* amazing. These last few weeks have been incredible. But ...'

But? Why did there have to be a 'but'? I was more than happy with her description of me as amazing. Her eyes fluttered shut as her cheeks reddened again. '... As you saw, I have certain, uh ... *issues*, which might not make moving forwards the easiest prospect.'

She sounded like she was apologising. It was *his* fault, that fucker, but I pushed that aside and decided to lay it all on the line once and for all.

'As far as I'm concerned, Caitlin, we're a team. You're my girlfriend. I'm committed to you, baggage and all. I don't care what issues you have as long as you think you might be able to share them with me one day. If that takes patience, then that's fine.' Running a hand through my hair, I prepared for the bombshell. 'What I'm trying to say is... I've been single a while, but over the course of my adult life, no one has ever made me feel the way you do. You're it for me, Caitlin. I'm not just looking for any relationship with you. I want commitment, baggage, the whole lot. I want this long-term. I want *you* long-term.'

There. It was out, and as I watched Caitlin's gorgeous hazel eyes widen in shock, I had no idea which way this was going to go.

# TWENTY-THREE

## CAIT

*Long-term.* Jack Felton wanted a committed, long-term relationship. With *me*. Up to now, I'd viewed this whole girlfriend/boyfriend thing quite sceptically – he had been saying the right things, but I'd kept thinking he'd realise what a freak show I was and change his mind at some point. I'd figured his patience would run out and he'd move on.

It would seem that I'd been wrong.

*You're it for me.* I didn't know what to say. Well … I did. I wanted to say yes. Shout yes. Scream it from the rooftops and fling myself at this patient and amazing man, but it was all a little overwhelming. So instead I sat there gawking like an idiot.

Smooth, Cait, really smooth.

Pulling myself together, I made a decision … a pretty monumental one. I was going to do something I'd never done before – tell a man the full, no holds barred story of my past.

'I … you know I want that too, but can I tell you about my past first? I feel like it's blocking me from moving forwards with you.'

'Of course. You can tell me anything, but know that it won't change my mind about you.'

I nodded, hoping his words were true. I felt fidgety and awkward, my hands moving restlessly on my lap. 'Would you …' Swallowing loudly, I dared to glance up at Jack as I spoke. '… Would you hold me again?' I whispered, surprised by how reassuring I found his touch.

Jack grinned, looking thrilled by my request, a smile so stunning that it made my heart skip. But then he paused, so I decided to just tell the truth. 'I feel so safe with you,' I whispered.

Safe. And so much more.

Attracted. Protected. Aroused.

Jack's face softened and without any further words, he opened his arms and gently helped me across the sofa and into his lap. Looping his arms around me, he cradled me against him as I relaxed against his strong chest with a sigh.

'Is this OK?' he enquired, still keeping his hold on me light and cautionary.

'It's perfect,' I murmured, absorbing the feel of his strength. And it really was.

'I don't know what he did to you, Caitlin,' Jack started and a shudder ran through my body as I thought of Greg being in LA. 'But please believe me when I say you can trust me. I will do everything in my power to keep you safe, sweetheart,' he murmured. His words and contact caused warmth to course through my body like an electric current, replacing the shuddering chill. It felt so good that I closed my eyes and allowed Jack's light to overpower the darkness and dread that Greg brought to my life.

'I know,' I murmured, and I really did. His careful, polite pursuit of me had earned my complete trust. I heard a hum of contentment rumble in Jack's chest and felt him drop the lightest of kisses on the top of my head.

A wry smile twisted my lips as I felt his lips linger in my hair for a second and a shiver of pleasure tingled across my scalp. I really couldn't believe that this was happening. After Greg, I'd never thought I'd open myself up to a man again, and yet here I was in the arms of Jack Felton.

Movie star.

Heart-throb.

My boyfriend.

Deciding to tell my story now, I cleared my throat, closed my eyes against the painful images that tried to crawl into my mind, and began. 'So, obviously you know that that guy was Greg,' I stated quietly, and in response I felt his body briefly tense below my fingertips.

Fiddling with one of the buttons on his shirt, I sighed. He said he wanted all of me, and now he was going to get it. Every sordid detail.

'I want to fill you in on the part that has really made me wary of men.

'We ... we met in a bar, not long after I'd graduated from my teaching degree. He was six years older than me, and charming, funny, and handsome.' At least I'd thought so at the time, but really, Greg was only average-looking at best, especially when compared to Jack's handsome features. As I spoke, Jack began to gently stoke my shoulder, his movements tentative and careful but filling me with the courage to continue.

'Well, at first he was, anyway,' I corrected. The change in Greg had been almost beyond recognition and a shudder ran through my entire body as I remembered how he'd gone from sweet and caring to possessive, abusive, and controlling. 'He was a sales representative for a pharmaceutical company based in Germany and he worked away a lot, so for the first nine months we barely saw each other. It was long distance, mostly over the phone. Every time he was home it would just be for a day or a weekend, and every time I felt like we were starting our relationship all over again.'

Turning my head so my forehead was on Jack's shoulder, I drew in a deep breath filled with his lovely, clean linen scent and tried to muster up some courage. 'Things didn't fully develop between us physically. He often tried to initiate sex, but the distance made me unsure and I never felt entirely comfortable with him. We did certain things, but never ...' I paused, clearing my throat and feeling my cheeks burn. '... We never went all the way.' I felt so juvenile describing sex like this but it was the best I could do without completely dying of embarrassment.

'Deep down, I knew he wasn't as great as my friends said, but they always told me how lucky I was to have a good-looking, rich boyfriend so I'd tried to stick with him. I should have dumped him as soon as I got worried, but I didn't.' I gave a small chuckle to release some of the pressure building inside of me.

'Only Allie saw through him from the start. She never liked Greg, and for a while that put pressure on our friendship. That girl has a radar for detecting bad men, always has done.'

Leaning back, I tried to lighten the mood. 'She bloody loves you by the way, so I guess that means you must be alright.' In response, the serious expression on Jack's face morphed into a shy smile and I realised just how small the space between our faces was. Literally just a few centimetres. I could kiss him so easily, and from the way Jack's gaze dropped to my lips and lingered there I could tell he was thinking the same.

Surprisingly, I *wanted* him to kiss me, and before another thought could pass through my mind I leant forward and placed my lips against his. Warmth coursed through my body and a groan rose in my chest at how good it felt, then I quickly leant back. I was seconds away from moving on from just a closed-mouth kiss to something more heated, but I had the distinct feeling that if I deepened the kiss it would distract me from my story, and I wanted to get it out in the open once and for

167

all.

Jack rubbed his nose against mine and then very gently ran his thumb across my lower lip before encouraging me to lie back against his chest.

'After we'd been together for about nine months, Greg's job changed and he became more UK-based. We suddenly had the opportunity to see each other more frequently, and immediately I saw a change in him. He became incredibly possessive. He got jealous if people so much as spoke to me when we were out. He started to get verbally abusive too, accusing me of flirting with other guys and being really critical about my body.'

*Scrawny little legs. Look at you, you're all skin and bone. You've barely got tits. No one else will want to fuck you, Cait, you're fucking lucky you've got me. You should appreciate that more than you do.*

I shuddered and gave the elastic bands on my wrist a few pings until Jack gently interlinked his fingers with mine. Squeezing his digits, I smiled fondly – my very own human stress ball.

'He began turning up at my work to make sure I wasn't chatting to any of the dads at home time, and if we were walking together he'd push my lower back or tug my clothes to keep me close and lead me where he wanted … he started to scare me.' I shivered and felt Jack hold me against him more firmly, his hand now circling my shoulder at a faster pace.

'He'd been based in the UK for about three weeks when I decided to end the relationship,' I whispered. Jack's hand had stilled in my hair, and I could feel his body turning rigid below mine.

'He was living at home with his mum until he found a place, so one afternoon I cycled round his house to finish things. His mum worked night shifts and was always home in the afternoon so I'd thought it was the safest time.' A small sob left my throat. 'That day of all days, she'd gone out to get her hair done,' I whispered.

'Greg was home and on the PlayStation with a couple of friends, so I figured if there were other people in the house I'd be OK.' A shudder racked through my entire body as I clung to Jack's shirt. I was nearly done. Just a few more sentences and he'd know it all.

'His bedroom reeked of weed, so I stayed in the corridor telling him we needed to talk. I finished things with him, telling him we'd grown apart while he'd been travelling, but he totally freaked out.' By this point I could almost see Greg's bedroom in my mind, could remember how red and angry his eyes had been, and I found silent tears streaming down my cheeks and soaking into Jack's shirt.

'Before I even knew what happened, Greg grabbed hold of me and threw me into his bedroom. I banged my head on the door and fell to the floor, but managed to get up.' I had to pause to get a proper breath, because by this point I was almost hyperventilating.

'Christ, Caitlin ...' His wheezy breath made me pause, but I couldn't look at him. 'You don't have to tell me, sweetheart, it's OK ...' he murmured, but I shook my head. I *needed* to get this out.

I squeezed my eyes shut and tried to focus on the soothing smell of Jack's shirt instead of the terrifying flashes of memory seeping into my mind like a poison. 'He pinned me to the wardrobe and told me that I'd been a ... a ... a fucking cock tease the whole time we'd been together so he'd fuck me before I left him.'

Jack drew in a sharp breath as his arms tightened around me, and I felt his hands ball into fists as if he were barely managing to contain his anger.

'He was so strong. He held my wrists in one hand and used the other to rip my T-shirt open, but he couldn't get my jeans down one handed because I was wearing a belt and struggling as hard as I could. He ... he asked his

169

friends to help him, said they could fuck me after if they'd help get my clothes off.'

At this statement, Jack stifled a pained groan and I actually felt his teeth snap together.

'I ... I thought they'd tell him to stop, or help me, but they didn't. They ... they joined in.'

'Fucking hell.'

'I couldn't understand it, but they didn't seem bothered that I was crying and screaming. Maybe they'd done more than weed because the next second they were ripping at my clothes too.' I took a hiccupy breath and shook my head. 'One took hold of me so Greg could take his trousers off and the other knelt down to work out my belt.

'I brought my knee up as hard as I could into the guy's face. Blood came bursting out so I think I might have broken his nose, I never did find out. Greg went totally mental and hit me in the face. His friend let me go, I think the force knocked me out of his grasp. So I took my opportunity and made a break for it.'

Pulling in several ragged breaths I licked my lips, tasting the salt of my tears and prepared for the home straight.

'Greg had already half dropped his trousers, so it took a second or two for him to give chase. He lived down a farmer's lane so there were no neighbours, but I knew if I cut across the wheat fields he couldn't use his car to follow me, and it would bring me out near the police station so I left my bike and went that way.'

I could see the field so clearly in my mind it was as if I'd been there last week. The feel of the spiky wheat heads scratching at my skin as I ran, the rough, bumpy soil slowing my escape ... shuddering, I shook my head. To this day I would never, ever forget the sound of the wheat stems behind me snapping and crunching as he caught up with me.

170

A strange gasp reared up my throat but I swallowed it down. 'I'd probably made it two thirds of the way across the field, but I knew he was gaining on me. He … he tackled me to the ground, and he was too big for me to fight off.' My memory was in overdrive, but I didn't tell Jack the gritty details. I could feel how upset he already was. It would be too much for him to hear that Greg had slapped me and given me a black eye as he'd smirked at me and told me he loved the thrill of the chase. He'd kissed me so viciously that my top lip had burst, and I still had a tiny scar there to prove it.

'I knew there was no point fighting it. I couldn't do anything without my hands, so I saved my energy and stopped struggling. Gradually, Greg thought I was giving in, and he released one of my hands so he could undo my belt. As hard as it was, I bided my time, letting him get inside my trousers and pull his own down so he'd think he'd won.'

I squeezed my eyes shut as I remembered how victorious Greg had looked as he'd shoved two fingers inside my underwear. I couldn't help squeezing my thighs together protectively as another sob leapt from my throat.

'Then he moved over me and started to push himself inside me …'

'Jesus fucking Christ … Caitlin …' Jack's voice was hoarse, swearing under his breath as he fidgeted, but he seemed unable to let go of me as he continued to clutch me tightly. I was so glad of his contact.

Images of Greg holding his shaft and pressing between my legs caused more hot tears to flow and bile to rise in my throat, but I swallowed hard and tried to maintain my composure. I would never, *ever* forget how invasive that moment had felt, to the day I died.

'Luckily he hadn't pulled my jeans down enough. He couldn't get my legs wide enough to get fully inside me.

171

As soon as he let go of my other hand to take my jeans off, I punched him as hard as I could in the side of the head. It didn't knock him out, but it certainly dazed him and as he leant up, I gave him a pretty good knee in the groin.

'I managed to get up and kick him in the face. He didn't follow me after that. I got my trousers up and ran to the police station.' God knows what would have happened if his friends had decided to follow him. It wasn't something I'd ever let myself dwell upon.

Suddenly, my words dried and instead, my tears began to flow in earnest. It was as if all my energy had been sucked from me.

'Shhh, it's OK, sweetheart. It's OK. You're safe. I'm here.' After what seemed like an eternity of Jack's soothing touch and whispered words he leant back so he could see my eyes, which felt so swollen from the hot tears still flowing down my cheeks that I tried to hide in the sanctuary of his chest.

'Can I touch your face?' he enquired, and I nodded, warmed by his gentle request.

Unfortunately, giving Jack permission to touch my face meant that he didn't allow me the reprieve of his soaked shirt for long, as he lifted one hand slowly and placed a thumb under my chin to lift me up to meet his warm gaze.

Instead of the pity I had expected, all I could see in Jack's gaze was concern. His eyes were glassy and red-rimmed too, but his expression was calm, showing none of the anger I could feel in his tightly clenched muscles.

Moving the same thumb, he wiped at the endless flow of tears streaming from my eyes and leant down to place a gentle kiss on both of my cheeks. 'I'm so sorry that happened to you, Caitlin,' he murmured huskily.

Keeping his face close to mine, he rested his lips on my forehead, leaving his mouth there for several seconds as if trying to control himself. The warmth of his skin made me quiver, not with nerves or fear, but with the sensation of being cared for by this incredible man.

Jack was doing and saying all the right things, but I knew he must be thinking over all I'd told him, and while I was still emotional, I actually found that I felt lighter. It was like a huge weight had been removed from my shoulders and now I could really make a fresh start.

Snuggling into his chest, I tried to come to terms with how our relationship had changed in the last few hours. Until today we'd only held hands, and now here I was sitting on Jack's lap. And instead of feeling scared or awash with sickening memories, all I felt was safe and warm and protected.

'I can't believe I let him get away. What happened to him? Was he charged?' Jack ground the words out through gritted teeth, and I winced, feeling guilty that I had unburdened my issues on to him.

I didn't want to continue reminiscing; I'd had enough of thinking about Greg for a lifetime, but it was clear that Jack needed to know. If he was looking for some closure, he was going to be disappointed.

I licked my dry lips before continuing. 'When the police arrived at his house, he and his mates denied ever having seen me, said they'd had a fight over a game and bruised each other up a bit. I couldn't understand it, but the police obviously thought three against one was more believable.'

Sighing heavily, I remember how long I'd been in hospital that night having endless test after test before Allie had taken me home. 'They couldn't prove anything, because he hadn't managed to get himself in properly for there to be any DNA evidence ...' Pausing, I flinched. 'The forensic guys couldn't find any trace evidence at his house to support that I'd even been there. My bike was gone. His house was spotless. He must

173

have gone back and really cleaned up.

'That first day, he went into questioning willingly. But as soon as they released him, he disappeared. He's never been seen since. There was no evidence to link him to the crime so I don't think the British police are even looking for him.

'He called at first, always from blocked numbers, and sounding drunk and angry and threatening, which is why I left to go travelling. Now I just get the postcards and letters every few months.'

'Christ, Caitlin,' Jack murmured, before placing another kiss on the top of my head and holding me against his chest so tightly it was like he was worried I was going to evaporate.

'I just can't believe his friends – guys I'd known from the village for years – were willing to help him. That just made me think that all men are intrinsically sex-crazed arseholes and that I was better off without them.'

'I understand completely.' Pushing some stray stands of hair behind my ear, Jack smiled at me and gently wiped away the last of my tears. 'We're not all like that. You can trust me, Caitlin. I will never hurt you like that.'

Leaning my face into his hand, I let out a long sigh. 'I'm starting to understand that,' I agreed, pressing my lips into his palm. 'Thank you for listening, Jack. You're amazing.'

'It's not me who's the incredible one here,' he murmured, as he cradled me and gently rocked us both.

'So this is really real, then?' I asked hesitantly, indicating between the two of us.

'Yep,' Jack confirmed with a grin. I felt my cheeks flame with lust. 'Look, I know you're not ready to rush into anything physically, and I want to reassure you that I'm happy to wait …' Jack said.

'You won't think I'm being a … a prick tease?' I

174

whispered.

'God, no. You take as long as you need to get comfortable.' Suddenly I wondered if his offer of waiting had anything to do with what I'd just told him. Had it put him off me? 'I … uh … I hope I didn't freak you out, telling you my past?'

He instantly shook his head, his dark eyes dragging me in with the intensity of his gaze. 'Not at all. I'm just so sorry you had to go through that, Caitlin.'

'You're not just being nice because you pity me, are you?' I couldn't stand the thought of that. Pity was one thing I hated. I might have a shitty past, but I was strong, and getting stronger every day. Support and care I could cope with, but pity? No.

Jack barked out a laugh before sobering his expression. 'Fuck no. Jesus, Caitlin, look me in the eye and see how I feel about you.' Gazing into his beautiful eyes, I saw nothing but emotion swirling in the chestnut hues, and I nodded jerkily, nervously chewing on my lip.

'I don't want to be with you because I pity you or feel sorry for you, or want to look after you,' Jack stated, his gaze becoming even deeper. 'I want to be with you because you attract me like no one else ever has. Your looks, your personality, your wickedly dry sense of humour … everything, Caitlin. *That's* why I want to be with you.'

I felt my shoulders relax even as my stomach jumbled into excited knots. 'I feel like that too, Jack. I've never met someone like you. You make me feel … Well, you make me feel things I've never experienced before. It's amazing.'

'So you're not just with me because I'm super famous?' he teased, his eyes twinkling as a devilish grin spread on his face.

I knew he was joking to lighten the mood, but I flushed nonetheless, well aware that I *had* fancied him

175

before I'd even met him. 'You know I'm not.'

'I know, sweetheart.'

'So, to clarify, we are together and this is most definitely real.' Jack gave me a determined smile. 'We don't need to revisit that topic any more, having said that, I am more than willing to wait. I won't rush you sweetheart. I've already promised you that, and I always keep my promises.'

I'd given him enough chances to take the easy route out and he was still here. I wouldn't repeat my offer any more. We were together. Officially.

# TWENTY-FOUR

## JACK

I felt full to the brim with anger towards her fucker of an ex but by the time Caitlin had calmed down, the police had arrived to talk to us. I'd called in my lawyer too, Benjamin Hobbs, to make sure everything was done correctly, and he was now sat on a chair beside us. There was no way I was letting her go through questioning alone, so I held myself together to give the support she needed.

Caitlin was incredibly brave as she ran through the story with them, keeping it brief and seeming to deal with the emotions far better than I did.

At one point she started to flick at her elastic bands, and now I knew the background, it became clear where the habit came from. I did, however, offer my hand to her in case she would prefer the contact. Glancing at my extended hand, Caitlin stopped flicking her elastic bands and immediately linked her fingers with mine. Her palm felt cool and clammy, but she tightened her grip and continued to give them the details of the detective in the UK who'd dealt with the case, and the subsequent letters she'd received.

The female detective leant forwards. 'I know it'll be hard to recall today's events, but can you remember what happened? What he said to you?'

Nodding jerkily, Caitlin gripped my hand even tighter. 'I wasn't very confident when I was younger, so I think he was expecting me to be the same shy walkover. But I'm not, I'm different now.

'I was by the lockers putting my phone away, and I felt a tap on my shoulder. It took me a second to realise it was Greg … I'd never expected him to be there … When it clicked, I thought I was going to throw up.' Caitlin paused, running her free hand through her hair, and I definitely saw a tremble in her fingers. 'I think he expected me to freeze, but I shoved him hard and tried to make a break for the door.

'He was closer to the exit than me, and caught me as I got to the corridor. I was going to keep fighting but he …' her face paled significantly, 'he drew a blade on me. Said he'd come armed so I couldn't fight him again. He pressed it right here.' Caitlin indicated the lower part of her rib cage with a trembling finger.

'He told me he could puncture my lung quicker than I could scream for help,' she whispered. I certainly hadn't seen a knife, but by god I wanted to find this son of a bitch with everything I had in me. 'It was a flick knife, I think. He pocketed it when he saw Jack.'

Caitlin shifted on the sofa, looking agitated. 'I should have kept fighting him, but I freaked out. I couldn't breathe properly.'

'Did he say or do anything else?' the detective asked gently.

'He said he found me because his friend overheard my mum talking to her sister about my new job.' Caitlin's eyes lowered and her fingers tightened around mine until her knuckles blanched. 'There was one more thing … he … he sniffed me,' Caitlin swallowed hard and shrugged. 'He ran his nose up my neck to my ear and said I smelt the same, and he said … he said …' Her eyes flickered shut and her words dried up as she gulped for air, which made me feel so helpless. '… He said he loved the smell of my fear.'

*What. The. Fuck?* Every muscle in my body exploded

178

with anger. I wanted to find that fucker and kill him. Rip him limb from limb until the smell of *his* fear was smeared across the whole fucking world.

'He said it was time we finished what we had started all those years ago.'

'You think he wants to continue where his last attack was interrupted?' the male detective asked. Caitlin's head bobbed up and down jerkily.

'He … he spat at me as he left, but he missed and hit the floor.'

The two detectives exchanged a look, and then the woman nodded. 'Get forensics to check that out, could be additional evidence. Can you think of anything else?'

Caitlin just swallowed hard and stared at the detective. She seemed unable to speak any more, as her head fell sideways and rested on my shoulder.

'This is incredibly distressing for Miss Byrne, surely you must have all you need?' Benjamin interjected sharply, making me infinitely glad I'd called him here.

'Yes, of course. If we think of anything, we'll call you.' The female detective dug into her bag and held out a business card. 'If you think you see him, call us immediately. My direct number is on there.'

Finally they left, and after I saw Benjamin out I returned to find the room blessedly silent again. Caitlin silently crawled into my lap when I sat down and I stroked her hair as she cried more tears into my shirt. I didn't know what else to do, so I reassured her with soft words until I felt her body go heavy. Looking down, I realised she had fallen asleep. The stress of the day must have really taken its toll on her.

Easing myself out from underneath her, I laid her down and tucked a blanket around her. Briefly I stood there watching her sleep and I made a silent vow – I would never let anyone hurt her again.

# TWENTY-FIVE

## ALLIE

Glancing at the clock, I saw it had been over two hours since Cait and Jack had holed themselves up in the lounge. Would she be brave enough to tell him everything?

I wasn't the most patient person when it came to waiting, and so many questions were going around my mind that I'd nearly burst in on them several times. The police had left five minutes before, and there had still been no word from the lounge. As I stood at the kitchen table, I wondered how long I should give them before I went in.

I was thrilled that Cait was letting Jack in, but seeing as she'd had a pretty major meltdown today I wanted to check she was OK. I knew Jack had her best interests at heart, but their relationship was still so new and as her longest friend I wanted to support her if she needed me. Plus, I was nosey, and desperate for the gossip.

Just as I was about to check if I could hear them talking through the door, the sound of Sean's key in the front door caught my ear. Within a minute he had joined me in the kitchen and immediately pulled me into his arms for a hello kiss.

A very thorough hello kiss.

Grinning, I let him have his way with me for a few seconds and after several moments of brief, hot kissing, he trailed small pecks across my jaw.

'Hello, my gorgeous girl.'

Burying my lips in his neck, I smiled as I soaked up his lovely smoky, spicy scent. 'Hmm. I could get used to this. I like finding you in my house when I get home,' he murmured breathily.

I rather liked it too.

Pausing in his exploration, he leant back and met my gaze, immediately looking just a little smug when he took in my flushed cheeks.

'Hi, you. Good day?' I murmured, my hands sliding around his waist and settling on his firm bum.

'Not bad. Better now I'm here with you.' He jerked his hips forward to thrust his growing erection at my belly and gave a wiggle of his eyebrows as he placed another kiss on my lips.

'It looked like Jack's car was in the garage, is he here too?'

'He is. He's with Cait in the lounge. We've had a very eventful day,' I explained with a grimace. Sean's eyebrows rose before he reluctantly let me go and walked to the fridge to pull out two beers.

'What's happened?'

Accepting the beer, I leant back on the counter. 'You know when Jack called you earlier and asked you to get me to help Cait?' Sean nodded. 'She'd had a panic attack. Her ex was at the studios threatening her.'

'What?'

'Luckily Jack was there and interrupted them before anything could happen. Greg and Jack fought, then Greg made a run for it.'

'Jesus. Jack was in a fight? Is everyone OK?'

'More or less. Cait was a wreck, but Jack's been amazing. They've been talking for two hours. We've had the police here too.'

Sean swigged on his beer, and had just opened his mouth to say something when the kitchen door swung open and Jack strode in. Both Sean and I turned to look

181

at his tense frame as he paced then leant against the wall, his eyes flicking around in agitation.

Cait had been a wreck earlier, but now it was Jack who looked messed up. His face was pale, his eyes red, and his hair an absolute state.

'Everything OK, mate?' Sean asked cautiously. Without answering, Jack looked at Sean, then his gaze flicked to mine before he closed his eyes and took several deep breaths through his nose.

Anxiety settled in my stomach and then I noticed how the entire left-hand side of his shirt was soaked to the point where it had gone see-through.

Jack's hand touched the wet cloth, causing my gaze to rise to his where I found him staring at me. 'Caitlin told me about her ex,' he murmured. 'She cried. A lot.'

'Oh God, is she OK?' I asked around a loud swallow, relieved when Jack immediately nodded.

'She was understandably upset, but she seemed to be really relieved once it was out. She's dozing now. I think the anxiety attack exhausted her.' Closing his eyes again, I watched as his fists repeatedly clenched and unclenched at his sides.

The tension in the room was palpable. 'Are *you* OK?' Sean asked Jack.

Gritting his teeth, Jack opened his eyes and turned towards the back door. 'Not really. Excuse me,' he muttered darkly. With that he practically ripped the back door from its hinges and took off down the steps to the beach.

Sean and I rushed to the windows and watched as Jack strode as far away from the house as he could before letting out the most pained, bellowed howl I think I'd ever heard in my life.

Holy cow. I gripped the kitchen surface, unable to look away as goose pimples flooded my skin. 'Does he often lose it like this?' I whispered.

'Never. He's the most laid-back guy I know,' Sean replied. Unable to forget my concerns about Cait, I quickly left the kitchen and poked my head into the lounge to check on her. Just as Jack had said, Cait was fast asleep on the couch and covered carefully with a blanket, a gesture I suspected was Jack's doing.

Dashing back to the kitchen I retook my position at Sean's side, linking my arm through his for reassurance as we watched his friend through the window. Jack was now pacing near the surf, but stopped, tilting his head toward the sky before roaring out several swear words and collapsing onto his knees where he slapped his hands against the wet sand, sending it flying everywhere as he continued to howl like a complete mad man.

*Ho-ly shit.*

'His arm!' I squeaked as I watched the bandage covering his burnt arm turn brown from the wet sand staining it.

'*Fuck.*' Sean swore beside me before urgently taking hold of my arm and forcing me to tear my gaze away from the beach. 'What exactly did Jack mean when he said Cait told him about her ex?'

Cait's past still wasn't my story to tell, but clearly Jack was having serious issues dealing with it and I needed to bring Sean up to date so he could help his friend.

'Let's just say that you were right when you thought Cait's ex was the root of her problems. She had a really bad experience. It ended up with him and his friends attacking her. It sounds like she told Jack, and I'm guessing he isn't coping very well with that news.'

'No shit,' Sean murmured as the sound of another wail resonated through the kitchen. Practically throwing his beer down, Sean headed toward the door. 'Let me go and talk to him before someone calls the police.'

# TWENTY-SIX

## SEAN

Apprehension roiled in my gut as I jogged down the
stairs toward the long strip of beach behind my
apartment. In all the years I'd known Jack, I'd never
seen him lose his cool. He was one of the most chilled-
out guys I'd ever met. Apparently not today. My eyes
fell on his knelt form just a few feet away, the back of
his shirt soaked with sweat and his shoulders rapidly
rising and falling. At least he'd stopped slapping the
sand.

'Jack?' Dropping onto my haunches beside him, I
placed a hand on his shoulder, causing him to glance at
me, his brown eyes now red and narrowed.

'Three of them went at her. *Three*. Then her fucking
ex chased her through a field, dragged her to the ground,
and tried to rape her again,' he growled.

I sucked in a sharp breath and felt my own anger
rising. Who the fuck would ever treat a woman that
way?

'She's so sweet and kind. How could someone do
that?' he asked me despairingly.

'Fuck, Jack. I have no idea. Is she OK?'

Nodding, he closed his eyes and lifted one sand-
covered hand to wipe his sweaty forehead, leaving a trail
of dirt on his brow. 'Yeah. As OK as she can be,
anyway. I think she's relieved she told me.'

Falling back, Jack lay in the wet sand, oblivious of
the water lapping around his feet. He stared at the sky,
looking dishevelled and a million miles away from his

usual smart self. 'It was a few years ago, but the fucker has been stalking her and finally found her.'

'Stalking her?' Goosebumps rose on my arms. God, this was so much more extreme than I'd ever imagined.

Crossing my legs, I ignored the water and sat beside him before absently picking at a shell. I couldn't even imagine how I would feel if I found out that someone had hurt Allie that way. I would want to kill them.

As if reading my mind, Jack clenched his jaw and gave a tight nod. 'I want to rip him to fucking pieces. I wouldn't feel one shred of guilt.' I nodded my understanding and then we both just sat there sharing a few minutes of silence.

'Cait talked to you today, though, so that must show she trusts you?'

Sitting up, Jack turned to me, his face calmer now, more hopeful. 'Yeah. She said I make her feel safe. I really care about her, Sean. I want to make this relationship work.' Jack drew in a long breath as I nodded. 'I just want to be with her.' A short, dry laugh left his lips and he shot me a vaguely amused look, 'I know that probably sounds soft as shit, so don't take the piss, Sean.'

Relieved to see some of Jack's usual humour returning, I gave him a smile. 'I wouldn't dream of it, mate, but it's good to know you'll be as under the thumb as me soon.' Jack took it well, blowing out another breath before looking at the state of his ruined bandage with a grimace.

'You OK now?' I asked tentatively. 'As OK as you can be given the circumstances, anyway.'

Nodding, Jack licked his lips. 'Yeah, sorry. I've never felt rage like that, Sean. I just needed to vent before I saw Caitlin again.' Chewing on his lip, Jack looked at me and I could still see some remnants of the anger swirling in his eyes. 'I swear to God if that fucker

185

had been in the room I would have crucified him.' Jack was a big guy, strong, broad, and tall, but he was the least violent man I knew. Right now though, as I looked at his serious face, I knew he meant every single word.

'But I'm OK. Caitlin has trusted me with her past and started to let me in, so I need to be calm and strong for her now. The police told me to leave it, but I've already called Flynn and asked him to start his own search for Lambert.'

Glancing at his wet, sandy clothes, Jack gave a sharp laugh. 'I look like I've been in a fight with a swamp.'

Chuckling, I stood up and held out a hand to him. 'Come inside. You can take a shower and borrow some clothes.' Jack accepted my hand and got to his feet.

'Thanks for the support, mate. Sorry I lost it for a minute.' We gave the torn-up section of beach a rueful glance before heading back inside.

# TWENTY-SEVEN

## CAIT

Pulling in a deep breath, I yawned, stretched, and opened my eyes. It took a second to remember where I was, but as soon as I did, I sat bolt upright and quickly checked the room for Jack. Much to my disappointment it was empty, Jack had obviously left me to sleep. I was tucked under a warm, cosy blanket, so he must have covered me up after I drifted off. The idea of him pampering me brought a cheesy grin to my face that I simply couldn't supress.

Rubbing at my tender eyes, I took a moment to go over all that had happened that day. Now that I'd let Jack in on my past, this morning's traumatic run-in with Greg didn't seem nearly as overwhelming. Perhaps it was sharing the burden of my troubles that made me feel a bit better.

I could hear voices in the kitchen, so I wandered in that direction, but as I entered the hallway I met Jack coming the other way. He looked weary and serious, but as soon as he saw me approaching his face immediately softened into a handsome smile.

'Hey, sweetheart. I was just coming to wake you for dinner. How are you feeling?' he asked.

I gave him a shy smile. 'A lot better now I've had a power nap. Thank you for covering me up.'

As my eyes greedily soaked up his appearance, I noticed he'd changed his clothes. 'You've changed,' I stated, pointing at the checked shirt and jeans.

'Oh ... yeah. I uh, spilt a coffee over myself. Sean leant me some clothes and Allie redid my bandage for me.'

I looked to his arm in concern, seeing the bright new strapping. 'You didn't re-burn it, did you?'

'Nah. It's all good.' He brushed off my concern with a shrug and jerked a thumb in the direction of the kitchen. 'So, are you hungry? Allie's made fajitas.'

Given today's traumatic events, I was surprised to realise I was ravenous, and I giggled as my stomach gave a loud growl.

'Let's feed you before your stomach complains again.' Jack replied with a chuckle. Reaching out for me, he slid one hand toward my hip, but accidentally brushed my lower back in the process, causing my teeth to clench.

He saw my reaction and immediately pulled his hand back with a grimace. Desperate to reassure him that it wasn't his touch I was reacting to, I grabbed his hand and held it. 'I ... I really like it when you touch me,' I murmured. 'But I ... I have a real thing about my lower back. Greg used to ...' A huff left my lips. I wouldn't use *his* name any more – he wasn't worthy of my time. '... That was where *he* would grab me. Could you not touch me there? Anywhere else, just not my lower back,' I asked in a croaky voice.

I watched Jack's shoulders slump. 'Shit, I didn't mean to touch your back. I'm sorry, Caitlin.' Raising a hand he ran it through his hair and gave me an apologetic smile. 'It just feels natural for me to want to touch you.'

'I ... I feel the same. I'm hyper-aware every time you're in the same room as me,' I confessed, my tone almost as heated as his. 'I want contact. I love the feel of it.' He made a small noise that sounded almost disbelieving, so I cut off any reply he was about to make

189

by plastering myself against him in a tight hug.

As I made contact, sparks seemed to fly across my skin, warming me from the inside out and causing a small gasp to slip from my lips. We'd already cuddled for over two hours, but touching him was just so new that I suspected I'd be gasping quite a bit from now on.

If I got this much of a reaction from just putting my arms around him, then letting him touch me in more intimate places could be incredible. Snorting an anxious laugh, I rolled my eyes – *One step at a time, Cait*, I reminded myself firmly.

When I risked a glance up at Jack, I saw that his lips were parted, cheeks flushed, and eyebrows raised. A small noise rumbled from his chest, one of appreciation, I think, and I felt him shift as he lowered his head and placed a gentle kiss on the top of my head.

'Shall we join Allie and Sean for dinner? Or do you just want to snuggle me some more, because I have to say, this is pretty damn amazing.' His question was jokey, but I could tell by the roughness of his voice that he was just as affected by my move as I was.

Clearing my throat, I avoided eye contact and stepped out of the hug. But I wasn't ready to give up my new hold on him just yet, so I tucked myself close into Jack's side, slipping an arm around his waist and guiding his hand to do the same, so it lay around me and rested on my hip. It felt good, really good. There was no fear, no flashbacks of *him*, just a lovely feeling of being wanted by this incredible man.

'Let's eat. I'm starving.' We were at the point that many couples probably found a bit boring and normal – walking along with arms slung around each other – but to me, it felt wonderful. I was almost cocooned. Even through his clothing, he felt so warm, and despite the fact that his grip was gentle, I could feel his strength almost pulse between us.

I felt completely safe. It was reassuring, but more than that, it was actually arousing, which wasn't a sensation that any man had managed to raise in me since before the attack.

As we walked into the kitchen, I noticed that both Sean and Allie did a double take when they saw the entwined position Jack and I were in, but he made me feel so good that I didn't even bother to feel embarrassed.

As we sat at the table, Jack swapped our arm in arm embrace for a hand hold. It was stupid just how good the touch of his palm made me feel, and I couldn't help giving his fingers a firm squeeze every few minutes as his thumb rubbed a gentle rhythm on the back of my hand.

It was just as well that Allie had pre-filled and rolled the fajitas, because as we started dinner it quickly became obvious that Jack wasn't willing to give up our contact. I tried to pull my hand away to serve myself some food, but Jack merely tightened his grip, refusing to let me go. Giving him a curious look, he just squeezed my hand, grinned at me mischievously, and used his free hand to offer me the plate of fajitas.

So that was how this meal was going to proceed? Giggling, I moved two wraps onto my plate and began to eat one handed. We must have looked quite a sight. I know Allie spotted what was going on because she could barely keep a straight face as Jack struggled to eat with his bandaged arm.

By the time Allie had served coffee, Jack had shifted his chair closer to mine and draped his arm over my shoulder as if he couldn't bear to be apart from me for a second longer. His fingers were gently trailing up and down my arm as he chatted with Sean, and I saw Allie watching his behaviour with a grin almost as big as mine.

It was silly, but the fact that Jack wanted the contact and was happy to eat and drink one handed in order to keep a hold of me actually made me feel pretty damn special.

# TWENTY-EIGHT

## SEAN

'So, seeing as I cooked, I think it's only fair you boys wash up,' Allie declared with a grin aimed at me. I narrowed my eyes, fairly sure her smile was because she loved having the power to make a film star get their hands soapy.

'Yeah, I guess that's fair,' I agreed, standing up and clearing the dishes. Most of this would go in the dishwasher, anyway.

'While the police look for Greg, it might be better if you stay here for a few days, Cait,' I suggested as I put the salsa in the fridge. I didn't want them staying on their own with Lambert on the loose.

'Or you could stay with me?' Jack suggested, in a tone that sounded decidedly hopeful.

'But you'll have to go to work during the day, Jack, it makes sense for Caitlin to stay here, then at least we're together,' Allie commented.

'That's true,' Cait agreed. 'Honestly though, our compound is pretty safe, I think we'd be fine to go back. I'll stay here tonight and Allie and I can decide what to do in the morning.'

Forcing myself to nod pleasantly, I felt my fingers tighten around the glass in my hand. There was no way they were going to be alone in that house. I'd have to talk to Allie about it later.

'Excuse me, I need the loo,' Cait said, attempting to stand only to have Jack hold onto her with a grin.

'Let the poor girl pee!' Allie giggled. I'd noticed the way Jack had held onto Cait all through dinner – it had cracked me up and I couldn't wait to rib him about it. Finally, after laying a kiss on her forehead, Jack released Cait and she practically skipped from the room, smiling like a lunatic.

It seemed that things were progressing well between them.

The door had barely shut when I turned to Jack, but he cut me off by standing up and giving me a wry shake of his head. 'Don't you dare say a word. Either of you,' he warned. 'I finally have her as my girlfriend and then I find out she had to endure all that traumatic shit. I can't believe she went through all that. I don't want to let her go for a second right now.'

OK, when he put it that way maybe he didn't deserve the ribbing.

Seeing the turmoil Jack was dealing with, Allie immediately went to his side and gave his shoulder a reassuring rub. 'I thought it was very sweet,' she murmured.

Jack blushed and tried to shrug off Allie's comment, but I could see the guy was clearly loved up. 'I already got Flynn on the case putting together a team to search for Lambert, and I hope you don't mind, but if Caitlin is going to be staying here, I'd like to get some extra security. I've even been considering getting Caitlin a bodyguard until he's caught. Do you think she'll go for it?'

'A bodyguard?' Allie squeaked, her eyebrows leaping up. I couldn't see Cait being thrilled by someone trailing after her all the time, but maybe today's encounter with Greg had scared her enough to make her consider it.

'I won't be able to concentrate unless I know she's safe,' Jack added as he carried the rest of the plates to me.

'I dunno. Maybe?' I offered, looking to Allie for insight.

'She comes across as shy, but she's stubborn and independent. Perhaps if you tell her it's to put your mind at ease she might go for it?' Allie suggested.

Jack nodded and pulled out his phone. 'I'll talk it through with her tomorrow, but in the meantime let me text Flynn and see if he can suggest anyone.'

# TWENTY-NINE

## CAIT

By the time I'd washed my face and freshened up, I found Allie, Sean, and Jack waiting for me near the front door.

Noticing that Jack had his jacket on, I immediately felt a pang of anxiousness settle in my stomach. Was he leaving? I didn't want him to go. Then again, I wasn't ready to share a bed with him either, so I could hardly ask him to stay and then make him sleep on the sofa.

Picking up on my expression, Jack gave me a soft smile and immediately stepped closer to me, slipping a hand to my hip and giving a reassuring squeeze. 'I better be making a move, sweetheart. It's getting late and I've got a pretty early start tomorrow.' He sounded reluctant, which made me feel a bit better about things; it wasn't just me. He didn't want us to be apart either.

I was so focused on Jack that I hardly even noticed when Allie and Sean discreetly moved into the lounge. Placing a hand on the doorknob, Jack paused in the doorway and looked at me intently. 'Call me if you need me, Caitlin. Even if it's the middle of the night and you can't sleep and just want to talk. OK?'

I *really* didn't want him to go, which was just ridiculous really, because we'd barely even begun our relationship yet. Talk about jumping the gun. It was *waaay* too soon to get that needy.

I had another need on my mind too. For once in my life I actually wanted a man to kiss me, really kiss me,

198

and after this morning, it would be nice to have a happy memory to finish off the day. I needed it.

Jack's gaze made the briefest flick to my lips and I knew he wanted to kiss me too. Even without the glance at my mouth it would have been obvious, because now we had actually started touching each other, the sexual chemistry between us was almost overpowering. All though dinner my body had been alive with sensation as he sat beside me. My skin tingled, and heat licked across every area he touched. It had felt so potent that I'd struggled to concentrate on the delicious dinner Allie had made us.

I wanted to kiss him so badly I was aching, but would my lack of skill show through? I hadn't so much as held a man's hand for over three years until recently, let alone kissed one … what if I'd forgotten how to do it properly?

Lifting my wide eyes to his handsome face, I found Jack watching me closely, his brown eyes warm and supportive and seeming to draw me closer. No doubt my thoughts were written all over my expression because he lifted a hand and gently smoothed some hair away from my forehead.

I didn't flinch away from the touch like I would have just a week ago. Instead I found myself leaning into it, which caused Jack to give a small murmur of approval. His noise somehow seemed to bolster my confidence because the next second I found myself throwing caution to the wind as I lifted onto my tiptoes, cupped his jaw, and drew my lips closer to his.

Tilting his head, Jack gently held me back and gave me a smile. 'Hey, no pressure, sweetheart. Please don't feel you need to push yourself into anything.' I nodded my understanding as I licked my lips and closed the gap between our mouths, gently placing my lips against his.

Warmth seared through me from the contact of our

mouths, causing my lips to open in a gasp of desire as our tongues tentatively touched in a slow, gentle exploration.

He was letting me lead the pace, but that didn't stop a groan resonating from Jack's throat as one of my hands slid into his hair and urged him closer still. Part of me desperately wished that he would just drag me to him so I could feel the full extent of his warm, hard body pressed against mine.

He was noticeably more delicate with me than he had been that day we'd kissed in the park. In fact, when I thought about it, his hands weren't even touching me. Really, this was just *me* kissing, and him letting me.

Was he not enjoying this?

Didn't he want to kiss me?

Suddenly feeling self-conscious, I leant back and examined Jack's face. His lips were moist, cheeks flushed, brown eyes heavy-lidded. He looked just as into it as I was, so why hadn't he touched me?

'OK, sweetheart?' he murmured.

'I am, but I was just wondering … uh …' God, now he had asked, I didn't know how to word it. 'When you kissed me in the park, you were quite … um … *heated.* And you held on to me …' I blinked as something like recognition seemed to dawn on his face.

'But I'm not now and you're wondering why?'

Biting on my lower lip, I nodded, and in response Jack threw his head back and barked out a hearty laugh. Lowering his gaze, he sobered his grin, tilting his head so our foreheads were resting together.

'Sweetheart, I wanted to hold you more than you could ever know, but you've only just learnt to trust me.' Giving me a rueful smile, he looked rather embarrassed. 'If I had allowed myself to do what I really wanted when you kissed me, you would be pressed against that wall with me completely smothering you.' My heartbeat rocketed in my chest at his words.

Hmm. I quite liked the idea of being smothered in kisses by Jack Felton.

'The only way I held back was by doing this,' he said, showing me where his hands were balled into fists and rammed deep into his jeans. I saw there was also a bulge in the front of his trousers that definitely hadn't been there earlier. Blimey.

Distracting me from his jutting arousal, Jack hunkered down so he could reinstate the contact between our foreheads as I stared into his dilated eyes.

He was telling the truth. He did want me as much as I wanted him. Gulping loudly, I decided that now I had made the decision to be with Jack, the idea of him pressing me against a wall and smothering me actually sounded pretty amazing, but just as I was about to tell him, we were disturbed by the lounge door opening as Allie and Sean strolled into the hallway laughing, before spotting us and coming to a standstill.

'Oh, oops … uh … sorry to interrupt, we were just, uh …' Allie didn't even finish her stuttered sentence before Sean flashed us a smile and dragged her into the kitchen.

'I think Allie is going to want the gossip tonight,' Jack joked. 'I didn't mean to make you unsure, Caitlin. I was just trying to do the right thing.'

My heart just about melted. He really was bloody amazing. 'Let's make a deal. You avoid my lower back but everywhere else is OK, and I'll tell you if something makes me uncomfortable. How does that sound?'

He paused, his eyes narrowing. 'That sounds pretty great, but you need to promise you'll tell me immediately. I can't lose you because I scared you off.'

Releasing a breath, I nodded and smiled. 'It's a deal. I promise. Now would you please kiss me goodbye properly?'

201

Jack grinned, did a mock salute, and nodded, his eyes sparkling. 'It would be my pleasure, sweetheart.' His hands rose and slipped into my hair and his lips sought mine as his large body moved forwards and gently eased me backwards until I was pressed against the wall. As his tongue pushed into my mouth and began to sweep across mine, I quickly realised it would definitely be my pleasure too.

# THIRTY

As soon as I heard the front door close, I practically threw down my cup of tea and raced into the hallway to get the gossip – much to Sean's amusement, as he looked up from his iPad and grinned.

Skidding into the hallway, I found my bestie leaning back against the front door. She had flushed cheeks, red lips, and a soppy smile on her face, and so all in all looked like she'd been kissed half-senseless. Seeing as Cait had confessed yesterday that she and Jack were still only at the holding hands stage, that would be a pretty major development within twenty-four hours.

'I'm going to show Cait the spare bedroom and get her settled,' I called through to Sean, who almost immediately popped his head out of the lounge door and eyed me with amusement.

'Yeah, sure.' Judging from the gleam in his eye, Sean knew exactly what I was going to do – dig for gossip.

Showing Cait the guest room, I quickly got her sorted with a spare toothbrush, a change of clothes, and one of Sean's old T-shirts to act as pyjamas. Then, once the technicalities were out of the way, we sat on the edge of her bed and I waited with bated breath to see if she was going to voluntarily spill the beans.

It didn't take long.

'I miss him already and he's only been gone ten minutes,' Cait blurted before blushing. 'That's stupid. We hardly even know each other.'

'It's not stupid at all. It's how you feel when you care about someone. Time scale has nothing to do with it – if you feel a connection with someone it doesn't matter how long you've been together, it's either there or it's not.'

Cait giggled. 'It's definitely there.' Dragging a cushion onto her lap, she hugged it as she grinned. 'I've never felt the things I feel when I'm with him. It's amazing.'

Grinning at her awe-struck expression, I couldn't help but dig. 'So did you two finally kiss?'

Cait's eyes fluttered shut, and then a long, contented breath slipped from her lips. 'Yep.'

Yep? That's all she was giving me?

'*And?*' My impatience was obvious in my tone, but I could answer my own question just by looking at her – Cait looked well and truly loved up. Her skin was still flushed, her eyes bright, and there was a continual smile tugging at her mouth. Yeah, it had been a good kiss.

'It was great.' Sighing, she absently tugged on a piece of hair as she continued to gaze happily into space. '*He's* amazing.' I watched as, turning to me, her face sobered and she blinked rapidly. 'He listened to the story of my time with Greg. I told him everything and he was incredible, so supportive.'

'It was really cute during dinner when he wouldn't let go of your hand,' I giggled. 'Or was it you who wouldn't let go, I couldn't tell?'

Cait laughed and flopped back on the bed. 'That was all him!' All I could focus on was the change in her. Happiness was radiating from every pore, and it almost took my breath away. For the last three years, Cait had been my withdrawn, skittish, quiet best friend, and suddenly, it was like seeing the girl I'd gone to college with. I'd almost forgotten how chilled out she'd been before she'd met Greg. Her entire demeanour seemed different; she was relaxed, happy, and clearly very, very into a certain Mr Felton.

I would for ever be thankful to Jack for giving me my real best friend back.

# THIRTY-ONE

## JACK

Jogging down the steps from Sean's apartment, I stopped at the railing that overlooked the sea and leant forward. Taking in several deep lungfuls of the salty air helped calm me, but every molecule within me wanted to turn back and return to Caitlin.

I tried to focus, and ended up staring at the horizon. The view was beautiful, but I struggled to see it with the lingering memories of Caitlin's kiss swirling in my mind. Finally I focused my mind on the outlook. The sea was calm, lit by a nearly full moon and breaking onto the sand in regular, almost hypnotic, lulling waves. Closing my eyes, I allowed the sound to wash over me.

When I woke up that morning I never thought for one second that by the end of the day I would have Caitlin in my arms for the first time as she willingly pressed her soft lips to mine. *Fuck*. That kiss had been incredible, my body was still alight from it, not to mention craving more.

Not dragging her off to a bedroom had nearly killed me. Talk about serious levels of self-restraint. I considered myself a gentleman, but even I was impressed with my control over the past few weeks.

Pushing back from the railing, I dug my hands into my hair in frustration, tugging at several chunks and letting out a low growl of irritation. I hated leaving her more than I could even understand. We'd only just stepped beyond friendship recently but already I felt such feelings of protectiveness that I was struggling to make myself move away from Sean's pathway.

In a twisted way, Greg's appearance today had fast-forwarded the progress of my relationship with Caitlin, but I would rather have waited another year for her to come to me willingly than ever put her through seeing him again. I couldn't believe he'd been right there in the same room as me and I'd let him go – not that I'd known who he was, but still, if I had a time machine I'd go back and kill the fucker for ever hurting her. No, scrap that, if I had a time machine I'd go way back to the day he had first met her, stop him from asking her out, and *then* rip him limb from limb.

Thinking about Greg on the loose somewhere in LA made me tense and glance around to check security. I could see Flynn on the driveway leaning on the bonnet of my car and talking to a guy I didn't recognise. Reluctantly, I strode towards Flynn and gave the new guy a look-over. He was decked out in black combats, army boots, and had a gun strapped to his waist. I could only assume that Flynn had come through on his promise to arrange some extra security.

'Jack, this is Edward Pearson of Pearson Private Security.'

'Mr Felton.' He shook my hand with a no holds barred grip, which I took as a good sign. I couldn't stand a weak handshake. In my experience it said a great deal about a man's character. 'Flynn has given me an update of the situation. We've passed out the target information and photograph and I have men situated at the road exit, pedestrian exit, and several on the beach. No one is getting in here tonight, sir.'

'Good. Thank you.' Turning, Pearson headed in the direction of the gate. His professional air went some way towards calming me, but I was still reluctant to leave. Until the police actually did something about Greg, I wasn't willing to take any risks with Caitlin's safety. She'd been through enough. Besides, it wasn't like I couldn't afford it. Considering my wealth, I lived a very frugal life. I wasn't an extravagant purchaser, so the least I could do was use it on something that actually mattered to me. And by god did Caitlin matter to me.

I held out a hand to Flynn. 'Let me see the photograph they're using.' He reached inside his jacket pocket and pulled out a small picture. This photograph was him alright, with his pointy cheekbones, floppy hair, and spiteful eyes.

'Pulled it off a police database. There's a warrant out for his arrest. He's still using Greg as a first name, but rotates between several surnames.'

A frown creased my brow as I handed the picture back. 'What's the warrant for?'

'Multiple charges, including several accusations of rape. It's more complex because of the multiple identities and because he's been moving between countries, but I have a guy working on putting together an international file.'

*Fuck*. It sounded like Caitlin was far from his only victim.

'How you holding up?' Flynn's voice had lowered, losing its professional edge. Opening my eyes I saw him watching me intently.

'OK, I think.' It was a hell of a lot to take in.

'And Caitlin?' We didn't speak about her very much, but Flynn was well aware of my soft spot for her, and so with a sigh I shrugged.

'She's better than she was. We've talked a lot and she's calmer now.' Since I had got out of the hospital I hadn't told Flynn that Caitlin and I were trying a relationship. I think he'd probably guessed as much, but given everything, it was best he had all the details.

'She's with me now, and I'll do everything in my

210

power to keep that fucker away from her.'

Flynn's eyebrows rose, but he nodded. 'She's with you? She's finally agreed to date you?'

This wasn't the type of thing I would usually talk about with Flynn, so I felt embarrassed and uncomfortable as I nodded and averted my eyes. 'Yeah, since I was in the hospital.'

The corner of his mouth twitched, and I just knew a sarcastic comment was coming my way any second now. 'Damn, I'm going to lose the enjoyment of watching her knock you back,' he grinned. I smiled along with him. 'Seeing her shut you down *every time* you asked her out was the highlight of my fucking year.'

'Tell me about it, my ego was seriously starting to wither away.'

Flynn crossed his arms and nodded slowly. 'Seriously though, I know the circumstances are shitty, but I'm happy for you, man. I can see how much you like her.'

Heat rushed to my cheeks and I cleared my throat to try and cover my embarrassment. 'Thanks.' Indulging in overly soppy talk with my bodyguard was not really my thing, so I looked around the compound and drew in a long breath. 'Are we locked down here?'

'Yep, security is as tight as an otter's ass.'

I snorted as Flynn levelled me with an intense stare. 'Do you think he's coming after her?'

I hated my answer before I'd even said it, but my certainty was bone deep. 'Yes. He's been trying to track her down for three years, so I can't see that he'd stop now he's finally found her. I don't think he'll be able to trace her to here, though, and even if he did, he's not stupid enough to try and get in. I don't want to take any chances though.'

Recalling her terrified expression when I'd found her, I let out an irritated hiss. 'Flynn, you should have seen her. She was catatonic.' Shoving my hands into my hair,

I threw my head back in anger. 'I was right there and I let him walk away.'

A firm hand landed on my shoulder and gripped tightly. 'You didn't know who he was then, Jack. We'll get him. You'll get your chance at him.' Flynn's quiet certainty quelled some of the annoyance inside of me and I lowered my head and nodded before sending another glance towards Sean's door.

'You don't want to leave her, do you?' he asked quietly.

'No.' I tried to rationalise how I felt, but it was no good – where Caitlin was concerned I was in deep. 'It's fucking stupid, isn't it?'

Flynn shrugged and crossed his arms. 'Not at all. You've just got with the chick and you find out she might be in danger, it seems logical that you'd want to stay close by.' I was actually surprised by Flynn's support; I'd expected my confession to prompt him into taking the piss. 'Why don't you go back and stay the night? I've got things covered out here.'

Giving his offer a moment's consideration, I nodded in thanks and headed back up the stairs, where the front door was being opened by Sean. 'I saw you out of the window. Wanna crash here?'

Nodding, I followed Sean inside to the empty kitchen where he grabbed two beers from the fridge and handed one to me. 'Thanks Sean. It didn't feel right to leave her.'

Clicking his beer bottle against mine, Sean nodded. 'I would feel exactly the same.'

We wandered through to the lounge, which was also empty. 'Caitlin wanted an early night but Allie went with her to get her settled. I expect they're gossiping,' he murmured with a knowing smile.

We sat in companionable silence for several minutes before Sean crossed one leg over his opposite ankle.

'Talking of gossip, you want to fill me in? You and Cait certainly seemed cosy this evening.'

Giving him an amused look, I rested my head back on the sofa. 'I think we've sped up our relationship a bit. She's really opening up.'

'I'm really pleased for you. You two look great together.'

I smiled and closed my eyes as I allowed weariness to get the better of me.

'Are you going to sleep in with Cait?' Sean asked. His words made my body tingle with the prospect of curling up with her in my arms, but I shook my head almost immediately.

'God no. After what she's been through, she's fragile.'

Nodding his understanding, Sean gave the sofa cushion next to him a pat with his hand. 'I'm afraid you're going to have to sleep on the sofa then.'

'The sofa is fine.' After everything that had happened today, I very much doubted I'd be getting much sleep, regardless of how tired I was.

# THIRTY-TWO

## CAIT

The last hour had dragged by. Every time I glanced at the clock on the bedside table, only another minute seemed to have passed. I was tired, but I literally could not sleep.

There was way too much going through my head for me to relax. It had all been a bit of an emotional overload, so it was no wonder my brain couldn't seem to shut down.

Checking my mobile for about the tenth time, I still found no messages from Jack. Scrunching up my face, I flopped back on my pillow with a sigh. I'd been hoping that he'd send me a goodnight text when he got home, but he probably hadn't wanted to disturb me.

Chewing on my lip, I debated giving him a call. I wanted to speak to him so badly but it was the middle of the night. I knew he'd said I could call any time, but I couldn't wake him up just to hear his voice. After laying there for another nine painfully slow minutes, I settled on sending a text.

*To: Jack F*

*Thank you again for saving me today. And for a lovely evening, I had a great time. I hope you aren't too tired for your shoot. Sleep well xx*

Once the message had sent I lay back, still clutching my

phone to my chest. Seconds later it rang, flashing up Jack's number, and I answered with a smile.

'Hey, sweetheart. Are you alright?' His voice was so rich and deep that I immediately shivered as an unexpectedly sudden shot of lust pulsed through my body.

Clearing my throat, I snuggled down in my duvet and then answered. 'Yeah, I couldn't sleep. Sorry if I woke you.'

'You didn't. I couldn't sleep either.'

It seemed easier to confess things in the dark, and my next words slipped out with barely a thought. 'I … I really wish you were here.' Down the line I heard him give a contented sigh and there was the soft swishing of material like he was rolling over in bed.

'Actually, I am. Sean invited me back after you'd gone to bed. I'm on the sofa, you can sleep in peace.'

He was here? In the other room? My pulse leapt at the knowledge of his nearness and I felt my skin heat with excitement.

'Oh, OK. Goodnight then.'

He had obviously misinterpreted my words and thought I wanted him here to feel safe, but what I'd actually meant was that I wanted him here because I missed him, missed being held by him and touching him … and kissing him.

Hanging up, I immediately slid from the bed, intent on setting him straight.

# JACK

I hung up with a sigh. I'd have given anything to go to her room and pull Caitlin into my arms, but I wouldn't rush her, so I closed my eyes and tried to calm my breathing enough to make sleep a possibility.

Who was I kidding? Sleep was nowhere in sight. All I could think about was the fact that Caitlin was here, in bed. Images of her lithe body curled beneath a sheet filled my head: chestnut hair spilling across her pillow, skin flushed from the heat of the room, nipples erect when she threw the sheet back ... I expelled a frustrated breath and ran a hand over my face. Fantasizing like that was not going to do me any favours in the sleep department.

Suddenly I heard a sound, which had my ears straining for more. A brief flicker of a shadow crossed the ceiling and I shot upright. Shit! Something was in the room. My heart rate flew up at the possibility that Greg might have got in, but as I bolted upright I saw Caitlin highlighted in a sliver of moonlight, standing in the doorway dressed in what appeared to be a long T-shirt.

The realisation that she had come to me had my already heightened pulse absolutely skyrocketing.

'Hey ... I feel a bit weird asking, but ... can I ...can I ...' Caitlin was stuttering like crazy and I wondered what on earth she was going to ask. 'Can I snuggle in with you while we sleep?' she croaked. 'I ... missed you.'

I felt like all my Christmases had come at once. That question she could ask me *any* day of the week. 'Of course, sweetheart.' I lifted up the corner of the blanket without hesitation and held out a hand.

The speed with which Caitlin practically flew across the room inflated my ego no end, and before I'd had time to register it, she was under the covers and snuggled up beside me. She placed a leg across my torso, before speedily shifting it down and settling against me. An immense sense of calm enveloped me as I inhaled her sweet scent, but as I wrapped an arm around her and gently pulled her closer I noticed that she was tense and shaking. 'Hey, you're trembling, are you cold?'

'No.' Her voice sounded strange, but it was too dark for me to look at her face. One answer sprung to my mind that had me kicking myself.

'Are you scared?' I swallowed hard. 'Of me?'

'No, no, it's not that.' Her immediate response reassured me, but I still wanted to know what was troubling her. Caitlin tentatively lifted a hand and placed it on my chest, but I could definitely still feel a light shaking. 'I just didn't expect you to … uh, be so … um, undressed.'

Shit, of course! I was naked! That must be why she had shifted her leg so suddenly, she must have felt my groin against her thigh. *Oops.* When I'd had my freak-out on the beach, my clothes had got soaked, even my underwear, so although Sean had leant me some clothes I'd gone commando all night.

Being with Caitlin felt so natural that I kept forgetting how carefully I needed to tread, but rubbing my naked body against her was definitely pushing some serious limits.

'Shit, I'm so sorry. Earlier when I … spilt the coffee … all my clothes got wet. Allie put them in the washer and I borrowed some off Sean, but I didn't really want to wear his underwear.' Pushing myself upright, I tried to hold the covers over my groin so I could climb from the sofa. 'He did give me some boxers, hang on.'

There was a second of awkwardness when I had to slide from under the sheet, but Caitlin looked away and I quickly pulled on the grey briefs.

'I'll put the jeans on too.'

'No, don't.' Caitlin's small hand reached up and gripped at mine, applying enough pressure that I had no choice but to abandon my jeans and rejoin her under the blankets. Once I was beside her, she pressed on the centre of my chest, seeming to urge me back down, and tilted her head up to meet my gaze in the moonlight. 'Just shorts is fine.'

These were pretty small briefs, which didn't do much to hide my modesty. 'Are you sure? I don't mind.'

'I'm sure. I trust you. Besides, you're cosy like this.' Closing my eyes, I tried to supress the smile that spread across my face at the way her fingers were giving my chest a tentative exploration.

As I settled myself down and carefully adjusted against Caitlin I realised I could feel the weight of her bare breasts against my chest. *Shit*. That sent a jolt of lust coursing through me and I felt my cock twitch then immediately start to harden. Damn. This was going to be the best, but most challenging, night of my life.

## CAIT

As I lay in Jack's embrace, two things kept swirling in my mind. Firstly, the feel of his hot groin under my leg when I'd accidentally rubbed against it, and secondly, our kiss earlier. It went round and around in my head: gentle lips, soft, warm caresses of his tongue, hands in my hair, my body igniting under his touch …

'Are you asleep?' I whispered, my voice sounding ridiculously needy.

'No. I can't sleep. Are you OK?' Jack didn't sound sleepy at all, so using the darkness of the night to bolster my courage, I propped myself up and used one hand to feel out where his face was. As soon as I was sure of my target I leant up and placed my lips on his.

Jack's response was immediate as a groan resonated through his chest, making my nipples harden and press into his side.

My lips moved tentatively at first, but the longer I kissed him, the surer Jack seemed to get, and after a few minutes his control seemed to shatter as his hands went from lightly resting against me to gripping my waist and tugging me against him. It was amazing. I'd never felt so wanted, so sexual.

There was one small issue nagging at me. Something I should have just told Jack about earlier, but a fact I had omitted.

I tried to push my worry aside and lose myself in the kiss, which worked for a few moments, but as his tongue worked skilfully against mine, whipping me into a frenzy, my worries came flooding back. Jack was older and far more experienced than me. Would he really want to bother when he realised just how inexperienced I was?

Overcome with horrendous self-consciousness, I rolled away to gain some space but only succeeded in rather clumsily wrapping myself in the blanket and falling from the sofa.

'*Oppff.*' The air flew from my lungs as I scrambled to sit up, but as I was pretty much a human sausage roll I ended up flailing and flapping for a good few seconds before managing to free myself. Ugh. I was such an idiot I could hardly bear it.

Propping myself against the coffee table, I watched in embarrassment as Jack – now completely and rather magnificently uncovered – hastily sat up. The briefs really were very tiny. Even in the moonlight his excitement was easy to spot tenting the front. I felt my cheeks flame at the impressive bulge before he grabbed a pillow and awkwardly shoved it over his groin.

Poor guy. My stomach churned as I wondered if perhaps I really was a prick tease. God, had Greg been right about me?

Feeling woozy, I lurched unsteadily to my feet, and saw the sanctuary of the balcony to my right. 'Sorry,' I muttered shakily. 'I just need some air.'

The walk across the room was surprisingly difficult, because after his amazing kiss my legs seemed to be the consistency of loose rubber bands. Thankfully my trembling fingers didn't let me down and I managed to flick the latch up before sliding the door open and feeling the cool of the night on my face.

'Umm, OK.' Jack's mumbled response was barely audible over the rushing of blood in my ears as I practically ran through the doors and sucked in a lungful of the refreshing sea air.

The balcony was heavy with shadows and I allowed the soft sound of the waves breaking on the beach to calm me as I attempted to steady my hammering heart.

I was mentally kicking myself. Firstly for getting so carried away, and secondly for leaving the room like an idiot. He was, after all, my dream man – practically perfect. If I couldn't bring myself to let down my final wall with him, I'd probably end up single for ever.

I stared out at the inky black waves and tensed as I heard the patio door open behind me with a quiet squeak.

'I'm sorry. I should have exerted more control,' Jack murmured.

Closing my eyes, I drew in a long breath and shook my head. 'No, it wasn't you. You didn't do anything wrong. I got carried away and now I feel … well, I'm way out of my depth here.' Finally plucking up some of my waning courage, I turned to Jack and saw that he was still shirtless, but had now pulled his jeans on. The top two buttons were undone and gave a tantalising glimpse of the teeny tiny grey shorts below.

'There's something I should have told you earlier,' I whispered. Once I'd told him this final nugget, he'd know every single one of my secrets. 'You're amazing, and I'm …' I was willing myself to say it, but my throat constricted so tightly that words didn't seem to fit out any more. Jack stepped closer and carefully placed a hand on my shoulder.

His touch soothed me, as it always did. 'I'm so ordinary and …' I felt wretched. Why was this so bloody difficult to say? Maybe being single was easier after all.

'What is it?' he encouraged.

Oh God, it was now or never. 'I'm a virgin, Jack.' I blurted the words out as quickly as I could and turned my burning face to the floor, examining the iron nails in the decking in great detail. 'Apart from … the attack, but I refuse to count that.'

Wrapping my arms around myself, I felt my face flush with searing heat and was immensely relieved that the porch was only lit by the soft glow from the moon.

Silence hung for several moments, but then I felt his thumb on my chin as Jack gently forced me to turn my face upwards. I saw that his eyes were full of tenderness and his lips had formed into a gentle smile.

'Oh, sweetheart.' His voice was hoarse and he gently gathered my tense body into his arms and held me to the security of his warm chest until I began to relax. 'Is that what you were worried about?' He sounded immensely relieved and even chuckled. 'That just makes you even more special,' he mumbled as he placed a kiss on the top of my head. 'And by the way, you are far from ordinary.'

Leaning back, I saw his expression was fiercely intense. 'Without one word of a lie, Caitlin, I can say you are the most amazing woman I have ever met. No one else has come close to how I feel about you ... and your lack of experience doesn't bother me one bit. In fact, if I'm being truly honest, I find it extremely attractive. It's a big turn-on,' he added in a lower, seductive tone that made my tummy flip over several times.

Well, that certainly boosted my self-confidence somewhat.

'So even before your ex ... there was no one?' Jack asked quietly, causing me to immediately shake my head. A smile cracked on my lips as I realised just how good it felt to finally get it off my chest. I hadn't told anyone my secret for years.

'No. I had boyfriends, but nothing serious. Then when I was old enough to be interested in the idea of sex I decided I would wait for the right man. He never really came along.' I shrugged, forcing images of Greg from my mind. For a few months I'd thought he might be the one. How very wrong I'd been.

'After a while of waiting, I met Greg, and then after the experience with him I stopped dating completely. So

222

here I am, twenty-seven and a virgin.

'So you know, no pressure or anything, but there's a vacancy in my life for a Mr Right.'

'No pressure at all …' he laughed, his arm immediately tightening around me as he laid his head on my hair and kissed my temple. 'How am I doing so far?'

'So far? Hmm, I'd say you're lining up pretty well,' I grinned.

He hummed his happiness, and it vibrated through me. 'Just being with you makes me feel like the luckiest man alive.'

He always said the most amazing things. With the way he made me feel, I had a feeling the wait might not be so long after all.

# THIRTY-THREE

## ALLIE

'Are you awake, babe? I'm heading off to work.' Sean's face floated above me as he leant over the bed, looking and smelling like some gorgeous Adonis that my sleepy brain had conjured up.

As he placed a lingering kiss on my lips, I giggled and pulled him in. 'Can't get enough of me, eh?' he quipped, before giving me exactly what I had wanted and deepening the kiss. He was real alright – no dreamed-up lover could ever be quite this good or this cocky.

After a few more seconds he leant up, looking flushed and amused at my protesting moan. 'OK. I'm going. I'll be home early, so I was wondering if you fancied going out somewhere.'

That certainly woke me up. Out?

Propping myself up, I rubbed the sleep from my eyes and looked at him. 'Like a date?' I asked, a nervous flutter rising in my belly and making my chest feel a bit tight.

'Yeah. What do you think?'

Wow. After the press conference we'd decided to give everything a while to settle down before going out in public together, but thinking about it, that had been a few weeks ago. It was probably time we actually left his house together rather than just hiding away and shagging each other's brains out. I'd get a vitamin D deficiency soon if we didn't start getting out and about more often.

'It sounds good …' I paused. 'But what about Cait? I

don't want to leave her on her own after the Greg thing, and Jack said he was working.'

'Good point.' Nodding slowly, Sean rubbed his jaw. 'You mentioned her friends from the studio were dying to see my house, maybe she could invite them over?'

I knew Mel and Lisa would jump at the chance to nosey around the beach house, so it seemed an ideal solution.

'That sounds perfect.'

'Glad to hear it,' he smiled.

'So ... where do you want to go tonight?' I almost felt shy, which was ridiculous.

Shrugging, Sean shoved his mobile into his jeans as he prepared to leave. 'I was thinking maybe see a movie?'

I found myself nodding at how normal, and lovely, that sounded. 'OK. Movies it is.'

Sean grinned from ear to ear, his eyes twinkling with happiness. 'It's a pretty fancy theatre, so we'll need to dress up. Oh yeah, don't forget that Jack's on the sofa.' Leaning in, Sean lowered his voice and gave me an intense look. 'And from what I saw when I dropped his clothes in, he's got company.'

'Cait's with him?' I asked, my voice rising in shock.

'I didn't exactly hang around to perv on them, but let's just say I could definitely see two sets of feet poking out from under the covers.'

Sean pulled open the bedroom door and wiggled his eyebrows. 'See you later for our date, gorgeous.'

Our date.

Oh my gosh.

# THIRTY-FOUR

## JACK

After Caitlin's confessions, we had stumbled back inside and made out on the sofa like a couple of randy teenagers until I'd had to practically peel her off of me.

After our heated kisses and some mild fondling, we had tried to settle down for sleep, but it hadn't been particularly successful. The sofa wasn't long enough for me, and I'd been tempted to steer her towards the spare bedroom, but with the way Caitlin affected me I was seriously concerned that I might not be able to hold myself back if I'd got to lay beside her in a bed.

So we stayed on the lumpy sofa. Don't get me wrong, it was a high quality leather suite, but definitely not designed to be slept on. Especially not by somebody of my height. Not that it really mattered, because I'd barely slept a wink, instead spending the entire night with images of her mouth and body running around my brain, and a rock hard groin as a result.

And now, at 4.56 a.m., I was still awake, and waiting for the 5 a.m. alarm on my watch. I could have got up and showered, but I was enjoying the sensation of having Caitlin in my arms far too much.

She was sound asleep, and during the night she had snuggled up against me, one arm thrown across my belly and clutching at my hip as if I was all that mattered in the entire world. At least that's what I'd like to believe.

And yes, I still had a throbbing erection. I'd been hard for so long that I was surprised I wasn't light-

226

headed. I probably would be when I stood up.

As if weirdly in sync with me, Caitlin began to stir, making a cute moan and raising one hand to rub at her face and push her hair back from her eyes before giving such a sweet smile that my heart actually ached.

'Morning, sweetheart.' My voice was embarrassingly gruff, but I didn't care. We'd both laid our cards on the table – she knew how into her I was.

'Morning. Do you have to get up?'

Grimacing at the thought of not only today's early start but the rest of my hectic week, I nodded, and couldn't resist burying my nose in her hair to inhale the floral scent of her shampoo.

'Unfortunately, yes.' I kissed her temple and sighed. 'The timing is really shitty, but I've got a really busy few weeks coming up so I might not be able to see you that much.' This was partly true, work *was* busy, but I was also going to be occupied working with Flynn to try and track down Lambert. I wasn't going to tell Caitlin , but that fucker wasn't going to get away with threatening my girl or fucking up her life any longer.

Caitlin made a small noise of protest and snuggled closer to me, burying her face in my chest.

'Sorry. We're still trying to make up for the days we missed when I was in hospital. I should still be able to see you on our coffee breaks, though.'

'OK.' Caitlin gave me a smile, but I could see it was forced, and I felt horribly guilty as a result.

Sitting up, I spotted a pile of clothes by the doorway and realised someone had left my dried clothes for me at some point. So either Sean or Allie had seen Caitlin and I curled up together. No doubt we'd face a curious interrogation later.

'I guess I should let you get ready for work.' She rolled from the sofa and stood in the nightdress that had acted as a barrier between full skin-on-skin contact all night.

Standing up, I saw Caitlin's eyes widen as her gaze ran up and down my still aroused body, clad only in the briefs, so I quickly walked to the doorway and pulled on my T-shirt and jeans to hide what I couldn't seem to get control over.

Worried that Caitlin would be freaked out by my inability to control my cock, I glanced at her, but instead of seeing fear in her gaze, I found her smiling at me, looking utterly thrilled by my predicament. The little minx.

As I grinned sheepishly back at her, I noticed that what I had thought was a cotton nightdress was, in fact, a Metallica T-shirt. 'Is that Allie's?'

Looking down, Caitlin fingered the faded material and shrugged. 'Nah, it's massive. Must be Sean's.'

Sean's. As stupid as it was, I really disliked the idea of her wearing his clothes. If she was going to sleep in anyone's T-shirt, then I wanted it to be mine. Keeping my face as neutral as possible, I peeled off the T-shirt that I had only just put on, and then held it out to her.

'Wear this one tonight.' I didn't word it as a question, because in my mind there was no other option. If she was wearing a man's clothes against her naked skin, then they would damn well be *my* clothes.

Turning away from her, I collected my watch, wallet, and phone from the table and pulled on the checked shirt that Sean had lent me. I was already running late so I'd have to grab a shower at the studio. Shoving my phone into my back pocket, I rotated back to Caitlin, and to my surprise, found her clad in my T-shirt, with Sean's discarded one lying on the sofa.

She'd been naked and I'd missed it. Damn it!

My mild irritation was quickly lost when I saw she had the collar held in her fingers and was sniffing it with a soft smile on her face.

228

I couldn't help myself from stepping toward her and easing her into my arms. There was no tenseness in her body, or gasp of shock as I touched her this time. Caitlin simply seemed to melt into my embrace until we were touching from our heads to our toes, leaving me feeling like I was on top of the frigging world.

'That's far better. You make my T-shirt look better than I do.'

Caitlin hummed her approval into my chest. 'I doubt that. But I like wearing it. It smells like you. You can think of me tonight, wearing it in bed … and nothing else.'

My eyes flew open and I definitely grasped her against me more firmly. Jeez. For a virgin she had a real way with words. And just like that, my cock was solid as a rock again and trying to push its way out of my jeans.

Marvellous.

'Tease,' I muttered, because quite frankly I couldn't think of one useful thing to say or do apart from go against all of my promises to be good and drag her back to the sofa with me.

'Because I won't be around much in the next few days, I'd really rather you stay here with Allie. Please don't go back to your apartment while … while *he's* still out there somewhere. OK?'

The teasing smile on Caitlin's face faded to tension as she swallowed hard and then nodded stiffly. 'OK.'

'Also, I talked to Flynn and he's recommended a bodyguard for you.' I tried to drop it in casually, but my words caused Caitlin to fly back and gawk at me in the early morning sun. Even gawking, she was still beautiful. God, I had it so bad.

'What? A bodyguard? No!' Caitlin's mouth opened and closed several times like a goldfish. 'No!'

'She'll just trail you, you won't even know she's there. I promise.'

'But … but … I'm a no one. I'll be fine, Jack, I don't need a bodyguard. The police said they'd keep an eye on me.' Yeah, but I knew for sure that 'keeping an eye on her' meant a phone call every day or so, which was nowhere near good enough for me.

'Sweetheart … it's for me, really. I seriously won't be able to concentrate if I don't know you're safe. Please?'

Caitlin absorbed my words, and I could see her processing them as she blinked and chewed on her lip. 'Fine. But she'll be bored senseless following me around. You did say "she", didn't you?'

'Thank you, Caitlin. And yes, it's a woman. Her name is Tanya, apparently she's ex-special forces, and holds a sixth *dan* in karate. She'll come along to meet you and Allie at breakfast, and then once you've done the introductions she'll melt into the background. You'll have her phone number. Program it into your phone and call her if you ever see Greg or feel unsafe, OK?'

Caitlin sighed again, giving the elastic bands on her wrist a ping before nodding. 'OK.'

'Come here, let's wipe that miserable look off your face.'

I'm proud to say that after five minutes of kissing, Caitlin did indeed look far perkier when I finally pried myself away from Sean's house.

# THIRTY-FIVE

## CAIT

I couldn't resist crawling back under the covers on the sofa and snuggling into them. I could smell his scent all over the cotton, and it brought a huge goofy smile to my face.

We'd kissed for what felt like hours, and we'd even had a tentative exploration of each other's bodies, and although I had very much enjoyed tracing the muscles on his chest with my fingers, I hadn't been quite brave enough to lower my hand and stroke over the bulge in his shorts. The *impressive* bulge in his shorts.

Maybe I'd do that next time. The thought had my cheeks heating, because surely once I started down that route, things would inevitably move to the next level. Funnily enough, now he knew I was still a virgin, the thought of progressing with Jack didn't scare me. I trusted him implicitly, and I knew he wouldn't hurt me, which made me think my V status would soon become a thing of the past.

Excitement tumbled in my belly at the idea of sex with Jack, and I had giddily buried my face in his pillow when I heard a giggle behind me. 'Cait? What are you doing?'

I nearly jumped out of my skin at the sound of Allie's voice and, leaping upright, I spun round and found her stood in the doorway with her hands on her hips and a knowing grin on her face.

Horrifically embarrassed to have been caught mid

sniff, I fidgeted and tried to avoid her gaze. 'Uh ... nothing ...' I couldn't help it if I loved the way Jack smelt, but getting caught was certainly a little humiliating.

'Yeah, right. You were sniffing his pillow, I saw you,' she announced smugly as she came into the lounge, pushed the duvet back, and sat down. 'Don't worry, I do that with Sean's stuff too,' she added, apparently looking to reassure me. It worked to some degree, so with a self-conscious shrug I smiled and plopped down next to her.

'So ... you stayed here last night then ...' she ventured carefully, her tone laden with curiosity.

'Yep.' I tried to keep my reply light, but a vision of Jack's lips locked with mine as his hand dug into my hair had me swallowing hard, so my reply came out all high and breathy.

Allie was staring at me as if she was trying to look right through me, and under such intense scrutiny I felt my cheeks heat further. 'And from that blush I take it there was more than just sleep going on, huh?'

'We mostly just snuggled,' I mumbled.

'Just snuggled? Come on, I wasn't born yesterday! I want more deets!' she exclaimed with a grin, and slightly reluctantly I explained how I'd come to share the sofa with Jack and that we'd then spent several hours talking, cuddling, and sharing some fairly heated kisses.

Beside me, Allie let out a wistful sigh. 'I kind of miss nights like that. Sean is great at sex, but sometimes it's nice to connect with talking, kissing, and a bit of a grope.' I couldn't compare, but I certainly hadn't had any complaints about the way our night had panned out, that was for sure.

'I told him I was a virgin,' I confessed, self-consciously averting my eyes even though Allie already knew my secret.

'Blimey. I bet he was totally cool about it too, huh?' she asked gently.

A giggle bubbled in my throat as I recalled the stunned look on Jack's face when I'd told him. 'Actually, he was pretty shocked at first.' I grinned at Allie. 'Then he said it made me even more special, and that he found it ...' I paused, my cheeks flushing again, '... he found it rather arousing.'

My bestie drew in a gasp and grabbed my arm in excitement. 'God, Cait, he is like the perfect man. I'm almost a bit jealous!'

'Yeah right, you're not exactly hard done by dating Sean, are you?'

Allie's expression softened in that love-struck way it often did when we discussed anything to do with Sean. 'We're going public tonight,' she confessed, chewing her lip nervously.

That was big news. 'Wow. Are you making an official statement or anything?'

'Sean said he wants to go to the movies, so I guess we're just going to start going out in public and let the press make of it what they will.'

Nodding my head, I wondered if I'd be so cool and calm when the time came for me and Jack to venture out in public together. The spotlight was far more up Allie's street than mine.

'Sean suggested you could invite Mel and Lisa over for a girly night if you'd like some company,' Allie offered, and I immediately felt myself relax a little. Not that I needed babysitting, but company would certainly be nice.

'That sounds great. Actually, I got a text from Mel last night asking if I was OK. She heard what happened,' I grimaced, imagining what the rumour mill was making of my meltdown. 'I bet everyone thinks I'm a complete weirdo,' I mumbled, my eyes dropping. 'Anyway, I'll

234

call her and invite them over.'

'Are you going to tell them about Jack?' she asked.

I gave a non-committal shrug. 'I don't know, maybe. Things are still pretty new, so I might keep it quiet for a while longer.'

'Fair enough,' Allie agreed with a nod, before bursting into a broad grin. 'So, looks like we've got a busy day ahead of us!'

Perking up, I wrapped my arms around my knees. 'Why? What are we doing?'

'I need to prep for tonight, and I need you to help. It's only a trip to the cinema, but seeing as he's a pretty famous actor and I'm an ex-primary school teacher, I think I should at least make some effort.' Allie scrunched her nose and gave me a funny look. 'I don't want people to see us together and wonder why the hell he's with me.'

Rolling my eyes, I flopped back on the sofa. 'Like that would ever happen. Besides, he's with you because he loves you. But I get what you mean. So what are you thinking? New outfit and a trip to the hairdresser's?'

'Yeah, I guess that sounds about right,' Allie paused and flashed me a look as she chewed frantically on a fingernail.

Raising a hand, I slapped the back of her wrist with a tut. 'Enough of that, you'll need those nails if you get a manicure.'

'Sorry, you're right. I just feel really nervous.'

Just as I was about to reassure her that everything would be fine, a knock at the front door interrupted us.

Frowning, I looked at my watch and saw it was still really early, just after 7 a.m., and then looked at Allie to see a matching frown on her face. 'Bit early for house guests, isn't it?' she murmured warily, standing up.

'Check the peep hole before you open it,' I warned, jumping up with her as a shot of anxiety sped through my veins.

Allie nodded as we approached the door. 'This estate is really safe, I doubt anyone could get in.'

Glancing through the peep hole, I let out a relieved breath when I saw Flynn standing on the steps with a woman beside him. 'Ah. It's Flynn, and I'm guessing the woman must be Tanya, my new bodyguard.'

'You said yes to that?' Allie queried in surprise.

'You knew about it?' I retorted, my voice equally as stunned.

Heat rushed to her cheeks and she gave a small nod. 'Jack mentioned the idea last night when you were in the loo.'

'I'm not massively keen on the idea, and I think it's unnecessary, but if it makes Jack happier then I'll indulge him.'

Pulling open the door, I watched as Flynn raised an eyebrow. It might have been my stunning case of bed hair that was entertaining him, or perhaps he had spotted that I was wearing Jack's T-shirt, because he certainly looked mildly amused, which was at odds to his usual stern expression.

After nodding a greeting at us, he promptly made the introductions. Tanya was almost as tall and broad as Flynn, and her manner was professional: calm and aloof, which was fine by me.

'You won't know I'm here most of the time. Just let me know in advance if you plan on going anywhere so I can make sure to accompany you,' she said, turning for the steps to leave.

'Actually, I'm going out with Allie today.'

Both Flynn and Tanya turned back with matching frowns. 'After yesterday's run-in with Lambert, I would strongly advise against that for now, Miss Byrne,' Flynn said, pulling out his mobile. 'Save going out and let the police track him down.' After giving me my dressing down, he called someone on his phone and turned away again.

I shared a look with Allie. I understood their concerns, but what was the point of having a bodyguard if I wasn't even allowed to leave the frigging house?

'Mr Felton would like to speak to you,' Flynn bit out, holding his phone toward me with a strict expression. Wow, talk about arsey. He'd gotten hold of Jack awfully speedily too. Normally I had to leave a message and wait for him to have a break in filming.

Walking a few steps away from my audience, I lifted the phone to my ear. 'Hey.'

Skipping his usual pleasantries, Jack got straight to the point. 'Caitlin, please don't go out. What's so desperate that you need a shopping trip today?'

'Allie and Sean are having their first public date tonight. She's nervous about the press so she wanted me to help her pick a new outfit.'

After a pause, I heard a heavy sigh down the line. 'OK, I understand, but after yesterday I just don't think it's safe for you to go out yet.' There was a brief silence down the phone and then a deep breath. 'I have an idea … Allie's the same size as you, right?'

'Yes, but my clothes are back at the apartment.'

'That wasn't what I was thinking. If I promised to arrange the most perfect outfit for Allie's date, would you stay in today?'

'I guess so, but how?'

'I'll arrange everything. Just get yourselves showered and have some breakfast and I'll get someone to come around and sort it out, OK?'

'What do you mean you'll get someone to come and sort it out?' I asked in confusion.

'Trust me.'

'You know I trust you, Jack. We'll stay here, I promise.'

I heard someone in the background calling Jack's name and him click his tongue in irritation. 'I've got to go, but I'll see you as soon as I get some time off from shoots. Bye.'

# THIRTY-SIX

## ALLIE

When Jack had said he'd 'get someone to come and sort it', what he'd actually meant was that he'd get the most exclusive store on Rodeo Drive to send two of its personal shoppers to Sean's house with a rail of beautiful clothes in my size.

Talk about overkill.

Tiffany and Brent were our personal shoppers for the day and they'd picked out the finest, most beautiful clothes I'd ever seen in my life.

The sound of a loud pop to my left made me flinch, but as I turned, I saw Brent holding a bottle of champagne aloft with a grin on his face as he began to pour it into two glasses.

OK, this was really surreal.

Brent was now holding a glass in my face, leaving me little option but to accept it.

Blimey. It was only ten, but seeing as he'd already opened the bottle, it would be rude not to have at least one glass, wouldn't it?

I glanced at Cait and saw a similarly bemused look on her face, but deciding to bin our doubts and enjoy the moment, I clinked it against hers and only just held back from shouting 'Let the show begin!'

Two hours later and we had seen so many outfits I almost felt a bit dizzy. Although that might have been the champagne, because Brent had cracked open bottle number two about twenty minutes before and it was going down rather well.

'Which ones do you like?' Tiffany asked Cait, but in reply my bestie simply laughed and shook her head.

'Oh no, this isn't for me. Allie is the one who needs a dress,' she replied.

'Actually, miss, the gentleman who booked us made it very clear that you are both to choose outfits. He said he'll be greatly offended if you don't both pick at least two each.'

He'd be greatly offended? I'd seen a couple of the price tags, and I had to say, the number of zeros greatly offended *me*. There was no way I could afford to pay Jack back for any of these.

'He mentioned to tell you that the clothes are a belated birthday gift to you, Miss Shaw, and an early birthday gift for you, Miss Byrne.'

Wow. Jack really had thought of everything. I hadn't been wrong when I'd told Cait that her boyfriend was amazing.

All I could manage was a weak, 'Oh,' before I looked towards Cait with wide eyes. Cait's expression held a similar look of disbelief, her eyes bugging as she downed the last of her champagne in shock and then winced from the fizz.

As much as I was enjoying this star treatment, I felt it only polite to inform them of what I actually needed the outfit for. 'Um ... I'm only going to the cinema ...' I stuttered, thinking this might all be a touch over the top given the casualness of my date. I mean, I wanted to look good, but I could hardly turn up wearing Prada.

'We have details of the location, miss, and we promise to only show you suitable outfits.' They knew the destination? I guess that meant Jack had spoken to Sean.

'So, what are your thoughts on this?' Tiffany asked,

pulling out a fabulous pale blue backless dress and matching high heels. My eyebrows rose. It was a gorgeous outfit, but if I needed to wear something that stunning, where exactly was Sean taking me?

Four hours later, I found out that the 'movie' Sean had mentioned was actually a frigging star-studded premiere for a new Hollywood release. Seriously? Could we not have done something a little more low key? We pulled up to the waiting area outside the theatre and my mouth dropped open as I saw the red carpet and probably close to a hundred people lining its edges. There were press everywhere, lights flashing, music blaring, and I suddenly felt sick to my stomach with nerves.

My palms felt sweaty as I clutched at the handle on the car door and gawped out of the window. The pulsing of my heartbeat in my ears was so loud it was almost drowning out the music outside.

This had to be the most nervous I had ever felt in my entire life. Trying to get my shaking under control, I swivelled on my seat to look at Sean and found him observing me with a broad smile on his face.

'Don't you dare laugh, Sean!' I squeaked as a sudden jolt of irritation ripped through me.

Softening his features, Sean leant forwards and took one of my hands. 'I'm not laughing at you, Allie, I promise. I've attended so many of these things over the years. My PR team insist I attend all the big events these days – awards, premiers, previews, you name it. But I hate them. You know why?'

Swallowing hard, I shook my head, unable to think straight.

'I'm never allowed to attend alone. I either have to team up with my current co-star or some up-and-coming actress that my agency represents.'

Great, a good dollop of jealousy was added to my

nervous irritation and I felt my eyebrows dipping into a deep frown. Was he deliberately trying to make me feel self-conscious?

'I have to put on a happy charade and the press always have a field day, harking back to my days as a troublemaker and printing bullshit stories about how I bed women and break their hearts. I've never once attended with someone I actually want to be with.' Sean paused and licked his lips. 'Not until tonight.'

OK, so that got my attention.

'I dread these things, but I'm actually excited about getting out of the car tonight. Do you know why?'

Clearing my dry throat, I shook my head. 'Why?' The throat clearing had been a waste of time because my voice still came out as a nervous rasp.

Sean smiled his Hollywood A-lister grin, dimples and all, then leaned in close to my ear. 'Because I'm here with you. I can relax and enjoy myself. For once it's not fake, and I can't wait to show you off and let everyone see how much I love you.'

Holy cow. That certainly made me feel a bit better about facing the crowd.

# SEAN

'Here, have a sip of this. It'll help bolster your courage.'
I poured a glass of brandy from the mini-bar inside the
limo and handed it to Allie.

She was nervous, but my gorgeous girl was living up
to her nickname, looking stunning in a pale blue dress,
delicate makeup, and with her hair long and sleek around
her shoulders. Because of the design of the dress, I knew
she wasn't wearing a bra underneath it, and it would take
all my self-control not to explore that fact once we were
settled in the darkness of our theatre seats.

Allie took a drink of the brandy, grimacing as the
fiery liquid went down but remaining silent, and I started
to wonder if this was a bad idea. When I'd suggested it
this morning I'd had visions of Allie enjoying the red
carpet, and the idea of showing her off as mine had been
too appealing to deny, but seeing how packed the
entrance seemed, maybe this would be a bit
overwhelming.

'If you don't want to get out, I can have David drive
us away. Maybe we could go for a meal instead?'

After another couple of seconds, and another hearty
glug of brandy, Allie shook her head. 'No. It was just a
bit of a shock, but I want to be with you, Sean, and I
understand this type of thing comes as a part of that.'
Giving another glance out of the window, Allie
swallowed hard, a bit of her bravado slipping. 'Just
promise me you won't leave my side, OK?'

Wild hounds would have had to drag me away from
her side tonight. 'Deal.' I sealed it with a kiss but
reluctantly leant back before it became too heated –

facing the press together looking dishevelled, flushed, and aroused probably wouldn't make the best first impression.

'Can I give them your name?'

Shrugging, Allie pulled out a mirror to check her lipstick. 'I suppose so. I guess it doesn't really matter.'

Popping the mirror back into her tiny handbag, Allie took a deep breath and straightened her shoulders. 'Let's do this.'

Sliding from the car, I ignored the shouts of my name and instead turned around and held out my hand to assist Allie. As she rose gracefully from the car, the calling and flashes of cameras intensified and I felt her fingers grip mine with almost feral strength.

Over the next ten minutes, I kept my promise and stayed glued to Allie's side, with her hand held tightly in mine. I couldn't have been more proud of her. She handled the questions, flashing bulbs, and screaming voices with the utmost calm, answering a few choice queries, smiling politely, and blushing beautifully when I announced that she was the love of my life.

All in all, it had gone pretty damn well.

No doubt we'd be all over the papers, but I was hopeful that for once the stories wouldn't be full of the usual bullshit, and would actually be pleasant for me to read, which let's face it, would make a bloody nice change.

# THIRTY-SEVEN

## ALLIE

The evening had been incredible. I'd thought I would feel overwhelmed with cameras flashing around us, but I hadn't. I'd felt immensely proud. Proud of the man by my side for not only his brilliant acting, but proud of the fact that he'd managed to overcome his fears from the past and move on.

Move on with *me*. The fact that we were together for real and the entire world would know about it tomorrow wasn't half as scary as I'd thought it would be. It was quite empowering. He was mine, I was his, and as of tomorrow no one would be able to doubt that.

My bra-less choice of outfit had gone down rather well, causing Sean to find multiple opportunities to fondle me throughout the evening, but much to his disappointment the theatre had been too busy for us to find a secluded spot to release our rising tension.

As a result, we were now entering his house feeling ramped up, turned on, and keen to celebrate our new-found publicity in his bedroom.

Hearing Cait's door close down the corridor, I realised she was still awake and wanted to quickly check on her before losing myself in Sean. Sean had other ideas, and was desperately trying to drag me into his room as I tugged myself from his grasp with a giggle.

'Just give me two minutes! Yesterday was really tough on Cait, I want to check that she's OK.'

Sean pouted, which made me laugh, because let's

face it, grown men pouting was always amusing. 'Two minutes?' He glanced at his watch then back to me. 'You better be quick, you've only got one minute, fifty-one seconds left.'

Rolling my eyes, I spun on my heel and went past the three doors that would take me to Cait's room. Giving a soft knock, I immediately heard movement, followed by her call. 'Come in.'

Entering the room, I found Cait already tucked up in bed with the bedside lamp illuminating the space. 'Hey, babes. Just thought I'd check in and see how your evening was.'

Propping herself up on the pillows, Cait smiled, but I could see she still looked tired. 'It was nice to see Mel and Lisa. We had a good time. They *loved* this place.'

I bet they did – this house was incredible. I perched on the edge of her bed, wondering how much of my two minutes was left and grinning at the thought of Sean getting more and more impatient. That wasn't necessarily a bad thing because Sean had proven in the past just how creative he could be when he was particularly wound up.

'How was the film?'

Breaking into a laugh, I updated Cait about my eventful night, giving her brief details of our 'trip to the cinema' and the fact that we'd done a full question and photo session with the journalists.

'Oh my God!' Cait was now sat bolt upright, her eyes wide. 'How was it? Did you freak out?'

I thought over my meeting with the journalists and smiled. 'Nowhere near as terrifying as I'd thought it would be. Having Sean by my side seemed to make it much more bearable.' It sounded sappy, but was completely true. He'd been like a wall of solid confidence and security by my side throughout the evening, there every single time I'd felt a nip of nerves in my belly. Knowing we were there as a team had calmed me completely, making the entire evening far more enjoyable than I'd expected.

'Do you think you'll be in the papers tomorrow?' she asked.

'Sean thinks so, so that'll make an interesting morning.'

Leaving Cait to sleep, I slipped from her room and headed back in the direction of my impatient man. It was about time I thanked him for making tonight so much easier than it could have been, and I had a pretty good idea how to do it.

Pausing outside the door to his room, I quickly shed my clothes and stowed them in a cupboard before opening the door and putting on my best attempt at a sultry expression as I entered.

Sean was sitting on the bed looking away from me as he removed his socks, so I closed the door and began a slow strut toward him. 'That was longer than two …' but Sean's complaint was cut off as he looked at me and his jaw fell open. 'Holy hell, Allie …'

I stayed quiet, looking at him from under my lowered lashes as I rounded the bed and then silently dropped to my knees before him. Biting on my lower lip, I slowly raised my hands and placed them on his bare knees, trailing up towards the only clothing he was wearing – his black boxers. I nearly lost my sultry expression to a smug one when I saw how desperately the material was straining over his excitement.

Dipping my fingers into the waistband of his briefs, I began to tug them down until he shifted his hips to help me. As soon as I had dragged them down his thighs his erection bobbed free and I wasted no time dipping my head and licking the crown of his cock while I pulled the briefs free and chucked them aside.

A groan ripped from his throat, but then his hand

landed on my shoulder and held me still. 'Allie … we've been teasing each other all night, I'm really wound up, babe …'

'I know. Let me make it better.'

He caressed my cheek with a soft smile, but I could see the red hot desire burning in his dark eyes. 'That's not what I mean … I had planned on being inside of you hard and fast …'

When I glanced up, I saw the tension in his muscles and realised he was worried about being too rough with me. I smiled, fondly remembering when we first got together and he was rough and hard pretty much all the time. Luckily I loved it like that too. Placing my hand on top of his, I guided it from my shoulder and into my hair before giving a teasing smile and a deliberately slow lick of my lips.

'Then you better use my mouth hard and fast,' I offered, my voice husky from my desire. Without waiting for him to debate this, I simply lowered my head and took him into my mouth, running my tongue around the steely heat of his arousal and then sinking lower until he bumped against the back of my throat.

'Jesus, Allie.' His voice was hoarse, but his grip in my hair increased as he urged me to continue. I didn't disappoint. Seeing as he'd said he wanted 'hard and fast' I didn't waste time with too much build-up and went straight for hollowing my cheeks as I sucked him into the back of my throat and cupped his balls with my left hand. My right wrapped around the base of his cock and I began a quick rhythm with both my hand and my mouth, bobbing up and down his length and loving how he groaned out his enjoyment and gripped my hair tighter.

'You're so fucking sexy, Allie … I'm close, babe.'

Tilting my head, I looked up at him as I carried on my strokes, and saw his face flushed with arousal and his eyes so dark they almost looked black. Keeping my fist pumping, I briefly lifted my mouth clear so I could speak.

'Do you want to come in my mouth, or on my boobs?' I knew Sean liked to spray his release on my breasts, but better than that, he loved it when I talked dirty during sex. It worked this time too, because he groaned, and his spare hand joined the other in my hair, urging my head back down. 'Your mouth feels so incredible …don't stop …'

His words were almost incomprehensible because his voice was so thick with lust. I often lost my head when Sean was doing deliciously naughty things to me, so I loved that I could also make him crazy with lust too. Doubling my efforts, I gripped his shaft firmer with my hand, and sucked him as deep as I could go. The speed and depth meant that I was slurping and dribbling more than usual, but Sean seemed to love this, his moans increasing and hips jerking more and more the messier I got.

Smiling triumphantly, I felt his cock thicken against my tongue and I knew he was about to come. Seconds later, Sean let out a garbled groan as I sucked him deep and hard and felt him pumping his release into my mouth in a series of hot, thick spurts.

'Holy fuck …' he gasped, his body collapsing onto the bed with a huge, long moan, leaving me kneeling between his legs as I smiled around his cock. From that reaction it would seem that I had done rather well.

Gentling my moves, I sucked until his cock stopped pulsing, and then licked him clean before looking up. His chest was heaving, but Sean sat upright, looped his hands under my arms, and dragged me into the bed before kissing me long and hard. He didn't seem to mind the fact that I tasted like him. In fact, it just seemed to fuel his lust, because he licked my lips, growled, and flipped me onto my back before speedily pinning me to the bed with his big body.

His face was between my legs quicker than I could even process, hot mouth licking and sucking my clit into his mouth with such delicious force that I yelled and bucked off the bed.

'So sexy. And all mine,' he declared against my clit, the vibrations of his voice travelling straight to my core as his warm breath tickled and teased my arousal even higher. 'After tonight, the whole world knows too.' His possessiveness had always been strong, but right now it felt potent and all-consuming. His hands pressed my legs wider, and his mouth worked me towards my peak with his tongue lapping and sucking in a near frenzy.

After the hours of teasing each other and the enjoyment of going down on him, I felt my own climax building at record speed, and as he sucked on my clit and thrust three fingers inside me I came undone, exploding into a flood of pleasure.

My body jerked and bowed off the mattress, but his firm hands kept me pinned as he continued with his onslaught, his hand now thrusting with determination and massaging my g-spot as his thumb pressed onto my clit.

'Again. Come again for me, my gorgeous girl.'

Again? Holy crap. I was barely dealing with the aftermath of the first mind-blowing orgasm, but like the slave to him my body was, it began following his demand as his fingers continued to thrust in and out. Two more deep thrusts and I cried out as I felt a second wave sweep over me, tensing my muscles almost painfully as my channel convulsed around his skilful fingers.

Jeez. My body was so alive with sensation that I almost couldn't deal with it and I found myself crying out his name and then collapsed into an exhausted heap on the damp sheets.

Sean growled his approval against my quivering flesh, and began to kiss his way back up my exhausted body until his smug face came into sight and he grinned at me.

Thankfully, after that explosive little number, Sean gave me a thorough kiss goodnight and pulled me into his arms to sleep.

# THIRTY-EIGHT

## CAIT

After the initial exultant high of being unreservedly desired by a Hollywood star, things changed dramatically in the following two weeks. I hadn't seen Jack *at all*. We'd arranged several dates but he'd cancelled them all, claiming he was completely snowed under with work.

I'd tried not to read too much into it at first. After all, he'd forewarned me that his schedule was going to be frantic, but he hadn't even managed to meet me for our usual coffee breaks, and I was starting to doubt that even he could be *this* busy.

Nibbling my fingernail, I frowned as I re-read the most recent text from him, which had pinged to my phone ten minutes before. Yet another cancellation.

*From: Jack F*

*I'm not going to be able to make dinner tonight, Caitlin, issues at work. Sorry for the late notice. J*

I didn't really care about the late notice, because all my focus was on two things: one, he'd called me Caitlin instead of his customary 'sweetheart', and two, he hadn't added a kiss like he usually would. Had Jack decided that with my baggage, psychotic ex-boyfriends, and complete lack of experience I was actually going to be too much work?

We'd spoken on the phone a few times, but after his romantic, affectionate behaviour when we'd been together at Sean's house, I had been shocked by the shortness of our calls, not to mention the briskness in his tone. I'd expected him to be just as desperate as me to move forward, and I'd had romantic visions of late night phone calls and snatched kisses by the coffee counter at the studio.

But none of that had happened, and I was feeling unsure and anxious.

Or perhaps I was just being paranoid and needy?

Flopping back on the sofa, I let out a dejected sigh as I heard Allie open the front door and walk down the corridor. We were both still staying at Sean's; I'd tried to move back to our apartment at the start of the week, but this had been vetoed by both Sean – very audibly stating his dislike of the idea – and Jack, who had texted to say he didn't want us to be alone until Greg was caught.

'Hey, chick. What are you doing still here?' Allie cooed cheerily, before pausing to take in my dress, make-up, and generally gloomy appearance. 'Has he cancelled *again*?' Allie asked as she walked over and sunk into the seat beside me, depositing a paper bag of what smelt like fried food on the table.

'Yep,' I replied, feeling a lump form in my throat. 'I don't get it. He told me he liked me and now he's nowhere to be seen. He's worried enough to get me a bodyguard, but can't make any time to meet up. I think he's changed his mind about me.'

Fingering the soft silk of the dress – one I'd chosen from the fashion show at our house – I shook my head. 'He paid for this dress but hasn't even bothered to come and see me wearing it. Maybe these fancy clothes were some sort of goodbye pay-off.'

The only vague positive I could see was that I hadn't made the final embarrassment and told him how I felt about him. It was however, startlingly clear – I was in love with Jack Felton. My heart had fallen for a man that no longer wanted to bother with me.

Grabbing my hand, Allie clutched it between hers. 'I don't care how famous he is, you're way too good to be stood up like this. Someone needs to have serious words with that man.' I took from her tone, and the way she was making a dive for my phone, that she meant *she* would be having serious words with him, so I quickly shook my head and reached out to grab her arm.

'No!' My squawk brought her up short. 'Thank you for trying to look after me, Allie, but I need to do this myself. I'll talk to him, and if he's changed his mind then I'll ...' *Be heartbroken? Curl up in a ball and cry?* '... I'll deal with it. He said he's working tonight, so I'll call him in the morning.' This was a delaying tactic on my part, but also true. Calling him while he was at the studios wouldn't do any good – we needed to speak in private.

Allie made a humming noise and gave in with a nod. 'Fine. OK. But make sure you do.' She then pointed at the bag she'd deposited on the table, pulled it closer, and grinned. 'So, you've caught me cheating on my diet. I figured as Sean was working and you were going out, I'd treat myself to some junk food. You want to share?'

I nodded and opened up the bag to peer inside. Yum. A bucket of chicken with a huge pile of fries and coleslaw on the side. Comfort food was just what I needed, although I had to say, this was a hellava lot of junk food for my slim as a rake best friend. 'Jeez, there's a mountain of food, were you planning on eating it all?'

Laughing, Allie grabbed two plates and rejoined me on the sofa. 'No! The delivery guy got my order mixed up, but he said I could just take it as they'd driven it all the way out here.'

It seemed like fate had known my dinner date was

going to be cancelled.

'All the better for me, then,' I agreed, accepting the drumstick and fries that Allie had plated up for me. Biting into the warm meat, I couldn't help but hum my appreciation. Things with Jack were up in the air, but the power of greasy, deep-fried food was truly unbelievable. I hadn't even thought I was that hungry, but in no time I was on my third piece of chicken and feeling much better for it.

Once we'd well and truly stuffed ourselves silly, we both collapsed back, groaning and clutching our full bellies.

'I'll wash these plates up and grab us a bottle of wine. If we're doing a girly night we should do it in style,' Allie announced, before refusing my offer of help and ushering me upstairs to change out of my dress.

Looking at my gorgeous outfit I sighed, nodded, and dutifully headed to change, trying to distract my mind from thoughts of Jack.

# THIRTY-NINE

## SEAN

I was on a break, drinking a strong cup of coffee and hoping we would be able to bring tonight's exhausting shoot to an early finish, when my phone vibrated in my pocket.

I saw Allie's name on the screen and quickly glanced around to see if my director was nearby. Phones weren't allowed on set, but seeing as Finlay appeared to be absent, I headed over to a quiet corner to answer it.

I couldn't help smiling at the knowledge that Allie would be at my house when I got in. I knew it was a tough time for Cait with her arsehole ex still on the loose, but from a purely selfish point of view, the girls' new living arrangements were working out brilliantly for me. I loved sharing my space with Allie, eating together, going to bed with her, waking up to her gorgeous sleepy eyes …

By the time I had lifted the phone to my ear I was grinning like a fool. Which was exactly what I was – a lovesick fool.

'Hey, babe.'

'Hi, I haven't got long, so just listen, OK?' Allie's irritable tone made my smile instantly morph to a frown as I began to conjure up all sorts of far-fetched reasons for her to sound so upset.

'Cait's gone to change, so I need to be quick. Do you know what the heck Jack is playing at? Since he and Cait were at your house two weeks ago he's not seen her

258

once, and he keeps cancelling the dates they've arranged.'

Wincing, I swallowed hard. I knew *exactly* what Jack was playing at; he was spending every spare second with Flynn working to track down Cait's ex. The poor guy was sleep-deprived but determined to ensure Cait's safety. He'd also made me promise that I wouldn't breathe a word to Allie or Cait. *Shit.*

'Uhhh … I don't know. Why, what's the matter?'

'She thinks he's avoiding her and wants to finish things between them,' Allie sighed heavily. 'Has he said anything to you?'

'He doesn't want to finish with her, Allie. He's crazy about Cait,' I stated with complete conviction.

'Well, he's not acting like it. She's putting on a brave face, but I think she's kinda freaking out. I thought he was a good guy, but after this I'm not so sure.'

Down the line, I heard some rustling noises and then Allie's voice came back as a rushed whisper. 'Cait's coming, I gotta go. See you soon.' And just like that, the line went dead.

Staring at my phone for a second I rubbed a hand over my face and decided to push my luck by making a call to Jack.

'Sean, hi.' He sounded distracted, as he had every time I'd called him recently, but when I'd pulled him up on it he'd apologised and said that he and Flynn were spending hours every day staring at CCTV footage and traffic camera feeds of the local area in the hope of catching Greg.

'I can't talk long because I'm due on set, but I thought you'd like to know that Allie just called me. Cait's getting upset by your lack of contact, she thinks you're avoiding her and want to finish things.'

'What!? Shit, I never thought she'd think that.' There was a pause down the line and I could picture Jack's face crumpling with worry. 'I've become so completely obsessed with finding fucking Greg that I guess I've neglected her. Fuck, I'm such an idiot.' I couldn't help but think this would all be so much easier if he just confided in her about what he was doing.

'Where are you?'

Down the line, Jack gave a dry laugh. 'I'm with Flynn in the surveillance van outside your house.' That was now where Jack spent most of his time. It was the only way he felt he could be near Cait but still work with Flynn on tracking down Greg.

'I know you didn't want to worry her, but just tell her what you're doing, Jack. She might worry but at least she'll understand. You and Flynn can set up base inside my house if you want. Use the dining room. At least that way you'll get to see her.'

'I didn't want to impose, but thank you. I might take you up on that.' I heard some muffled noises and the slam of a vehicle door. 'I'll sort it out, thanks for letting me know, Sean.'

# FORTY

## CAIT

Ten minutes later, I returned after a shower and change of clothes, in the mood to well and truly drown my sorrows.

Trotting down the steps that led to the lounge, I was surprised to find the lights in the living room off and no sign of Allie. I peered through to the kitchen, which was also in darkness, and I caught sight of a flickering light coming from the deck out the back. Allie had obviously decided to take our night outside so we could enjoy the warm evening.

Stopping in the kitchen to pick up the bottle of wine and two glasses that were sitting on the counter, I wandered through the lounge to the patio doors. Using my hips, I pushed through the magnetic fly screen door and on to the balcony.

Unfortunately, I immediately became hopelessly tangled in the hanging fly cover over the door. Bugger. Why was I so clumsy?

I couldn't help but laugh as I attempted to de-tangle myself from the fly screen, which had become caught round the wine bottle, but the laugh promptly died in my throat when I saw that it wasn't Allie sat waiting for me, but Jack, lounging on the sofa with his eyes shut.

Two thoughts fought for space in my brain: 'Bloody hell' and 'Holy crap'. Even looking as tired as he did, Jack Felton was seriously, *seriously* good-looking.

'Uh … hi?' My throat felt so dry that I only just

managed to speak. My brain had already jumped to the conclusion that he was here to finish things with me.

Jack seemed to wake as he heard my voice, and after opening his eyes and blinking sleepily he lifted his head with what looked like great effort and gave me a tired smile. 'Hey, you.'

Jack patted the cushion next to him, indicating that I should join him, which, if he was about to dump me, wasn't exactly where I wanted to be sitting. Seeing as the only other chairs were loungers down the far end, I put down the wine and glasses and cautiously joined him on the sofa.

It was a two-seater, and a fairly small one at that, so I found I couldn't leave much of a gap between us and I immediately felt the heat radiating from his big body. Being this close, I immediately found myself getting lost in his intoxicating smell too, clean linen and spice. Probably my favourite ever scent.

Oh man. Sitting beside him brought back to me just how attached to him I was.

He'd looked tired from across the balcony, but now I was closer I could see exactly how exhausted he was. His skin was pale and drawn, there were little purple marks under his eyes, and he had a touch of stubble gracing his jaw.

I didn't know what to say, so I sat there silently praying he would get it over with quickly so I could slink off and cry. Instead of speaking though, Jack lifted his right arm, wrapped it around my shoulders, and pulled me in close so I was practically lying on his chest. Then he rested his cheek on my hair as he snuggled me closer.

Right. Now I was confused. This wasn't the behaviour I had been expecting. He was being all cuddly, and at complete odds to the man that had barely bothered with me for the past two weeks. What on earth

263

was going on?

'It's so good to see you,' Jack mumbled into my hair, before placing several light kisses there that sent my skin tingling in all sorts of directions and my brain spiralling out of control.

'I'm sorry I've had to cancel on you so many times, Caitlin. I …' Jack paused then sighed. 'Work has been crazily busy. I … I had some unexpected night shoots to do.'

Hmm. As glad as I was that he wasn't finishing with me, something didn't add up. Sitting up so I could see his face, I drew in a short breath at his handsomeness. Even with his tiredness he appealed to me on a primal level that made my heart constrict like a tight fist in my chest.

'There weren't any night shoots on the props roster,' I murmured, and even as I said it, I knew it sounded like I had been checking up on him – which was exactly what I *had* been doing.

Jack lifted an eyebrow and smiled down at me before drawing in another huge breath. 'No, there weren't, you're quite right.' Licking his lips, Jack raised a hand and stroked my cheek before letting out a heavy sigh. 'OK, that was a lie. Truthfully, I haven't been at work quite as much as I've been making out.'

My stomach plummeted. If he hadn't been at work, then where had he been? My panicking brain could only come to one conclusion: another woman.

Jerking myself away, I frowned, and found myself crossing my arms defensively. 'Where have you been then?' I snapped, surprising myself with the sharpness of my tone.

'I didn't want you to worry, so I didn't tell you.' Pausing, he ran a hand though his hair and scrubbed at his stubble before dropping his hand into his lap. 'I … I've been trying to track down Greg.'

264

Greg?

He was looking for Greg?

'What … how … but …' I stuttered, unable to form a coherent sentence. Remembering the blade Greg had held against my skin, I shuddered, a chill flooding my veins. 'You shouldn't be endangering yourself chasing him down, the police are looking for him.'

Practically leaping from the sofa, Jack lost his usual demeanour and started pacing back and forth. 'Yeah, and a great job they've been doing. How long has it been? Three years? And he's *still* out there? Fuck, Caitlin, I'm not having you in danger one more day if I can help it.'

Jack strode to my side and dropped to his knees, immediately pulling my hands into the warmth of his grip. 'I'm sorry I shouted … I'm just tired.'

'He's seriously unstable, Jack, please let the police do their jobs,' I pleaded, gripping his hands so tightly that my knuckles turned white.

'I can't do that, Caitlin. You mean too much for me to leave it in the hands of someone else.'

I felt tears building behind my lids, and to my embarrassment, my lower lip began to tremble.

'Oh God, sweetheart, please don't cry. Come here.' Still on his knees, Jack shuffled himself closer and gently pulled me into his arms, his lips seeking mine and pressing small pecks across my face until my trembling subsided. Resting his forehead against mine, he looked into my eyes.

'Flynn is trained in tracking and surveillance. All we've been doing is looking for Greg, mostly by monitoring CCTV feeds to see if he's made an appearance near your house or the studios. It killed me being apart from you, so I stayed as close as I could.' Grinning, Jack chuckled. 'You know the black van on Sean's driveway?' I nodded, but still sat in muted silence. 'I've been inside that for most of the week, staring at a TV screen.'

'Really?' I hated how tiny and needy my voice sounded.

'Really.'

Blinking several times to erase the tears, I stared into his gorgeous brown eyes and felt myself begin to relax.

'I've been so focused on finding him that I've completely neglected you. I'm so sorry, Caitlin, please forgive me.'

His behaviour had been upsetting, but now he had explained, I couldn't hold it against him. He'd been doing it for me. To protect me. 'You don't need to apologise, Jack.'

Using a gentle grip on my chin, he lifted my gaze to his. 'Yes, I do. I should have been there for you, or at least have made more time to call you, and meet you ... but I just got ... so ... obsessed, I guess,' he confessed, looking mildly embarrassed.

'So all this time I thought you were avoiding me, but you were sitting in a van just outside,' I mumbled quietly. 'I thought you wanted to finish with me.'

'What? Why on earth did you think that? I told you how serious I am about you, Caitlin. How serious I am about *us*.' He sounded confused and I felt my stomach muscles relax as I laughed with embarrassment.

A hot flush shot up my neck as I gave a self-conscious shrug. 'I thought maybe once you'd had time to think about me being a ... a virgin, it might have put you off. I mean, I already have a shit tonne of baggage, add that to the mix and it hardly makes me an attractive package.' My voice was no more than a whisper, but Jack immediately shook his head as he maintained the grip on my chin, not allowing me to look away for even a millisecond.

He smiled, such a tender expression burning on his face that my breath caught in my lungs and my heart clenched.

'I told you that doesn't bother me,' he whispered. Suddenly, my view shifted as Jack moved like lightening to stand us up, and arranged us on the sofa so he was sitting down and I was straddling his lap.

Letting out a shriek of laughter, I steadied myself by resting my hands on his shoulders, enjoying the feel of his strong muscles underneath my fingertips.

'Quite the opposite, in fact,' he continued. 'I find the fact that your body is untouched *very* attractive … a huge turn-on.' Jack paused, running both hands gently over my clothes. His fingers trailed practically everywhere before coming to rest on my thighs as he sighed contentedly. The pleasure of his delicate touch sent a shudder through my body, and Jack smiled lazily.

'And to be frank, if I wasn't so dog-tired after filming every day and spending practically every night working with Flynn, I would lay you down right here on the deck and show you exactly how much you turn me on.' As he spoke, I began to feel through his jeans exactly what he was talking about as his erection pressed against my crotch.

Crikey. My cheeks felt like they were completely burning as an embarrassed grin spread across my face.

Jack joined our hands, interlocking the fingers and gently twirling our thumbs together. 'Are we OK?' he asked.

'Yes.' My answer came without hesitation. 'But no more secrets, OK?'

Jack nodded immediately, his hair flopping over his brow and causing me to immediately tangle my fingers through it and push it back from his face. 'Of course. I promise. I hated not telling you, but I thought you had enough on your plate as it was.'

Rolling my eyes, I frowned and chewed on my lip. 'And don't take any stupid risks. If you track him down,

I want you to promise me you'll call the police and let them deal with it.'

Jack noticeably tensed, and as I stared into his eyes, willing him to agree, I saw a tick develop in his jaw as his eyes clouded over. I understood that he wanted to avenge the things Greg had done to me in the past, but I couldn't lose him, not now that I'd finally found him.

'Caitlin …' His low tone had a touch of warning to it but I didn't let it deter me, and instantly shook my head. Wrenching my fingers from his grip, I poked at his chest. 'Feisty. I like this side of you,' he murmured, his lips tweaking with a seductive smile which I expected was supposed to distract me from the topic at hand. It was a close run thing. Jack giving me the sultry 'come hither' eyes was a pretty appealing sight, but this was way too important for me to lose focus.

'No! No, distractions or excuses, Jack. You could get hurt, and I can't stand the thought of that. Besides, if you find Greg and do something to him you could end up in prison!' My voice had gone high and panicky, so I paused to draw in a breath, swallowed hard, and lowered my eyes. 'I can't lose you, Jack. I … I need you.'

As much as I loved the connection between the two of us, I also slightly resented it because it was everything I always swore I would never be: clingy, emotional, reliant, needy … Ugh. I sounded like some limp rom-com character. Jack, however, didn't seem repelled by my pathetic confession at all. In fact, his reaction seemed quite the opposite as his hands settled on my hips before his face crumpled into a soft, sweet smile.

'Caitlin, sweetheart, you have me. Believe me, you have me.' His voice cracked a little as he leant forward and placed his lips to mine. He didn't kiss me, exactly, just joined our mouths as he closed his eyes and held me tightly.

Leaning back a touch, he spoke, his warm breath

fanning across my tingling lips. 'I'll be careful. And if we find him, I'll get the police involved. I'm not going anywhere, I promise.'

Taking in a deep breath, Jack raised his eyebrows and briefly flicked his tongue over his bottom lip. 'While we're on the subject of our relationship ... I wanted to discuss going public.'

'Going public?'

Grimacing, he nodded. 'We'll probably be spotted together pretty quickly. If we don't make some sort of statement to the press they'll make our lives hell.'

I couldn't seem to breathe quite right. My lungs were almost frozen with the idea of the world knowing my business. I'd lived the past three years so carefully hiding my every move that going to the complete opposite pole seemed like utter madness. What if Greg found out?

'No. I don't want anyone to know. Not yet.'

'No?' Jack repeated. 'I know you wanted to keep quiet in case Greg tracked you here, but he knows you're in LA. It doesn't seem a valid reason to keep quiet any more.'

I could see he was disappointed, and I hated to be the cause of that, but I just couldn't do it, not yet. 'It's not that I don't want people to know, Jack, I do ... but ... well, I can't put you at risk by being linked to you. He knows I'm in LA, but he doesn't know I'm dating you. He's totally nuts, if he finds out, he might target you. I couldn't live with myself if something happened to you.'

Jack looked like he was about to protest at my words, but running his gaze over my worried face, he paused and sighed. 'OK. We'll keep it quiet for now, but don't think I'll hold off for ever, Caitlin. I want the world to know you're mine.'

Shivering, I nodded as desire shot through my

system. Somehow knowing that he desired me that much made my lust rise like a volcanic eruption, and after sitting pressed together and breathing the same air for a few seconds, Jack locked our lips and moved beyond a simple touch to something far more heated as his tongue immediately sought access to my mouth.

'God, I've missed you,' Jack muttered, before skipping gentle and moving straight to desperate and hungry as he groaned, slid a hand around the back of my neck, and pressed his tongue into my mouth greedily, taking all that I would give. I melted into his embrace, giving just as much to the kiss as he did.

Our hands began roaming, touching each other over our clothes and getting me so worked up I found my body instinctively starting to grind against the hard bulge I could feel below me. Jack thrust his hips upwards, making me groan at just how good it felt, but then, after whipping me into enough of a frenzy that I very nearly insisted he took me to bed, he pulled back and gave me a tired smile.

'Sorry. I got a bit carried away,' he admitted sheepishly.

If he hadn't looked so knackered, I might well have attempted my own form of seduction, but he really did seem exhausted, and so when he began to help me off his lap I shifted to his side and watched as Jack opened the wine and poured two glasses.

Handing one to me, Jack sipped his before putting his glass down, moving sideways, and laying down with his head resting in my lap. The sofa was far too small for this type of position, but Jack tucked his legs around the end and balanced them on the adjacent side table in what appeared to be a comfortable position before letting out a long sigh.

Utterly relaxed, I sat with my wine in one hand and began to stroke Jack's hair. After only a minute, I heard his breathing change and deepen as he seemed to fall asleep. A smile curved my lips as I continued to play with his hair while he snoozed. It still amazed me that I could feel this relaxed with a man in my presence, so I sat blissfully absorbing the quiet time, revelling in this new development.

Staring out at the moonlit beach behind the house, I shook my head in disbelief; we were so comfortable in each other's company that it felt like we had known each other for years, and I was starting to like the feeling of togetherness very much indeed.

Jack must have dozed for about half an hour, because my glass of wine was long finished when he made a quiet humming noise in my lap and stretched an arm out. Blinking, he pushed himself up, yawned, performed an even bigger stretch, and looked across at me sleepily. 'Sorry, I didn't mean to fall asleep. It's not been the most exciting evening for you, has it? I should probably just have napped in the van instead of spoiling your night with Allie.'

My head shook of its own accord as I cupped his cheek where he had creases from sleeping. Gently rubbing the marks with my thumb, I smiled at him. 'No,' I whispered. 'I'm really glad you came in and cleared this all up. I feel so much better now.'

'Good.' Jack leant across and placed a quick kiss on my lips then gave a glance at his watch before grimacing. 'I've got to be on set in seven hours,' he groaned, flopping his head back on the sofa and closing his eyes.

Without really thinking it through, my mouth suddenly went into auto drive. 'Would you like to stay? You're tired and it will save you the drive home,' I offered, trying not to panic about what might happen if he actually said yes.

But panic I did. Oh God, what would it be like to lie

beside him in a bed, cradled in his arms?

Beside me, Jack sat up, breaking my panicked haze, and took my hands, grinning broadly. 'You're only offering because you know I'm so tired that your virtue will remain safe,' he joked, and I immediately faked an expression of shock. Deep down I knew a little bit of what he was saying was true – I *was* getting nervous about our first time.

'Cheeky!' I giggled, as a pleasant warmth spread through my body. This man made me feel so good.

'I really appreciate your offer, Cait. I'm so tired I think I could sleep standing up.'

'Well, you won't need to. Sean's spare room has a double bed, you know.' I gave him another impish grin, which seemed to make his eyes sparkle, and I stood up. 'In fact, it might even be king-size,' I pondered, as I pulled him along by the hand and led him inside.

Pausing inside the lounge, I locked the patio doors and we silently made our way through the house.

'I'm not sure I'm Allie's favourite person any more,' he murmured, casting a lopsided grin over his shoulder, which caused me to frown. 'When I arrived tonight she gave me the filthiest look I've ever seen and proceeded to lecture me about how you deserved much better than being stood up.'

Ha! I could imagine Allie laying into him! Jack's lips twitched in amusement, but then his expression changed, morphing into one of regret. 'She's right. I'm so sorry, Caitlin. I wasn't thinking straight, all I could focus on was getting you safe. I never in a million years thought you'd take my absence as an indication that I wasn't interested. You mean everything to me, Caitlin.'

My pulse was thumping so hard that I wondered if he was actually able to hear it. I didn't know what else to say, so I opted for staying mute and simply wrapping my arms around him.

'Me too. I'm so glad we met.' My words were choked and I had to swallow hard to try and prevent tears from escaping. As soon as I made contact with his firm chest, Jack made a mumbling sound in his throat and pulled me against him.

We stood like that until Jack leant back, stifling yet another yawn, and smiled at me. 'I hope you don't think I'm being too forward, but if you don't mind, would you take me to bed now?' Beneath the joking exterior I could see his smile was forced, so I nodded, led him upstairs, found him a spare toothbrush, and directed him to the en suite.

While Jack was brushing his teeth I dug under my pillow to retrieve my pyjamas. I eyed them critically before my nose wrinkled in distaste. They were comfy, but these baggy old PJs certainly weren't something I wanted to expose Jack to. Swiftly depositing them in the wash bin, I exchanged them for a dark blue nightdress that I wore when the heat was oppressive. It had thin straps, revealed a bit more breast than was probably decent, and fell to mid-thigh. It was cotton, not exactly sexy lacy lingerie, but it was pretty enough and about the best I could do. There was no way I was spending my first night in bed with a man wearing holey old PJs.

As he reappeared from the bathroom, Jack immediately paused as he narrowed his eyes and took in my scantily clad figure. I stood motionless and holding my breath as his eyes darkened and ran down my body and back up again, before releasing my breath in a rush.

His heavy-lidded gaze locked with mine, and he stalked toward me, placing his hands firmly on my hips before lowering his head and kissing me firmly on the lips. I'd have to buy more nightdresses if that was the reaction they triggered.

'God, you make it hard to breathe,' he whispered against the corner of my mouth, before kissing his way

273

down my neck and nuzzling the soft skin of my earlobe. His touch was so light, yet so confident that it immediately sent a shudder of pleasure ripping through my body, causing goose bumps to rise over my skin as my head spun with desire.

Grasping his upper arms, I giggled nervously and wobbled on my unsteady legs. 'Go to the bathroom, before I have my way with you.' He was teasing, but the air between us was thick with sexual tension, and I was fairly sure that if I lay on the bed and offered my body it wouldn't have taken much persuading to get him to join me.

Letting out a shaky breath, I licked my lips and turned towards the bathroom, which made Jack give a low growl. 'It's backless? Christ, Caitlin, you're killing me,' he groaned, before tugging me back into his arms and kissing me again, his tongue plunging into my mouth and ripping any remaining air from my lungs.

He gripped me tight as he continued with the thorough exploration of my mouth, but eventually, and reluctantly, he let me go and nudged me in the direction of the en suite.

I was in such a daze that I barely registered using the toilet or brushing my teeth. I did take a moment longer to thoroughly wash my face, though – I didn't want to wake up next to Jack in the morning with smeared make-up all over my pillow, or my face … or him, for that matter. Although there was a certain temptation in the idea of exactly how the make-up might get smeared and whereabouts on his body it might end up.

I'd never felt so wanton in my life.

I took a second to peer into the mirror. Even without make-up, my cheeks were flushed and my eyes were sparkling. Is that how a girl looked when she was preparing to lose her virginity? I wondered if I'd look different after we'd done the deed. Would I appear more experienced? More mature?

Instead of standing there like an idiot thinking about it, I decided it was time to head back to Jack and see where the night took us. I tried to suppress my nerves, knowing the most probable outcome would be that Jack would continue to be the honourable gentleman that he had been so far.

Even trusting Jack implicitly, my heart was hammering in my chest when I finally plucked up the courage to open the bathroom door and enter the bedroom again. The room was mostly in darkness, and it took my eyes a few seconds to adjust. Jack must have turned off the main lights and replaced them with one of my tiny bedside lamps, because once my eyes had recovered I noticed the room was lit with a soft, warm glow that crept across the bed and floor.

Softly shutting the door behind me, I padded over to the bed and couldn't help but smile at what I found; Jack was flat on his back and fast asleep under the covers. I watched him for a few seconds, taking in his handsome, relaxed features, and the way his hair fell carelessly across his forehead, and then slipped carefully under the sheets next to him.

As I lay back I felt my muscles slacken, and was glad that my earlier nerves were mostly dissipated. As I lay there listening to his soft breathing and smelling his lovely scent I felt a different flutter in my stomach – unreserved curiosity.

Glancing at Jack, I couldn't resist looking under the covers. Biting my lip, and knowing this was wrong, I gave the covers a quick lift, which allowed me to glance down and see his gorgeous chest. A happy sigh slipped from my lips as I took in the dusting of brown hair. Letting my eyes slip lower, I saw that Jack was just in a black pair of boxer shorts, tight enough to give me a nice view, which caused me to instantly put the blankets down. God, I couldn't believe I was perving over him while he was asleep!

With the image of his glorious body lingering in my mind, I turned off the bedside light and lay down, feeling mighty contented at my bed partner. Gathering the covers around myself, I fell asleep in no time at all with rather pleasant dreams of Jack and I rolling around my brain.

# FORTY-ONE

## CAIT

The sensation of something heavy pressing down on me woke me up. It felt like a tree branch was laying across my chest and I felt fear seeping into my sleepy mind. Why was I being held down? After another attempt to breathe only succeeded in gaining a small gasp of oxygen, my terror increased and my groggy eyes flew open.

Looking down, I saw a brown head of hair resting on my shoulder, and after a millisecond of confusion, I was then filled with rushing memories of last night and an overwhelming feeling of relief and safety. Jack! His left arm was the cause of my breathing difficulties because it was flopped casually across my chest, but given his large build the thing felt like it weighed an absolute tonne.

In actual fact, he had me pretty much pinned to the bed, because his left leg was also bent and casually laid over both of mine.

Jack Felton liked to snuggle in his sleep, who'd have guessed?

After a few more breathless seconds I decided that if I wanted to live long enough to enjoy Jack a little more, I *did* need to breathe, so I tried to adjust his arm and shift it carefully down.

At first I managed quite successfully but then he began to stir. The offending arm lifted, and he ran his fingers through his hair. Jack's eyes opened, blinked a few times, then eventually settled on me.

The way his expression changed was hilarious. He started off with a smile, but as he fully woke up and took in his sprawled position, his eyes opened wider and he began scrabbling in the blankets to push himself up.

'Oops. I must have shifted in my sleep,' he muttered, grumbling when his legs got even more tangled in the sheets.

I simply wrapped my arms around his shoulders and pulled his lovely warm body back down. 'Don't apologise, I like it,' I murmured softly, rubbing a hand over his chest and causing Jack to relax with a happy sigh and a growl that made my heart race.

After years of being so isolated from anything remotely sexual I really was quite shocked at my recent bravery. It was like Jack had managed to erase my memories and fears with his goodness.

After a few seconds of lovely cuddling, an unfamiliar noise made its presence known somewhere in the room with an annoyingly high-pitched beeping. Jack buried his face in my neck with a groan. 'I wish I didn't have to work today.'

Propping himself on his elbow, he gazed at me, his eyes working their way around my face as if committing the details to memory.

'God, you're so beautiful,' he murmured, causing my cheeks to heat. It was first thing in the morning; I hadn't brushed my hair, teeth, or washed my face. But on top of that, I wasn't used to being showered with compliments all the time, especially by a Hollywood star.

'Don't blush, it's true,' he said, smiling lazily, 'I would like nothing more than to stay in bed with you all day,' he mumbled as he placed a light kiss on my lips that caused my stomach to tumble with excitement. But before we'd got to the good stuff, his alarm went off again.

'Damn it. I'm sorry, Caitlin, I'm going to have to go.'

Caressing my cheek, he grinned. 'I slept really bloody well last night. Apparently you make an excellent pillow,' he added softly, making me chuckle and blush even redder. At this rate I'd be the colour of a beetroot by the time he left for work.

'So, in an effort to make amends for my seriously appalling behaviour I think we should spend some time together. Sound good?'

It sounded *am-az-ing*. I tried, and probably failed, to look cool as I nodded my response.

Jack slid from my arms and stood, before turning and gazing down at me. His body was stunning in the bright morning light, and my eyes were trying to take it all in so desperately that they must have looked like a marble zooming around a pin-ball machine, and even though I knew it was rude to stare, I couldn't stop myself.

'Glad you like the view,' he joked. And boy, was he right. I seriously loved the view. And the way he smelt. And the feel of him curled around me in bed. And … well, the list was pretty endless.

'Sorry,' I replied, even though I wasn't really sorry at all.

'Don't apologise, I got my own eyeful last night when I saw you in the tiny thing you call a nightdress,' Jack teased as he began slipping on his shirt. 'I'm busy all morning, then I've got a golf lesson with Sean at lunch then a few more hours at the studio, but can I see you later? Maybe we could have dinner at my place?'

He was willing to have another night off from his Greg search so he could spend time with me. Nodding happily, I struggled unsuccessfully to avoid the distracting sight of Jack bending to pick up his trousers, so I was another few notches redder by the time he dropped another kiss on my lips and donned his shoes.

'It's Saturday tomorrow and I know you're off work, so bring an overnight bag and you can stay.' Seeing my raised eyebrow, Jack smiled sheepishly. 'No funny business, I promise. I'll be more than content just to have you with me.'

'I know. I actually find it funny how hard you're trying to be honourable,' I joked.

'Well, your honour is important to me,' he fired back smoothly.

My stomach was tumbling with excitement so frantically that I pulled my pillow down and hugged it to my belly. As I did so I saw Jack's eyes narrow and then an affectionate smile curved his lips. I wondered what his look was for as he sunk down onto the mattress beside me and reached above me for something.

'Are these mine?' he questioned.

Looking at his hand, I suddenly felt my stomach drop when I realised what he'd been reaching for – his two handkerchiefs. The ones he'd given me when I was crying that I'd never returned. Oh shit. Much to my mortification he'd discovered my collection, which still resided under my pillow for some stupid reason.

'Ummm …' What could I say? The truth would make me sound like a stalker, because the reason I'd kept them was simple; I'd been so madly infatuated with him that I'd liked keeping them close.

Thankfully, Jack spotted my rising mortification, because he simply re-folded the cotton squares, placed them on my bedside table, and gave them a little pat. 'I'm glad you like them. You keep them,' he whispered.

OK, that hadn't been nearly as embarrassing as I'd expected.

'Right, I gotta go, sweetheart. I'm running late. See you later, hopefully we'll wrap up at about six.'

'OK, sounds good.' Barely stifling a yawn, I stretched out lazily under the covers.

Jack shook his head at me, clearly jealous at my chance to stay in bed. Then after blowing me a kiss he left. I heard him quietly making his way through the house and out of the front door before I allowed myself to grin and roll around in the sheets that still held his gorgeous scent.

# ALLIE

I had literally been sitting on the edge of my bed for half an hour, waiting to hear Jack leave so I could grill Cait on what had happened last night. Sean had left twenty minutes ago, and finally, one minute ago, I had heard the front door open and close again.

Not wasting a single second, I leapt up, still in my pyjamas, and dashed towards the spare room where Cait was staying.

'I'm awake!' called Cait cheerily before I'd even had a chance to knock.

'How did you know I was out there?' I asked, as I burst in to find Cait still in bed, sitting up against the headboard as she smiled ruefully at me. 'You sounded like a herd of elephants running down the corridor, it would have been pretty hard *not* to hear you.'

'Oh.' Perhaps I had been just a little keen to get here. 'So, come on, fill me in! I assume from the fact he stayed the night that things are back on track?'

I could see Cait was trying her best to look nonchalant but failing miserably; her face was lit up with excitement, her eyes twinkling with happiness.

'Yep, things are good.' She paused and grinned. 'Really good.'

Cait gave the elastic bands around her wrist a ping and I couldn't help asking the obvious.

'Did you two ... you know ... do the deed?' Cait's cheeks flushed at my question, giving the distinct impression that they might have had sex, and I found myself so thrilled by the juicy gossip that was unfolding that I could hardly stand still.

Jumping onto the bed, I flapped my hands impatiently before grabbing a pillow and hugging it to my stomach. 'Come on! Tell me, Cait!' I exclaimed desperately.

'No, we didn't sleep together … well, obviously we shared the bed, but you know what I mean, we didn't … you know … do *it*.' Cait's cheeks were bright pink now, so I suspected something more than just sleeping might have taken place.

Seeing my questioning look she grinned and dropped her head into her hands, laughing. 'This is so embarrassing!' Rubbing her face she looked up at me again. 'We kissed and we had a bit of a cuddle and a … well, we had a bit of a feel of each other, but he was really tired so that's all we did.'

I nodded thoughtfully, actually rather glad that Jack was living up to the gentleman status I'd given him.

'Is his body as nice as it looks through his clothes?' I asked, unable to help myself.

Cait almost gurgled with laughter, her cheeks blooming with so much heat I could almost feel it from where I was sitting. 'Yeah … he's pretty ripped, actually.'

Grinning, I only just supressed the urge to high five her, but decided to tone down my excitement before Cait got too overwhelmed. 'So, when are you seeing him again?'

She drew in an excited breath before licking her lips. 'Tonight, after work. I was actually just writing a text to him asking if I can go to our house today with Tanya to get some clothes. Do you want to come?'

'Definitely. It'll be good to grab a few more bits and pieces. I need some clean undies! I'll meet you there.'

After a full exchange of gossip, I left Cait to get ready for work and decided to spend the morning writing some of my much neglected novel.

# FORTY-TWO

## CAIT

It felt strange sitting outside my little rental house after so long. With both Sean and Jack insistent that Allie and I didn't endanger ourselves while Greg was still on the loose, I'd had to spend the last few weeks making do with some clothes and bits and pieces that Sean had picked up for me.

After Jack left me in bed that morning, I'd thought about our upcoming date and messaged him to persuade him to let me come back to pack a bag properly. It was only dinner at his house, but it would be nice to have my own make-up and choice of clothes. Allie would be joining me soon too, but I'd come straight from work and it seemed I'd beaten her to it.

Jack made me promise that I'd get Tanya to check the house out first. Just a few minutes later, she arrived back at the car and knocked on my window so I unlocked the door and got out. 'It's all clear inside. No evidence that anyone has been in since you left.'

Now I had the all-clear, she told me she'd wait in the car while I ran inside and grabbed my stuff. After asking Tanya to keep an eye out for Allie, I headed to the house, and I was so ridiculously happy at the prospect of getting some of my own things back I almost skipped across the car park.

Grabbing my phone, I lifted my bag onto my shoulder and decided to call Jack to thank him for arranging Tanya for me. I'd not really been thrilled to have her around at first, so I'd hardly been appreciative, but I had to admit she did make me feel so much safer.

Scrolling for his number as I walked, I couldn't help the grin that broke out on my face. I wasn't able to get him out of my head: his handsome face, the devastating grin that seemed to be able to simultaneously make me heat with warmth *and* blush with arousal, his gentle hands, his gorgeous body ... I had a feeling that soon, maybe even tonight, I was going to jump the final hurdle and sleep with him.

*Mmmm*. A shiver of pleasure ran through me, and my smile turned to a full on smirk as I imagined what it would be like.

I was a lucky girl, that was for sure.

With my phone in one hand, I slid the key into the front door and shoved it open with my hip. Stepping into the cool interior of our little house, my attention was still on my phone, but a small, muffled cry brought my gaze up and my heart seemed to come to a stop as my entire world froze.

*Greg*.

Greg was here. In my house.

But ... but Tanya had literally just said it was OK ...

What had I just been saying about being a lucky girl? I must have laid a serious jinx on myself.

My lungs felt like they were freezing up. Icy panic slithered through my system, clenching my muscles and trying to take me away from reality towards the darkness of a panic attack.

It had been my body's response to fear for so many years, as if my brain understood that it was the only way for me to cope, but I couldn't give into it today, because to my utter horror, Greg and I weren't alone in the room.

Allie was here.

The sight of her on her knees in front of Greg shot terror to my heart. She was facing me as he stood behind her with an ominously sharp blade pressed against her throat. Considering how easily panic attacks usually came to me, it was incredible how much clarity the sight gave me. Greg was my ultimate nightmare, but I needed to dig into my recently bolstered confidence and be strong, for both myself *and* Allie.

'You have a personal security guard?' Greg sneered derisively. 'Not a very good one, though, she didn't even check the coat cupboard in the downstairs toilet.'

As I stood there, my breathing seemed to completely fail me, but my eyes desperately sought Allie's.

Her blue eyes were swollen and red as tears streamed down her face, plastering her hair to her cheeks and soaking the strip of grey fabric that had been shoved between her lips as a gag, but her eyes seemed to be urging me to run as she darted constant looks towards the door.

There was no way I was leaving her. *No way.* I knew just how screwed-up Greg was. He didn't just have a few screws loose; he was barely held together, and about as unstable as they got. If I ran away to get help, then God only knows what he might do to her.

'I skipped the pleasantries, didn't I? Hello, Cait.' The snide, oily quality of his voice slid over me, making my stomach turn with disgust and causing the hairs to stand up on my arms. Fuck, fuck, *fuck* … what the hell could I do? How long would it be until Tanya thought to check on me?

'Drop the phone and keys. Right now.' His tone left little room for manoeuvre so reluctantly I put my only possible lifeline down on the table and placed my keys on top with a shaky hand.

'Lock the door behind you.'

Saying goodbye to my freedom, I clicked the lock in place as my mind raced.

'Let her go, Greg. Allie has nothing to do with this,' I

stated, totally fucking amazed that my voice sounded as rock solid as it did.

'I don't think so, *sweetheart*.' The blood in my veins chilled until I shivered. Sweetheart. He'd called me *sweetheart*. Was that a sick coincidence, or had he somehow heard Jack and I together?

I felt well and truly thrown. Pulling myself together, I schooled my features into a blank mask.

We were in a locked room with a psychotic man and his large blade. I was really struggling to see an outcome where this didn't end badly for me, but the only thing I could hope was that I could keep Allie and Jack out of it.

'Well, at least put the knife down,' I tried again, but this time a sick leer spread across his face as he shook his head, his long hair brushing around his shoulders as he did so. *Ugh*. I couldn't believe I'd ever found him and his lanky hair attractive, it looked like hundreds of slimy rats tails.

'Nah.' He twirled the knife with skill before placing it back against Allie's reddened skin. 'This might be your house, but we play by my rules.' My stomach plummeted and Allie's breathing audibly increased until she was panting through the gag.

Greg seemed to notice her distress too, as if he'd suddenly remembered she was in the room, and with a sneer he lowered his head next to her ear and whispered, 'If you scream, I'll slice you.' Then he slid the gag from her mouth.

Allie stared at me, her tears dry for the moment while she sucked in deep breaths and gave me a helpless 'what the hell are we going to do' look.

I had no fucking idea.

Where the hell was Tanya?

Whichever way I looked at it, there seemed to be only one way out of this, and it wasn't going to be pleasant. It was time to suck it up and be brave. He wanted me.

Sucking in a deep breath, I said the words I'd never thought I'd say. 'I'm here now. You can do what you want to me, Greg, but let Allie go.'

Greg's eye's visibly dilated, his ego almost becoming tangible as his chest puffed up and his shoulders straightened. 'Nice offer, but no deal.' His piggy eyes trailed down the length of me and back up before he licked his lips.

'But I'm glad to see you offering yourself to me. Not that you needed to bother, you should already know. You're mine, Cait. You've always been mine.' His words held a clarity, and I struggled for breath as his eyes pierced into me from across the room. After three years, he really believed that I was his?

'Come a little closer.' His instruction was low, but all I could think was that it took me further away from the door and the slim chance of escape.

'Have you been good these past three years? Mmm?' Keeping the blade pressed to Allie's neck, he raised his free hand and caressed my cheek. The feel of his cool fingers on my skin made me shudder, but I did my best to mask it. 'I tried to keep an eye on you, but you made it very difficult. You always did like to play hard to get.'

I didn't know what to do. My obvious reaction was to scream and flail, but the blade in his hand held me back. Should I fake feelings? Was he nutty enough to believe me?

'I ... I've been good.' Now I was closer I could smell the same aftershave he used all those years ago and my confidence began failing as my throat tightened with the rush of terrifying memories.

'Really?' He looked intrigued, and I nodded jerkily. 'What about the guy who interrupted us? Mr Glamour-Boy and his fancy car?' I desperately fought to keep my features blank. 'That's right, Cait. I've been watching you. He's been touching you, I saw him.'

290

Greg leaned in close, his movement pressing the blade more firmly against Allie's neck and causing her to let out a terrified squeak. Greg didn't seem to notice and I panicked that he really didn't even acknowledge that she was there. 'Touching what was *mine*.'

'We're just friends.'

His eyes narrowed. 'Is it just him? Or have you let other men touch you, *sweetheart*?' He drew in a breath that flared his nostrils. 'How many men have you fucked when you should have been fucking me?'

I could barely breathe. A cold trickle of sweat ran down my neck and onto my spine as I tried to formulate an answer that would please him. Before I could even speak Allie wriggled below us, drawing our attention.

'She hasn't slept with anyone, you fucker!' she spat viciously. 'You left her too screwed up!'

My entire body tensed, sure that Greg was going to punish her for her anger, but instead, her words drew the opposite reaction.

He looked … *thrilled*.

'Is she telling the truth?' he demanded, his demeanour completely changing before my eyes as his jaw slackened and eyes widened. 'Have you really saved yourself? *For me*?' Christ, he really was deluded. In a twisted way he was partly right – I hadn't slept with anyone because the memories of him had been too horrific. I certainly hadn't been saving myself for him, though, but it was just possible I could use this to my advantage, and so I chewed my lip, trying to look contrite and shy and then nodded slowly. 'Yes.'

'You're still a virgin?' he asked in a shocked whisper, causing me to nod again as my cheeks bloomed with an instinctive blush.

The room filled with a tense silence. Allie was still on her knees, and Greg was staring at me as if trying to look through my skin and see if my hymen really was still intact.

'Let Allie go, then you and I can go upstairs, just the two of us. If you want?' I asked, trying to make my offer sound inviting, even though the very thought of him touching me was almost enough to make me vomit. I was willing to go through with it, though, if it meant saving Allie.

For a few moments, I thought Greg was about to agree – his grip on the blade visibly loosened, and he momentarily let go of Allie's shoulder.

'I won't fight you, I promise,' I declared, knowing full well that as soon as that knife was away from Allie's skin I would be fighting tooth and nail. I should have kept my mouth shut, because my words seemed to snap him out of his reverie and he looked at me with an evil glint in his eye.

Fuck.

'As tempting as that sounds, I think we'll keep Allie here. Now get undressed,' he ordered, his wide-eyed look gone, replaced with nothing but malicious intent. Fuck, fuck, fuck.

Frozen to the spot, I couldn't do it. My body was like a lump of rock, ignoring all commands.

'Now, Cait. Strip those clothes off that gorgeous body of yours.'

'Leave her the fuck alone!' Allie sobbed, but neither Greg nor I looked down.

All my fight left in a rush and I felt like a wreck. 'Please, Greg, not like this. I … I can't …' My voice was pleading and pathetic, but it didn't impact Greg at all. Instead, he calmly put the gag back into Allie's mouth and flashed me a grin.

'Try harder.'

Unclenching my hands, I stuttered out a breath and felt a tear escape from my eye as my useless body continued to fail. Now that I was faced with my

292

imminent de-flowering at the hands of a man I despised, I really, *really* wished I'd slept with Jack. At least then my first time would have been with a man I loved.

'I thought you might be a touch reluctant. Now, here's what's what's going to happen. I'm going to fuck you,' he paused and grinned again. 'And you can either make it easy for me, or fight me.'

The adrenaline rushing through my system told me I would be fighting all the way, something Greg must have picked up on, because he smirked and threw his head back and cackled. Then, as I watched helplessly, he raised the blade in his hand and swiped it near Allie's scalp, causing her to flinch and squeal behind her gag.

At least I had *thought* it was above her head, but to my horror I watched as a bright red stripe of blood suddenly escaped from her hairline and began to run across her forehead.

Holy fuck, he'd cut her? I dived forwards to protect my friend, a scream tearing from my chest, but he raised the blade to her throat and pressed it to her skin, sneering as spittle collected at the corners of his mouth.

I froze mid step, his threat enough to make me instantly hold my hands up. My eyes made the trip back down to Allie's face and I swallowed loudly.

Oh. My. God.

Blood. There was so much blood.

He'd actually cut her.

And pretty badly, judging by the quantity of blood now dripping from her eyebrows. Immediately I began to desperately pull at the buttons of my shirt. 'OK! OK! Please don't hurt her, I'll do it.' My fingers were so shaky I could barely undress and I ended up grabbing the collar and ripping my shirt open in frustration before I chucked it off and threw to the floor in despairing panic.

'Thank you, Cait.' He sounded so calm, as if I'd just

offered him tea and biscuits. His greedy eyes travelled to my bra and I cringed and watched with growing dread as he bit on his lip and let out a lusty growl. 'You always did have lovely tits. A little on the small side, but fucking lovely none the less.'

Allie was bleeding, I was shit scared, but he sounded like there was not a care in the world. He was way, way more deranged than I'd ever thought.

'This first cut here,' Greg explained as he paused and pointed to Allie's bleeding scalp, 'is nothing, really. Head wounds bleed excessively but it's not life threatening.'

My blood was pounding in my ears.

'Allie's survival will completely depend upon you, Cait,' he stated, a look of confidence crossing his sharp features.

'But … but you said that cut wasn't life threatening …' I stuttered as I fumbled with the button for my jeans.

'It's not,' he confirmed. 'But you're a fighter, so I plan to use Allie as my insurance policy. Sorry, Allie, you were just in the right place at the wrong time.'

His hand moved in a blur and before I could even let out a scream, he had plunged the blade into Allie's side. My whole body erupted to throw myself forward, but I held back. Allie screamed behind her gag, her eyes widening with terror as blood instantly bloomed on her white T-shirt.

My head was thumping and the room around me began to spin. This was a nightmare. It had to be. My vision went hazy, and I would have liked nothing more than to float into unconsciousness, but I forced myself to stay conscious for Allie's sake.

'Now *that* wound will bleed like a bastard,' Greg stated smugly, watching as the side of her T-shirt quickly became saturated with crimson. 'It's a shame her hands are tied, because someone *really* needs to stem the blood flow.'

'Please … Greg, don't do this. Help her,' I begged, the words falling from my tongue.

'If you make things easy for me, I'll let you see to her wound after we're done with round one.' *Round one?* I didn't care about myself, or my long-held virginity any more. He could fuck me a hundred times as long as Allie survived.

'Tell you what. If you make it good for me, I'll suture her cut myself. But if you struggle?' He gave a casual shrug. 'If you struggle, she'll probably bleed out while I'm still burying my cock inside you.'

White lights were flashing before my eyes as I desperately tried to steady my shaking limbs and rip my remaining clothes from my body. Even as I undressed I couldn't tear my eyes away from my best friend. She was slumped sideways, moaning in her throat, and the blood had started to soak into her jean shorts.

She couldn't die, not because of me.

My skin bore scratch marks where I had urgently disrobed, but finally I was naked, and I looked Greg in the eye and stepped towards him, desperate to get it over with.

'I'll be good, Greg, I swear to God. I won't fight you.'

Greg cast a gloating look at Allie and reached out and caressed my cheek again. 'I know you won't, *sweetheart*. Now lie down and spread those legs so I can finally claim what's mine.'

# FORTY-THREE

## JACK

Sean was getting better and better at this, and it was starting to put me to shame. Watching as he selected his club and set another golf ball upon the tee, I crossed my arms, trying not to look as if his increase in skill bothered me. But it secretly did.

I'd been playing since I was six, had numerous lessons throughout the years, and even managed to win the odd amateur tournament. *I* was the one who had introduced him to golf in the first place. It stood to reason that I should be better than him. But I wasn't, not any more.

Flynn gave me a nudge in the ribs and I glanced across to see him watching me carefully. 'Got a bit of the green-eyed monster?' he remarked.

'Mmm. A touch, perhaps.' I aimed for nonchalant, but probably came off as prickly. 'Looks like he could beat us both,' I added, trying not to let my ire show.

'Yep,' Flynn agreed amiably, 'although I've only started playing this idiotic game since I've been working with you, so I don't put in half as much effort as you do.'

Nice. Leave it to Flynn to further batter my ego.

Sean swung his club, connected with the ball, and sent it sailing off into the distance in a near perfect straight line. Bastard. My tee shots always went to the left, no matter what I did.

'Pretty good, huh?' Sean enquired with a cocky grin.

'Yeah. Not bad,' I conceded, packing my clubs away.

'I told Allie I'd meet her after golf, but do you wanna grab a coffee before we head off?'

'Yeah, sounds good,' I agreed. 'I'm meeting Caitlin tonight. Before you know it we'll be going on double dates.' We were sharing a laugh when my phone vibrated in my pocket. Pulling it out, I saw Caitlin's name and grinned. 'Speak of the devil.'

'Did you know you blush like a little girl whenever she calls?' Sean teased, before Flynn released a snort.

'Yeah, yeah. I'm under the thumb too, I get it.'

Clicking the screen to accept her call, I raised it to my ear. 'Hey, sweetheart.' There was no reply. 'Caitlin?' I tried, but after listening for a few seconds I shrugged and checked the screen to see if the call was active. 'Huh. She must have pocket dialled me.'

'Happens to me all the time. I always forget to lock the screen,' Sean said as he packed his golf clubs away and pulled off his glove.

Lifting the phone to my ear to check once more, I heard voices, but they were faint.

*'Drop the phone and keys, right now. Lock the door behind you.'* There were some muffled noises and the sound of some keys rattling.

Shaking my head, I drew the attention of Sean and Flynn. 'This is a really weird call, there's a man's voice. Listen to this,' I murmured, putting the phone on speaker.

Sean smirked. 'A man's voice on Cait's phone? You sure she hasn't got another guy on the go?' he teased. I couldn't even muster a laugh, because a strange, sickening feeling was forming in my stomach. Sean must have sensed my unease because the smile dropped from his lips and he leant in closer.

Suddenly Caitlin's voice came over the line. *'Let her go, Greg.'*

Greg? That fucker was there? I *knew* I had recognised

297

that voice. 'Fuck! She's with Greg!'

Caitlin's voice interrupted my rising panic as she spoke again, *'Allie has nothing to do with this.'*

Allie was there?

'We need to move, right now! Flynn, call the police!' Sean yelled as he threw his hands up into his hair.

'Wait! Flynn, call the police but keep them on hold, we need to know where they are before we go careening off. Call Tanya too and find out what the hell is happening.'

'Fuck waiting! Let's go to the studio! That's where he was last time!' Sean yelled, his impatience drawing the attention of several other nearby golfers.

'Cait had work today then she was going to get some stuff from their house but I'm not sure when, so they could be at the studios, your house, or their old place. Just listen for a second, please,' I implored him, desperately trying to listen for any noise or sound that would give me their location.

Flynn stepped away to make his calls just as Lambert's lecherous, vile voice came over the line again. *'I don't think so, sweetheart.'* My stomach roiled. That was *my* nickname for *my* girlfriend. How fucking dare he.

*'Well, at least put the knife down.'*

'Knife?! Jesus Christ!' Sean expelled.

My ears were ringing with every second that passed, but I kept my cool until finally Lambert gave me what I needed. *'Nah. This might be your house, but today we play by my rules.'*

'He's at their house, move!' The three of us deserted our golf clubs and started sprinting for the exit like there was a tsunami on our tail. It must have looked like a scene from a movie as we all leapt over golf bags, threw people aside, and yelled to clear the pathway. As we reached the car, Flynn had his mobile pressed to his ear as he ordered police and an ambulance to Caitlin's house, so I jumped in the driver's seat and gunned the motor.

My phone was still on speaker, and through the receiver I heard Caitlin's voice again. *'I'm here now, you can do what you want to me, Greg, but let Allie go.'* Oh God. My brave, beautiful girl was offering herself up in return for her friend's safety. It was exactly what I knew she would have done, but I couldn't help the dread rising up in an attempt to drown me.

'Tanya? What the fuck are you playing at? Cait and Allie are inside with Lambert! I don't give a fuck how it happened, we're one minute out, go around back and await my call,' Flynn grated though clenched teeth, pocketing his phone.

My reflection in the rear-view mirror was one of barely concealed desperation. Thank God Flynn was here, sitting beside me holding his gun with a look of grim determination on his face.

Hold on, Caitlin. I'm coming for you, sweetheart.

# FORTY-FOUR

## SEAN

The drive from the golf range to Studio City felt like an absolute age. We'd only been in the car nine minutes, and we were nearly there, but nine minutes was a long fucking time when you knew the woman you loved was in a room with an armed maniac.

Drawing in several deep breaths, I cursed myself again. I was supposed to have had lunch with Allie at twelve, but I'd delayed it so I could get my golf lesson in. I should have been with her. I wasn't, and now Greg had her and Cait at knife point.

I should have been there, but I wasn't – it was my history with Elena repeating itself.

If anything happened to Allie, I would never forgive myself.

Visions swum in my mind and I felt my grip on reality fading as a panic attack reared up on me, sucking me in with its cloying, inky darkness. My breathing altered to short, sharp pants as I struggled to get the oxygen I needed and I clawed at the leather seat.

No. *No*. I needed to pull myself together right fucking now. For Allie's sake. My girl was going to need me to be firing on all cylinders when we arrived, so that's what I'd do. Straightening my back, I felt my anxious adrenaline turning into a more constructive fuel, one that tightened my muscles and had my fists clenching in my lap. That was much better.

Flynn had called ahead to gate security and informed

them that there was an emergency, so when we arrived just a few seconds later the gates were open, allowing Jack to careen straight into the compound, tearing up several neat gravel paths as he went off-road and cut two corners to get to the girls' house in the quickest possible time. We'd calm any angry gardeners with a reimbursement later.

There was a compound security guy running up to the house as we arrived, but no police cars in sight, so we must have been first to arrive on the scene. The three of us shot from the car in a mass of pumped muscles and barely contained fury, but just before we reached the front door, Flynn held up a hand to stop us, indicating for the compound security man to join us. 'Wait! If he's armed and we burst in, he could injure one of the girls by mistake. I told Tanya to check the back entrance and wait for my call, you, go around and back her up,' he ordered the campus security. 'The rest of us will go in through the front. The curtains are drawn, but check if you can see anything through the gap.'

Jack and I crept to the front window and tried to peer through. My vision was blocked by the handle of the window, but Jack, crouched below, must have seen something because the next second he erupted, shooting from his crouched position and slamming his massive body into the door with a guttural roar.

Holy fuck. I strained to look inside, and finally caught a glimpse. Caitlin was on the floor, and a man was pinning her down as he writhed on top of her. Jesus Christ. As Jack exploded at the door again, I watched Greg look up with fury on his face as he began to stand, and as he moved I saw what had been hidden behind him.

Allie. Oh my God, Allie. Her body was slumped in a pile in the corner. She was covered in so much blood she was hardly recognisable.

He'd killed her.

Sense went out of the window as a red mist rose before my eyes and I threw Flynn aside to join Jack at the door, slamming myself against it in time with his shoulder barges. First the frame began to give way, then the door shifted, and finally, the door, frame, and several huge lumps of plaster went crashing inwards in a cloud of dust, allowing the three of us clambered inside.

'He went out the back door!' Cait screamed, causing Flynn to sprint away in pursuit. I couldn't think of anything except Allie, but as I flew across the room I found Cait already there, crouched beside my girl and pressing her tiny hands to the blood-soaked fabric at Allie's side.

Oh God. She looked dead, like a lifeless doll. Some sick, blood-covered image from a horror movie. Her hair was strewn across her face, but there was so much blood it almost looked red.

She couldn't be dead. I couldn't lose her. She was so important to me that I couldn't imagine how I would go on without her. Lifting a trembling hand, I pressed two fingers to her neck to check for a pulse, but her skin was so slick with blood that my fingers kept slipping.

If it weren't for all the blood she could almost be asleep. My panic was rising at my inability to find a pulse, when I suddenly felt a flicker. Struggling with the slippery skin, I finally honed in on a beat.

She was alive! Thank fuck. I could barely believe it, but it was definitely there, a faint but steady pulse.

'Get an ambulance, now!' Caitlin yelped.

'We already called one, but I just checked their ETA and they're one minute away,' Jack said, as he threw down his phone onto the sofa and came to kneel beside us, gently working on the rope that had Allie's hands tied behind her back.

One minute. Thank God.

'Sean, help me. We need to put pressure on the wound,' Cait begged.

Tearing my T-shirt off I wadded it into a ball and took over from Cait, pressing firmly onto Allie's side and leaning down low.

'Allie? Baby? I'm here, my gorgeous girl. The ambulance is on its way. We're gonna get you all fixed up.' She might not have heard the words, but I needed to say them for my own sanity. She had to be OK. She had to be.

# FORTY-FIVE

## CAIT

As I'd lain compliantly below Greg, waiting in dread, I had never in a million years thought I'd escape from him for a second time. Before he'd even had time to take his boxers off, there was a squealing noise outside and just moments later a thunderous bellow of rage before something huge hit the door.

It was so loud that it sounded like a battering ram trying to force its way in, then the entire room shook as a second blow landed and I heard a voice that had my heart squeezing. Jack.

Jack was here. And doing his best impression of a bulldozer against our door.

Just knowing he was the other side of the door filled me with hope, and I began to fight like a hellcat, shoving Greg and slapping at his face as he jumped to his feet and tugged his trousers up with a curse. Another slam came to the door, this time with another male voice screaming alongside, and with one hatred-filled glance Greg spat at me and ran out towards the back.

The door began to give way, so I quickly crawled over to Allie.

Fuck, fuck, fuck. I hardly knew where to start. I focused my attention on her side and pressed my hands to where I could see the blood bubbling through a rip in her shirt.

Allie mumbled as the door behind us crashed open, but I barely even flinched as wood splintered and chaos erupted around me.

Within seconds, Jack, Sean, and Flynn were inside. 'He went out the back door!' I watched as Flynn dashed in that direction with a gun in his hand, and couldn't help but hope he caught up with him. After what he'd done to Allie, I wanted Greg to hurt.

'Get an ambulance, now!' I begged.

I felt a warm hand land on my shoulder and immediately drew some strength from Jack's closeness. 'We'd already called one, but I just checked their ETA, they're one minute away,' Jack murmured before kneeling down beside me and untying Allie's hands.

Sean looked completely stricken, but I couldn't do this alone, so I urged him to assist me, hoping that giving him a task might stop him falling into one of the panic attacks that I knew he was prone to. 'Sean, help me, we need to put pressure on the wound.'

He immediately peeled his T-shirt over his head and used it as a pad to help stem the flow of blood, which would be far more effective than my hands had been. As soon as he was in control of her bleeding I collapsed backwards onto my arse as my entire body began to shake.

I wanted to be strong, but as I stared at my blood-coated hands I started to cry uncontrollably, my body jerking with the huge sobs.

Big, fat tears rolled down my nose and cheeks and began to drip onto my breasts. It was only when I felt the warm drops run across my chest that it occurred to me that I was completely naked in front of not only Jack, but Sean too. As I looked at Allie's bloodied body and heard Sean whispering to her, I realised I didn't even care.

Jack, however, did, because I felt some material being draped across my shoulders and buttoned up at the front of my neck. He'd covered me in his shirt and proceeded to drag me into his lap as I clung to him like he was a life jacket. Which he was. He'd saved me from the unthinkable.

Jack leant down close to my ear. 'Are you OK, sweetheart?'

Instinctively, I nodded, because really, when compared to Allie, I was OK. Physically, at least. Mentally, I felt a million types of fucked up.

'How did you know?' I asked, immeasurably thankful but surprised nonetheless.

'You pocket called me. I could hear Greg in the background.' Jack grated.

'Oh … I was going to call you. I guess I must have pressed dial by mistake.'

'Thank God you did,' Jack breathed, clutching me a little tighter. Thank God indeed.

Jack placed a kiss on my temple, and it was as his lips quivered against my skin that I realised he was shaking all over.

'Did he …' Jack paused, unable to continue until he rested his forehead into my hair. 'Did he … hurt you, Caitlin?' I could understand his hesitation – 'rape' wasn't a word that flowed easily from my tongue either.

'No. You got here just in time,' I whispered, thoughts of Allie at the forefront of my mind.

'Really?' he breathed. 'You can tell me, Caitlin.'

'Honestly, Jack. You got here in time. I swear. Thank you. Thank you, so much. You saved me.'

Jack's arms squeezed me closer, and then, in a voice so soft I barely heard it, he whispered into my hair, 'I love you, Caitlin.'

He loved me. I could barely comprehend it. I loved him too but I was too overwhelmed to reply, and simply proceeded to cry against his warmth with massive, jerky sobs.

After crying until Jack's chest had been slick below my

cheek I pulled myself together and existed in a blur of flashing lights, uniforms, and endless questions as the time passed at a surreal, warped pace. It seemed to drag, but fly by at the same time.

It felt so unreal.

In amongst the chaos, one thing stuck in my mind – Greg had got away. Flynn had informed us that after a tussle with Greg, Tanya had been knocked unconscious on the back porch and Greg was gone. The compound security guy had given chase but lost him once they hit the parkland behind the complex. Flynn had then disappeared after murmuring to Jack that he was going to 'put out some more feelers amongst his contacts', whatever the hell that meant.

The paramedics then arrived, rushing Allie and Sean to hospital while Jack and I sat with the police for what seemed like an eternity. The forensic officers took swabs from my skin and under my nails, and even managed to get a spittle sample from my hair from where Greg had spat at me as he'd left.

After I refused a check-up at the hospital they finally left, thanking me for being so strong, telling me they'd arrange an escort to ensure my safety, and assuring me that they'd be in touch.

Apparently the police escort would be more visible than Tanya, sticking with me whenever I wasn't with Jack.

Apart from my initial tears I hadn't allowed myself time to fall apart. Once the police had left I'd refused the shower Jack offered me, and dragged on my clothes so we could get to the hospital as quickly as possible to see Allie. In my rush, I had dressed before washing my hands, which had led to smears of my best friend's blood staining my clothes, but ignoring them with a grimace, I'd dashed from the house.

So here we were – two film stars and me, my best friend's blood engrained under my fingernails. Jack looked ridiculous in one of my hoodies because his shirt was covered in blood. Sean was holding on tightly to Allie's hand – and miraculously, Allie was awake and smiling. Albeit weakly.

To my shock, the doctor had informed us that both of Allie's injuries had been relatively harmless. They'd bled a hell of a lot, which could have caused serious complications if she hadn't been treated so quickly, but as it was, there was no damage to any vital organs.

It was either miraculous or Greg had been scarily precise with that blade of his. I wasn't sure I really wanted to think too long about how he'd got those skills or where he'd practiced them.

'But you were unconscious, surely that hints at quite extreme blood loss?' I pressed her, wondering if Allie was just making out she was alright for my benefit.

Allie gave a small chuckle. 'Actually, that was from the sight of the blood. I've always hated it, you must remember? There seemed so much of it and it made me light-headed. Then I must have passed out.'

It had been a hellish day, but *somehow*, it seemed both Allie and I had got off lightly when compared to what might have been.

I'd wanted to stay longer with Allie, but after we'd sat with her for an hour she'd insisted Jack and I leave so she could get some rest and spend some time with Sean.

As we walked out to the car, Jack insisted that I stay with him until Greg was caught. I couldn't think of anywhere I'd rather be.

# FORTY-SIX

## ALLIE

Once Cait and Jack had said their goodbyes, I gingerly set about shifting myself across the bed. It wasn't ladylike and it wasn't graceful, and my struggling immediately caused Sean to leap to his feet. 'Woah! Take it easy! Are you uncomfortable?'

'Yes,' I murmured, still gingerly moving myself to the left inch by inch.

'Careful, you'll hurt yourself. What can I do to help?' he enquired, hovering around me and faffing with my blankets. Bless him. I'm not sure I'd ever seen him so flustered.

'You can get in here and hold me,' I informed him, patting the space I'd now made. I was feeling decidedly needy.

'W … what?' he spluttered, as he gawked at me. It wasn't a look he could pull off very attractively.

'I'm not in pain,' I promised, which was true – the super strong pain meds were seeing to that. 'But I'm uncomfortable because you're too far away.'

'But I don't want to hurt you.'

'You won't. I promise to tell you if I get sore.'

Sean made a noise in his throat, and it immediately struck me as being almost exactly the same humming he would utter when in the midst of love making. The thought didn't help to lower my pulse rate one bit.

'OK … but only if you lie still. We can just hold hands. I don't want you to reopen the stitches.'

'Deal,' I agreed, giving his hand an impatient tug. Sean began to kick his shoes off before climbing up onto the bed. He was wearing some pale blue hospital scrubs the nurses had gifted him with when they'd seen the blood-covered state of his clothes, so he rustled every time he moved. At least I wouldn't lose him if the lights went out.

Sliding carefully beside me, Sean rolled onto his side so he was facing me and pressed himself against me as much as possible. Finally he reconnected our hand hold and let out a long, heavy sigh.

Ever since I'd become conscious and found Sean with me in the back of an ambulance while silent tears wet his cheeks, there had been an unspoken urgency for contact. In fact, until the moment he'd climbed on my bed I don't think we'd actually broken our touch once. Even when the doctors had been working on me and patching me up he'd been there, gripping my hand.

'Did ... did you and Jack get there in time to stop Greg?' I asked hesitantly. I'd wanted to ask Cait but been too scared to find out the answer. I had a vague recollection of Sean whispering to me when I was bleeding on the floor, but the last thing I properly remembered was Cait being naked and Greg demanding she lie down. I'd felt so helpless.

'Yeah, she said he hadn't managed to ... *you know* ...'

Thank God for that.

'I love you, Sean. So bloody much,' I gushed, unable to hold the words back a second longer. I guess it was the whole 'life flashing before my eyes' thing, which had made me so desperate to tell him and had solidified what I had already known, which was that Sean was the single most important thing in my life.

'I'm so, so sorry, Allie,' Sean blurted, burying his head in my shoulder.

'What on earth for?' I asked.

'I should have been there for you.' His words were choked, and I couldn't see his eyes but I would have placed money on the fact that he was crying. 'I delayed our lunch … I should have been there.'

'Don't you dare apologise, Sean!'

Sean didn't raise his head so I persevered, desperate to make him see that he hadn't let me down. 'Just when I felt so weak that I could give up, I heard you whispering to me. Hearing your voice kept me strong. You saved me, Sean.'

Finally his head began to rise, and we sat staring at each other for what seemed like an eternity. 'When I looked through that window and saw you … there was so much blood …' Sean gruffly cleared his throat. 'I thought you were …' This time he scrunched up his eyes and I watched as a lone tear escaped and ran down his cheek. '… I've never been so terrified in my life.'

Nodding, I wiped his tear away and placed a chaste kiss on his lips as several tears slipped from my own eyes. I'd thought I was going to die. Swallowing hard, it was almost impossible to distract myself from the myriad of images in my mind.

'Marry me.'

Wait … That certainly distracted me. Did he just ask me to marry him? He'd spoken against my lips, but I was pretty sure I'd heard them correctly.

'Did you just ask me to marry you?'

Sean was now staring at me with complete determination on his face. 'I did. Not because of what happened, but because you're the most important thing that has ever happened to me, Allie, and I don't want to live one more day without you being properly mine.'

'Yes!' I squealed. He said he wasn't asking because of today's events, but I was answering because of them. Yesterday, if he'd asked me, I'd have been hesitant, but

312

after genuinely thinking I was going to die my life had taken on new focus.

Life was precious, so every moment was to be treasured, I could see that now. Sean was the most amazing man I'd ever met, and I wanted to spend my moments with him. I couldn't think of one reason why I wouldn't want to be married to him.

'Yes? Really?' Sean was sitting up on the bed now, clutching one of my hands and grinning like an idiot.

'Yes,' I replied. 'I love you, Sean.'

'I love you too,' he replied, his face moving closer to mine. 'But can we keep this between you and me until I've spoken to your dad?'

'You're going to ask his permission to have my hand in marriage?' I asked in surprise.

He looked embarrassed, his cheeks reddening as he gave a shy shrug. 'I thought it would be a nice gesture, seeing as I haven't really met them properly yet.'

I instantly agreed, even though I knew keeping it from Cait would kill me.

'The future Mrs Phillips,' Sean murmured, gently stroking his knuckles across my cheek. 'I really like the sound of that,' he murmured, and I had to say, I really liked the sound of it too. From the smug grin on his face, I fully expected to hear that title a lot from Sean in the near future, but the look left his face a second later as he sealed our engagement with a scorching kiss.

# FORTY-SEVEN

## JACK

Pulling up outside my house, I hopped from the car and hurried around to open the passenger door for Caitlin. My teeth ground together as my eyes settled briefly on her bloody clothes, before I reached up a hand to help her out of the high seat and to the safety of solid land. As she descended from the cab she stumbled slightly and I pulled her against my chest.

We stood like that for several seconds, both content to absorb the warmth and protection that the other had to offer.

I ushered Caitlin inside, closed the door, and sent a text to Flynn to let him know we were home and locked up for the night. I knew he'd be working the perimeter with the extra security guys, but I doubled locked and bolted the door just the same.

Turning, I found Caitlin stood in the centre of my lounge. Seeing her in my space immediately felt right, and regardless of the shitty circumstances I was relishing the idea of having her here with me for a while.

'I'll give you a tour later, but do you want to jump straight in the shower first?' I was very aware of the fact that Caitlin would want to wash away any lingering memories of Greg's touch, not to mention the blood stains.

Caitlin wrapped her arms around herself and nodded. 'That sounds great.'

Leading Caitlin upstairs, I avoided the guest

bedrooms and took her straight towards my room. It had the biggest en suite in the house. I was secretly hoping she'd be happy to sleep in here tonight too, that way I could keep an eye on her, and get to have her close.

Grabbing some fresh towels, I showed her how to operate my shower and left her to it. 'I'll be out here if you need me.'

Pulling the bathroom door shut, I immediately set about peeling off my jeans before chucking them aside. When I'd knelt beside Allie, the legs had soaked up a fair amount of blood and I grimaced when I saw my skin was also stained with red.

What a day. It had been like some horrific movie, except instead of fake blood and special effects, it had all been real. Too real. Blowing out a long breath, I tilted my head back to the ceiling as I struggled to control my emotions.

'Jack?'

As soon as I heard Caitlin's tentative call, I rushed back into the bathroom to check on her. Caitlin was now undressed and wrapped in a towel, the straps of her bra visible on her shoulders to indicate she was still wearing underwear.

It was the expression on her face which caused me to stop in my tracks. She was smiling, and for all appearances seemed to be feeling ... playful. Was I misreading it? Weariness, sadness, or fear I might have expected, but she had a definite twinkle in her eye.

'I ... uhh, I was hoping you'd help me in the shower. I strained my shoulder today and it's a bit stiff.'

'Your shoulder?' I queried, had Greg hurt her? Reeling in my anger towards Lambert and levelling my voice, I gently reached out to touch her. 'Is it sore?'

'It's OK, but washing my hair might be a bit tricky.'

My throat suddenly felt tight when I considered the idea of sharing a shower with Caitlin. I needed to get a grip, but this was going to severely challenge my self-control. Swallowing hard, I nodded. 'Of course.'

Caitlin nodded her thanks jerkily, stepping to the shower, and then facing away from me she hung her towel up on the hook beside it.

My eyes couldn't help doing a quick sweep of her back profile as she stepped inside and turned on the water and my pulse jumped in response.

Pulling off my jumper, I dumped it in the wash basket and joined her, deciding to follow her lead and keep my boxers on. Not that the thin cotton was going to hide how my cock had begun to thicken, but at least it gave some kind of barrier.

Caitlin was still facing away from me, letting the main jet spray on her face, so couldn't see how hard I was battling with my arousal. After Greg's attack the last thing I wanted to do was scare her with my raging hard-on, but we were in the shower together, and there was no way my body could not react to the sight of her soaping herself. Gathering my resolve, I smoothed her hair down her back, picked up my shampoo, and began to gently work it into her scalp. Caitlin braced herself on the wall as I worked, leaning her head into my touch and making several throaty moans that didn't help my arousal in the slightest.

Once her hair was washed and rinsed, I set about carefully soaping her shoulders, arms, and back, although I avoided the lower part where she disliked contact. Even with the water raining down on us, she had one or two places where I could see lingering smears of blood. I set about washing her, trying my best to focus on getting her clean instead of absorbing how soft and perfect her skin was, or looking at how her cotton knickers had now turned see-through and were clinging to her amazing arse.

'Would you help me undo my bra, please?'

The desperate moan I made in response must have been audible to Cait, but she didn't react, so I complied and undid her bra before carefully slipping it from her shoulders. It fell to the floor and Caitlin began soaping herself and cleaning her body.

The knowledge that she was massaging my body wash into her breasts had me as hard as I could ever remember being in my entire life. Glancing down, I rolled my eyes at the sight of my shorts, which were now struggling to cover my straining erection.

I tried to distract myself by thoroughly washing my body, but it didn't help my arousal one bit, because bending to clean my legs just brought me closer to Caitlin's heated skin.

Leaning back on the shower wall, I closed my eyes and drew in several long breaths. 'Can I tell you a secret, Jack?' Caitlin's words brought me back to reality, and after swallowing yet another giant lump in my throat I nodded.

'Of course. You can tell me anything, Caitlin.'

'I ... I told a little fib. I haven't hurt my shoulder, I ... just wanted you in here with me.' Caitlin turned towards me, her hands covering her breasts and her bottom lip firmly between her teeth as she watched me anxiously.

It occurred to me that I should probably attempt to cover my jutting hard-on, but seeing Caitlin glance down at it, flush, and look back to my eyes, I realised I was too late.

'Please don't be worried, Caitlin. I can't help my response to you, but I promise I'll behave, sweetheart.' I was still pressed against the wall like a limpet, attempting to draw breath into my straining lungs and doing an utterly wretched job of making my erection calm down.

'I know.' Caitlin chewed on her lower lip one more

time then gave me a shy smile. 'Seeing as you saw me naked today, I guess I don't need to hide myself, do I?'

'I wasn't looking, Caitlin. I just wanted to help, I promise.'

Caitlin gave a small laugh, and then dropped her hands to her sides, leaving her topless and wet before me. Bloody hell. I could barely comprehend the fact that this was actually happening, let alone act on it. Caitlin eyed the bobbing bulge in my briefs and looked up at me with complete calm on her face. 'I trust you, Jack. Completely.'

Suddenly, to my total shock, Caitlin extended her right hand and tentatively wrapped it around the bulge in my boxers.

*Ho-ly fuck.*

It felt like every single nerve end in my body had centred in my shaft and exploded into bright, flashing lights of pleasure. Burning heat spread through my body as my cock thickened and lengthened below her touch, causing a gasp to slip from Caitlin's lips and a gurgled moan to rise in my throat.

As much as I wanted her hand to stay exactly where it was, I instinctively reached down and gripped her wrist.

'Caitlin, what are you doing?' I asked, my voice hoarse.

'I would have thought that was pretty obvious,' she whispered. 'Unless I'm doing it wrong?' She sounded tentative, but her hand refused to budge, instead giving another grip on the base of my cock that was so good it nearly made my brain explode.

'I … I want you to make love to me, Jack.'

Bloody hell. They were the words I'd wanted to hear since we'd got together. But not tonight, not like this.

I swallowed, not once, not twice, but three times, still finding myself unable to speak. She was gripping my cock now, and starting to move her hand slowly up and down, it was incredibly distracting.

Finally, I clawed at my ever receding willpower and gently tugged her hand away. I missed her heat immediately, but instead had to focus on the way Caitlin looked momentarily hurt before covering her breasts and starting to turn away from me.

'Hey, come back here,' I gently coaxed, although she was stubbornly refusing to meet my gaze. 'I want that too, sweetheart, more than you can imagine, but it's been a really stressful day. It's hardly the right time.'

My words brought Caitlin's face up to mine and the flash of strength and determination I saw surprised me. 'It's *exactly* the right time. He doesn't get to screw my life up any more. Please make love to me, Jack. Make me yours.'

At her quiet plea I suddenly recalled the statement Caitlin had given to the police. When they'd asked if Greg had said anything to her, she'd said he kept repeating that she was his.

'You're mine anyway,' I murmured, meaning every word.

'You … you said you loved me. I … I love you too, Jack,' Caitlin confessed softly. She loved me? My heart leapt in my chest and I instinctively reached out and stroked her cheek, relishing the way she leant into my touch.

'This has nothing to do with *him*. It's not a rash decision, this is about you and me. I'm sick of waiting. I want you to make love to me.'

It was starting to get difficult to deny her.

Caitlin continued on her very effective seduction by taking a step back and swiftly removing her panties.

So many expletives were now running through my mind I almost felt dizzy as I looked at her. Her skin was paler down there, highlighting the tan she had everywhere else on her body, and instead of the natural look I had expected, her hair was trimmed into a neat landing strip. Beautiful. She really was just beautiful.

Then she stepped toward me and slipped her thumbs into the waistband of my boxers and before I could stop her she'd dropped to a crouch and whipped the wet material down my legs.

Holy hell. Caitlin was now on her knees, staring at my cock with her mouth hanging open. If I were less of a man I might have been having thoughts about leaning forwards and pressing it to her lips right about now, but I was a gentleman, or so I kept telling myself, so I leant over and practically dragged her upright.

Kicking my boxers aside, I slid both hands up to cup her face so I could stare intently into her gaze, admitting my defeat. 'You want to stop at any point you just have to say so, OK?'

'OK. Please kiss me, Jack.' I liked women taking the lead just as much as I enjoyed leading, but hearing Caitlin begging me did something insanely primitive to my insides.

I was going to take care of this woman for the rest of our lives, and no fucker would get the chance to hurt her ever again.

Before common sense could persuade me to stop, I leaned down and kissed her softly on the lips. She seemed to like that I was making the first move, because as soon as our lips touched she wrapped her arms around my neck and let out a little mewl as she allowed me to pull her more firmly into my embrace.

Another groan rose up my throat as I felt the soft heat of her breasts against my chest, her nipples hardening like little stones against me as my cock nestled happily against her stomach. Jesus. I don't think I'll ever forget how amazing this moment felt.

Her hands began to roam across my back and hips and a shiver of lust ran over my skin at her tentative exploration. Suddenly she arched forwards, inadvertently causing the tip of my cock to slip down and wedge between her legs, and I felt myself almost buckle from the pleasure. We were slippery from the shower water, and I knew that if I rocked my hips just a little then I could be between her legs in no time, but I held back, enjoying the sensation of heat throughout my body.

Suddenly light-headed, I pulled back, my breath ragged and coming in short, hard pants.

Caitlin's face was glowing and her pupils were dilated with desire. 'This feels so good Caitlin, but I will be perfectly content just to hold you tonight.'

Caitlin looked at me, and the depth of emotion I could see reflected in her expression nearly winded me. 'I know, but I'm tired of waiting, Jack.'

As amazing as it was to be here with Caitlin naked in my arms, I didn't want her first time to be some rushed affair against a shower wall.

I quickly bent and scooped her into my arms, but almost immediately I had to hoist her higher in my grip because my arousal ended up bumping against her arse, driving me almost insane with lust.

With her cradled in my arms I headed back through to the bedroom and strode toward the bed before lying her down. We were dripping wet, but I didn't care.

Standing back, I greedily allowed my eyes to rove across her body. Her skin was like flawless silk, breasts the perfect size, waist like an egg timer, and then there was that little landing strip of hers. Fuck. Caitlin really was perfection.

Caitlin blushed under my scrutiny, and the gorgeous flush crawled all the way down her neck until it covered the top of her breasts. Her confidence seemed to have left for now, but she was still smiling at me as she raised a hand in invitation to go to her.

I took her hand and felt the slight tremble in her

fingers as I let her tug me onto the bed. I was going to make sure this was incredible for her, well worth her wait, and good enough to erase any remaining memories of Greg and the years of shit he had put her through.

No pressure then.

The idea that I would be the first man to be inside her was so potent it was almost enough to make me come on the spot and my cock gave another enormous lurch which caused Caitlin to giggle and blush even more.

I'd be her first lover.

And her *only* lover, if I got my wish.

## CAIT

Jack accepted my trembling fingers and came willingly to the bed, where he knelt beside me. He wasn't in a rush, his eyes lazily trailing across my body, so with a loud swallow I timidly let my gaze lower and skim him over properly too.

This was the first time I had seen him completely naked, and it was quite a stunning sight. He was all tanned skin and firm muscles, covered in trails of water as they ran across his body and caused the fine covering of hair on his chest and arms to look thicker than usual. His chest was my favourite part. It was so broad and masculine, and felt so good below my hands when he cuddled me.

Letting my eyes drift lower, I followed the trail of soft downy hair on his belly that led to his manhood before my eyes widened.

OK, maybe I now had a new favourite part. It was bigger than I had expected. Quite a bit bigger than it had seemed in the dimly lit shower, that was for sure. I couldn't help the gasp that slipped from my lips as my eyes remained glued to his cock, and I found myself swallowing nervously.

How would that fit inside me? Whenever I pleasured myself I always felt really tight around the two fingers that I used, but Jack's shaft looked to be far thicker than two of my skinny little digits.

Picking up on my rising nerves, Jack laid himself down next to me and cupped my jaw, bringing my gaze back to his warm brown eyes. 'Hey. You have nothing to worry about. I promise I'll be gentle.'

Instead of feeling ridiculously nervous, I found that, actually, being with Jack made it OK. I was starting to enjoy myself, finding that for the first time in my life I completely trusted the person I was with. If I said stop, I knew he would.

'I don't want to change my mind,' I whispered. Jack nodded then smiled before lowering his lips to mine and setting about easing my tension with a deep, exploring kiss.

Out tongues moved together, and one of his hands slid into my hair to hold me close. Already I could feel my whole body was alive with hot, tingling sensations, and such a deep yearning had built in my belly from my increased excitement that I was actually finding it difficult to stay still.

Leaning back to watch my excitement with apparent pleasure, Jack grinned at me before he let his free hand move from my hair to my shoulder, where he took a second to caress the sensitive skin, sending a shiver of delight though my body. He moved to a kneeling position and lowered his head, where he started to kiss me again, but this time his lips followed his fingers, trailing down my neck to my shoulder and leaving my skin hot and tingling from his attention.

Lower and lower his fingers went until he found my breast and an uncontrollable gasp leapt from my lips as he gently brushed the nipple with his thumb. It was so sensitive it almost felt painful as he repeated the caress, but then he soothed my nipple with a hot lick that caused me to arch off the bed with a groan.

I felt him chuckle as he drew my nipple into his mouth and sucked, but I was far too lost to the sensations to care that he was finding my reactions amusing.

As he moved his attention to my other breast, I decided to do a little exploration of my own and gingerly reached down to brush my fingers along his happy trail until I came to his thick shaft. My fingers wrapped around him, marvelling at how the skin could feel so soft when the muscle below was as solid as granite.

From the way he lurched in my palm I could only assume he was enjoying himself a great deal so I tightened my grip, which caused Jack to rip his mouth away from my breast and let out a hoarse moan of pleasure.

Ha! This time it was my turn to chuckle.

Like a true pro, it didn't take Jack long to recover his composure, and he continued with his delicious teasing as his fingers slipped lower until they found an area that until now had never been touched by a man in a pleasurable way. I tensed as flashes of Greg's painful intrusion with his fingers popped into my mind, but as Jack slowly circled a finger around my clitoris, all bad memories evaporated as waves of pleasure swamped my brain.

It felt so good. 'Oh God, Jack …' was all I managed to whisper, but it was enough to halt Jack's lips and bring his flushed and smiling face up to meet mine.

'OK, sweetheart?' he asked, his voice hoarse.

Nodding, I slid my fingers into the hair at the nape of his neck. 'More than OK.' His pleased grin was reward enough, but then Jack decided to up the pleasure stakes even more by slipping one finger inside me. He watched me carefully, only starting to move it when he saw my eyes roll back in pleasure. I knew my own body so well that I couldn't believe he could pleasure me better than I could, but he did. His finger curled, and continued with his lazy massage of thrusts, using the heel of his hand to rub my clit and cause a rising pleasure to burn through my veins.

I wasn't conscious of the precise moment it happened, but as we lay together touching and kissing and moaning, my body started to take over, and I found myself rolling into his body to deepen the contact of his fingers, and even grinding my hips slightly against his hand.

Jack left his knelt position and lay himself alongside me so we were practically touching from head to toe. The feel of his cock pressing into my belly was new, but I liked it, and on top of that, I *loved* that it was me that had gotten him so excited.

The longer we touched the more I could feel an ache of desire building in the pit of my stomach and demanding to be satisfied. Jack's hand was working me towards a peak, but I wanted more. I wanted all of him.

I started to squirm against him, my fingers sliding around his shoulders and digging into the skin of his back in a desperate attempt to get him closer. We were pressed together from our tangled legs right up to our clashing lips, so there really was only one way we could be closer.

I needed him inside me. Jack was still taking his time, presumably to make sure I was ready, and God was I. I really, really wanted this.

'Jack, please ...' I begged, breathless and desperate for him to ease the deep ache in my core.

His lips were reddened and his eyes dilated with desire as he reached up to brush a few stray hairs from my face. 'We can just use our hands tonight?' he suggested, ever the gentleman.

'No. I want you inside me,' I stated, surprised at the force behind my words. Jack watched me for a few seconds and nodded eagerly before pressing his lips to mine once again.

After kissing me until I was lightheaded with desire, Jack paused for breath, placed a quick peck on my nose, and leant to the bedside table to retrieve a condom. His hand was shaking as he ripped open the packet, and the sight thrilled me, reassuring me he was just as affected by this as I was.

'Jack …' I gasped breathlessly. He responded to my plea by shifting his position so he was propped over me.

'I love you, sweetheart, so much,' he murmured, and proceeded to manoeuvre the tip of himself gently inside me. Oh! It stretched me, but in a way that felt so good that I found my own hips lifting instinctively. With some gentle rocking he slid in another inch, and I gasped at the fullness as I felt something blocking him, my noise causing Jack to stop immediately.

'I love you too. Don't you dare stop.'

'This might hurt,' he whispered, but deciding it was now or never, I planted my feet on the mattress and helped him by lifting myself up as he dissolved the barrier of my virginity. I gasped again, but from the fullness rather than any actual pain.

One more thrust allowed him to slip fully inside and as his stomach settled upon mine we let out moans of pleasure as we were fully joined together for the first time. It felt incredible. Whenever I'd touched myself in the past I'd always been amazed that the human body could focus so many sensations in such a small area, but sharing that intensity with Jack was almost overwhelming.

After recovering himself, Jack kissed me, his tongue moving lazily against mine before he lifted his head, stared deeply into my eyes, and began to move more purposefully.

His thrusts were deep but controlled, each one causing delicious tremors to flow through my entire body. The sensations blurred into one long, hazily beautiful swirl as he worked both my mind and body towards a peak that I'd only ever experienced from my own hand. I felt myself tighten around Jack, and a deep, pleasurable ache settle in my core and I knew I was close, then a second later, as he thrust back inside me

327

once again I exploded into a climax so strong it had me grasping at Jack as I writhed against him, convulsing around him like a fist.

Jack moaned in pleasure, and I let out a hoarse cry as my orgasm seemed to go on and on, and then seconds later Jack thrust in deep and paused, a guttural groan escaping his throat as I felt his cock jerk and twitch inside me.

It took me a long while before I was remotely ready for speech, and in that time all I could manage was to gently trail my fingers through the damp hair at the nape of his neck as Jack panted on top of me.

'That … was … amazing,' I gasped. Jack leant up on his elbows and gazed at me with a grin.

'It certainly was,' he murmured. His forehead was damp, but his eyes were twinkling with happiness. Gently easing himself out of me, he rolled to my side with a laugh and kissed my shoulder and collarbone, making me shiver once again, dropping another soft kiss on my lips before he slid from the bed. 'Stay there.'

Returning a second or so later with the condom gone, Jack grabbed a box of tissues from the bedside table and held them out to me. Accepting them with an embarrassed blush I grabbed a wad and wiped between my legs, only to flush further when it came away with a pinkish smear on it. The last remnant of my lost virginity.

To my further embarrassment I noticed that Jack saw this too, and frowned. 'Are you OK?' he asked.

'I'm fine Jack, it didn't hurt,' I whispered, my cheeks absolutely flaming.

'Shall we take another quick rinse and get some food?' he asked.

'Sounds good. I'm starving.' I really was. Sex must have burned a whole load of calories because my stomach was actually grumbling audibly.

'Me too.' Jack looked at me and winked. 'I think we've worked up quite an appetite.' Laughing at how well he had mirrored my own thoughts, I allowed him to take my hand and pull me behind him into the bathroom.

As I stood behind Jack, waiting for him to get the temperature right, I watched the muscles in his broad back flex and felt my fingers itch with the urge to explore them. Swallowing, I refrained, but I couldn't stop my gaze moving over the rest of his body. He really was such a prime specimen. I suppose it was a by-product of needing to stay trim for filming, but there didn't seem to be an inch of fat on him anywhere. He was muscular, with corded arms and thick, strong legs, and an arse that was too good to be true.

Suddenly, as I stood there comparing my lanky, scrawny body to his near perfection I started to feel really self-conscious. The adrenaline had passed, leaving me feeling … almost vulnerable.

Turning toward me, Jack paused, and then frowned as he took in my awkward stance with one hand wrapped around my belly and the other covering my boobs.

'Hey, you don't need to hide from me, Caitlin.'

Averting my eyes, my past insecurities crept up on me all at once and I found myself shrugging awkwardly. 'I, um, I don't really like my body.'

Jack's eyes boggled at my statement. 'What? Why on earth not?'

I didn't really want to bring *him* up again, but Jack knew I carried a lot of baggage, most of which stemmed from Greg. 'Greg always used to tell me my breasts were too small, and my legs were too skinny and …' My list was interrupted by Jack as he closed the gap between us and dragged me into his arms.

'Fucking hell,' he cursed. 'I hate that he screwed with you so much, Caitlin, but you have to believe me, you are gorgeous. *Utterly gorgeous.* Unbelievably so. Please don't feel embarrassed, I love every single part of you.'

That was exactly what I needed to hear.

My hands dropped away from my breasts and wrapped around Jack's warm body. We seemed to fit together perfectly. This was where I was meant to be, and finally I'd fully accepted that fact.

# FORTY-EIGHT

## ALLIE

Staring at the phone in my hand, I grimaced at the idea of calling my parents. I normally loved chatting to my mum and dad, but this was one call that I was dreading. How did I break the news of Greg's attack without sending them into a complete tailspin?

*'Oh, hi, Mum and Dad, what's new? Me? Oh, I'm not too bad ... Friday was a bit of a bummer, I got stabbed by a psycho who attempted to rape Cait, but my boyfriend broke down the door and saved us, and then the knife-wielding lunatic escaped and is currently on the run ... Oh yeah, and my boyfriend proposed to me in the hospital and I said yes ...'*

Hmmm, no. I think my mother would pass out on the spot.

There really was no easy way to break this kind of news. All I could hope was that the sound of my voice would reassure them that I was OK.

Just as I plucked up the courage to bring up their number my mobile rang in my hand, illuminating the screen with four simple words: *Mum and Dad – Home.*

Shit. They'd beaten me to it. Was this just a regular catch up call? I supposed there was only one way to find out, so I took a deep breath and pressed the answer button.

'Hi.'

I tried to sound bright and breezy, but I only got one word out before my mum's panicked voice interrupted me. 'Allie? Oh thank God! We got a call from Cait's parents, are you alright?' Her voice was high and wobbly as if she had been crying, which I suppose she probably had.

'Calm down, Mum, I'm OK.' Well, as OK as I could be. I was in hospital, in fairly significant pain, but my mum didn't need to know that when she was thousands of miles away.

She didn't heed my request to calm down, though, because as soon as I had said I was OK she started sobbing, sniffling, snivelling, and hiccupping all at the same time down the line. Wow, was my mum a loud crier.

There was a muffled noise and then the calm voice of my dad filled the line. 'Allie, sweet pea, I'm so glad to hear you're OK. That phone call gave your mother and I quite a shock.' Hearing him call me sweet pea made me start to well up, and I found myself reaching for a tissue before I turned into a snivelling mess like my mother.

'Yeah, it was a pretty shocking day here,' I mumbled, not sure what else I could say.

'We're coming over, and Cait's parents too.'

I suppose it was only natural that they'd want to be near us. 'Dad, that's not necessary, we'll be fine. Honestly.'

'Yeah, that's what Cait said too, apparently. You girls are so stubborn it's unbelievable. We want to come.'

'OK. It'll be great to see you. When are you flying?' I was desperately hoping he would say a few days' time so I would look a bit perkier, and hopefully be out of hospital.

'We're not sure. As soon as possible, but flights for today and tomorrow are booked up, so probably Monday or Tuesday. I'm waiting for a travel agent to call me back.'

Just then, Sean burst into the room with a harried

expression on his face and a cardboard cup in his hand. Seeing me sitting up and talking on the phone, he immediately relaxed, and closed the door behind him before holding out the cup to me.

I had to chuckle. He hadn't left my side since I'd arrived in hospital, but when the doctor had given me the all clear for eating and drinking normally I'd immediately begged him to go and get me a cup of coffee – a decent cup of coffee, not the sludgy muck they served on the cart that came round the wards. He had refused at first, adamant that he wanted to stay with me, but after I'd threatened him with taking back my acceptance of his proposal if he didn't get me some java within the next fifteen minutes he had disappeared on his mission. From the delicious aroma wafting from the cup, he'd done a great job.

I mouthed a thank you to Sean as he took a seat beside me, gently stroking my thigh as I tried to re-focus on what my dad was saying. Even feeling as rough as I did, Sean's touch was still remarkably distracting.

'Cait was adamant that she was fine and told her parents not to come, but as it's her birthday soon they said they want to make the trip. It's going to be a bit of a surprise for her. I'll text you as soon as we have our flight details.'

'OK, Dad, sounds good.'

There was a chirruping noise in the background and the sound of my dad moving. 'My mobile's ringing; I think that might be the travel agent. I better go. We'll be in touch soon. Take care of yourself, sweet pea.'

The lump in my throat immediately reappeared as I nodded and had to force my words out. 'I will, Dad, see you soon. Bye.'

Once I had hung up, Sean took the phone from me, placed it on the bedside table, and linked his fingers with mine. 'How'd your parents take the news?'

I gave a watery-eyed shrug and gripped his fingers. 'Not too bad, I guess. They called me, apparently Cait's parents phoned them with the news this morning, so I guess she must have phoned home.' Pausing, I dabbed at my eyes and pulled in a deep breath. 'My mum was a bit of a state, but I think they were both just glad to hear my voice. They're coming over in the next few days.'

Sean nodded, and indicated for me to try my coffee. The deliciously warm beverage definitely had me smiling in no time.

I noticed Sean starting to get fidgety. First he stood up, then his fingers started to rhythmically squeeze mine, and the final giveaway was his eyes, which began to dart around the room restlessly.

Something was up.

'What's the matter?' I asked, putting my unfinished coffee down.

Sean chewed his lip for a second and then his cheeks flushed. 'This is going to sound so selfish …' Rolling his neck, he cleared his throat. 'I … well, I was just wondering if this means you'll be going back to the UK? Are your parents flying out to take you home?'

My eyebrows shot up. I hadn't even considered going back.

'Because I can't leave until filming finishes for the season, and I … I really don't want you to leave,' Sean whispered, his eyes lowering away as if he were embarrassed. It still amazed me how a man as strong and confident as Sean could also be so vulnerable.

'Sean, look at me.' After taking a deep breath, he followed my request and raised his eyes to mine. 'I *am* home. We're together, home is wherever you are.'

Sean raised an eyebrow and, after releasing a breath of relief, leant in closer to me. 'We're more than just together, my gorgeous girl. We're engaged. Don't forget that.'

335

As if I could! I giggled at the way he wiggled his eyebrows, but then he exchanged his grin for a more serious expression as he dug in the pocket of his shorts and pulled out a small, black velvet box.

'Speaking of which … I bought this a while ago. One of my security guards was kind enough to fetch it for me this morning.'

Popping open the box, Sean revealed a diamond ring that caused me to suck in a gasped breath. It was a simple band, which appeared to be platinum, and on the top were three square-cut diamonds nestled together and sparkling in the light. It was the most beautiful ring I'd ever seen.

'I'd rather not be doing this in a hospital room, but I want to make it official, so here goes.' Sean kept hold of my left hand and knelt onto one of his knees. Clearing his throat, he swallowed and grinned. 'I've been practising this in my head all morning.'

Drawing in a deep breath, he licked his lips and gave my hand a squeeze. 'Allie, you are without a doubt the most amazing thing that has ever happened to me. I love you more than you can ever imagine, and I want to spend the rest of my life with you. Will you make me the happiest man alive and agree to marry me?'

Seeing as he'd already asked, I shouldn't have been anywhere near as emotional as I was, but after the call with my parents, tears soaked my cheeks within seconds. 'Yes. I love you, Sean. I can't wait to marry you.'

Sean leapt up and planted a hard kiss onto my tear-stained lips before helping me to slip the ring onto my finger. 'I'm glad you said that, because I don't want to wait long to make you my wife. As soon as you get out of here we can start making plans.'

# FORTY-NINE

## CAIT

Being a nature geek, I always tried to spend as much time outside as possible, and so the morning after I had (temporarily) moved in with Jack, I went exploring, and discovered that his house offered me multiple ways to do so. There was a beautiful garden, a sunroom with side windows that opened out in a concertina so you were almost outside but still under the glass roof, and also not one, but two sprawling balconies.

I'd spent the best part of the previous hour exploring the private estate he lived on – complete with a gym and bar for the few residents – and was now relaxing on a sun lounger while I waited for Jack to finish a conference call with his director. I didn't have any spare clothes – Jack had washed yesterday's outfit for me and promised we could collect some from my own house today – so I'd stripped down to my bra and panties, deciding that they were basically the same as wearing a bikini anyway.

My eyes were closed and I was almost drifting off to sleep when I felt two warm hands trail across my belly. 'Hmmm. I could get used to seeing you with so few clothes on,' Jack murmured, dropping to his haunches and placing a kiss where his hands had just been.

Giggling as his lips tickled my belly, I rolled onto my side and noticed that he'd changed out of his swimming shorts and was now in grey jeans and a T-shirt. 'Are you going somewhere?'

He smiled at me ruefully. 'I'm ashamed to say it, but my cupboards are bare. If we're both staying here, I need to run out to get some food. I won't be long.'

Sunbathing was fine, but there was only so much I could do without getting bored so I quickly jumped up, keen to join him. 'Wait, I'll come too.'

Besides, the thought of watching a Hollywood superstar pick out groceries had a certain appeal to it. I pulled on my faded jeans and a T-shirt as fast as I could. 'Ready.'

Jack grinned, so I looked down at myself critically. I looked a little scruffy, but these were the only clothes I had here, and besides, we were only going shopping. 'What? Do I look OK?'

'You look gorgeous, as always. It's nothing. Come on, let's go.' I gave myself a final assessment, but saw nothing wrong with my outfit, so I shrugged, picked up my bag and a sunhat he had leant me, and followed him through to the Jeep.

After just ten minutes, Jack pulled his car into the carpark of a small supermarket. Well, it was small compared to the Walmarts I'd been to, anyway. As I gazed around I spotted what looked like several photographers lazily sitting in the sun by the trolley bays.

Seeing my look of concern Jack smiled and patted my knee. 'They're often here. This place is used by all the rich and famous of L.A. Well, the ones like me who do their own shopping,' he chuckled.

Oh God. I'd never considered that something as mundane as shopping would be of interest to the press, but thinking about the gossip magazines I read in the hairdresser's, I realised how naive I'd been. Jack was famous – *everything* he did was interesting to journalists.

So much for a quiet trip to the shops. Now I realised what he'd ben chuckling at earlier – my first meeting with the press and I was wearing a crumpled T-shirt and scruffy jeans. 'You could have warned me!'

Jack gave me his best cheeky chappy look and then shrugged as if it was no big deal. 'I already told you that you look gorgeous, and I meant it.' Leaning across, he gently swept a wayward piece of hair from my face and smiled at me so adoringly that I couldn't find it in me to stay irritated with him.

This was not good though, because after Greg's attack, I was now even more reluctant to be seen publicly with Jack.

Besides, I didn't want to be introducing myself to the world as the significant woman in his life when I looked like this: I had no make-up on, my face was shiny and red from sunbathing, and my clothes looked like I'd pulled them out of a bin bag.

There was only one solution. I was going to have to go incognito.

Digging around in my bag, I pulled out my large sunglasses and pulled on the floppy sun hat. It was a bit worse for wear, but it would do the trick – once I had these on, there was no way anyone would be able to recognise me.

Shaking his head, Jack fingered the rim of the hat. 'Is being seen in public with me really so awful that you have to hide?' he joked. Although there was humour in his tone, I could detect a hint of resignation. I knew he still wanted to go public, and it was obviously niggling him that I was holding back. I wanted us to be more official too, of course I did, but I was still adamant that my reasons for staying quiet were valid.

'You know it has nothing to do with you, Jack,' I murmured, tugging on the hat and making sure it was firmly on my head. 'But until Greg is found I'm not willing to put you at risk. The hat stays for now.' Flashing one more determined glance at Jack, I opened the door and dropped from the step onto the warm tarmac of the car park. I knew I was being paranoid; Jack had Flynn to watch over him, after all.

Slamming the door behind me, I saw some of the photographers glance my way, but not recognising me, they continued to lounge in the sun. Huh, this wasn't so bad.

A second later, however, it became a completely different story as Jack emerged from the other side of the Jeep and casually grabbed a trolley. He was wearing just his aviator sunglasses, so with his tall frame and familiar floppy hair he was instantly recognisable, and his mystery brunette in tow – me – became the centre of the photographers' day.

*Shiiiiiiiit.*

I had never seen a group of people get up so fast, and suddenly the photographers were on their feet and firing questions at us thick and fast. 'Jack! Jack! Is this your girlfriend? Sister? Friend? Miss? Hello, Miss?' This tirade was shortly followed by, 'Is this the new girlfriend you're rumoured to be seeing? Can we get a name? A picture?'

God, they were relentless!

'Jack! Who's the lucky lady?' called another. Randomly, amid all the chaos, the thing that really stuck in my mind was this comment – 'Who's the lucky lady?' Seriously? Did being taken to a supermarket get you classed as 'lucky'? I shook my head in disbelief, stuck close to Jack's side, and was immensely relieved that I had his hat to hide away underneath.

'Morning, guys … oh, and gals – hi, Jennifer,' Jack said, acknowledging the one female journalist with a nod. 'We're just doing some shopping. No other comments, thanks.' Jack was so at ease that I found myself in awe of his laid-back attitude to the whole situation I had found myself plunged rather unceremoniously into.

Once we had pushed through the shifting line of cameras, I released a huge breath and glanced nervously at Jack. 'Will it always be like this?' I muttered, decidedly flustered.

'Nah, once we go public there'll be a few weeks' interest and then it'll die down. We'll become old news. It's their job – they need a story, that's all.' He tugged on the trolley, which had a dodgy wheel, and gave a shrug. 'They don't know who you are. Once they get some answers or something to photograph they'll loosen up.'

Hmm. That sounded a bit more bearable. Narrowing my eyes, a plan began to form in my mind. It was pretty out there for me, but seeing as I wouldn't speak to them, maybe I could give them something to photograph …

Knowing the press were watching as we approached the shop, I took a deep breath and slipped my arm around Jack's waist. There, photograph that. And did they! Behind me, I heard a flurry of cameras clicking wildly, but Jack paused and smiled, his face glowing with happiness.

Suddenly overwhelmed with this new confidence, I slid my hand from his waist down into the back pocket of his Levi's, where it sat happily over his firm bum. I loved his arse. Even knowing that at least four people were watching, I couldn't help but give a firm squeeze.

Jack laughed, morphing into a huge grin. He seemed thrilled by my gesture, and reciprocated by lifting his left hand from the trolley handle and swinging it over my shoulder to pull me close to him.

Managing to steer the trolley one handed, Jack shifted his hand to the rim of my hat, where he tilted it back and dipped down to plant a kiss on my forehead. Wow, the cameras *really* loved that. I was feeling a giddy buzz of excitement in my stomach from Jack's affection *and* the idea that we were caught on camera, but I found myself relieved when he popped my hat back in place with a rueful grin.

Once we were safely inside the shop, Jack told me that no photographers were allowed inside, and after furtively glancing around, I removed my hat and glasses and placed them in the trolley before running my hands through my hair to fluff it out.

Glancing up at Jack, I fully expected to see a look of exasperation on his face, but instead I found him smiling at me with that sweet, soft, affectionate smile on his face that I loved. That look spoke volumes about his feelings, but it didn't scare me like it had when I'd first glimpsed it. Now I loved it.

'Anyone would think it's you who's famous, wearing a disguise,' he remarked with a grin, making my cheeks flush. 'Right, let's shop.'

And just like that, he changed the subject, removing me from the spotlight effortlessly and turning the trolley towards the fruit and vegetable aisle.

Referring to a handwritten list, Jack gave me a few items to get, which I dutifully set off to collect. As I picked out a cucumber I glanced down the aisle and watched as Jack filled a bag with apples. It was so domestic, and he seemed so at ease, but with his film star looks it made quite an incongruent image. Just then, he looked up from the bag and grinned. 'Cait, grab a red pepper too, please.'

I paused, realising it was the first time he had shortened my name. Huh. I wasn't sure I liked it. He was the only person who ever called me by my full name, and I'd kind of gotten used to it.

As I continued to pick out the items I'd been charged with finding I couldn't escape how weird this was. Well, no, actually it wasn't weird – shopping with Jack was normal, and that's what made it bizarre. It was normal.

We were out together, like a real, non-famous, boring, everyday couple.

No one was running up asking for his autograph or trying to take my picture. The other shoppers were completely ignoring us. They were simply shopping, buying fruit and bread and coffee, not hiding round corners to avoid cameras or sneaking into cars like naughty teenagers.

Maybe this would be OK in the end after all. I felt my shoulders relax and I smiled. Maybe he was right, maybe I should just let the press find out who I was. Jack was well protected from Greg, and it would mean we could get our relationship started properly. It was certainly something to consider.

I wasn't trying to fool myself, I was sensible enough to know that if I really wanted to try to share my life with Jack Felton, it would never be run-of-the-mill, but at least I wouldn't feel so exposed all the time.

After half an hour, I had almost forgotten about the journalists corralled outside. Almost. But as we made our way towards the exit I let out a quiet cry as I glanced out the doors and saw that the small group from earlier had at least doubled in size, no doubt as a result of the press grapevine in downtown L.A.

Diving into the trolley, I retrieved the hat and glasses and resumed my disguise before we exited into the bright, Hollywood sun. God, this was weird.

I had taken it upon myself to look after the trolley, perhaps because steering it meant I didn't have to look too hard at the journalists, but as I came to them, I cleared my throat and let my irritation out. 'Excuse me, please.'

I sounded polite, but my words were apparently an invitation to bombard me with questions. Three lousy words, but it was all they needed to dive on me like a free meal.

344

'Was that an English accent? Are you from the UK?' I swallowed hard and tried to ignore the hounding as I continued to push the trolley forward.

'Jack! Jack! Do you know each other from home?' Emerging from the other side without another word, I glanced at Jack.

'I spoke to them. Happy?' I muttered, decidedly flustered by the encounter.

Instead of picking up on my annoyance, Jack casually swung an arm around my hips and pulled me towards him so strongly that I – and my trolley – careened into his arms clumsily, no doubt giving the photographers more than enough time to snap another photo of Jack and his 'mystery girl'.

# FIFTY

Apart from running trips to the coffee shop for me, Sean was still opting to remain glued to my side. I'd been in hospital for two-and-a-half days, so we were falling into a bit of a rhythm, but that morning when he returned with my coffee he also had a stack of papers and magazines under one arm.

Grinning as he lay them out on the bed, he nodded, looking pleased with himself. 'You're going to want to see this.'

After briefly checking out the closest paper, I raised my eyebrows and exchanged a surprised glance with him. He was right. I *definitely* wanted to see this.

It was just as well Cait was due to visit, or I'd probably explode with questions. A few seconds later, right on cue, the door opened and, after a policeman briefly poked his head inside to check the room, Cait entered, shutting the door behind her.

Letting out a breath, she leant against the door, smiling thinly at Sean and I. 'He's a nice enough guy, but I'm getting really sick of having a babysitter.'

I couldn't help but smile. It had only been two days since the attack and the decision that she should have a police guard, but obviously the novelty was already wearing thin. She'd found Tanya's presence just about bearable, but clearly she'd been too far in the distance seeing as Greg had managed to get to not only Cait, but me as well. My smile tightened as images of him leaping

346

out from the kitchen sprung to my mind and sent fear crawling over my skin. With a deep breath, I forcefully pushed them aside and focused on the present – we were here and we were safe, that was all that mattered.

Sean frowned, his posture stiffening as he stood up. 'It's for your own safety, Cait.'

Cait sighed and nodded before walking over to join us. 'Yeah, I know. I'm not going to do anything stupid, don't worry.' Pushing her hair off her face she turned to me and narrowed her eyes. 'So, enough about me. How's the patient?'

Shrugging, I smiled at her, trying to hide my excitement about my engagement – the ring was hidden in the bedside drawer. 'Pretty great, all things considered. My head feels fine, and the stiches in my side don't itch any more. The painkillers are working well, so I just feel a bit stiff when I move.'

Glancing at Sean, I grinned and pulled one of the newspapers toward me. Ideally, I would've liked to be alone with Cait before starting to dig for gossip, but given Sean's superglue-like company I didn't think I'd be able to persuade him to leave the room.

Clearing my throat, I fingered the paper and opened it to page four. 'So, you've been shopping?' I asked casually. Cait looked confused, frowning and shaking her head. 'What do you mean? Was I supposed to bring you something?'

Instead of replying, I simply held up the page of the newspaper and turned it so Cait could see.

It seemed to take a second for her to acknowledge what she was seeing, because initially her face remained blank, but then her eyebrows shot up and her mouth popped open as she gasped loudly.

I glanced at the paper again, smiling at the pictures; there, in all its glory, was a half-page picture collage of Cait and Jack in what appeared to be a supermarket car park. Well, Jack was recognisable, and presumably the brunette with him was Cait. If it wasn't then he was going to be in big trouble.

In the main picture they'd been photographed from behind and were arm in arm, with him tilting her hat back and placing a kiss on her forehead. Above the picture was the headline "Jack's Mystery Girl."

'Oh my God! They actually put it in the paper!' Cait blurted, her cheeks turning beetroot red as she ripped the newspaper from my hand and scanned the article.

Sean chuckled and flicked through the pile to select another magazine. 'That's nothing, Cait. You two made the front cover of *L.A. Celebrity News,*' he said, handing the glossy magazine across the bed to her.

'Front page?' squeaked Cait, looking a bit like she was actually going into shock.

'Uh-huh. But they got a different photo,' I giggled as Cait stared at the cover, which had a similar shot of them walking from behind, but this time instead of showing the kiss it had a close-up of Cait squeezing his bum.

'Oh my God ...' Cait whispered, before flicking her elastic bands several times. 'The headline ... have you seen it?'

I had to say, it was genius. "Jack's new girl gets cheeky." With a lovely arrow pointing to where she was gripping his arse.

'It's quite imaginative,' Sean commented, trying to hide the grin from his voice and completely failing.

'How many papers are we in?' she asked cautiously as she started to look at the titles spread on the bed, which included the *L.A. Times, L.A. Daily, L.A. Herald,* and of course, *Celebrity News Magazine.*

Sean shrugged and grinned teasingly. 'No idea, these are just the ones they had in the hospital shop.'

'Your arse-grabbing shenanigans have made bigger headlines than Sean and I did when we went to the cinema together!'

Groaning, Cait grabbed a stack of the papers and sunk into a chair as if her legs could no longer support her body weight.

After nearly an hour of reading and exchanging the best bits, which were mostly harmless and by Cait's own admission, quite amusing, Sean threw the last one down in disgust. This particular piece was incredibly derogatory about celebrity lifestyles and the use of fame to find sexual conquests.

According to Sean, Jack had always been relatively selective about his dating, so I wasn't sure why they'd chosen to link this to him and Cait, but I could understand why Sean was upset – it was way too close to how he used to live his life. Thinking about his more less than salubrious past made me a little uncomfortable, so focusing on the fact that he was a changed man – not to mention my fiancé – I looked to Cait with an understanding smile, desperately wishing I could tell her about our engagement, but I wouldn't. I'd honour Sean's wish to keep it to ourselves until he'd spoken to Dad.

'Does this look like me?' Cait asked, holding up one of the articles that was running with the title "Do you know this woman? Reward, $200." It was accompanied by a zoomed-in shot of Cait's side profile with her hat tilted back, but it was blurry and, to be honest, could be just about any woman in L.A. with brown hair.

'Nah. But it's tempting. $200 could come in quite handy,' I quipped, which would have certainly earnt me a punch in the arm if I hadn't been laid up in a hospital bed. It turned out that being poorly had its benefits.

# CAIT

Just as I put the final paper down, my mobile began to ring in my handbag. Pulling it out, I saw Jack's name and wondered if he'd seen the papers too.

Wandering to the window, I lifted the phone and answered. 'Hey.'

'Hi, sweetheart. How are you?' Jack sounded quiet ... no, not quiet ... *worried*. He sounded worried, and I would almost place money on the fact that he had seen the papers and was concerned about my reaction.

My suspicions were furthered when I heard the rustling of paper in the background, which filled my mind with images of him on a coffee break and having a quick read of the juicy gossip.

Ignoring his question, I fired one of my own. 'You seen today's papers?' I drawled in a deliberately un-amused tone.

'Um, yeah, I'm looking at one now.' He paused, the concern in his tone so deep I could picture his grimace. 'Don't worry about it, it'll pass soon enough. Besides, you can't see who you are.'

After another moment of silence from my end, Jack spoke rather urgently, 'Caitlin?' Now he sounded *really* worried, so I put him out of his misery.

'Yeah, I'm here. It's OK, after grabbing your bum yesterday I kinda figured it might make one of the papers. I just didn't expect it to be such big news ...'

'I've been single a long time, a hot brunette grabbing my arse *is* big news to the journos.' After another pause, Jack cleared his throat. 'Seeing as the pictures are in the papers, can I get my PR team to release that statement?'

His words instantly removed my playful smile and instead filled my veins with dread. 'No!' My voice came out far harsher than expected, but I had Allie behind me covered in stiches as real-life proof of how insane Greg was. I couldn't risk putting Jack in hospital. Or worse. 'Greg stabbed Allie, for fuck's sake. I don't want your name linked to me until he's caught.'

'Caitlin, I have a great security team, I'd be fine –'

'No! Jack, please, just give the police a while longer to find him, please.'

I heard a heavy sigh down the line, 'OK, sweetheart. I'll tell them to hold off on the statement for now.'

I had a feeling that Jack didn't want to wait too much longer, so all I could do was pray that the police found Greg before Greg could find us again.

# FIFTY-ONE

## CAIT

Allie's parents arrived in L.A. the next day, but as she still hadn't been released, I volunteered to look after them. Along with my police escort, of course, who was already getting on my nerves because he was at my side *all the flipping time* like a second shadow.

Looking after Allie's folks was quite a good distraction for me because Jack was busy making up the shoots he'd missed while in hospital and I was off work at the moment after Di, my manager at the studio, insisted I take a sabbatical.

I'd told my parents not to visit, but after seeing the emotional reunion between Allie and her parents I was slightly regretting my decision. Perhaps I'd have to see if Jack could take some time off so we could take a trip to the UK. If he wanted to meet my parents, of course.

After becoming a suitably irritable patient, it was finally Allie's release day. She was allowed home on the condition she take it easy for the next few weeks. As I entered her room I found her being her usual stubborn self and refusing a wheelchair, even though Sean and her parents were trying to argue with her. To her credit, she walked slowly on her way out to the car, but her refusal to take the easy option caused Sean to faff around hilariously. I'd never seen him so on edge; he was like a little girl, and I couldn't help my grin as he finally sagged against the front door once he'd got her home and inside his house.

I stood back and allowed Mr and Mrs Shaw to enter while I re-tied my sandal, then stood up to follow them indoors.

I wouldn't be kidding if I said the sight that met me in the lounge completely took my breath away.

'Surprise! Happy Birthday!' In front of me stood our group from the hospital; Sean, Allie, and Mr and Mrs Shaw, but along with them were Mel and Lisa my friends from the studios, then *my* parents, and Sarah, my other friend from the UK.

What the heck?!

I shrieked with joy, and seconds later was bundled into a teary hug by my mum, who was somehow managing to sob and laugh simultaneously. After that followed hugs from Sarah and my dad before I was finally allowed to step back and get some air into my lungs.

Still amazed at the gathering, I cast Allie a rueful glance and found her grinning with delight. It was clear from her smug smile she had been in on this surprise.

Linking her arm through mine, she leant into my ear and whispered, 'We thought we could all do with a happy distraction, I hope you don't mind the surprise?'

Shaking my head, I barely managed to contain my grin. 'No, this is amazing. Just what we needed.'

Sean strode back into the room with a bottle in one hand and a fistful of champagne flutes in the other. 'Right, who'd like some fizz?'

The quiet room erupted into replies of 'Yes please', but before I'd even had a chance to get a drink in my hand I heard the front door ring.

Through the excitement I registered that the knock on the door would be Jack – I was still sleeping at his house so we'd arranged for him to pick me up from here once he'd finished work – and a sudden pang of panic shot through me. Jack was here – and so were my parents! I

353

hadn't even told them I was dating anyone, let alone a frigging film star who was over ten years older than me!

Given my strictly single years as spinster Cait, I suspected it was going to be quite a shock. It still surprised the hell out of me when I sat and thought about it.

Grabbing Allie's arm, I gave her panicked look. 'Does Jack know my parents are here?'

Allie frowned and shook her head. 'Uhh, I don't think so. Sean arranged the get together, I think he told Jack it was a surprise party.'

Great.

'Bloody hell, do you think he'll want to meet my parents?'

Allie chewed on her lip and gave a useless shrug. 'He's nut's about you, I'm sure it'll be fine.'

'Fine' wasn't exactly the reassurance I'd been looking for, so my face contorted into a panicked grimace as Allie shrugged casually. 'There's only one way to find out, go and let him in!'

Seeing Sean head for the door, I quickly stepped across and attempted a smile. 'I'll get it, you keep serving the drinks,' I stammered. Things had progressed between Jack and I pretty speedily, and our relationship was certainly intense and serious, but we'd hardly been together long. Normally the parents didn't get involved until wedding bells were in the air.

Leaving the bustle of the lounge, I entered the long hallway and made my way towards the front door with butterflies in my stomach. At least the door didn't open directly into the lounge, so I'd have a minute to prepare Jack, or wave him off as he ran away shrieking …

I was met by the most enormous bouquet of flowers I'd ever seen. Despite my nagging concern, I couldn't help but grin as his head popped out from behind the flowers.

'Hi, sweetheart. Happy birthday ... again.' He'd wished me happy birthday that morning with a scorching kiss, a beautiful pair of diamond earrings, and then a delicious quickie in the shower. 'These are for you,' he smiled as he handed the flowers to me.

'Thank you, Jack. Wow, they're stunning.' I accepted the flowers, practically staggering under their weight as I wondered where the heck I was going to put them.

Jack went to step forwards, but I hesitated, blocking the doorway. 'What's up?' he asked.

'Well, I know you're here for the party, but I think I should warn you that we have a few unexpected guests ...'

His eyebrows rose as he leant sideways on the doorframe and tucked one hand into the front pocket of his jeans like a frigging *GQ* model.

'My parents.' I gestured over my shoulder with my thumb. 'Allie and Sean arranged it.'

'Wow! What an amazing surprise!' Jack looked thrilled for me.

'Yeah, it is, but ...' I paused, not sure how to word it. I didn't want him to feel forced into meeting them if he didn't want to.

I watched as Jack's face suddenly fell. 'I get it, you don't want me to stay.' His crestfallen expression went some way to soothing my fears.

'Of course I want you to stay!' I blurted, my cheeks flushing. 'I just wasn't sure that you would want to get involved in family stuff yet. I know meeting the parents can be a big step, so if you don't want to then I totally understand.'

Jack's face remained passive, but one eyebrow was quirked up. 'How many ways can I tell you I'm here for the long haul?' he murmured softly.

'So, you ... you would like to join us?' I ventured tentatively.

To my relief, Jack smiled broadly and leant down to place a chaste kiss on my lips. 'Very much so, if it's OK with you?'

'It's more than OK!' I grinned, delighted by his reaction, and jumped up to twine my arms around his neck and place a long hard kiss on his lips which was far from his chaste effort and caused Jack to growl against my mouth.

Before I could step away, I heard Sarah's voice from down the corridor. 'Cait, this is supposed to be your birthday party! Where are you?'

Grimacing in anticipation of Sarah's reaction, I looked apologetically at Jack. 'My friend Sarah flew in from the UK.'

Before I could add any more, Sarah charged down the corridor before coming to a stuttering halt. 'Oh, sorry, I didn't realise you had someone here.' Sarah looked at the huge bunch of flowers in my hand, and then assessed my rather cuddly proximity to the man by my side before her eyes boggled.

'Oh, bugger! I didn't realise you had *him* in the hall! Sorry! I'll give you a minute.' With that, she spun and disappeared in the direction of the lounge.

'Just give it five seconds,' I murmured.

'Give what five seconds?' asked Jack, but no sooner had he spoken than there was a communal shrieking from the lounge followed by a desperate 'Sssshhhhhh, they'll hear you!'

'Five seconds for Sarah to tell everyone you're here,' I grimaced. 'Apart from Allie and Sean, no one knows I'm seeing anyone.' Jack slid an arm around my shoulders, clearly at ease with the impending meeting with my nearest and dearest.

'Sarah's a big fan of *FireLab* too, so there's no way she wouldn't have recognised you. She's lovely, but quite ... uh ... abrasive, and she swears like a trooper.

Two of my friends from the studios are here too.'

Jack smiled. 'I'm sure I can hold my own. Are you OK with them knowing?'

'Yes! Definitely. I want my friends and family to know, it's just the press I want to avoid.'

'OK, sweetheart, whenever you're ready.' He gestured towards the lounge, but I could tell he was referring to making our relationship public, too.

Taking a deep breath, we made our way along the corridor. I paused by a side table to lay down the flowers and stepped into the open space with Jack just behind me. As I looked around, I saw Allie and Sean grinning, Mr and Mrs Shaw smiling, and five very expectant faces staring at Jack and I.

'See? I bloody well said it was him!' Sarah blurted before slapping a hand over her mouth.

My mum would usually have chided Sarah for swearing, but she obviously had more important things to concentrate on, like why I was standing next to a film star and looking pretty damn cosy with him.

'Uh, this is my mum and dad, Alison and Jeff, and you know Mel and Lisa. And this is Sarah, who you met in the hall.' I tried to relax and throw a look of disapproval Sarah's way, but she was oblivious, practically jigging on the spot, and merely gave a jaunty wave.

'Everyone, this is Jack,' I said simply, his fame rendering any further introduction unnecessary.

The entire group remained silent. In fact, the only noise was a faint 'splat' as the mini-quiche my mum had been eating dropped from her fingers and hit the floor.

'Well, hello, Jack ...' my mum stammered, wiping up her quiche and turning her beady eyes on me. 'So, Cait, how do you know each other?' she asked. I smiled, knowing full well that if you ran this sentence through a Mum translator, this is what you'd get:

*Input: How do you know each other?*
*Translation: Are you dating him?*

I was intensely aware of the eyes staring at me and completely lost track of my thoughts under their scrutiny. I knew exactly what I wanted to say: 'He's my boyfriend.' Short, concise, and to the point, but what came out instead was a load of nonsense. 'Ummm, we … well, we've … I mean we're … ummm …'

I looked desperately at Jack, who was smiling broadly, obviously amused by my reaction. Bastard.

'You seem to be struggling, Caitlin, do you want me to help?' he asked quietly, and I immediately nodded and gulped down a nervous swallow of champagne that Allie had shoved into my hand.

I'd expected him to address the room, but instead Jack kept his eyes on me, his voice clear and calm and a million miles away from my cracked composure.

'What was it you said, Caitlin? *"We, we've,* and *we are"*? *"We"* met when Caitlin first arrived in L.A. *"We've"* been spending quite a lot of time together.' This caused my mum to shove my dad in the ribs so hard that beer almost shot out of his nose. I would have laughed, but I was still quite stressed. Jack's voice brought my eyes immediately back to his.

'And lastly, *"we are"*. Well, there are several ways to finish that, so I'll let you choose – *we are* seeing each other, *we are* dating, or *we are* a couple, although they all pretty much mean the same thing,' he stated with a grin so sexy that I instantly flushed.

Since we'd recently extended our relationship in the bedroom too, there were a few more ways we could finish that last sentence – *we are* sharing a bed, *we are* sleeping together, or *we are* having some incredibly hot sessions between the sheets – but they were way too crude to announce in front of my parents.

Judging by the heated look Jack was giving me, I

suspected his mind was travelling along similar lines, but instead of saying anything he laughed and slipped an arm around my waist so we could face the barrage of questions together.

Sarah, Mel, and Lisa gave several whoops of excitement, while Allie, Sean, and her parents watched on with broad grins. My mum and dad were the funniest of the lot, because my dad just nodded his head while my mum gawked at us. Her mouth was actually hanging open like a flytrap. It was probably the most inelegant pose I'd ever seen her in.

Thankfully Sean saved the day by choosing to raise a toast to Jack and I, and to Allie's speedy recovery, and the spotlight moved away from us as the room once again filled with easy conversation and laughter.

Over the course of the next few hours, both Sean and Jack presented themselves as the perfect boyfriends in front of our gathered friends and family. It was quite amusing just how keen they seemed to impress, and was certainly something I would be ribbing Jack about later.

Sean seemed a little tense, but Jack was the total opposite and looked completely at ease. He'd taken the time to chat to everyone, and patiently talked to my parents as Mum got herself more and more flustered with excitement.

Walking into the kitchen to get a refill of my drink, I topped my glass up and turned to find I'd been cornered by Allie and Sarah. 'Hey, shouldn't you be sitting down and resting those stiches?'

'They're fine,' Allie dismissed with a wave of her hand. 'I think perhaps you might have some juicy gossip for us?'

Sarah nodded her agreement and smirked. 'That's exactly what I was thinking! You know me, Cait, I can sniff out gossip from ten miles away, and I'm getting a big whiff right now.' Sarah glanced over her shoulder into the lounge where Jack was talking to Sean, and then looked back to me with a gleam in her eye. 'That's one very handsome, not to mention very *famous*, boyfriend you have there,' she added with a grin. 'Come on, catch me up! How long have you been seeing him?'

Predictably, being the focus of their attention had caused me to blush bright red. Nonchalantly flicking my elastic bands, I shrugged. 'A while. We were friends first, but it's developed into more in the last few weeks.'

'Wow. Well, I gotta say, you two look great together, and he's obviously totally besotted with you,' Sarah commented.

'He is pretty special,' I agreed with a further blush.

'The question is, is he special enough for your very high bedroom standards? Because I have to say, you have a different look about you. I thought it at the hospital but Sean was with us so I didn't want to ask.' Allie raised her eyebrows and waggled them, making it crystal clear what she was referring to. Sex. God, this was so embarrassing, but they were my best mates so if they wanted the gossip, I might as well give it to them.

Giving them a knowing look, I nodded. 'He is,' I paused, smiling, drawing out their wait, '… and we have.'

'*You have?*' Sarah repeated in astonishment, gawking at me. 'Does that mean what I think it does? That you've finally gone and done the deed?'

I was so red now that if I turned off the kitchen light I suspect I would illuminate the entire room, but I gave an embarrassed shrug and nodded. 'Yeah. On Friday night.' I could feel the heat of my blush spreading down my neck, as if so much blood was flowing to my face that it had nowhere else to go and was having to back track. 'And Saturday, and well … everyday between then and now.'

'Wow … You've gone from being a virgin to humping his brains out!' Sarah blurted gleefully, thankfully managing to maintain a whispered tone as she congratulated me.

'Oh my God, Cait! This is so great!' Allie added, '*And?*' she asked expectantly, barely containing her obvious need for the gossip.

'And it's great … he's great,' I said simply. 'I may have waited a long time but it was worth it.'

'I have sixteen stiches in my side, but there's no way I'm not hugging you. Come here.' Allie pulled me into a one-armed hug which Sarah joined and we shared a group cuddle before rejoining the party.

# FIFTY-TWO

## JACK

Across the room, Caitlin giggled at something Sarah said, and the pair of them burst into raucous laughter until Caitlin was clutching at her stomach and wiping tears from her eyes.

Her happiness made my own lips curl into a smile as I watched her. She was happy and relaxed, and seemed to have put the stress of the last week behind her, even if just for tonight.

She looked gorgeous too, in a pale pink skirt that went to mid-thigh and a white blouse with short sleeves. I'd noticed she'd started to expose more skin than she used to, but when I'd questioned her she'd just shrugged and said she didn't feel the need to hide away any more. I'd cornered Allie and asked her, and she'd said she thought it was my influence making Caitlin braver, but whatever the reason, it was amazing to see her coming out of her shell more and more.

Just as I was thinking that perhaps I should stop staring at her like a lovesick puppy, I felt someone come up beside me, and looked down to find Caitlin's mum also gazing across the room at her daughter.

'I can never thank you enough. You've brought my daughter back to me,' she murmured, her eyes glistening. 'When Caitlin was younger, she was so full of life. Then she met … *him*. She changed, withdrew from me and her dad, and then after …' This time her pause came with a small sob that indicated the deep pain she felt, a pain I imagine only a mother could feel. 'Well, after things with Greg finished she was a totally different person.'

Alison sniffed, and as she wiped a stray tear away from the corner of her eye I placed a reassuring hand on her shoulder.

'Seeing her tonight, with you, she's like the daughter I had before. She's so happy, so confident again.' Alison turned her face towards me and smiled, a full to the brim kind of smile that almost made me feel a bit teary myself. 'Thank you, Jack. Thank you so much.'

Wow. The praise was totally undeserved. After all, all I'd done was fall in love with her daughter. The rest Caitlin had done herself.

'Caitlin means the absolute world to me, Mrs Byrne. I'm in this for the long term. Please know I will never, ever hurt her, or allow anyone else to.' I watched her chin wobble as more tears threatened, but then she gathered her control and nodded with a huge smile.

'I can see that.' She stared me directly in the eyes and the trust I saw there was quite overwhelming. 'She told me how you saved her from … *him* …' She spat it out with the same level of hatred I held.

'I'm just glad I got there in time.' In truth, I wish I'd got there sooner. A shudder wracked through my body as I clenched my teeth. I wished with all my heart that I could have been ten minutes earlier and prevented Caitlin from having to experience that horrific nightmare for the second time.

My body was thrumming with energy, but surprisingly I felt the hatred I had for Greg completely surpassed by my love for Caitlin.

Alison clicked her tongue in the dismissive way that only a mother can, and shook her head. 'You downplay your part, Jack. You're a good man, and you saved her that day, and Allie too.'

Alison excused herself, saying she needed to sort out her make-up, and I decided it was time to get some contact with my girl. It had been far too long since I'd felt her skin against mine.

# FIFTY-THREE

## SEAN

Gradually our happy group of visitors moved around the table in preparation for the Mexican meal I'd ordered from a caterer. It looked delicious: chilli con carne, nachos topped with melted cheese and jalapeños, black beans, and a stack of spicy chicken tacos, but I was too nervous to think about eating.

I was hungry, but there was no way I could focus on food yet, not when we still had our big announcement to make.

Out of our gathered group, two people now knew of our engagement: Allie, and her dad Simon. We hadn't even told Cait, because I'd wanted to be a bit traditional and speak to Allie's parents first. I'd pulled Simon to one side earlier and asked his permission to wed his daughter, and I'm not kidding when I say it was the most shit-scared I'd ever been in my entire life. Admittedly it was a bit belated seeing as I'd already asked Allie, but thankfully he seemed to appreciate the sentiment, and after giving me a brief 'she's my little girl and you better take care of her speech' he had said yes.

Thank fuck for that.

Once everyone was seated, I stood up and picked up my bottle of beer. I'd already discussed with Allie what to say , and we'd decided that the Greg incident shouldn't be mentioned any more – it had been horrific for all involved and would need to be raised again in the future, but for tonight, mentioning it would only put a dampener on everyone's mood.

'It's time for a toast. Firstly, Cait, happy birthday. Let's all raise a glass.'

After a pretty tuneless rendition of happy birthday, we all toasted Cait, who was now blushing as red as a tomato, and when everyone took their seats again I remained standing. 'Actually, I have one more announcement to make.' Looking down at Allie sitting next to me, I found her grinning at me expectantly, her eyes glowing with happiness.

'Or perhaps I should say *we* have an announcement.' Taking her hand, I pulled her to her feet and watched as she quickly slipped her engagement ring on – it had been hidden in her pocket all night.

'I'm extremely proud to announce that I asked Allie to marry me last week, and she has agreed to be my wife.'

After a split second of shock, the room exploded into cheers and whoops as Allie's mum – Bethan – who had had no idea about any of this, burst into happy tears and rushed around the table to embrace Allie and myself in a trembling hug.

Next was Cait, who threw a fake look of annoyance at Allie and narrowed her eyes. 'I can't believe you didn't tell me!! If I wasn't so happy for you, you'd be in big trouble!'

After congratulations were given all round, and everyone had ooh-ed and ahh-ed over Allie's ring, we finally got around to eating the delicious spread. I couldn't help but tuck Allie at my side at the table and grin like an absolute buffoon for the rest of the meal.

# FIFTY-FOUR

## JACK

I was staring at Caitlin again, watching her across the table as we ate, and not even caring if everyone here could see how bad I had it for her.

This girl had fast become my whole life, and ever since Sean had announced his proposal to Allie I hadn't been able to get the idea out of my head. I desperately wanted that level of commitment. She was my soul mate. I had no doubts in my mind that she was the woman I wanted to spend the rest of my life with.

Lambert's attack had allowed me to see with complete clarity just how important Caitlin was to me, and it had unleashed an urgency to solidify that bond that was so powerful I could almost feel it as a tangible thing.

Mel reached across and touched Caitlin's arm, breaking me from my thoughts. 'I can't believe you two are really together!' Her eyes were wide and flicking between Caitlin and I with a gleeful twinkle. 'I mean, Lisa and I had seen you together at the coffee stand but we thought you were friends – we had no idea you were dating!'

Caitlin gave a chuckle and glanced at me, her cheeks pink with a blush from either the wine or the unexpected attention, I couldn't be sure which.

'She didn't make it easy,' I commented dryly.

'Keeping him on his toes!' Mel giggled.

Leaning across, Lisa gave us a speculative glance.

'You've kept it so quiet, how come we've not seen an announcement?'

This question seemed to get the attention of the entire table as everyone went silent and turned their gaze towards us.

'Ummm ...' Caitlin fidgeted and just when I thought she was going to flick her elastic bands she reached across and linked her fingers with mine. Such a simple action, but it had my chest compressing with the intimacy – she was turning to me for support.

Licking her lips, Caitlin let out a low breath and shrugged. 'Everyone around this table knows what's happened recently with my ex ...' She paused, seeming to work through her words before she spoke, and I gripped her fingers in silent support. 'He's still not been caught, and I ... I didn't want to put Jack at risk. Greg might be nuts enough to target Jack.'

There were a few murmurs around the table and Sarah nodded. 'So you guys are going to go public once Greg's caught?'

Caitlin blinked then shrugged. 'Yeah, I guess so.'

'It's so exciting!' Mel chipped in. 'It's like the celebrity magazines but real life! How are you going to do it? Be seen in public? Or make a statement? Attend a big glitzy event hand in hand?' Mel was getting really excited. The added atmosphere seemed to be having the opposite effect on Caitlin, and I watched as she squeezed her lips together in a tight line. 'We haven't really thought that far ahead yet.'

She hadn't, but I had. I wanted a press release and then I'd use every opportunity to have Caitlin on my arm in public.

Caitlin smiled and stood up as she turned towards the kitchen. 'Right, I'll get the puddings.'

Something about her voice didn't sound quite right, and as she walked away I saw her hands clench into fists by her side. Hmm. I excused myself from the table and followed her into the kitchen, where I found her leaning on the counter with her eyes closed.

'Hey, what's up, sweetheart?'

Caitlin's eyes sprung open as she jumped in surprise. 'Hey. Nothing, I'm fine.'

Crossing my arms, I raised an eyebrow and shook my head. 'You're a self-confessed bad liar, Caitlin, don't try to fool me. What is it?'

Caitlin swallowed and leant back onto the kitchen surface again with a sigh. 'I've spent the last three years trying to be as inconspicuous as possible. I've had no social media, barely taken any photographs, hardly even used my e-mail account. I ... I guess the idea of going from that to the polar opposite is just freaking me out a little.'

Her words reassured me, because of course she would be nervous about joining me in the exposed life that I lived. 'You'll be at my side, though, sweetheart, we'll deal with it together.'

'Yeah.' Caitlin set her gaze on mine. 'I think I've been in a bit of a bubble up until now. I mean, I know you're famous, but I hadn't really considered the long-term meaning of that. Then announcing us as a couple to everyone and seeing how giddy they all got ... it's just given me an insight into what the future might be like.' Drawing in a stuttering breath, Caitlin averted her eyes. 'I guess ... occasionally I just wonder why you're with me when you could have an actress on your arm. What if you meet someone glamorous? It'd be so much easier for you.'

Easier? Wow. Her words had stunned me into silence. I couldn't believe she could doubt my commitment like that, let alone how shallow her words made me out to be.

'I can't believe you could even say that,' I blurted.

370

'Do you really think so little of me? That I would just drop you if someone "perfect" came along?'

'No, I mean … I don't know. I've never been in a proper relationship before, and now I've met you and … you know I've fallen pretty hard, pretty quick.' Even through my irritation my heart swelled at her words. 'If you left me it would be awful enough, but if we go public and then you leave it would be even worse because I'd have the whole world watching …'

Jesus. I couldn't bear to listen to another word, so I covered the space between us in two steps and gripped the tops of her arms. 'Enough. Where has this come from, Caitlin? You know I love you, I'm not leaving you, sweetheart, *ever*.'

*I want you to marry me.* I only just managed not to say the words out loud.

'Let me be frank with you. I've been in this industry a long time, I've met and dated "perfect" women, and if I wanted to be with one of them, I would be.' She blinked, hurt expanding in her pupils at my words. 'But I don't, Caitlin. I want to be with *you*.'

Unable to bear the gap between us for a second longer I dragged her against my chest and felt my shoulders relax when her body melted into my embrace. Lowering my lips to her ear, I kissed the hair there, inhaling her scent.

'You are perfect.' It was simple. She made me whole. 'This doubting needs to stop. I don't care how long you want us to remain a secret, but I need to know that you understand that you are it for me.'

Caitlin pulled back, and then she nodded

'I'm sorry I freaked out … *Again*.' Rolling onto her tiptoes, she placed a kiss on my lips. 'I still can't entirely believe this has happened, but I promise I won't doubt it any more. I love you, Jack. You're it for me too.'

# FIFTY-FIVE

## CAIT

Once Jack had finally let me go, we walked hand in hand back to the dining room, grinning like idiots and carrying a dessert in our free hands.

'So, while you were in the kitchen, we decided how you should out yourselves to the press,' declared Sarah.

Oh God. Here we go. Sarah always had a hair-brained scheme up her sleeve.

Jack caught my eye and smiled at me, but then squeezed my hand reassuringly.

Breathing a sigh of relief, I turned to Sarah but Jack intervened again. 'I'm sure it'll be a great plan, Sarah. But I think we'll let Caitlin decide when she's ready to have her picture in the papers.'

'Oh. But my plan was really elaborate ...' Sarah commented with a fake pout.

'Actually, I think I've decided,' I announced, much to the delight of my friends and the surprise of Jack. Even Sarah seemed to lose her disappointment and looked perky again. 'Spill the beans then!' she urged.

'My parents are here for a few weeks, so let's use that time to settle into things and see what's happening with the police investigation, and then ... I'll go out for dinner with you anywhere you like and the press can take as many pictures as they want. We can even make a statement.' I looked directly at Jack and watched as a smile of delight spread on his lips and extended all the way up to the crinkling corners of his eyes.

'Really?'

'Yep,' I nodded.

'No disguises?' he continued.

'No disguises, I promise,' I whispered with a grin.

'Sounds like a deal,' said Jack, nodding proudly and sealing it with a kiss, and even though all my friends and family were watching I couldn't help but join in.

The evening passed in a lovely, warm blur, and in no time, my parents and Mr and Mrs Shaw were piling into a car and being driven to their hotel. Mel and Lisa were going to get a cab later, Sarah was sleeping on the sofa, and Jack and I had got lucky and been allocated the spare room.

Leaning out of the door to wave them off, I returned to the lounge to find Jack waiting for me. 'As always, I've got an early shoot in the morning, so I'd better get to bed.'

'Aww, look at his face! He doesn't want to leave his girlfriend!' Sarah teased, her drunken state making her even more candid than usual and causing her to pronounce it like 'guurlfrieend'. 'You can go to bed if you want, Cait, we promise not to listen to your rampant shagging!'

My mouth dropped open. Mel and Lisa giggled, looking a little embarrassed, and Allie and Sean melted into a fit of laughter before disappearing into the kitchen to mix some birthday cocktails.

God, Sarah could be *so* embarrassing.

Grimacing, I looked up at Jack, expecting him to look mortified, but he seemed totally unfazed, and to my utter shock he closed the gap between us with a purposeful expression on his face.

'In that case ...' He winked at me impishly, scooped me up and tossed me over his shoulder, resulting in a cheer from my friends and a shriek from me. 'I shall have to take her to the bedroom and have my wicked way with her,' he remarked, before giving my bottom a resounding slap, causing laughter to echo around the room.

Jack got about halfway down the corridor towards the bedroom and then carefully placed me on the ground before giving me quick peck on the lips. 'As much as I would love to worship you, I won't. It's your birthday party, you should stay up with your friends and celebrate in style.'

Hmm. Being worshipped sounded pretty good, but Jack was right, it was fairly early and I did have a room full of people here who had all come across for my birthday.

Once Jack had given me a lovely goodnight kiss and disappeared into the spare room I briefly fanned my face and stepped back into the lounge. As my gaze travelled over my friends, an expectant grin spread on my face. I knew they'd all want to deliver their verdict on Jack, and they certainly didn't wait long to deliver it – they liked him, *a lot*, and thought we made the perfect couple.

I had to say, I wholeheartedly agreed.

# FIFTY-SIX

## JACK

Thankfully, ever since the party, Caitlin had stuck to her promise and been far more relaxed; she'd stopped doubting herself, and had promised me several more times that we'd go public once there was more news on Greg.

She was now cradled against me, snoozing after we'd spent the evening lazing with a movie. Her parents were staying with us before flying home at the weekend, but they'd opted for an afternoon out shopping and still weren't back – which I suspected was their discreet way of giving us some privacy, something we'd both appreciated and made immediate use of by spending two-and-a-half hours in bed.

For the movie we'd chosen a release I was actually looking forward to seeing, but we'd barely gotten past the intro when she'd started kissing me, and obviously I was never going to try and stop her when she pounced like that. Caitlin was becoming much braver with initiating things, telling me exactly when she was horny and often just walking in and dropping to her knees if she fancied giving me a blow job.

Her new-found boldness was a real fucking turn-on.

Predictably, our kisses had turned to another round of lazy lovemaking, and the lovemaking had ended with us dozing on the sofa and missing pretty much the entire film.

Her fingers were rhythmically trailing back and forth

across my chest and it felt so good that there was no way I was going to disturb her. The movement was hypnotic, lulling me toward sleep even though it was only just gone 8 p.m.

The noise of my phone caused her to jump, before she gave a laugh and sat up, pushing her wayward hair from her face and looking so adorable that it made me want to start kissing her all over again.

'I almost fell asleep,' she said, her face still looking warm. I loved the way she flushed when she was aroused. The fact I knew I was the only man to ever make her look this way was an even bigger turn-on, and I couldn't help the satisfied smile that spread on my lips as I sat up and reached for my phone.

Seeing the number on the screen made my smile die on my lips and I felt my heart accelerate until it was pounding in my ears. It was Edward Pearson, one of the private detectives working with Flynn, and there could be only one reason he would be calling.

'Hello?' I tried to sound casual, but it was bloody difficult with my entire body on full alert.

'He's still in L.A.'

Fuck. Edward's words caused my blood to turn to fury in my veins.

## CAIT

I wasn't entirely sure what had happened in the last ten seconds, but Jack had gone from relaxed and happy to radiating tension.

I fidgeted on the spot, unsure whether I should leave him to his call, or wait for him to finish.

'You're sure?' Jack demanded, the flush in his cheeks seeming to drain away, leaving him looking pale and drawn.

'When?' Seconds later, Jack's eyes closed; presumably he had heard an answer he didn't like, and I found myself getting frustrated. What the hell was wrong?

'Where?' Nodding, Jack began to awkwardly shrug into his shirt. 'Text me the address and stay there, I'll be straight over.'

Quickly pulling on his jeans, Jack ended the call and immediately dialled another number, leaving me practically bouncing on the balls of my feet in irritation.

Shoving his foot into one of his Converse, he didn't even bother to tie the laces, just pushing them under the tongue instead. 'Flynn? Get the car here now, I'll be out in a minute.'

Dragging my dress on, I stepped backwards, bumping into the couch and resting my thighs on it to support my wobbly legs as I found myself flicking at my elastic bands nervously. Whatever the call had been about, it was obviously important.

Hanging up, Jack pocketed his phone, fastened his jeans, and turned to me. His eyes immediately went to my wrist and I saw him wince and soften his tense expression.

'Hey.' Coming over to me, he brushed the backs of his knuckles across my cheek so gently it was as if he thought I was going to flinch away. Which, after witnessing his bristling anger, I nearly did.

'Enough of this,' he whispered, taking a loose hold on my wrist to halt my flicking. Lifting it to his lips, he dropped several soft, slow kisses on the reddened skin, before lifting his head and looking into my eyes.

'I'm sorry if I scared you, I've just had some news about a situation that I need to attend to, but it's absolutely nothing for you to worry about, OK?'

Just seeing his confident look reassured me a little and I let out a breath I didn't know I'd been holding. 'OK. But you looked really pissed off. Is it something to do with Greg?'

'It's work stuff, but I don't have time to explain now. We can talk about it later, I promise.' His left eye flickered into a wince just slightly, and I began to wonder if that was a sign that he was lying. 'I have to go, sweetheart.' Picking up an old hoodie that he usually wore for running, he dragged it over his head and gave me another look.

My stomach twisted with nerves even though I didn't know what it was I was feeling anxious about, but I nodded anyway and followed him to the front door.

'Stay here and relax with your parents when they get back. I'm not sure how long I'll be but I promise to come back tonight.'

Surely if it was to do with Greg he would have told me? Something in my gut told me that whatever it was wasn't good, so instinctively I found myself reaching out and gripping his arm as he tried to leave.

'Be careful,' I whispered, my voice reedy and thin and infinitely pathetic.

Jack turned back, his face creasing with worry, and in

a split second had me hauled up against him in a tight embrace.

Placing a firm kiss on the top of my head, he leant back and repeated the action on my lips. He pressed his tongue into my mouth where it massaged against mine until I moaned and then he stepped back. 'Hold that thought. We can pick this up as soon as I get home.'

Just like that, he was gone. Hurrying out of the front door and down the path, Jack didn't even glance back at me once. If he had, he'd have seen me flicking my elastic bands again.

# JACK

'That was longer than one minute,' Flynn grunted by way of greeting as I jogged to the car and practically threw myself into the passenger seat.

'I know, Caitlin sensed something was up.' I forced the seat belt into the lock and made an impatient gesture with my hand. 'Get going, haven't got a second to waste.'

Flashing me a narrow-eyed stare, Flynn followed my instructions and started the car. 'You wanna explain what the fuck is going on? You call me up in the middle of my night off, demand I get here, and when I do you look like someone's shoved a poker up your ass.'

Pulling out my phone, I found the text from Pearson and began programming the satnav with the address he had sent me. 'They found him. Lambert, he's still in L.A.' Flynn had been working every spare minute on tracking down Caitlin's ex, so this would no doubt be music to his ears.

There was a second of silence as Flynn digested my words, and then his foot stamped onto the accelerator so hard that I was thrown back in my seat. 'Let's go get the miserable fucker,' he suggested.

'My thoughts exactly,' I agreed grimly. Every fibre in my being was screaming at me to go to Lambert and rip him limb from pitiful limb. Gregory fucking Lambert. Caitlin's abuser, Allie's attacker.

After stabbing Allie and attempting to rape Caitlin for the second time, I'd thought he might have scarpered, but the arrogant fuck had hung around. All the better for me, but I was going to make him regret that decision.

From the reports that Edward had supplied last week, it was clear Lambert's abuse of Caitlin was far from a one-time thing; in fact, there were multiple allegations against him for sexual assault, rape, and attempted rape. Enough to fill four A4 pages, spanning a period of over nine years.

It seemed he got his kicks from mistreating women, and Caitlin's sweet, innocent perfection had caught his eye and turned into an obsession.

How the tables had turned, I thought, because now *he* had caught *my* eye.

# FIFTY-SEVEN

## JACK

'How do you want to approach this, Jack?' Flynn asked, breaking the silence that had fallen between us. 'Your face is far too familiar to go storming in and kicking the shit out of him. You need to be careful or you'll end up in jail. I'd be happy to do it for you.' I knew very well that Flynn's offer was no word of a lie. Back in the army he'd been a violent fucker, known for his fighting skills and lack of a conscience. It didn't matter if he was unarmed, he had more than enough imagination and training to be a veritable fighting machine if given the chance.

Rolling my head from side to side, I tried to loosen off the bunched muscles in my neck. It was no good, I was wound so tight I could feel every tic and jump of the tension flowing around my body. I actually found Flynn's offer quite touching; coming from a guy as unsentimental as he was, I knew it showed how much he respected me and the bond I had with Caitlin, and that knowledge meant a great deal to me.

'I appreciate that, Flynn, thank you. But unfortunately it's not going to be quite as simple as that.'

Giving an acknowledging grunt, he gripped the steering wheel a little tighter. 'Never fucking is. You ready to fill me in on the details from Edward?'

Clearing my throat, I pulled my phone from my pocket and scanned the messages. 'I paid that private security team you hired a little bonus to help us track down Lambert. They managed to trace a lot of his movements over the past few years. It seems that while he was happy to abuse and attack other women, he was still constantly searching for Caitlin. She obviously caught his eye more than the rest.'

'The one that got away,' Flynn grunted.

'Yeah, that's what I thought. Caitlin has made herself as invisible as possible. She has no social media, a burner phone, and no other obvious means for him to follow her, so it made tracing her tricky. He entered the states a little over six weeks ago, but the trail went dead until he surfaced at the studios and hit me. Then he managed to drop under the radar again until the attack on Allie and Caitlin.

'A little over half an hour ago, a report of a sexual assault in progress was filed from a downtown apartment. The woman who called said her flatmate was being attacked by a guy she had been on a date with, and gave his name as Greg Lambert.'

'Holy shit,' Flynn cursed under his breath. We must have been breaking the legal limit by quite some way. 'He's still using his real name?' Flynn exclaimed, letting out a sharp breath that was almost a scornful laugh. 'Arrogant fucker deserves what's coming to him.'

'He does,' I agreed, my voice thick and low. 'Apparently the flatmate got home from work early and heard her friend screaming so she called the police. Edward's people had been tracking the police radio in case Greg's name came up, so I guess we got lucky.'

Checking the satnav, I saw we were just three minutes away from our destination, so I pulled up the hood on my sweater and donned my shades. It wasn't the best disguise ever, but it would have to do. 'The police are already on the scene, but one of Edward's guys is too. He's pretty pally with the detective leading the case so he thinks he might be able to get me a minute to speak with Lambert.'

Flynn took his eyes off the road long enough to fix me with a hard stare. 'You better do more than fucking speak to him, or I really will shove a poker up your ass.'

'Don't worry, I plan to,' I replied as I saw the red and blue lights flashing in the road ahead.

As Flynn pulled the car to a stop by the police tape he looked at me and tutted. 'You're still recognisable.' Leaning across, he pulled out a black woollen hat and threw it in my lap. 'This rolls out into a balaclava. Don't forget to use it when you're with him, we can't have your name getting dragged into this.'

Nodding my thanks, I pulled the beanie hat on, replaced my hood, and slid from the car.

Edward's guy on the scene knew our car and must have seen us coming, because he was standing beside me before I'd even taken in the scene. I hunched my shoulders, still with my hood, hat, and glasses on, and watched as the tall, broad man pulled some ID from his wallet to prove he did indeed work with Pearson Security.

'Jack, my name is Wilson.' Pearson and his team all knew who I was, but a very large upfront payment could get you pretty much anything you needed these days, discretion included. 'Our suspect, Mr Lambert, is to be taken to the central police department for further questioning over tonight's attempted assault. I've managed to delay his departure. At the moment, he's inside with two uniformed officers. I'm familiar with Detective Jacobs and he's keen to move things along. I haven't mentioned your name; but I've told him you're a friend of mine.'

'Thank you, Wilson.' Nodding curtly, I followed him as he began to lead me towards a heavily built guy in a suit who was barking orders at a forensic team and looking almost as harassed as I felt.

'Jacobs, this is my friend. He'd like a quick word with you.'

Jacobs sized me up, no doubt taking in my shades and hood with suspicion – it was night-time, after all – before finally holding out a hand to me. 'Thank you for speaking to me. I know you need to get him to jail, but that fucker in there attacked my girlfriend and has been making her life hell for the last three years.'

I could tell my words were not the ones he had been expecting, and before my eyes, the detective's face lost its suspicion and moulded into understanding. 'He's a scrawny runt and looks so unassuming, but he's got a list as long as my fucking arm.'

'Did you work the attack in Studio City? The two girls? One was stabbed and the other only just escaped a rape?' I asked, watching as the Detective's eyes narrowed and then he nodded.

'My girlfriend was one of the victims. Again. This is the second time he's tried to rape her.'

'Christ, I'm sorry to hear that. I did work that case …'

Every muscle clenched in my body. 'Will he go down for this? Or is there a chance he'll get off?'

The detective gave a thin, satisfied smile. 'There's no chance. We have some possible links between him and a few attacks on students several years ago, but since he's been back in the US he's become sloppy; we've got DNA evidence from several of the victims, including a spittle sample from the attack on your girlfriend, and tonight we have him at the scene with two viable witnesses. Seems like his MO is to target younger women who he can impress by splashing them with cash. Often students or recent graduates. If I get my way, he won't be getting out for a very, very long time. If ever.'

My shoulders sagged in relief that Caitlin would

finally be free from the shadow of this monster.

'What exactly can I do to help?' the detective inquired.

It was now or never. I doubted the guy would give me what I wanted, but I had to try. 'I want one minute alone to speak to him.' Jacobs' mouth thinned into a tight line as he continued to appraise me, and I quickly realised that I needed to do some more persuasive talking. 'Do you have a girlfriend, or a wife?'

Jacobs nodded, and rubbed his chin. 'Yeah, a wife and two girls.'

'Then I'm sure you can understand how intolerable I find it to know that the woman I love was hurt, and *still* hurts, because of that piece of shit in there.'

I saw from the spark in his eyes that Jacobs understood exactly what I was saying. 'Wilson says you were in the military for a time back in the UK?' I nodded my reply, too tense now to speak without demanding that he quit the small talk and just take me in there.

'Me too, US Army. Served a term before getting out and changing to policing. Easier to enforce real justice in the army, if you know what I mean.' I just kept quiet and nodded.

Jacobs drew in a long breath and scratched at the back of his head. 'You want to *talk* to him, huh?' he repeated, one of his eyebrows rising.

'I do.' I pulled off my sunglasses so the detective could see the desperation in my eyes. 'My girlfriend was a virgin the first time he tried to force himself on her. She's still messed up from it now,' I confided, my voice dropping as I struggled to contain my emotion. Donning my shades again, I tried to blink away the moisture I found forming in my eyes.

'Girl tonight was a virgin too,' Jacobs confirmed. His use of *was* made my gut twist sickeningly. Cracking the knuckles of one hand, Jacobs glanced down the street.

'My eldest daughter is studying at the local college. She lives in that block just over there, the grey brick one. This so easily could have been her.' Shaking his head, he turned back to me and sniffed loudly.

'You were never here, you never met me, and this never happened,' he stated, before cocking his head toward the house. 'Come with me.' My heart rate rocketed through the roof. He was actually going to take me inside, and all I could do was try to keep calm as I followed him. Jacobs led us through the house – it was cluttered and messy and looked just like the student digs I'd lived in back in my college days. Jesus, Greg was in his thirties now, I couldn't believe he had attacked a student.

My thoughts were broken when we climbed the stairs and arrived at a closed door. Jacobs pushed it open and ordered the room to be cleared before two uniformed officers traipsed out. Turning to me, Jacobs gave me a long, hard stare. 'I'll give you your minute. Try not to leave any visible bruises, and he better be alive when I come in.'

Nodding once, I pulled off my shades and pocketed them, then, as soon as Jacobs had turned away, I unrolled the beanie so my face was covered and entered the room to come face to face with Gregory Lambert.

As I stepped inside, I could smell sweat, sex, and cheap aftershave. My nose wrinkled from the odour. Lambert was half dressed, standing in only his jeans with his hands cuffed behind his back. His tall, wiry frame was covered in numerous poorly executed tattoos and a couple of claw marks. His ratty little eyes turned towards me, and I'm sure from the sudden widening of his pupils that he knew what was about to befall him. The balaclava was probably enough of a giveaway.

'Who are you?' he demanded, as he backed towards a wall.

389

I lunged forward. It was only sixty seconds, but I intended to use each and every one of them.

The detective had said to leave no visible bruises, so with one gloved hand I gripped his shoulder and brought my knee into his groin as hard as I could.

I'm a big guy, so the force of my leg was pretty impressive, even if I do say so myself.

Lambert let out a startled yelp, followed by a long groan of pain as he slumped forwards, but I held him up by his armpits. Once I'd started, I couldn't stop. Images of Caitlin's scared, trembling body filled my mind, and with every knee to his groin I tried to extract some revenge for her.

I must have hit him in the nuts at least ten times, and I was panting heavily when I finally drew away. As soon as my support was gone he keeled forward, collapsing to his knees and spewing vomit so violently that I had to jump back to avoid it as it spattered across the threadbare carpet.

I quickly moved behind his collapsed form and wrapped my gloved hands around his neck.

'Please, no! Leave me alone!' he yelped, his voice high and panicked. 'Who the fuck are you?'

'Who am I? I'm your shadow. Stay away from Caitlin, you understand? No more letters. No more postcards. No visits, phone calls, nothing. You get me?'

'Whatever …' he sputtered, another mouthful of vomit spewing from his mouth.

'I'm not sure you're taking this seriously, Gregory,' I stated. 'If you ever, *ever* contact her again, I'll kill you before you even see me coming.' Adjusting my grip on his neck, I pressed two fingers into the pressure point I wanted. 'If I apply pressure here, you'll be unconscious within eight seconds. If I keep that pressure, you'll wake up brain damaged, if you wake up at all.' I began a quiet countdown for Greg's benefit.

'Eight ... seven ... six ... five ... four ... three ...'

'Fuck! I'm getting spots before my eyes! OK! OK! Fuck! I get it, no more contact with Cait!'

Shoving Lambert forward so he fell into the puddle of vomit, I stepped over him towards the door.

'I'm glad we have an understanding. You better stick to it, Gregory, because I'll be watching. Your prison phone calls, your mail, *everything* will be checked.'

With that I strode from the room, feeling marginally better. I had murderous thoughts towards this fucker, but I wasn't a killer. I'd had retribution for Caitlin, and Lambert would get locked away. It was a winning situation all round.

Flynn didn't say a word as I silently got into the car beside him and ripped off the balaclava, nor did we speak as he pulled the car away from the curb. In fact, we probably sat in silence for at least five minutes, the only noise in the small interior being my slightly raised breathing.

Finally, it seemed Flynn could take no more. 'All sorted?'

Seeing Flynn glance my way, I gave a solemn nod. 'Yes.'

'What did you do to him?'

Flynn no doubt wanted the gory details and a step-by-step run-through, but I wasn't really in the mood for talking, so I kept it short and sweet. 'Let's just say his voice will be really high-pitched for a while and his nuts are now residing somewhere in his chest cavity.'

Removing my shades, I tucked them into the neck of my jumper before running my hands over my face. 'I couldn't do too much, the detective was already putting his neck on the line for me as it was so I didn't push my luck, but I feel a whole lot better now. Plus, the detective told me Gregory will be going away for a long time, probably a life sentence because of the evidence they have on him.'

'Fucking right too.' Flynn agreed. 'Good call with the gloves, by the way. So, you wanna go for a drink to help relax you, or you want me to take you home?'

'Home, I want to see Caitlin,' I responded immediately.

Flynn nodded once and the car dropped into silence as he put his foot down and drove me home to my girl.

# FIFTY-EIGHT

## CAIT

I woke up pleasantly warm and rolled over with a satisfied sigh. It was only as my hand stretched towards Jack's side and felt the stone-cold sheets that I realised he wasn't back. Startled into immediate wakefulness, I sat up and turned towards the clock on the bedside table.

3.27 a.m.

Blinking, I checked I had read it correctly and hastily began to untangle myself from his soft sheets. He promised he'd be back, so where was he?

My stomach twisted as I fumbled for the bedside light so I could check my phone.

No calls, no messages, and it was over six hours since he'd left the house.

The cool of the room mixed with my concern and made my skin pop with goose pimples, so I grabbed Jack's navy dressing-gown from the back of the door and slipped it on, lifting it up to stop myself tripping as I headed pnto the landing.

Soft light permeated the hallway below, pooling on the carpet from a crack in the lounge doorway. Was he there? Nervous flutters added to the already tense feeling in my stomach as I began to cautiously descend the stairs.

I paused as I reached the lounge door. What if it wasn't Jack inside? What if I pushed open the door and discovered a burglar? My heartrate leapt before I let out a soft, shaky laugh and rolled my eyes. I knew the extent of the security in this compound, and I knew it was top-notch – nothing, or nobody, could get in without permission.

Mind you, that's what I'd thought about my place in Studio City, and Greg had managed to get in there, hadn't he? A shudder ripped through my body, causing me to draw the dressing-gown tighter around myself. It was the only thing keeping me vaguely calm, because the fabric was surrounding me with Jack's reassuring scent.

Calming my erratic breathing, I gripped the collars of the dressing-gown as I poked my head around the gap in the door.

I felt my entire body relax when I saw Jack's familiar profile in the soft glow of a solitary lamp. *Thank God.* My shoulders slumped as I gripped the doorframe and released a slow breath. I must have moved with the stealth of a mouse because Jack didn't appear to have noticed me.

Taking a quiet moment to observe him, I ran my gaze over his features; he was sitting in an armchair, staring at the empty fireplace, with a tumbler of amber liquid in his hand, and a sheath of papers splayed on the coffee table in front of him. His posture looked relaxed, but I could see from the dip of his eyebrows that he was troubled, and that made me reluctant to approach him.

Staying by the door, I cleared my throat to catch his attention. 'Hey. You're back.' My words broke him from his trance and caused him to turn his head towards me. His big, brown eyes lazily trailed up and down me, before his lips twitched with a smile.

'I like you wearing my clothes, but I think I need to buy you a dressing-gown that fits,' he commented. He was right, his dressing-gown was *waaay* too big for me, heaping on the floor by my feet and hanging over my hands, and I couldn't help but giggle self-consciously.

'Did I wake you? I tried to be quiet.'

Shaking my head, I maintained my position by the door. 'No. I woke up because the bed was empty.' And that was totally true; I now disliked sleeping on my own.

'What's up?' I asked tentatively, hoping he'd share his burdens, just as I'd shared mine with him.

Jack placed his drink on the side table and opened up his arms. 'Come here, sweetheart.' There was no hesitation on my part. I went to him keenly, pausing to peel off the dressing-gown so I was just in the T-shirt I wore in bed, and then climbing into his lap.

I seemed to fit against him perfectly, like our bodies were made for each other. Jack wrapped me in his arms, pulling me closer, ever vigilant not to squeeze too hard. But it was never too much. In fact, it was never enough. I wanted more of him every time I was with him, like only constant contact would be enough.

'I'm sorry about earlier. I hope I didn't alarm you.'

He *had* alarmed me. I'd been skittish and fidgety all evening with my parents until they'd gone to bed and I'd forced myself to try and sleep too. I'd lain awake for hours, though, until I'd rolled over and buried my head in his pillow, which had eventually calmed me enough to fall asleep. But he was back now.

'Where did you go?'

There was a second or two of silence, and after expelling a long breath, he cleared his throat. 'We found him.'

I ran his words through my sleepy mind several times, and I got a sickening sensation in my gut as my skin chilled and my throat began to close up.

Greg. He had to be talking about Greg. I knew Flynn had been working to find Greg, but I hadn't actually expected them to have any success. Even though I was almost one hundred per cent sure who he was referring to I found myself asking anyway.

'Who?' God, if my voice got any squeakier I'd be giving chipmunks a run for their money.

Jack spent a few moments stroking down my hair until my erratic breathing had eased and then placed a gentle kiss on the top of my head. 'Greg. We found him.'

Greg. Fucking Greg. The man I had been trying to get away from for the past three years. For several moments, my mind couldn't comprehend it. I wanted to escape thoughts of him, not be reminded ever, ever again, and I found myself pushing away from Jack's lap and stumbling across the rug to the middle of the room.

'That's the police's job. You promised you'd leave it … why … why would you do that?' I could hardly comprehend what he was saying.

I felt simultaneously chilled to the bone and overheated with panic. Somewhere in the fogginess of my brain I knew I was slipping towards an anxiety attack, but I couldn't steer myself away.

I wasn't aware that I had fallen into full on panic mode until I felt warm hands grip my shoulders. 'Breathe, it's OK, Caitlin. *Breathe.*'

I tried to, I really did. My lungs were too tight, and my throat too sore to pull any air in. My cheeks felt wet and my vision was blurry, and the room around me seemed to swim in the lamplight. Squeezing my eyes shut to avoid the disorientating sensation – not to mention the images of Greg that were flooding my mind – I tried to curl my body into a protective ball as a loud, gurgling wheeze tore its way up my throat.

'Wh … what if he'd hurt you?' I wheezed, panic flooding my entire system. The hands on my shoulders began to grip me with force, and I was aware that I was being pulled upright.

'*Caitlin.* Look at me. I'm fine. We're OK.' A hand caressed my cheek, familiar in its warmth and size and I

397

felt a small amount of my fear slide away as Jack's strength seeped into me. 'It's Jack. I'm here, and I'll keep you safe. Look at me, *right now.*' I found myself forcing my stinging eyelids open and trying to focus on his blurry image.

'There's my girl,' he murmured, and he carefully wiped below my eyes to clear the flood of tears that must have fallen from my eyes.

Blimey. That anxiety attack had flared from zero to nuclear level in the blink of an eye. Pulling in a much needed breath I heard just how affected my breathing was and licked my dry lips.

Jack urged me forwards into the safety of his chest, and even though I was still winded, I stepped forwards and buried my face in the warmth of his body. My fingers snaked around his waist, gripping handfuls of his shirt like it was the only thing keeping me grounded.

One of his hands slid to the back of my head, cradling it with infinite care. 'I'm so sorry I upset you, sweetheart. That was never my intention, I swear. But I promised you no more secrets, so I had to tell you where I'd been.'

'I just panicked. I kept thinking about how he'd hurt Allie, and then I imagined you getting injured …' I murmured, my voice thick and low.

'I had to know you were safe. The police were trying to trace him, but Flynn and I carried on our search too.' Jack gave a small shrug as if there had been no other option for him, and then bent forwards to scoop me into his arms and carry us both across to the sofa.

Lowering himself down, he settled me on his lap and gazed into my eyes, his face soft as he watched me. I was no doubt puffy, snotty, and red, but Jack didn't seem to notice or care.

'You are too important to me, Caitlin. I won't ever let anything happen to you. I knew there was a risk he was looking for you. He'll never be able to attack you again, sweetheart.'

'Where is he?'

'He's in police custody. He's going to jail tonight to await trial, but he'll be going to prison for a very long time.'

'What for? The attack on Allie and I?'

Jack's face crumpled into a sad frown. 'I'm not sure you want to know the details, Caitlin.'

I absolutely did. I hated that man more than I'd thought humanly possible, and there was no way I wanted Jack keeping the details from me. The resolute expression on my face had Jack sighing heavily before he flicked a hand towards the papers on the coffee table. 'Multiple accusations of sexual assault,' he muttered quietly.

Multiple? It wasn't just me? Swallowing loudly, I shifted myself on his lap so I could reach the table and gave the papers a more thorough look over. There were pictures of several women on the top sheet.

As my eyes lingered on the papers I felt a sickening chill wrap itself around me as my eyes moved from girl to girl. 'Oh my God. They … they all look like me.'

Scrabbling from his lap, I grabbed the top papers and gazed at image after image of girls who all had similar looks to mine. 'They have my eyes … and all have long, brown hair …' There had to be twenty or so girls here.

Flicking a glance at Jack, I saw him give a grim nod as his nostrils flared, but an even more horrifying thought occurred to me and my hands began to tremble so hard that I dropped the papers and gripped them in my lap instead.

'Oh my God … It's my fault.' I jumped up, my hands digging painfully into the hair at my temples. 'All these girls. If I'd just let him have me … all those years ago then he wouldn't have attacked these other girls!'

Suddenly, my legs gave way and I fell to my knees on the rug as fresh tears sprung to my eyes.

Jack was on the floor in the blink of an eye, wrapping himself around me and pulling me into his arms. 'No, sweetheart, it's not your fault. At least eight of the attacks happened before you even met him.'

Before me? I needed to know he was telling me the truth, so I struggled to swivel in his tight embrace and saw the solemn look in Jack's eyes. 'He's always had a thing for brunettes with green eyes.'

God. After the way he'd treated me I'd always known that Greg wasn't quite right in the head, but I'd never suspected he was this deranged. 'But we dated, we were together a year …'

Nodding, Jack pulled me to him again. 'Yes. The detective I spoke to said you were one of the exceptions. There was one other girl he was with for a while, but most of his victims didn't know him.'

Oh my God. This was so much worse than I'd ever imagined.

'Come on, it's late. Let's go to bed. We can talk more about it tomorrow if you want.'

I didn't feel particularly tired any more, but I could see from the dark circles under Jack's eyes that he needed to rest even if I didn't.

Jack placed a kiss on my temple. 'You're safe, sweetheart. You can sleep soundly. You don't have to look over your shoulder any more. You're free to live your life without fear.' I could barely digest his words. I'd lived carefully and quietly for so long, and I'd assumed I would always have to live that way, but now I was free. Free from the memories of my past.

From Greg.

It felt like a twenty tonne weight had been lifted from my shoulders. He'd been caught. Three years I'd been living in fear. Three long years, and now I was free. It was an odd feeling, and one I suspected would take a while to get used to. A huffed breath left my lungs and I suddenly had to stifle a yawn as overwhelming exhaustion crept up on me. Perhaps I would sleep well after all.

# FIFTY-NINE

## ALLIE

Using the key Cait had given me, I let myself into Jack's house and immediately started to search. 'Cait?!' My voice was shrill as I ran through his house. Where was she? 'Caitlin?'

Finally I heard a noise down the corridor that led to the garden and saw Cait appearing from the patio with a towel around her body, her hair damp. Of course. Typical! The pool was the one place I hadn't checked.

'Jeez, Allie, you sound like you've inhaled a canister of helium, what the heck is the matter?'

She had a point. My voice had gone seriously high-pitched as I'd grown impatient in my search for her.

'Why are you here so early?' Since Greg's reappearance we'd taken to spending most of our free time together as a safety measure. If Cait wasn't in Sean's spare room then I'd head over here after breakfast. Admittedly, I was fairly early today.

Dashing up to her, I immediately dragged her into my arms, pushing aside the remaining twinge of pain in my stiches. 'Sean just called, he said he spoke to Jack and that Greg was caught last night. Why didn't you tell me?'

'It all happened in the middle of the night. Jack didn't get back until after three this morning. I was going to tell you over coffee.'

'So it really happened? He's finally in prison?' I asked in a hoarse whisper.

'Yep. Well, he's in jail while he awaits trial, but Jack said there was so much evidence against him that it's basically a done deal. Greg won't be getting out anytime soon. If ever.'

Cait seemed incredibly calm. Almost too calm. 'You don't have to run from him any more. How are you feeling?'

Cait used the towel to dry her hair and nodded slowly, pulling a T-shirt and pair of shorts over her quickly drying swimsuit. 'I had a bit of a cry last night. But today I feel ...' she shrugged, seemingly lost for words. 'Free. I guess.'

Free. My best friend was free. I immediately burst into tears, clutching Cait again as great, big sobs wracked my chest.

'Woah ... hey, it's OK. We're OK, Allie.'

I sniffed hard to sort myself out. 'Yes. We are. God, this is amazing news, Cait, I'm so relieved for you.'

Nodding, Cait let out a long, low breath as if releasing the last three years of pent-up anxiety. 'Yep. Now, let's make a deal. We put this behind us and don't mention *his* name again, OK?'

There were questions I wanted to ask, but I could see Cait needed to put the subject to rest, so I matched her smile and nodded.

'Deal. So where's Jack?'

'He's at work. He wanted to stay, but I forced him out the door. I wanted some quiet time to think it over. He's coming home early, though.'

'You done with your workout?'

Cait nodded and gave a shrug. 'Yeah, I was just swimming off the last of my edginess. I feel a lot better now.'

'Coffee?' I offered.

'God yes. I'll dig some croissants out of the freezer as a celebratory breakfast too.'

Linking my arm through hers, we made our way toward the kitchen. 'You won't be able to stop Jack wanting to go public about you any more, you know that? I bet he'll be whipping you up the aisle before you know it.'

'Ha! The aisle? Yeah, right,' Cait chuckled, but I could see the interest in her gaze. 'I should be happy he's so keen to tell the world we're together, but after so long of living under the radar it just feels strange.'

Giving her a narrow-eyed stare, I drew in a breath. 'You still want to be with him, don't you?'

'Of course I do, Allie. I love him,' she confessed. I was sure Cait loved Jack as much as I loved Sean – an all-consuming, stomach-flipping love, and with greater depth than I could even comprehend.

'Then making him wait is crazy, Cait. Most women would *pay* to be seen in public with Jack Felton,' I declared. 'After being forced to hide my relationship with Sean I can tell you that being out in the open is so much better. The press don't even bother with me any more.'

'Clearly you're still a supporter of "Team Jack", then,' Cait commented with a smirk and I grinned back.

'But you're right,' she nodded, and clearly deciding there was no time like the present, Cait retrieved her mobile from the table, and dialled Jack's number, putting it on speakerphone for my benefit.

'I'll leave a message on his answerphone.' After two rings, we heard the click of the call being connected and Jack's voice came over the line.

'Hey, sweetheart, what's up?'

I felt a bit weird being included in the call, but seeing Cait supressing her grin as she jigged back and forth on her toes in excitement made me smile with her.

'Hi. Nothing in particular.' Cait swallowed loudly. 'I … I was phoning to see if you were free to take me out to dinner tonight?'

There was a long pause, and I'm pretty sure both Cait and I held our breath as we waited for a response. There was quite a long pause. Maybe Jack needed a second to regain his composure, or possibly he had fainted and was currently picking himself up from the floor, I wasn't sure.

'Of course … o*ut*? As in a restaurant, *in public*?' I could tell from Jack's tone that he was smiling.

'Yes, out, at a restaurant. I think it's time to go public.' After a brief pause she giggled. 'And I won't wear a hat, I promise.'

# SIXTY

## CAIT

'Maybe you could ask Jack to send those lovely folks from Rodeo Drive over again to help you with an outfit for tonight?' Allie asked keenly.

Shaking my head, I gave Allie a rueful look. I already disliked that Jack had spent so much on my outfits that day – they'd added up to nearly three months' of my pay cheques.

That day had been great fun but I couldn't do it again. 'Nah. He still hasn't seen the black dress, and my parents got me two lovely new dresses for my birthday so I'm sure we can pick one out of those.'

'Oh! That black dress was gorgeous!' Allie chipped in, her hands clapping in excitement. 'And it'll look perfect with those heels you got!'

Fingering the ends of my hair, I grimaced. 'I'll book into the hairdresser's though, I desperately need a cut.'

At five minutes past six, five minutes after Jack's shoot had been scheduled to finish and halfway through re-straightening my hair, my phone rang. I felt my stomach flip-flop in excitement when I saw Jack's number on the screen.

'Hi.' There was a definite tremor in my voice, and I desperately hoped he hadn't heard it.

'Hi, yourself,' Jack replied smoothly. With Jack sounding that appealing, maybe we didn't need to go out tonight after all – staying in sounded just as good to me, if not better.

Clearing my wanton thoughts, I focused my attention on the call, knowing that tonight was really important to Jack.

'Sorry I haven't called until now, the shoot was hellish.' There was a pause. 'We didn't arrange a time for our meal ... assuming you still want to go?' He sounded tentative.

'We can leave it if you've had a bad day?' I tried to keep my tone light, but was incredibly aware that my whole body was tingling with nervous apprehension.

'You're kidding, aren't you? I've been looking forward to it all day!!' Jack exclaimed.

'Shall we say seven thirty, then?' I suggested, which would give me time to finish getting ready. 'Where shall I meet you?'

Down the phone, I heard Jack laugh softly. 'This is a date, Caitlin, we'll go together.'

'Oh ... I'm at Allie's at the moment, we spent the afternoon going through some wedding brochures. I can get a cab to your place.'

'*Our* place,' he corrected, making my chest feel incredibly tight. Our place. I quite liked the sound of that.

'But don't get a cab, I'll pick you up from Sean's front door, make it like a real date,' he murmured. I hadn't considered that as an option, which, now that I thought about it, was completely stupid. Of course he'd want to pick me up at the door.

'I better go. I need to get home to freshen up.' He paused briefly, as if choosing his next words with ultimate care. 'Remember, we're just going to dinner, you have no reason to be nervous, Caitlin.'

No reason at all. *Yeah, right.* I could still recall the journalists yelling at me outside the frigging supermarket, but still, I appreciated his attempt.

'OK,' I replied, but my mouth already felt as dry as a sandpit.

'See you soon, sweetheart,' Jack murmured, before I heard the click of his phone closing down the line.

'Allie!' I yelled at the top of my voice, desperate to get some help with my make-up. 'He's coming in less than two hours! I need you to do my face!'

Once we were finished, with fifteen minutes to spare, Allie stood back and gave me a thorough once over before letting out a long, low whistle.

'You're always gorgeous, but *wow* ... Jack's gonna blow a gasket when he sees you.'

Which was precisely the reaction I was hoping for. If I had to face the press, I wanted to look good. For Jack's sake, and maybe a little bit for myself too.

The doorbell rang at exactly half past seven. I had expected no less; if Jack agreed to something, he stuck to it rigidly. Allie gave me a silent thumbs up from the hallway, blew me a kiss, and then discretely disappeared.

Here we go.

I was left alone in the large hallway, more nervous than I had been in a long while. I pulled the door open to find Jack on the doorstep in a breathtaking grey suit, holding a beautiful bunch of red roses in one hand.

I grinned like an idiot, loving that he was making this exactly like a first date, even though the scary part of any first date – the kiss at the end – would be the easiest bit by far tonight.

Jack sucked in a long breath. 'God, Caitlin, you look stunning.' His voice was low and thick as his eyes skimmed over my dress.

Jack flashed me one of his customary winks and held the flowers towards me. 'These are for you.' Accepting the bouquet, I couldn't help but sniff them and smile timidly as I realised that this was only the second time in my entire life that a man had bought me flowers, and both had come from this amazing man.

'You look so handsome, Jack,' I whispered, but my voice had dried up with nerves and I wondered if he had heard me.

As if answering my question, he stepped towards me and placed a kiss on my lips. 'Thank you. I knew I would have to dress smartly so I didn't show myself up next to you.'

Ha! Sometimes flattery will get you everywhere, I thought with a shy smile.

Once I had put the roses into some water, Jack took my hand and escorted me out to his car, where I saw Flynn waiting expectantly. Jack insisted on opening the back passenger door for me, and didn't let go of my hand until I had climbed into the high cab of his Jeep.

I desperately tried to tamp down my growing nerves on the drive. It was useless, of course, because I was really nervous. After driving through some incredibly exclusive neighbourhoods, Flynn turned the car onto a road that ran along by the seafront. Even with the sun close to setting, the view was beautiful. Crystal clear sea and sandy beaches stretched for what seemed like miles, interrupted by only one building, which I assumed was our destination.

'Wow Jack, this place is phenomenal,' I whispered as we neared it. The building itself was away from the mainland, built on a pier supported by thick wooden stilts, and seemed to be accessible via a small, white bridge that spanned the crashing sea and swayed slightly in the breeze. The restaurant was built from smart, white-slatted wood and a collection of decorative lobster pots and fishing nets adorned its walls.

'So, are you ready?' Jack asked. I looked over his shoulder and I could already see several photographers loitering in the background. They were safely restrained behind the fence to the car park, but I felt a tingle of nervous excitement in my belly at the prospect of walking past them on Jack's arm.

'I guess this is another of those places that attracts celebrities, and therefore journalists, huh?' I murmured.

Jack's face softened and he leant in to place a gentle kiss on my lips. It was soft and sweet, and just what I needed. Leaning back, he then gave me his best reassuring smile and caressed my cheek with his thumb.

'Yeah. But don't worry, sweetheart, the press aren't here for us … no one knows we're coming here. This restaurant is exclusive and has a reputation for being high-end. The press know if they sit outside, they're bound to snap someone famous eventually.'

Exclusive and high-end? I was so glad Allie had talked me into the fancy high heels and smoky eye make-up. At least I looked the part, even if my stomach was currently attempting a loop-the-loop.

'Right. Great,' I muttered. Seeing his eyebrows tweak with concern, I realised that my nerves were probably making it look like I wasn't keen on being seen in public with him. Which I was. I was just nervous as hell, so I reached across and took his hand.

'I'm ready, and I'm really looking forward to spending the evening with you,' I whispered as a smile broke through my nerves. 'I'm just a bit nervous about them,' I added, with a nod in the direction of the press.

'I understand. That's why I picked this place, once we're across the bridge, that big security guard will make sure they can't bother us.'

I glanced at the pretty bridge again, covered with trailing flowers and delicate fairy lights, and noticed the rather large, scary-looking bouncer blocking the gate. His trunk-like arms folded across a well-built chest which looked almost as wide as a car. Hmm. Yep, he looked like he'd do the job rather nicely.

Giving me one more reassuring smile, Jack then jumped out of the car and walked around to open the door for me. With a final gulp, I accepted Jack's outstretched hand and climbed out, smoothing my little black dress with lightly trembling fingers.

It was almost sunset, but Jack was wearing his sunglasses, so I chose to keep mine on too to give me a small protection against the prying eyes. I'd promised him I wouldn't wear a hat, but there had been no mention of sunnies in our deal.

I held onto Jack's hand tightly as we walked towards the bridge, partly because of nerves, but mostly because my stupid heels were way taller than I usually wore and I was terrified of falling over.

As we approached the press, I saw a tremor of excitement run through the photographers as they recognised Jack, and I saw various cameras quickly being raised in our direction. Before I even realised what was happening, Jack had smoothly swapped positions with me, moving from my left to my right, wrapping a protective arm around my shoulder and effectively shielding me from the cameras.

Voices began calling out, desperate for us to pause for a photograph, and the sound of camera shutters rose to a cacophony of near constant clicking and tapping.

The closer we got to the pack of journalists, the more I could feel my senses becoming wound up; everything seemed to be getting brighter, louder, and scarier by the step, the sun felt as if it were searing through my glasses, directly into my retinas, the gravel under our feet was screaming at me with each step, and if it hadn't been for Jack's firm, reassuring arm around me, I felt certain that I would have turned and run for the safety of the car a long time ago.

'Do you want to stop for a picture?' Jack asked quietly, but I immediately shook my head. This was

411

already starting to overwhelm me. I desperately wanted to get inside and chug down at least one glass of wine to dissipate my nerves.

'Can we do it after the meal? I think I'll be more relaxed then,' I suggested, to which Jack agreed with a nod.

'Jack, who's the lovely lady?' I could hear all number of voices calling out for Jack's attention but he calmly raised a hand, and with a polite smile we advanced towards the imposing-looking bouncer who glanced at a reservations book and then immediately stepped aside to let us in.

'You do realise that by not posing for photos, they're probably all snapping pictures of your lovely arse right now, don't you?' Jack teased, causing me to gasp and clench my buttocks for the remains of the walk. Great – enlarged close-ups of my bum would probably be all over the papers tomorrow – that was the last thing I wanted to see with my morning coffee.

When we arrived at the doorway, a shy, pleasant girl introduced herself as our waitress and asked us if we could wait on the deck for a few minutes while she finished laying our table.

'Jack, this is beautiful,' I whispered as I gazed around at the lovely restaurant and sea view behind us.

'That's just what I was thinking,' murmured Jack, but as I glanced at him I saw that instead of looking at the view, Jack's attention was firmly concentrated on me, causing me to look away in embarrassment.

As we waited for our table I was aware of the distant noise of journalists' calling out across the bridge, and even though it was faint, it was starting to irritate me, and probably some of the diners inside too, no doubt.

'Just try and ignore them, sweetheart. You won't hear them once we're inside,' soothed Jack calmly.

'Don't you ever find it weird that those strangers are

so desperate to know all about you? Every little detail of your life?' I asked, wondering how on earth he had lived most of his life like this when I was losing my temper at my first real encounter.

'At first, maybe, but it comes with the territory. To be honest, I've not had much attention from the media lately. That seems to have changed since you and I were spotted at the store, though,' he added with a proud smile.

'So once they know who I am, will they leave us alone?' I questioned, contemplating a horrendous lifetime of putting up with paparazzi following me everywhere as I dived from shadow to shadow trying to avoid them like some clumsy ninja.

'They'll be satisfied for a while, yeah,' he said.

I'd wanted wine for confidence, but what I really wanted was to enjoy my meal with Jack in peace. Weighing up my options, I huffed out a breath and turned to the bridge. 'Sod it. I'll be right back,' I announced, sounding far braver than I felt.

Before I could change my mind I marched with false confidence across the bridge with my heart practically in my mouth.

As I approached the group of photographers, I paused just short of them and leaned up to whisper to the bouncer. After a second his stern exterior relaxed as he grinned at me and stepped forwards towards the buoyant crowd.

'Quiet down, guys. This little lady is here with Jack Felton and says she wants to make a deal with you.' The press quietened as an expectant flutter ran through them. 'She said she'll pose for photos, tell you her name, and answer two minutes of questions if you'll then leave them to eat in peace.' Stepping forwards, he crossed his arms and glared at the crowd, 'Do we have a deal or what?'

God, what the hell was I doing?

Unsurprisingly there was an uproar of agreement, so after a nod of encouragement from my new bouncer friend, I removed my sunglasses.

As soon as I looked at the gathered faces, a multitude of cameras bulbs started to flash in front of me, temporarily blinding me, and I immediately began to regret the decision.

A frenzy of questions were being fired at me from every direction, and I started to feel overwhelmed. Why had I thought this was a good idea? My eyes widened, and my heart was thundering under my skin as I desperately tried to get some moisture back to my desert dry mouth.

Swallowing a lump of pure terror, I returned my wide bug eyes to a normal size, lifted my shoulders, and smiled calmly at the reporters.

'Tell us your name!' yelled several of the reporters.

At least that question was easy to answer. 'Ca ...' Well, it should have been easy. My mouth was so dry that I actually wondered if I'd even be able to speak at all.

Clearing my throat and licking my lips, I tried again. 'I'm Caitlin Byrne.' Wow, my calm voice surprised even me and I raised my chin proudly under their scrutinising gazes.

'How did you meet Jack, Miss Byrne?' called another.

A smile flitted to my lips as I recalled the jog in the park. Gosh, that seemed like a lifetime ago now. 'We literally ran into each other.' I gave a laugh and my smile grew. 'We were out jogging and we bumped straight into each other.'

'Did he ask you out straight away?' called another.

'No. But I got a job at his studios and ended up on the set next to Jack's. We started to see more of each other and it went from there, really.' Which was pretty much the truth.

'So are you an actress, Miss Byrne?'

'God no!' I stifled a giggle, 'I work in the Props Department.'

At this point I was starting to feel well and truly under the spotlight, so I glanced over my shoulder for Jack, desperately wishing he were at my side. He was still across the bridge, leaning against the frame of the door with his arms folded. With the sun setting behind him, he looked like a flipping supermodel – or more accurately, the Hollywood hero in a romance film.

Lifting my brows, I made a small jerking motion, hoping he would understand my silent plea of 'Please get the hell down here' and watched in relief as he casually pushed off from the frame and sauntered towards us.

A rustle of excitement ran through the little pack as they all jostled for the best place to get a good close-up of the new couple together, and much to their apparent joy, Jack stopped behind me, slipped his arms underneath mine, and joined his hands around the front of my belly so his front was firmly pressed against my back.

Blimey, I'd wanted him to join me, but he'd taken up just about the most intimate position he could without actually humping in front of them.

With a shy smile, I inclined my face up and to the side so I could see his. 'It was getting a bit much, I wanted your support,' I murmured. In response Jack dipped his head to whisper in my ear, which caused camera flashes to go wild, presumably because they had been anticipating a kiss.

'You're doing amazingly … besides, I didn't want to steal your spotlight,' he joked, giving me a playful squeeze, and even with all the photographs I definitely felt his groin twitch against my bottom.

Oh my God.

Surely he couldn't get an erection here, in front of the press? Quite apparently he could, because over the next few seconds the pressure and warmth of the hardness grew until he lowered his head and chuckled.

'Oops. See what you do to me?'

I nearly choked. What I do to *him*? The soft flutter of his breath tickling my ear caused a matching rush of desire to surge through my own body, and I was hugely thankful that at least mine wouldn't be visible like his.

'Right, well … I've answered your questions, so it's time for you to calm down and let us eat in peace,' I announced. Given my current state, not to mention the distracting erection digging into my bum, I sounded remarkably calm. I was actually quite surprised when two photographers actually did what I asked and turned to leave almost immediately; one more called out a thanks. Maybe they weren't the heartless scavengers they were made out to be after all – or perhaps they were just keen to head off so they could be the first to get the story to their publishers.

'One more question for the two of you … you both look so happy, could this be the real thing? Is it love?'

Yikes, I hadn't thought they'd get quite so personal.

Jack didn't even hesitate to answer, leaning around me and pulling me even more firmly against him. 'Yes. One hundred per cent.' Two journalists were now scribbling like mad, but as Jack leant down and placed a kiss on my lips, their notes were forgotten as flashbulbs popped.

'Thanks for your time, everyone, we have a dinner to get to. Goodnight.'

With Jack's polite dismissal we turned around and Jack guided me back toward the restaurant with his arm still protectively wrapped around my shoulder.

'I'm so proud of you,' he murmured as we walked.

416

As I thought about what I'd just done, I had to admit I felt pretty proud of myself too.

Instead of going inside as I'd expected, Jack tugged on my hand and pulled me around the corner of the decking to an area where we were out of sight of any onlookers.

Without warning Jack suddenly moved me so I was pressed against the wall, and then rested his hands on either side of me so they were effectively caging me between the building and his body. Leaning in close, I could smell the musky scent of his aftershave, and feel the strength of his body surrounding me.

'You were incredible. So brave.' Leaning down to kiss me, his tongue swept over mine with such tenderness that I ended up moaning into his mouth.

'And I am so turned on right now it hurts,' he added, thrusting his hips against me so I could feel the hard length of his cock. 'I need a minute to cool off before we go inside.'

I wasn't sure that grinding against me would help him 'cool off', but I was enjoying it too much to point that out to him.

'I love you.' Jack's lips brushed against mine with every word and I felt a rush of goose pimples appear all over my skin. I would never tire of hearing those words.

Jack maintained his close proximity, pushing his body even closer to mine. This was all so intimate I could barely contain myself; I knew I was bright red, but I smiled anyway, before wrapping my arms around his waist and gripping tightly. 'I love you too,' I whispered, 'more so than I ever thought possible.'

It's amazing to consider the significance that generations of humans have placed on the words 'I love you'. But even though we'd said them to each other multiple times, the impact was immediately evident, because no sooner had I spoken them than Jack was

417

kissing me again. It wasn't just a gentle exploration this time but a feverishly strong and passionate kiss.

His hands grasped my hips and pushed me against the wall. Both sets of our hands set about roaming over each other's clothes and soon my skin was burning from his touch. From the jerking thrusting of his hips, it seemed that Jack shared the same sentiment.

Suddenly, Jack ripped his lips from mine with a ragged breath and rested his forehead against mine, as we clung to each other and tried to regain control.

'If we weren't in public with the possibility of journalists or CCTV cameras, I swear, I would have my way with you right here against the building.'

As tempting as that sounded, we were interrupted by our waitress as she poked her head around the corner and told us our table was ready. The poor girl blushed even redder than I did when she saw the intimate position Jack and I were in.

Taking my hand, Jack led me inside and we took our seats, our flushed waitress giving us our menus and then dashing away with her eyes averted.

We had the most stunning view of the coast, but instead of gazing at it, I accepted the glass of champagne that Jack handed me and grinned at him, feeling ten tonnes lighter after my encounter with the press.

I knew we'd be all over the papers the next day, but I didn't care – there was no risk from Greg any more and from the gigantic grin on Jack's face I'd obviously made my man very happy.

Both of us were grinning like idiots, and stuck in a bubble of happiness because we were hardly speaking as we looked at the menu, just constantly touching and gazing at each other as we chose our food.

'By the way,' Jack murmured, gaining my attention from the menu, 'we're not staying for dessert, Caitlin,' he announced, flashing me a heated look. 'With the way

I feel right now, there's no way I can spend much longer without getting you back in our bed.'

Wow. I loved that I could affect him so potently. I think Jack was probably expecting his words to make me blush and look away in embarrassment, and although I did flush a little, I decided to see if I could shock him for the second time in one evening.

Licking my lips slowly and seductively, I nodded. 'I'll provide you with dessert at home, Jack, and I guarantee you'll like it more than anything on this menu.' Slipping my foot from my high heel, I ran my toes up the inside of his thigh until they came to the warmth of his groin, then I wiggled until I felt his thighs tensing and his cock hardening.

Jack almost sprayed his entire mouthful of champagne out, and I sat back with a cheeky grin on my face as I picked up my menu, nonchalantly pretending to read it.

# SIXTY-ONE

## ALLIE

I couldn't believe I was about to do this, and as a result I was fidgeting on the sofa as I clutched my iPad to my chest and waited for Sean to walk into the room to join me.

He must have sensed my discomfort, or perhaps it showed on my face, because as he dropped onto the couch beside me he gave me a curious look. 'What's up?'

Shaking my head, I felt my flush spread down my neck in a rush of embarrassed heat. 'Nothing's wrong, I … uh … I just wanted to show you something.'

'OK … what is it?'

I wasn't sure what to say, so instead I turned the iPad toward him and winced at the astounded expression on his face. 'You're shopping for sex toys? Seriously?'

'Kind of … seeing as it's your birthday soon I wondered if you'd like to pick a present …?' I let my words trail off and my offer sink in.

I'd been wracking my brains wondering what I could get him for his birthday; he was super rich, so if he wanted something, he just bought it.

Then it had hit me. He was keen on sexual exploration, as was I. If I opened up the idea for discussion, maybe I could find the perfect gift, something he would never buy for himself, but would love all the same.

Shock spread on his handsome face as he licked his

420

lips and keenly took the iPad from me. 'Really?'

'Mmm-hmm,' I agreed, absorbing the thrilled look in his eyes. 'That's a shopping basket of things I'd be happy to try, so you can take your pick.'

Sean swallowed, and shifted on the sofa as he reached down and adjusted a growing tent in his shorts. 'Jesus, Allie, you constantly surprise me.'

A pleased smile curled my lips.

'So I can pick any of these?' he asked, scrolling through a page of items which included nipple clamps, ribbons designed for bondage, leather cuffs, and rather bravely, some small butt plugs. Seeing that last item, Sean pursed his lips and looked at me with a wicked twinkle in his eyes. 'This looks interesting,' he murmured thickly.

Rolling my eyes at his predictability, I nodded.

He let out a deep groan and almost threw my iPad down before closing the gap between us and pouncing on me like a man possessed, his lips sucking, licking, and tugging on mine as his hands began to trace over my clothes almost desperately.

It seemed that my idea was already going down rather well, and I hadn't even completed the order yet.

Before we'd got to the really good stuff, I heard the familiar chirruping of my Skype ringtone filtering through from the iPad buried somewhere between us. Groaning, I tried to remove it, but was halted by Sean as his lips descended to my neck.

'Ignore it,' he demanded, but I wriggled again and tried to sit up.

'I can't,' I panted, managing to push back. 'Cait texted me this morning to say she had important news and was going to call me. I think this is her.'

'You better make this a bloody quick call, because I'm in serious need of assistance here,' Sean quipped, eyeing the bulge in his shorts and giving it a quick rub.

Giggling, I quickly flattened my hair. 'Hold that thought. I'll be quick, I promise.'

Pressing accept, I waited for the screen to load. Finally, the image popped to life and I saw my bestie grinning at me from the screen.

'Allie! Hi!' She sounded pretty exuberant, and as the camera stilled I noticed that she looked gorgeous, with her make-up done and her hair partially pinned up.

'Hi. Cait. Wow, you look lovely.'

'Thanks.' Cait then squinted into the camera. 'You look a bit flustered, have you been running?'

Beside me Sean grunted his amusement. 'Uh ... no.' I didn't know what else to say, so I quickly changed the subject. 'How come you're not just calling on your mobile?'

'Jack surprised me with a trip away so I thought I'd show you ... can you guess where I am?'

A trip away? The screen shifted as Cait rotated the phone to show me her location. I saw a large sunlit square full of people; a fountain at the centre bubbling water across a cascade of steps; cafés lining the edges; and somewhere in the distance it sounded like someone was playing an accordion.

The scene had a distinctly European feel to it. 'Uhhh ... I don't know, France?'

Cait's face came back to the screen, grinning from ear to ear. 'Close. Italy. We're in Florence, and it's even more beautiful than I imagined.'

A soft smile tugged at my lips. Cait had always wanted to go to Florence.

'I have so much to tell you.' Cait paused. 'Let me show you something, hang on ...' There was another pause, and then Caitlin started to walk, the camera shaking and giving me brief glimpses of a cloudless blue sky.

Beside me, Sean was getting impatient, one of his

hands running up and down my thigh as his right hand continued to stroke his groin. Jeez. Talk about distracting.

Through the iPad there was a low creak. It looked as if she was going through a door, and then more blue sky appeared.

'Let me put this on the table.' The camera finally steadied and I could see she was in a beautiful, walled courtyard with flowers everywhere, small water fountains, and a pergola decorated with white ribbons in the background.

'Please, don't be mad, Allie ...' Cait begged as she stepped in front of the camera and held her hand out to something off the screen.

I saw Cait giggle and tug on whatever she'd reached out for. I realised it was Jack as he joined her in the shot and wrapped his arm around her shoulders.

Wow, Italy obviously suited them because they both looked great; Jack was decked out in dark grey suit trousers, a white shirt with his sleeves rolled up, and a grey waistcoat, and Cait was wearing a beautiful, sleeveless cream dress that accentuated her slim figure to perfection.

Jack leant towards the camera and greeted us with a wave. 'Hi, guys!' Glancing at Cait he then turned back beaming from ear to ear. 'I'd like to introduce you to the new Mrs Felton.'

Huh?

Mrs Felton?

Wait, *what?*

'We got married ten minutes ago. It was so beautiful, Allie, I wish you could have been here!' Cait blurted gleefully.

Married ... now the ribbon strewn pergola made sense. Sean stopped his fiddling and, after gawking at me, shuffled closer to look at the screen with me. 'Wow!

Congratulations!' he said, breaking my stunned silence and making me realise I needed to say something.

Bouncing up and down on the sofa, I slapped a hand to my forehead as the news finally sunk in. 'Oh my God! Congratulations! I can't believe it!' I giggled. I really couldn't, I mean, this was Cait – she was probably the worst secret keeper in the world. How the heck had I not known that something was going on? 'So, was it planned? Did you elope?'

'No! It wasn't planned at all. We were out for a meal on our first night here and Jack proposed on the spur of the moment!' Cait beamed at Jack, who shrugged and looked well and truly pleased with himself.

'I couldn't hold it back any longer. Luckily Caitlin said yes. I did a bit of research to see if a wedding was feasible, and when I saw this venue I asked Caitlin if she'd like to tie the knot while we were here. Luckily she said yes to that too.' The grin on Jack's face couldn't be any larger.

'The ceremony was just the two of us, the marriage official, and some poor unsuspecting Spanish tourists that we dragged in to act as our witnesses.' Jack continued. 'I don't think they recognised me, so they might be a bit shocked to see themselves in the papers tomorrow.'

'Papers?' Sean asked. 'You had press there?'

Jack shook his head and stuck his free hand into the pocket of his trousers. 'Not really. I have a college friend out here, Antonio. He went into journalism a few years ago, so I invited him and gave him an exclusive. My PR team are going to make a discreet announcement, but we've kept it all very low-key. It'll be interesting to see how long it takes the news to spread.'

Discreet and low key, exactly how Cait would have wanted it.

Cait moved forward so more of her face took up the

screen and I could immediately see the worried look on her face. 'You're not mad, are you, Allie? I know we were supposed to be bridesmaids for each other, but when Jack suggested we get married here it just seemed so right for us.'

Wiping a happy tear away from my eye, I laughed, wishing I could hug her. 'Of course I'm not mad! I'm so happy for you both! And you're right, this is perfect.'

# SIXTY-TWO

## CAIT

The moment I hung up, my new husband pulled me up into his arms with a growl. 'Now, we've called your parents, my parents, and your best friend. Am I finally allowed to have my new wife to myself?'

Looping my arms around his shoulders, I giggled and leant up to lay a kiss on his lips. 'Definitely, Mr Felton.' Extending the kiss into something more heated, I rested my forehead on his, thinking we should stop before we got too carried away in the garden.

It seemed that Jack had other ideas, because as I tried to pull away, he clung on.

'Uh-uh, you're not going anywhere, *Mrs Felton*,' he murmured with a wicked grin. My heart beat accelerated at the naughty glint in his eye. Joining in with his smile, I raised my eyebrows wondering what he had planned.

Keeping his eyes locked with mine, Jack crouched, and after shifting his hands to my bum, he tightened his hold on me and stood up again, lifting me clean off the floor. Yelping with surprise and delight, I gripped his shoulders and slid my legs around his waist as he began to walk.

I was fairly certain he was going to whip me back to our hotel room so he could have his way with me, but instead, he began heading away from the gate and towards the back of the courtyard.

'Where are we going?'

'Somewhere I can pounce on you.'

Hmm, I liked the sound of that, but we were in a walled garden, so I couldn't imagine what he meant. Confused, I leaned back and gave him a curious look.

'Well, you always refer to me as your perfect gentleman,' Jack began, striding with purpose towards nothing but a wall, 'and I thought that as we are married now it was only fair to warn you that I'm not always quite as gentlemanly …'

Oh wow. That sounded rather promising.

He reached the corner of the courtyard and used a foot to kick open an ivy-covered door, disguised in the wall.

Craning my neck, I saw a small shed-like room hidden behind the door, but I didn't get much chance to look around because Jack launched me from his arms and up into the air.

A shriek flew from my lungs as I flailed my arms, but I landed on something soft that cocooned my body and broke my fall. I realised I was on a huge stack of sun lounger cushions, topped with blankets and pillows.

Jack flicked a switch to his left and promptly attacked me, falling over my body with a lusty rumble and kissing me with so much passion that I could do nothing but arch into his touch and groan my appreciation.

A few seconds later, when he allowed me to come up for air, I briefly glanced around and saw the stone room was illuminated with fairy lights, the little trails of bulbs twinkling from almost every available surface.

'I may have prepared a little in advance,' he admitted with a grin, kissing me again as one hand began to explore down my body.

'So you're showing me your impetuous non-gentlemanly side but you prepped beforehand?' I enquired, teasing before I lost the ability to speak.

'Hmm, yes.' Nibbling at my neck, I felt him chuckle against my heated skin. 'What can I say? I want to be a

427

bad boy, but I'm just a good guy at heart.'

Jack was good through and through, but this was a lovely surprise. 'That you are, but I believe you promised me a pouncing, Mr Felton?'

Instead of continuing to kiss my neck, Jack gave a small nip to the tender skin below my ear and laughed again, this time lustier. 'I did, didn't I, Mrs Felton?' he smirked. 'Let's see about that, shall we?'

Raising onto his forearms, Jack immediately gripped my left wrist, pulling my hand to his mouth and placing a lingering kiss on my wedding ring before he pinned the hand above my head and repeated the action with the right arm.

His head lowered to mine, trailing kisses across my cheek to my lips and then licked and nibbled across my gasping mouth and slid his tongue inside.

As we kissed, his right hand explored my body, across the silk of my dress, with several appreciative hums before pausing on my breast and pulling away with a grumble.

'Too many clothes.' Using the hold he had on my wrists, Jack pulled me to a sitting position and let go of me as he rose gracefully to his feet and immediately began to strip his clothes off. 'I should have undressed you first. I'll remember that next time I plan a pouncing,' he informed me with a wicked glint in his eye.

Once he was naked, and splendidly aroused, he held out a hand and pulled me to my feet. I was nowhere near as graceful, because my legs were decidedly wobbly after watching his strip tease. He didn't let go of me as his other hand reached around and swiftly pulled down the zip to my dress. Moments later, his hands were splaying on my shoulders and he slid them inside the dress and helped it fall from my body.

The beautiful lace underwear set Jack had given me

428

as a wedding gift was next to be removed, and then I was standing wearing just my wedding garter. Jack gave it a brief caress before helping me back down to the soft blankets and beginning to kiss his way down my body.

We were naked in a shed, and I really couldn't have cared less.

His lips rested on the garter and he tugged at the lace with his teeth before looking up and grinning. 'I like this. Very traditional. I think it can stay on.'

I was about to say I was glad he liked it, but my eyes rolled shut as his lips moved from the garter, working higher until they focused on a very different target. 'Oh God ...' His tongue immediately flattened against my clitoris, sending sparks of pleasure shooting through my body as his large palms slid up my thighs and pressed my legs open wider.

Shifting one hand, he introduced a finger, circling it around my sensitive flesh before running his tongue down to join it until I was writhing below his touch and mumbling incoherently. Gradually, his mouth worked its way back up to my clit and he sucked the bundle of nerves into his mouth, causing a gurgled mumble to slide from my lips as my hands buried into his hair and gripped.

My body arched into his touch, wishing the sensations would never end but desperate for release at the same time.

'Patience, Mrs Felton, we'll get there soon enough,' he whispered against my quivering flesh before pressing one finger up inside of me and crooking it so it rubbed at my g-spot. I certainly would get there soon if he kept up that amazing move.

Just when I was on the verge of exploding into a climax he stopped, but before I could complain, Jack was donning a condom and shifting his body over mine so the tip of his cock was resting where his fingers had been. Hmm. His fingers were good, but this would be better.

'I love you, Caitlin,' he murmured, right before he pressed his hips forwards and sunk inside me. The contact of his pelvic bone against my clit added to my already heightened state, triggering an instant climax that had me screaming and clawing at his back.

As lost in the moment as I was, I forced myself to grip his biceps and return his sentiment. It was our wedding day, after all. 'I love you too, Jack.'

With my body still convulsing, Jack remained deeply planted inside me, just giving the smallest circles to help me ride out my orgasm, and once I'd come down from my high he grinned and lowered his head for a deep kiss.

I felt his cock give a jerk inside as if urging him to move, so I sunk my fingers into his hair and pulled his head back. I could see a film of sweat on his brow, so with our eyes still locked I began to grind myself against him.

Jack quickly got the message, beginning to move his hips and dragging his length slowly out before pressing back in again with a low groan. His control was fast deserting him, because he only managed to go slow for a minute or so before his eyes intensified, along with his movements, and his thrusts sped up.

Even though I'd only just climaxed, I could feel my desire building again as every one of his strokes managed to rub directly on my g-spot as well as stimulating my clit. Our desperation to come became more evident in our breathing and clawing hands, and then suddenly Jack made a low moan and his hips jerked against me as he came, his body shuddering above mine as I felt his release inside of me.

The jarring of his body against my over-sensitized clit triggered my own second release and I gasped, my skin overheating as I clamped around him and felt spasm after spasm spiralling through me.

Well, that was our marriage well and truly consummated. I almost felt stunned from the intensity of it.

Jack supported his weight, panting desperately but still trying to peck small kisses across my damp brow. 'Incredible,' he murmured. 'You are just incredible.' He had done wonders for my confidence, but as always, his compliments made me blush and smile.

Once we'd recovered enough to move, Jack slid from me and handed me a hanky, which made me smile and think of my little handkerchief collection.

We re-dressed, both of us giggling and blushing as we tidied up the shed and quickly removed the fairy lights.

'Do you want children?' Jack suddenly asked.

A few months ago, I'd never thought I'd ever have a husband, let alone kids, but deep down I'd wanted both since I was a teenager. Would Jack want kids? We'd only just tied the knot, so I picked my reply carefully. 'I think I would … how about you?'

Jack's face softened into that sweet, soft expression that I loved and I even saw his cheeks blush. 'I would, very much.'

I felt a warm, deep sensation of love building in my chest as I imagined mini versions of Jack or myself running around.

'Guess we can start skipping condoms at some point then,' I joked, before sobering my expression and giving his waist a squeeze. 'You'd make an amazing dad.' The words slipped from my mouth, but Jack seemed utterly thrilled.

'You think so?' He looked glued to my answer, his face serious as he waited for my confirmation.

Nodding my head, I cupped his cheek and smiled at him, hardly able to believe this stunning man was really my husband. 'I know so.'

'If we have kids they'll be very lucky then, because you'd also be a great mum.' My cheeks flushed, and Jack lowered his head and kissed me.

I'm not sure if it was the talk of children, the fact that we'd just got married, or the insatiable bond between us, but his gentle kiss quickly started to turn into something more heated as our hands began exploring again.

Dragging his head up with a groan, Jack grinned, his face flushed with desire even though we'd only just sealed our marriage five minutes before. 'I'd like our next time as a married couple to be in a bed. Shall we head back to the room?'

My only reply was a keen nod. Sliding his hand down my left arm, he pulled my fingers to his lips and placed a lingering kiss on my wedding ring before interlocking our hands and turning for the door.

As we emerged from the shed into the light of day, it hit me what I'd just done – had steamy sex in a shed – and I laughed, setting Jack off until we were both giggling like naughty teenagers.

Jack tried to tug me towards the gate, but I paused, and pulled my hand free. There was one final thing I wanted to do today, and it seemed fitting to do it in the place where I'd married my amazing man. Touching the elastic bands around my wrist, I slid a finger under them, only to have Jack reach over and stop me with a frown.

'Hey, you haven't pinged those for a while, why now? You're not having second thoughts, are you?'

Smiling at his complete misunderstanding, I shook my head then tugged both elastic bands off my wrist.

Jack's mouth fell open in surprise as he watched me dispose of them on a table and rub at my empty wrist.

'I don't need them any more,' I murmured softly as Jack moved closer to me, still gaping at my move. 'I have you to keep me grounded now.' Rolling up onto my tiptoes I closed the final gap between us and pressed my lips to his.

'Yes, you do,' Jack confirmed gruffly, pulling me against him and dragging my arm up so he could kiss the now bare skin on my wrist.

Reluctant to give up the contact between us, I stepped back but slid my fingers down and linked our hands. 'Shall we head to the hotel?'

Jack grinned his sweet, affectionate smile and I just about melted, almost unable to believe that he was real.

I'd truly believed that the attack by Greg had irreparably changed my life. But now Greg was behind bars – at his trial last month he'd been given two life sentences – and I was relaxed, happy, and married to an amazing man.

Hollywood heartthrob, Jack Felton.

My saviour.

My husband.

'Thank you for organising today, Jack. You've made me the happiest girl in the world.'

Looking around the courtyard, I sighed happily. Considering we'd put it all together in fewer than seven days, it had been everything I'd wanted and more. I'd never craved a huge wedding. The idea of being the focus of attention was terrifying, and as Jack and I had got closer in our relationship and discussed getting engaged it had quickly become clear that he didn't want a big wedding either; he lived his entire life in the spotlight – he didn't want our wedding to be in one too.

When Jack had proposed at the start of our holiday it had just seemed like the ideal timing. Jack had taken charge and planned it all, right down to moving us to the beautiful hotel in the centre of Florence with its garden that was licenced for weddings. And its shed, which probably wasn't licensed for the things we'd just done inside it …

Allie had described our wedding as being perfect, and as I allowed Jack to pull me to his side and lead me onto the streets of Florence, I had to say I couldn't agree more. It really had been perfect. The prefect day. The perfect man. The perfect start to my new life.

# EPILOGUE

## ALLIE

Just as Sean had promised several months ago when he'd made his dramatic declaration on his balcony, we were married on the beach behind his house in a ceremony that was more beautiful than I could ever have imagined.

Sean and I being together was obviously meant to be, because things couldn't have gone any smoother. It had been an utterly beautiful day; the weather was perfect, and we'd decorated the beach and wedding area with lanterns and delicate bunches of white and yellow wild flowers, all buried in artistically arranged piles of shells and driftwood.

The pergola where we'd exchanged vows was wrapped up with ribbons and more flowers and as we'd held hands and said 'I do' we'd been able to smell their sweet scent on the warm sea breeze.

In true beach style, I'd walked to my fiancé in bare feet, and, instead of a wedding dress, I'd worn a cotton sun dress, but this hadn't been just any old sun dress – Sean had paid a local designer to help me get it exactly right, and I'd been completely thrilled with the outcome. I'd debated about going for knee-length because of the weather, but in the end had gone for full-length white cotton to retain a part of the usual wedding tradition. Tiny shoulder straps opened out into a backless dress. After the fitted top, the dress plunged to the floor in floaty, airy layers which kept me cool but still looked gorgeous.

435

Sean, always a fan of me in backless, bra-less dresses, had loved it when he'd finally been allowed to see it. He'd also enjoyed taking me out of it later, when we'd snuck up to the house for a quickie to consummate our union.

I'd opted for three bridesmaids: Cait, Sarah, and Sean's sister Evie. All three had had a dress of similarly simple style: full length, pale blue cotton with capped sleeves and a curved neckline. Cait had still wanted her back covered for the ceremony, and even though she was far braver with her clothing these days, I guess some of her engrained habits would take longer to get over than others.

We exchanged vows as the sun set behind us, and danced the night away on the beach surrounded by our family and friends. It was the perfect day, made even more perfect because I could see just how happy Cait was too.

And all because I'd covered that cleaning shift for Sarah and ended up snowed in with Sean. It was incredible to think that something as inconsequential as helping out my friend had led me to meeting the love of my life. Destiny must have been shining down on me that day.

Even with the twists and turns that our relationship had taken, I couldn't help but think that everything had worked out perfectly for us. I had my amazing husband and a life in the sun, and Cait, the bravest woman I knew, had found her protector and soul mate, and could leave behind the ghosts of her past. It really was like our very own Hollywood blockbuster – complete with dashing heroes, loved up heroines, and a happily-ever-after ending.


The End

21830991R00257

Printed in Great Britain
by Amazon